OH, FAE!

First Published in Great Britain 2022 by Mirador Publishing

Copyright © 2022 by John Westbrook

First edition: 2022

A copy of this work is available through the British Library.

ISBN: 978-1-914965-43-2

Mirador Publishing
10 Greenbrook Terrace
Taunton
Somerset
TA1 1UT

OH, FAE!

By

John Westbrook

Acknowledgements

THIS TOOK A LOT LONGER to write than intended for more reasons than I would care to mention. So special thanks to the family for the forbearance and encouragement when there were long gaps in the writing process.

I hope I have managed to finish this in time for my granddaughters Maddie, Rosie and Fion to enjoy having it read to them, or even for them to read it themselves. It was a great help having such wonderful girls around to watch and listen to and get ideas for how Milly might talk and act in her formative years. It's been far too long since my own lovely kids were at that critical stage of their development – although perhaps the odd memory from those days may have just have crept in to the story from time to time?

Thanks again to Margaret (Mash) for her amazing patience during all those times when I have disappeared into the study to be away with the faeries. I'd like to say I'm back now, but I'm not so sure.

Prelude

RALPH STOOD BESIDE THE ROAD. The pedestrian crossing lay just a few metres to his right but he had never used it. He rarely even crossed the road. He just stood, feet planted solidly a few inches apart and wrapped in thin strips of old blanket. The remains of his boots were placed tidily behind him, side by side against the wall, where they wouldn't get in peoples' way. He was very particular about that.

This morning he was agitated. He was agitated every morning – and every afternoon and every evening. He waved his supermarket plastic bags at almost every car that passed.

"One of you, just one of you. 300 grams. Spare the horses. Fill it up, fill it up. Here comes the bus now. Every 10 minutes. Come in number 15 your time's up…"

Two young men walked past, slowing as they did so.

"Give it a break, Ralph. You'll wear yourself out." They moved on laughing. "He's away with the fairies, that one!"

Ralph put down his bags and ran mittened fingers through his matted hair.

"Pity there ain't more of us, eh Barry?" He spoke to his left shoulder.

"Too right, Ralph. Still, maybe when Milly grows up it'll be a bit different. In the meantime, keep up the good work. I'd better get back to the village and open up the Royal Oak. Doesn't do to keep the patrons waiting."

And with his parting words, Barry Goodfellow, Sprite of the village of Whimbury, climbed down from Ralph's shoulder and set off back home.

In a dark wood in another part of the country, an interview panel of Nixie commanders was putting a special recruit through his paces. He was unlike them and they were uneasy. He didn't share their deep purple colouring. He didn't look evil to his core and his eyes were unnaturally bright, lacking the traditional Nixie piercing quality. In short, the panel was confused. And they hated being confused, especially when the source of their confusion was their only hope of preventing the Crossover child from fulfilling her potential.

"Are you quite sure that you are a true Nixie?" The Commander in Chief took control of proceedings.

"My parents are both Nixies from the warrior class, but I have a genetic abnormality. I am what is known as a 'Greeno' - perfectly normal in every way except for my green skin colouring and white eyes. Otherwise, I think and act like a Nixie, and desire only to further the cause of my people."

"That is why we sent for you. There is a mission that only you can carry out for us. You must become like one of the fairies of Whimbury and earn their trust. Then when the time is right, you can prevent the Crossover child from completing the process to its full extent. This is our only hope of keeping a wedge between the fae world and that of the humans. Are you ready for this?" The C-in-C stared at him, as much in hope as authority.

"I am." Only the tone of his voice identified him as a Nixie - strong, dominant and assertive to the point of aggression, and beyond.

"Good!" The C-in-C breathed a little easier. "Then you may progress immediately to the Reconstruction Training Centre. From there you will proceed to Whimbury. You do realise that the whole process will take years rather than months?"

"I do." Nothing else needed to be said.

****

Two years later.

Will Hope sat in the front garden of Over Cross View. He loved the late spring evenings, or at least the sunny ones. Across the road, behind and to the side of Green's Farm Machinery Repairs workshop, Whimbury Wood was in full leaf. Much of it was protected ancient woodland and it appealed to his need for security to think that it had almost always been there and would continue to be so. The May blossom was still hanging tenaciously to the smaller trees and hedgerows around the village, and the sparrows and tits were jockeying for position around the bird feeders and fat ball hangers in next door's garden. He couldn't identify the different varieties of bird but he vowed to learn to do so before Milly reached the age of questioning.

More than anything, he loved to watch Milly picking daisies from the overgrown lawn. He sat on the fallen log beside the front path and waited patiently as she brought each daisy to him, one at a time. He pinched the base of each stem as the posy grew and dreamt of the time when she would be old enough to be taught the traditional art of daisy chain making. He had already washed out the Marmite jar in preparation for the floral arrangement.

"OK, princess, make that the last one. The vase won't hold any more."

Will was pleased with himself. The small jar meant that Milly couldn't pick too many daisies, and he saw that as a conservation measure. He was both proud and fond of his eco-patch front garden – proud because it was "of its time" and fond because it involved less formal planting and therefore less chance of things going wrong. If truth be told, Will was not a natural gardener but he did like nature, and if nature desired a small foothold in the village then he was happy to oblige.

Milly showed a keen interest in the garden, particularly – and this bemused Will – in woodlice, which she would watch crawling over the decaying log for long periods of time. She would never touch them, but she did talk to them, and seemed to integrate them into her play.

Will watched as she toddled back to the lawn, knelt down on the grass and peered for signs of life. He smiled as she sat back on her heels, gestured with her hands in animated and knowing fashion, and tilted her head at a jaunty 45 degree angle.

"I wonder why she does that?" Will picked up the jar of daisies. "Probably talking to the fairies."

Chapter One

"YER SEES, BAZZA, I GOT arfritis in some of me joints." Larry the woodlouse waved his antennae in the general direction of his legs. "It all started in the third to fifth pairs and uvver bits are goin' the same way. So it's getting' more difficult movin' ararnd in the cellars. 'Ad to appen sometime I s'pose. None of us is getting' any younger."

Barry knew his louse friend inside out, and was well aware that he was about to break some bad news as gently as possible. He'd been half expecting a moment like this to come, ever since Larry had returned from the latest visit to his family in the east end of London, several months back.

"So what are you saying Larry?"

"I s'pose I'm sayin' that I don't fink that I'll be able to do all the clearin' art and sortin' darn here like I used ter. It's a pity, cos I've developed a bit of a taste for algae and the like, an' I feels pretty much at 'ome here nar - but nuffink lasts for ever does it?"

"You'll be hard to replace Larry." Barry was genuinely upset at the news. Larry had become a close friend as well as a good worker in the unglamorous bowels of the Royal Oak, cleaning the barrels of ale and their pipes, and generally helping Barry to comply with the complexity of environmental health regulations relating to fay public houses, without the need for expensive magic.

"Well that's where I might be able ter 'elp." Larry turned his antennae and gestured to an as yet unseen accomplice. A smaller version of Larry emerged from behind one of the barrels. Other than some slightly lighter patches of grey on his scales, he looked the very image of Larry, though, in truth, Barry had never been good at distinguishing the subtle differences between members of the louse family.

"Junior 'ere would love the chance ter take over my place in the greater scheme of fings, if yer knows my meanin'." Larry's son and heir pointed his antennae to the floor in a show of mild embarrassment.

"I hadn't realised that he was so interested. You've never mentioned it before - or even brought him in for that matter. As I recall, the nearest he's got so far is to sit in the lobby with a packet of soggy crisps watching the Happs play darts!"

"Yers, well, 'e's only young, in't 'e. I've no idea what the legal age for comin' into a fairy pub is, but I fort as since 'e's just been frew 'is fird full moult, 'e's probly ready ter come and work like. 'E's bright enough - asks all the right questions about what I does, 'ow ter strip algae an' clean up detritus an' stuff. And 'e's getting strong nar - strong as I ever was, and......" At which point, Larry indicated that he wanted to speak in confidence and Barry beckoned him up onto his shoulder.

"In troof, Bazza, yer've bin real good ter me, and I've really enjoyed the work 'ere - give or take the odd khazi cleaning duties, which 'ave pushed my antennal capacities to their limits at times."

"After curry nights I presume?" Barry offered an explanatory interjection to avoid further and more detailed description.

"Heggsactly!" Larry continued. "But nar I feels as if I 'as a kinda responsibility to the place. I've built up a level of expertise that takes time an' effort, an' it'd be sad ter let it all go, as it were. Junior already knows a lot and I could mentor 'im like, and all you'd need to do would be to keep 'im up ter date wiv new technologies an' the like. 'E's reliable and an 'ard worker, an I'll still be ' ere fer a while, I 'opes, to keep an eye on 'im and act in a sorta liaison type capacity. What d'yer say?"

"Well, I'll need someone to replace you, and it would be a pain having to train a new worker up from scratch. Would I have to put up with the same theatricality every time I gave him a job to do?" Barry was in playful mood and knew just how to wind Larry up.

"What d'yer mean, featricality? Just cos I'm cultured and study the classics. That ain't no bad fing." He slipped effortlessly into luvvy mode. "Keep theatre live, that's what we say. Reclaim the heritage of our literary past. Give Shakespeare the acknowledgment and honour he deserves. All the world's a stage and......"

Barry gently gripped one of his flailing limbs to cut the speech short. "I'll take that as a yes then shall I? He is indeed his father's son?"

"Well actcherly, Bazza," Larry dropped back into hushed tones, with the merest hint of embarrassment. "Junior don't like the classics. They're all a bit old-fashioned for 'im. Can't understand the Elizabefan language an' the like. I've tried me best ter heducate 'im, but 'e ain't got the patience. Ter tell you the troof, he's been a bit rebellious recently - they do say that the third skin is the 'ardest and that's when yer needs ter keep a close eye on 'em. But when 'e's not wiv me, 'e's fine. Don't seem ter feel the need to show off so much and try ter prove that 'e don't 'ave ter follow my hinterests."

"So what is he into then? If not Shakespeare?" Barry had seen enough of Junior around the village to know that he was a good louse at heart, and he was enlightened enough as an employer to want to know as much about his employees as possible, so that he could keep them happy. A happy staff was a productive and reliable staff. To his surprise Larry seemed embarrassed and reluctant to pass on any more details.

"Come on Larry, spill the beans. We're old friends, we've always shared our concerns. And you know that I am the epitome of discretion in personal family matters."

"Iber n ifn." Larry turned his antennae away to distort his signal.

"What was that Larry? Missed it." Barry was a Sprite and knew when to twist the knife to achieve maximum embarrassment.

"Iber n alifn." Larry's antennae took on a life of their own in a successful attempt to make all meaning as obscure as possible.

"Larry, kindly take full control of your communicating faculties and give me a clear answer." Barry smiled a kindly smile that contained just the requisite mix of forbearance and false sympathy.

Larry sighed and heaved his armour plating in despair.

"Gilbert and Sullivan!" He gave his response a slight barbed edge, but kept the volume down so as not to bring down the wrath of his son.

Barry placed his hand surreptitiously over his mouth to stifle a grin.

"Wow, Larry, now that really is rebellion of the highest order! I mean, I like a bit of light operetta myself, now and again, but – well to someone of your highbrow artistic tastes, it must be difficult for you? Have you tried counselling?"

"Oh very funny, Bazza. Yer should be awarded a Doctorate in Sarcasm or somefink. Well if yer not interested we might as well go." Larry turned to Junior and made a gesture that was intended to give the impression to Barry that they had been insulted in better places than this and were now going to return to such places as a matter of choice.

Barry realised that he had hit a raw nerve and that the time was now right to ease off.

"Sorry Larry! Couldn't help it. Seriously, it would be great if Junior could take over. I'd be more than happy to maintain the family connection and for you to train him up in the ways and methodologies of cellar life. This part of the Royal Oak has never been run better or more efficiently, and we've been through so much. When do you want to start the handover process and how long will it take?"

Larry rose to his full height and turned to face Barry. He placed his first two right-side limbs across his thorax and spoke with the authority of one who feels he has both the upper hand and a need to enunciate very clearly to establish a point of principle.

"It is a wise father that knows his own child! We may differ on matters of taste, but my son is bright and quick to learn – as was, and is, his father. As I developed a set of procedures to bring this shambles to a semblance of order, so I can pass them on to the next generation, such that the order may be preserved or even enhanced with the effluxion of time." Larry utilised all available limbs to elaborate his points.

"How long?"

"Abart a week, Bazza. Just so's 'e can pick up the different priorities on a day-to-day basis."

"You're on! He can start – under your supervision – as soon as he wants. Same terms and conditions."

Larry looked temporarily perplexed.

"I never 'ad no terms and conditions!"

"And I guarantee that Junior will have nothing worse, despite only being a trainee for the first week."

"Well that sarnds fair enough, Bazza." Larry turned to his son. "Shall we start nar, buddy?"

"Why not, Pops?" Junior broke into song. "For duty, duty must be done, the rule applies to everyone."

Larry smiled apologetically and hustled Junior off in search of algae.

******

Will and Miranda Hope stood at the Whimbury village bus stop outside of the old station building. Milly sat quietly in her pushchair gazing up High Street towards the Celtic Cross at the far end, where the road split around it. Her view was channelled between the buildings lining the road, such that the Cross seemed like the end of the known world. She could also see it from the window-sill of her bedroom, when her father lifted her up there to point out the landmarks of the village – the Cross over to the left, the edge of Whimbury Woods opposite, Green's Agricultural Machinery Repairs workshop to the right, and beyond that the "Ever Been Fleeced" wool and fabric shop and "Shearings" the hairdresser's.

Whimbury had a long farming history and Will would often take Milly out for a walk beyond Home Farm to the last remaining water meadows in the area, where they would watch the sheep grazing. He would explain to her the process of getting the wool from the sheep to the shop. In truth he was a little hazy on some of the detail, but he knew enough to stimulate the imagination of a small child. He had been pleased when, just the other day, Miranda came home with Milly after a visit to the wool shop and laughed as she told him how his daughter had spent several minutes graphically describing the origins of the balls of wool that were laid in disorderly fashion on the shelves and the floor.

"The whole shop fell about laughing. It was as if the whole shearing, spinning, dyeing thing was some sort of magic trick."

"Busy in the shop, was it?" Will was constantly amazed at how the wool shop kept going. It was small and totally chaotic – rather like the village itself.

"Well, there were three of us, Mrs Patterson herself, of course, and then me and Evadne. But there again, you can't really fit more than that in at any one time."

But today, the family was off to town. Whimburton was a compact, sleepy town, though it had a range of shops and a market twice a week. It also boasted a wine bar and a tattoo parlour and was therefore seen by many of the inhabitants of Whimbury as the devil's playground, on a par in the moral depravity stakes with Sodom and Gomorrah. The Hopes were prepared to risk the dangers and the corruption once a week to visit the food market and have afternoon tea out. They were up and out early to catch the first, and indeed only, bus from the village. Over the years the frequency of the buses had been continually reduced and reduced such that only a day trip was now possible. That was hard on some of the older folks who had no access to a car, but the Hopes enjoyed their outing, and it gave Milly the opportunity to try out some different play equipment in the large playground behind Whimburton Market Square.

"It's late again!" Will looked at his watch and across to Miranda, who was busying herself attending to Milly's sun hat.

"It's only a minute or so late, just be patient and be glad we have a bus service at all. Use it or lose it is what I say. Once a week we can relax a little, forget the car and spend some time with our little princess. We're lucky. Your job is flexible and we can go when it's all a bit quieter." Miranda shaded her eyes against the morning sun as she looked down Station Road in the direction from which the bus would come.

"I guess so. You are right as usual, my little May blossom. I'll just pop over to the Mission Church notice board and see if there's anything interesting. Shout me if you see it coming." Will ambled across the road and perused the notice board outside of the little wooden chapel building. After just a few seconds, he was called by Miranda and he jogged back to the bus stop ready to lift Milly onto the bus.

"Did you see anything interesting on the notice board?" Miranda settled down beside Will on the front seats of the bus with Milly in her pushchair in the space allocated, looking back at them.

"Didn't get much time to read it all, but apparently there's a meeting in the Village Hall tonight to discuss some plans that the Council have for new housing around the Whimbury area. I'll read it more carefully on the way back."

Miranda pondered for a moment. Will gazed lovingly at Milly, as he often did. Milly stared back at Will and then smiled, as she often did. Then she turned her attention to the beagle laying obediently on the floor of the bus across the aisle from Will. Mrs Brown often took Charlie into Whimburton with her on market days and it had become something of a social occasion with friends and acquaintances from neighbouring villages meeting up either on the bus or in the Market Tea Room.

Charlie raised one eyelid as if aware that he was being looked at. It wasn't that he was tired, but dogs get bored on a bus when there's nothing organic to see or smell other than humans, and he had long since been made painfully aware that it was not appropriate behaviour to go around Mrs Brown's companions sniffing their bottoms. He noticed Milly and opened the other eye. His tail began to twitch a coded message, which indicated to anyone versed in the language that given the right encouragement a full-scale wag could follow. Milly leaned forward in her pushchair and waved her finger in the general direction of Charlie. He, in turn, gave a low contented growl while his tail moved into stage two twitch mode. Milly turned her head at 45 degrees and gave him a quizzical look.

"Funny how dogs and small children seem to have a special way of relating to each other, isn't it?" Will had noticed the wordless exchange between his daughter and the beagle, and used the opportunity to strike up a conversation with Mrs Brown.

"Yes. I've often wondered about that. Perhaps dogs realise that children are still innocent enough to accept them as fellow inhabitants on the planet and equals on that basis?" Mrs Brown worked part-time in the "Fur Coat and No Bickers" pet grooming salon in Whimbury. It was one of the few shops in the village, all of which were having financial difficulties and all of which, barring Potts' General Store and Post Office, opened only on selected days during the week. In the case of the grooming salon, that did not include Whimburton market day, which suited Mrs Brown just fine. She jiggled her fingers around Charlie's ears, neck and throat in comforting fashion. He moved his head to allow further such attention, yawned an extensive yawn and looked across at Milly, who burst out laughing with an infectiousness that had the rest of the passengers joining in for the pure fun of it all.

****

In Whimbury Woods, Percy Grumplet was giving his Wild Garlic hedge a final prune of the season. The flowers had long gone, but the leaves were still smooth and green. The fresh pungent garlic smell was past its peak, but Percy still enjoyed the aroma of the newly cut plants, and sniffed long and hard as he gazed along the top of his hedge to check for any irregularities in line and height. From his vantage point at the top of the step-ladders he could check on activity along the byways through the woods and, if the need arose, he could use his periscope to see over the undergrowth and between the trees to the High Street beyond.

Today there was little happening to catch his attention. He kept a look out for new butterflies and moths in the vicinity. The Brimstones and Speckled Woods were already in evidence, but he would expect to see more very soon. They were useful sources of information of what was going on in and around the wood, even if they did occasionally lapse into existentialist panics about previous lives and forms. "Flutter by name, flutter by intellect" was how the fairies of Whimbury referred to them, though not of course directly to their antennae. Most of the inhabitants of Whimbury Wood believed whole-heartedly in Chaos Theory, and didn't want to risk devastation in some far-flung part of the world by causing a local moth to fly off in a disgruntled flap.

Then Percy became aware of a distant singing. Not by any means tuneful, but nevertheless cheerful and honest. He ducked down slightly as the disturbance approached.

"If'n I were not a fishergnome, an 'unter I would be.

What would you 'unt? I'd 'unt a most ferocious bumble bee.

Ohhhh………. Buzz, buzz, buzz, buzz, buzzy buzz buzz, buzzy buzz buzz…"

"Everard Gnappins!" Percy, from the safety of his own garden, allowed himself the luxury of a little jape and shouted at the top of his voice as a fishing rod passed right in front of him above the top of the hedge.

"Bloody Oberon's wingtips!" Everard exclaimed, jumped and broke wind in perfect unison. "Whom the noddin' donkey be that?"[1]

"It be I." Percy reverted effortlessly to default grumpy mode once contact had been established, "As you would well know if you had taken any kind of notice as to your progress through the woods. Even a mere cursory glance around you would have identified the fact that you were passing my estate, surrounded in your own inimitable style by a clattering of impedimenta and a cacophonous wail that totally destroyed the peace and quietude of the neighbourhood on this pleasant late Spring morning."

"By the 'allowed knees of Titania, Percy, you'm be on top form today, though oi feels I ought ter tell thee that you'm be losin' yer grip a little bit, moi cantankerous old friend."

"Why be that, exactly?" Percy wasn't about to relinquish the argumentative high ground without a struggle, but he was just a little put out by Everard's opening gambit. Both he and Everard were elder statesgnomes of the Whimbury Parish and they understood each other perfectly. Percy was up for a good battle of miserable banter, and he knew that he needed to gather sufficient ammunition before going onto the attack.

"Cos'n I actcherly understood quoite a few o' the words that'n you'm be a usin'. Normally, oi wouldn't 'ave a clue what on earth you'd be talking about, but as oi understands it, you'm be a moanin' that I be a noisy ol' bugger whoilst in the presence o'your good self. Now, am oi roight, or am oi roight?"

"Much as it grieves me to say so, Mr Gnappins, you are roight, I mean right. Now, judging by the fact that you are greatly weighed down by a fishing rod, tackle, baskets and a picnic hamper, I would hazard a guess that you are off fishing for the day?"

"Spot on, Sherlock. Off to the pond fer a day's recreational activity." Everard was being lulled into a false sense of security by Percy's deferential and pacific demeanour.

---

[1] The use of fossil fuels of any kind to produce energy, when there were so many natural sources, was a matter of bewilderment and concern to faeries. Hence "Nodding Donkeys" was one of the worst expletives they could conceive of.

"Activity seems like a rather overambitious description for setting up a seat, rod and stand, and then falling asleep for the rest of the day." Percy and Everard actually got along very well, especially since the day of the birth of Milly Hope, when they earned a great deal of mutual respect from each other. But much of the fun in their relationship derived from the foreplay of insult and counter-insult when their paths crossed.

"Now, Percy, you'm knows full well that oi don't doze off until I've 'ad at least one catch, even if it only be of them there Sirens wot lives around the fountain in the middle."

"Are they still there? Last time I went to that pond it was almost full of weed and algae, and the fountain didn't look as though it had worked since well before Crossover Day."

"An' it still don't!" Everard came over just a little wistful. He and his family had been fishing in the village pond for generations, catching a wide range of tadpoles, water-boatmen, larvae and the like according to the season. Now it was just a way of passing the time. If he was being brutally honest, he would tell all prepared to listen that the pond had been in decline ever since the local human District Council had reduced its Environment and Amenities budget in response to the requirement to cut back on unnecessary public expenditure. "Communityism" they had called it. A chance for the community to take control of its own daily life. Forge the community spirit through group activities like cleaning the village pond.

In fairness, Evadne Potts, wife of Kenneth, the village Postmaster, had tried to organise just such an activity one day soon after the birth of Milly Hope, some two years earlier. Her motives were perhaps only partly community spirit and partly a response to the amount of alien life forms she had found in the coat of her poodle Spot after he had bounded into the pond that day, for who knew what reason.

On the proposed Pond-cleaning Action Day, only herself, Kenneth and their son Adrian had turned up. Spot had been securely tied to the old fire hydrant while they waded in and threw out piles of weed, lager bottles, a cricket bat, and two wire baskets that had been taken from outside of Kenneth's shop many months previously. After an hour of churning up mud and miasmatic gases from the floor of the pond, they gave up and spent the rest of the day taking the bottles to the recycling bank and cleaning the wire baskets for subsequent re-use.

The following day, friends of the Potts' had been profuse in their apology for forgetting the event, or giving excellent excuses such as colds, flu, other communicable and non-communicable diseases, loss of waterproof clothing and boots, need to work, need to do the weekly shopping, need to spend quality time with children/spouses/parents/grandparents etc as appropriate, allergic reactions to algae, birthday/christening/stag/hen etc parties, taking the car for its service, playing sports (some of which were even in season, which impressed Kenneth), and oversleeping – the last of which was exceptionally galling for Evadne since the event had been scheduled for 2 o'clock in the afternoon.

The net effect of this expression of community spirit was that the pond remained something of a no-go area. But Everard returned daily, as much out of habit as expectation.

"Well I've just finished trimming my hedge, so why don't we pause in our daily routines for light mid-morning refreshments on my terrace. Percetta will be busy most of the day setting up her new knit'n'needle club, so we could have our very own moaning session without fear of disturbance." Since handing over the Chair of the Family Grump Dispute and Disquiet Group to his nephew Victor, Percy had become almost sociable, though only in private and with a few selected trusted friends.

"Don't moind if'n oi do." Everard was easily distracted these days and he and Percy had plenty of tales to relive time and time again since Crossover Day, tales that grew in fancy and elaboration at each telling. And Percy had a good stock of early vintage Innkeeper's Choice that he was as happy to share as Everard was to quaff. "Be that the new version of the Stitch'n'Bitch club that she used to run?"

Requisite preliminaries completed, the two friends ambled over to the terrace for what had become their regular update on events in the village.

****

Robin and Trixie Goodfellow sat on the wall of the Potts' front garden in

~ 21 ~

earnest conversation with Spot, the family poodle. Spot stood on his hind legs with his front paws on the wall. To all intents and purposes he was watching the world go by, or at least that limited part of the world which passed his Whimbury home in the middle of a late spring morning. In reality he was deep in the metaphysical patterns and processes that linked his world with that of the fairies of the parish.

"So Barry and I reckon...."

"And me!" Interjected Trixie, who had no intention of being marginalised.

"Yes, well of course and your good self, my little relativity bender." Robin just stopped himself from patting her knee in loving manner as he remembered the cost of such patronising behaviour. Trixie was a most surprising and unsettling pixie, with remarkable transportational powers along with a sense of fun to rival his own. This was what had first attracted Robin to her, and also what kept him on his toes. He had always prided himself on the fact that he would never settle down or moderate his pranksterism, but meeting Trixie at the time of the Crossover had caught his emotions unawares. Once his brother Morris had continued on his travels, Robin had stayed and become a stalwart of the Whimbury fairy community.

"So as I was saying, Barry and Trixie and I reckon that we need to begin the process of educating young Milly in the ways of the Fae. She'll have to join us before her 7th birthday to complete the Crossover and she has a lot to learn. You've talked with her as much as anybody, what do you think?"

Spot looked up and down the road to find something suitable to bark about. Whilst Robin and Trixie would be able to understand him, any humans in the vicinity would simply hear barking and assume he was mad. His excuse appeared in the form of a cyclist, replete in garish Lycra top and shorts proclaiming his support for the Gira d'Italia, though his portly appearance and slow progress rendered his participation in said event extremely unlikely. Spot let rip.

"She already understands much of the balance between the human and natural world. It's remarkable how human children have an innate feeling for other species, long before they are encouraged to see themselves as special and above the rest of creation. Larry and Junior have had words with her and sown seeds of creativity. They see great potential in her. And her parents will be sympathetic, I'm sure. They were well chosen - open and caring, receptive to tradition and free from unworthy ambitions."

There is much contained within a few barks for those prepared to listen to the subtle modulations and nano-pauses within the overall structure.

Robin and Trixie looked over their shoulder in unison to watch the cyclist pick himself up and, satisfied that no serious damage had been done, they responded to Spot's encouraging remarks.

"We've made contact of course. At first, she just seemed to look straight through us but now she focuses on us with those sparkly eyes of hers and she appreciates that we're here. It's just difficult to know how much to pass on. We don't want to overburden her with information, not in these early years. It's hard enough for her to take everything in from her own world." Robin was by nature an impatient sprite and he had to be regularly restrained by both Trixie and Barry from trying to hasten the education process.

Spot responded with another sudden loud bark. This one was not intended for fairy conversation but was delivered more in a spirit of devilment, having seen the effect of his previous outburst on the passing cyclist. It was greeted with what Spot presumed, correctly, was a human gesture of defiance and serious rudeness.

"Behave yourself young poodle." Trixie stifled a laugh as Spot turned to her and stuck out his slobbery tongue which indicated intense happiness and fulfilment. In truth, so little happened on a day-to-day basis in Whimbury that discomforting a cyclist was a matter for celebration.

"The truth is that none of us are certain exactly what will happen when she finally fulfils her potential." Trixie was sensitive to the unspoken detail of the Crossover legend and favoured the precautionary approach when it came to developing the Fae side of Milly's character. All that anyone knew for certain was that she would be able to be both human and faery, and cross between the two whenever she chose. That was what would differentiate her from those few humans who already could communicate with faeries but who were unable ever to fully enter their world. The legend was clear on one point however. She must achieve the first crossover before she became 7 years old or the chance would be missed and she could only be, at best, a human with very special powers.

"So we're going to need you and Charlie and all your animal comrades to teach her as much of the non-human natural world as you can, as quickly as possible. Help her to appreciate the subtleties of the animal and flower community, along with the insects and Crustacea of course, to add to what she needs to know about the largely unseen and unknown worlds beyond." Robin couldn't help himself. He was active and a doer, a resourceful charmer with a big heart. Trixie had been won over by him and his ways, but knew enough to realise that her task from now on was to provide him with boundaries in as subtle a way as possible. What they both agreed upon was that their little community had a major part to play in bringing about the Crossover correctly and on time. It accepted the responsibility and the privilege, but it had no experience of such matters and it was going to take all its resourcefulness to bring it about. Robin for one was in his element, and he had the welcome ability to pull others along with him.

Spot recognised the importance of what Robin and Trixie had said and barked his affirmation both to them and to a sadly empty stretch of road.

Chapter Two

WILL AND MIRANDA EXTRACTED MILLY from her pushchair and watched her run to the slide. She always ran first to the slide because it meant she had to ease through the mouth of an elephant and project herself down its bendy trunk onto the rubber mat below. This she enjoyed greatly and was prepared to repeat the process time and time again while her parents made appropriate whooshing noises and other encouraging statements until they felt it was time to move onto an alternative piece of equipment. She was less enthusiastic about the swing and roundabout, probably due to the fact that they were not designed around animals. She liked animals and reserved her most infectious giggles for the chicken on a spring that swung this way and that with just a sufficient degree of unpredictability to appeal to her more adventurous side.

Miranda sat on the bench and smiled as Will held Milly's hand to steady her across the wooden logs that formed the wiggly snake in the middle of the playground. He was so protective of his little princess and shared much of her childish innocence. Once Milly had tired of the little childrens' playground, Will would take her to the older kids' area and carry her down the big slide with him. That was his treat for the day. Miranda's treat was to find other mothers to sit and talk to. She got on well with almost everyone in Whimbury but there were no other families with a child of Milly's age and she missed the comparing of development and the tales of new accomplishments. Her only other opportunity was the Mother and Toddler aquaerobics session at the Whimburton Baths every fortnight, but this was a busy time and she was on her own with Milly, so the benefit of having Will along to attend to all of their joint needs once a week was a greatly anticipated luxury.

Playtime over, they moved from the playground to the main part of the town park where they laid down a picnic rug beside the flower beds and opened up the cool bag with its store of sandwiches and drinks, carefully assembled earlier in the morning before setting off for the bus. To this was added a cream cake that they bought from the bread and cake stall in the market square. This was the one concession to debauchery that they allowed themselves during the week - a dietary eccentric in the otherwise level playing field of good honest healthy food that they set out for normal mealtimes. A cake from the same stall each week because it alone used all organic ingredients, and somehow organic cream and carbohydrates seemed so much better for you.

Milly was satisfied with one little bite of cake and then moved off to explore the surrounding lawns and flowers for wildlife. She would find woodlice to talk to and butterflies to watch intently. She stared at the bees hovering around the lavender bushes and found a patch of grass with no daisies in it to sit upon and ponder the wonders of nature with her chin in her hands. Occasionally, she would point her finger at one part of the flower bed as if to direct the traffic towards a currently under-exploited source of pollen. Will and Miranda sat and studied their daughter in a relaxed manner.

"Funny how she seems so contented in her own little world outside and yet can get so frustrated when she has to stay inside." Will lay back on his elbows taking in the sun and colour of the park with the parish church in the background, its bell-tower encouraging his eyes heavenward for a moment.

"We'll let's hope for a good summer, and she can play out in the garden." Miranda loved the Spring for its promise of new life and good things to come. Will loved the Spring up until the moment that his hay-fever exploded into action and he was reduced to a slobbering wreck with a comic red nose and a pocketful of drenched tissues. He was just glad that this visit to Whimburton had not coincided with the cutting of the grass. Any time now he would begin to be laid low in the mornings and evenings with a never-ending bout of sneezing and dribbling that abated but little during the main part of the day. He'd tried all the remedies: local honey - to desensitise himself to the pollen;

vinegar and lemon infusion - to make him realise that there were worse things than sneezing; regular showers and baths - to wash the pollen off his skin; Vaseline up the nose - to trap the pollen before it hit the nasal receptors; enough chewing gum to equip the whole of the US military - to promote the production of saliva and distract the brain; and, as a last resort; tightly screwed up tissue in each nostril to block the pollen and soak up the mucus. Tablets gave him strange reactions and he'd once misdirected a nasal spray with dire consequences to those sitting opposite to him at the time. Nothing really made any substantial difference.

"Perhaps I should make her a sand pit this year? I could easily get an old tractor tyre from work, wheel it across the road and just lay it in the front garden – then fill it with sand. It would be quite safe."

Miranda was about to utter her approval for the idea, when she became aware of a loud muttery-type of shouting from the entrance to the park. She turned her head to see what was going on. Striding along the path in their general direction was an unkempt man in an ill-fitting and ragged suit, carrying a supermarket bag and waving scraps of a newspaper in angry fashion at nothing and no-one in particular.

"What is it?" Will lay back and waited for Miranda to put him in the picture.

"It's that man Ralph! You know? The one who's often walking through town, and who we saw once sleeping in the doorway of the old Picture House. He's heading our way and seems upset."

Will sat up instantly and looked anxiously across at Milly who seemed oblivious to any disturbance.

"Maybe I'd better head him off before he gets near Princess?" Will adopted his best protective mode and prepared to get up.

"Everyone says he's quite harmless. Just leave him and let him walk past without any fuss. That's probably safest."

Will sat on his haunches and bounced on his heels ready to leap into action. Miranda watched as Ralph approached and concentrated to try to make out what he was saying. He seemed lost in his own thoughts, totally unaware of the existence of anything outside of his own little bubble.

"Parting the Red Sea! That was a miracle! Need a miracle. Listening, lost art – talk, talk, talk. No substance. Empty. Spin the bottle, spin the arrow, spin the news. All in a spin. Square the circle or lose the battle. No bees, no honey. No sweet, all sour. Bee hive – behave, won't behave. To the barricades, mes amis. What's amiss? What did I miss? The point. What's the point? What's the answer? What's the question? What's the future?"

Will and Miranda, tense and unsettled, attempted to look without looking and listen without listening. Ralph had been around for years, but since they only came into town once a week, they rarely came across him, and if they did it was usually at a distance or while he was asleep or quietly playing with items from his bag. To the best of their knowledge he had never caused any offence or harm to any other person, apart from those who were affronted by anyone who was out of the ordinary and who failed to conform to the norms of decent society. But this time he was clearly troubled and they had no experience of this side to Ralph.

Ralph continued up the path until he was level with the band of Hopes. Will concentrated his brainwaves to encourage him to carry on walking forward and ever onward into the safety of the far distance. But Ralph stopped suddenly. His hands, earlier waving in all directions with a mind of their own, fell to his side. His hunched shoulders rose and his head tilted back. His manic eyes softened and his mouth formed the beginnings of a smile. After a few moments of assessing the situation, he turned his face towards Milly. At that precise moment Milly stood up and turned to look directly at Ralph. Their eyes met.

Will and Miranda would never forget the pregnant pause as their daughter and the parish outcast stood looking across at each other, a safe distance apart in terms of metric or imperial measurements, but with an emotional closeness that Miranda could sense coursing through every fibre of her body. Ralph stood erect and his face broke into the broadest of grins. He put down his paper and bag and tugged his matted forelock before bowing to Milly elaborately and gracefully. She laughed, picked a daisy from beside where she had been sitting, and proffered it in his general direction. He turned to Will and Miranda and opened his arms in a gesture of welcome and friendship. They stood bemused before him. He swivelled back to face Milly.

"Of course, of course, at last." He picked up his paper and bag once again and moved on. Milly waved at him and continued to wave until he reached the far entrance to the park, where he turned and waved back. Milly sat down and resumed her conversation with the flowers and the insects.

****

Barry cast his eyes over the bar in the Snug at the Families Grump, intense in their attempts to navigate their way through a game of dominoes with two dominoes missing. He had recently introduced a new dimension to the game by revealing the identity of only one of the absent dominoes. This placed a significant hurdle in the way of the less mathematically minded of the players. Barry had realised a couple of years back that to keep the Grumps moaning and complaining (and therefore, by definition, amused and contented, if only inwardly), he had to come up with new frustrations and annoyances at regular intervals. The mark of a good and successful pub manager was incremental innovation. Too much or too quick and the conservative tendencies of the customers would be pushed beyond their limits. Too little or too slow, and they would get bored and drink more slowly. Neither scenario was good for business.

For those in the Snug, dominoes had been a way of life for generations. But by the time that Barry had taken over as publican at the Royal Oak, whingeing about the routine vagaries of the game had undergone several rounds of the multiplier effect involving moaning about there being nothing new to moan about, and then moaning about having to moan about nothing in particular, or the effort expended in having to find something new to moan about. After a while, and when he considered that the regulars were primed and ready for a new challenge, Barry began to remove a random domino from each set before handing them out. Then when the participants had grown used to this ploy, he removed two. Initially, he had told each team which ones were missing and then sat back and watched as the gnomes first grew agitated and then more aggressively animated as game succeeded game. Over a period of time, he grew to recognise the signs of a need for change. In this case, one or two of the players began to show initial signs of moving from their state of agitation into one that threatened a degree of enjoyment at the intellectual stimulation provided by the situation. As soon as Barry spotted the merest suggestion of a grin or smile from one of his customers he knew it was time to move on. A cheerful Grump could result in an unstable atmosphere and that was something to be avoided at all costs.

And so he manipulated the rules of engagement just enough to keep things tense. He just prayed to Oberon that, for the foreseeable future at least, he would be able to maintain gentle step changes to the prevailing status quo, and not have to re-introduce Darts. [2]

Barry turned his attention to the public bar where more raucous behaviour was the order of the day. The Families Happ were assembled into small huddles, joking and laughing at the previous day's events and/or the Grumps, both of which were popular topics. It was too early for the main activities of the evening which tended to revolve around a quiz, or faeryoke, or pool or bar billiards competitions, or illustrated talks (usually on the subject of alcohol or having an alcohol-related theme). The bonhomie of the bar attracted other fun-loving fae species including sprites and pixies. Barry was proud of the eclectic mix of his customers. There was room for everyone and everyone was welcome, including newcomers.

Over there, a table full of Gnappins, most, including Everard, with their heads resting on beer mats, hands still firmly grasping their glass of Innkeeper's Choice, and the others laying back in their chairs, facing the ceiling with open mouths and snoring vigorously. In the corner, Trixie's mother and father with assorted other relatives were playing table skittles, and by the window Eric O'Shy was quietly reading his newspaper. Eric, quiet and apparently introverted by nature, had established himself as a regular over the past few months and had become a fount of knowledge on parish matters and faery politics over a wider area. His ability to remember trivia was a much-appreciated quality when teams were short of players on quiz nights.

"It's building up to a good night!" Barry stood between Trixie and Damon behind the bar and put his arms around them. He counted himself blessed with

---

[2] Barry had decided on a "temporary" ban on darts a year back, when he finally ran out of filler paste for the holes in the wall, some of which were worryingly close to the bar.

two reliable and hard-working employees. Trixie was fast, smart, efficient and full of energy, while Damon was, well, reliable and hard-working.

"Busy already, Barry. Good job we changed those barrels earlier on." Damon was polishing glasses and preparing himself for the evening onslaught. Whilst not the brightest of Sprites, he knew his job and ploughed on regardless whatever the state of play. He could spot a potential affray from afar and had the right techniques to deal with it. His worldly-wise approach made up for the lightweight nature of his academic intellect.

"Indeed it was, Damon, indeed it was." Barry prided himself not only on his intimate knowledge of his customers, their customs and their peculiarities, but also on the cleanliness of his cellar and the quality of his ales. On their most recent visit to the cellar, Barry had been pleased to note that Junior was doing a good job keeping the algae and other organisms under control down amongst the roots of the tree, while his father continued teaching him the more advanced tricks of the trade. The work-rate of the young woodlouse was impressive and he was a quick learner. Barry had to suppress a grin every time he went down and heard Junior regaling Larry with excerpts from such favourites as the Sprites of Penzance, Ruddiheck, and, on that particular occasion, The Gnome Men of the Yard.

"Ter tell yer the troof, Bazza," Larry had confided, "I'll be glad when I've finally taught 'im all I know. All this light opera stuff is givin' me the willies. I can't be doin' wiv it meself. Still if that's what 'e enjoys. Must be 'is muvva's doin'. It's nuffink ter do wiv me, that's fer sure." Larry had given the woodlouse version of a grimace, and replaced his antenna sound-proofing lichen-muffs. Once Barry and Damon had returned to the bar, he went back to reading up on his classics and merely issued instructions to Junior as and when necessary.

"Hello, here comes trouble!" Trixie looked over to the door as Mack and Trevor Stout swaggered in. Mack had never been short of self-confidence and bravado, while Trevor had always been short of brain cells. For all of his outward gusto and bluster, Mack had no serious harm in him, but he did have a reputation to maintain, particularly since his valiant and game-changing stand against the powers of evil on the day of the birth of Milly Hope. Today he stood in the doorway, as always, his hands raised to shoulder level, palms outwards, silencing the standing ovation that hadn't materialised since around two weeks after his heroic exploits. To a backdrop of overwhelming apathy, he "John Wayned" his way over to the bar and smiled at Barry. Only a palomino thoroughbred and a large Stetson could have enhanced the image of superstardom that he presented to anyone that was prepared to look. No-one was.

"A large Innkeeper's Choice for me, my good fellow, and a small Sarsaparilla for my partner here." Mack leaned on the bar and barked his order, looking Barry squarely in the eye and winking as he did so. Trevor leaned on the bar next to him, then removed his elbow from the slops tray and wrung out his shirt sleeve.

"Certainly Mr Stout, and would you like them in your usual jugs?" Barry knew how important it was for Mack to maintain his persona, and he presented his question with sufficient volume and gravitas to ensure that the rest of the public bar appreciated the status of his current customer.

In truth, Mack had remained a little confused since the confrontation with the Nixies that had scrambled his atoms and reassembled them several days later, not necessarily with all the right connections. He knew that he was tough, intolerant, aggressive and loud – the other regulars told him so on a daily basis - and he knew that Trevor depended on him and, to a certain extent, needed his protection, but he couldn't get to grips with the occasional lapse into humility when he least expected it. From time to time he realised that he had begun to assess situations from both perspectives and this was most disconcerting. In the absence of any close friends to confide in, he had taken the only obvious course left open to him and allowed the pub manager inside his defences. Barry for his part had developed a grudging respect for Mack and was happy to help him through his nagging self-doubts – particularly if it meant he kept drinking and livening up the atmosphere.

The necessary preliminaries over, Mack engaged Barry in surreptitious conversation.

"So how do you think this Crossover girl is coming along?" He offered up the question discreetly from the corner of his mouth facing Barry, whilst simultaneously adopting a hard-faced, half-manic smile from the corner facing the rest of the bar. Barry, by now, was used to this disjointed pose and gave an appropriate and similarly two-pronged response from behind his bartender's towel, tactically raised to allow an exaggerated cleaning of an already sparkling glass.

"From what I've heard she's proving very responsive. Still too young to understand much, of course, but Larry says she watches and learns from him and his mates whenever she's in the garden, and Spot and Charlie reckon that she knows what they're thinking before they do. She sees us quite clearly and just accepts us as part of the background to life, so all seems well so far. Now that she's starting to put proper sentences together, we should be able to begin the process of real communication in the very near future."

How long before she can cross over fully?" Mack had thrown himself selflessly into the battle to complete the Crossover ceremony and had laid his heart and soul on the line to enable it to happen. He'd never really understood it, but he knew how important it was and felt a need to get to grips with the next stage of the process.

"A few years yet, Mack. It should happen by her seventh birthday or it will never be fulfilled in the true sense of the word. It's reaching the stage when it's all down to us again. This has got to be our one and only focus from now on."

Mack downed his Innkeeper's Choice and looked into the far distance. He gave Trevor a playful clip round the ear and smiled.

"No pressure there then. Bring it on!"

****

In the Village Hall, the Parish Council was resolutely failing to come to order. Evadne Potts, the Chair, was tapping her pencil in agitated fashion on the table as each apology for absence was debated in depth regarding potential reasons, previous occurrences, the health and welfare of close and distant relatives, and whether or not each absentee had been allocated to bring refreshments that evening.

"Can we please get on to the "Matters Arising" item? We do have a guillotine at 9 o'clock and, as I can confidently predict we will cease to be quorate after that time due to the announcement of the results of the first semi-final of "Strictly go Ping-Pong" on the Telly at nine-thirty, we must get cracking."

"Shall I put the kettle on? We're probably ready for a cuppa aren't we?" Lucinda Patterson rose and then sat down immediately as she caught the frosty gaze of Evadne out of the corner of her eye. "Or perhaps in a few minutes!"

"The only matter arising is an update on the council's consultation on the proposed new Local Plan. If you remember there was a rumour last month that the district council were intending to recommend releasing some land in the Parish for additional housing. This was a matter of great concern to us all and Fred agreed to go to the 'Economic Development, Growth and Sustainability Sub –committee' meeting last week and report back." Evadne eyeballed Fred Butterworth, erstwhile village schoolmaster and now part-time churchwarden. Evadne's eyeballing was akin to having a knuckleduster waved in front of one's face by an ex-rugby prop forward with facial elements described in terms of a vegetable allotment and a largely toothless grin.

Fred broke out into a cold sweat. He paused as if searching for just the right word to serve a very specific situation, which in fact it was. He raised his pencil to emphasise the point that was about to be made, but no point materialised.

"You didn't go, did you?" Evadne cut to the chase and brought prevarication to a halt. She knew her fellow council members from way back and could predict their behaviour and thoughts before they themselves knew.

"Well, you see, it coincided with the final of the all-Whimshire indoor bowls championship, and it was on satellite TV, and I only intended to watch the first few ends but the excitement got to me and before you knew it was 20-all and this youngster – he can't have been more than 40 or 45 – had an easy upshot to beat the reigning champion and he just feathered one of his own bowls on the way through and ended up with two of his own bowls in the ditch and giving away a winning position. They were both playing amazingly well, some incredible draw shots – the weight and direction impeccable – and it was tense all the way through. My little heart was pounding away......."

"So you didn't go!" Evadne cut the thread with a somewhat judgemental and very loud exclamation. She never bore grudges but expected a high standard of dependability from her peers, and she was not slow to let any such peer who proved to be less than dependable know exactly how she felt about it.

"No, sorry!" Fred sat chastised.

"Then we are no further forward on that particular matter, or at least we would not be had I not contacted one of our own local councillors for her take on the situation. She doesn't sit on that committee but she does hear what goes on from a colleague who informed her that the Council has to find a lot more land for housing across the District to meet its targets, and that Whimbury is one village that could be earmarked for quite a substantial expansion. This, of course, is a matter that we must take very seriously and we must try to find a consensus opinion on what we think about it so that we can respond to the consultation in a sensible fashion. So any questions?"

"Who actually won the final, Fred?" Lucinda was aware of the unwritten rule that Evadne frequently threatened to invoke – "three strikes and you're out", where each strike was here represented by one of her frosty gazes. Lucinda belatedly realised that she was now on two and resolved to keep quiet for the rest of the meeting.

"Any questions regarding the housing situation?" Evadne threw out a general offer whilst looking directly at, and through, Lucinda. Lucinda smiled and shrugged, and looked around for support in the form of a relevant question that would deflect attention from herself. None was forthcoming.

"Right, well I've put the topic down as an agenda item anyway so we can come back to it." Evadne remained focussed and totally in charge. Once she sensed that she now had everyone's undivided attention, she moved on to the main concerns of the meeting.

"Item One relates to the village bus service – and I have a suspicion that as we consider this, we may well find a connection with the housing issue. Now I was hoping that someone who uses the bus regularly might come along tonight to throw some insights into the mix, but there wouldn't appear to be anyone here – perhaps a combination of Whimburton Market Day and the TV Ping Pong?"

A nervous laughter rippled around the table. Fred Butterworth, anxious to earn some bonus points, opened up the debate.

"Well the issue seems to me to be that all the services that us old 'uns need are in Whimburton. There's nothing much left here any more. The school's closed, the local boy scout troop has folded, there's no-one left to run the crèche, and the cricket team haven't had anyone run out in the last two seasons cos they're all too old to run. The vicar turns out if they're short, but he can't fit into his whites any more, and he can't see as far as the stumps the other end anyway, so he's a bit of a liability to be honest. Well-meaning of course, but it's getting embarrassing. I've taken over doing the scoring, but that's not difficult when we never get into double figures – there's one section of the scoreboard that's got sun-bleached because no numbers get put on those hooks. Obviously it would only take a little bit of blackboard paint to sort it out, but….."

"So in a nutshell," Evadne felt a sudden urge to summarise the main points expressed thus far, "you're saying that we need the bus service to enable us to get to facilities that are no longer available in the village."

"Exactly, nicely put Madame Chair. I've asked at Green's the Machinery Repair place if they've got any black paint that would do, but they haven't so I'll have to go to A-Z Decorating Needs in Whimburton before I can sort out the scoreboard."

"Quite!" Evadne butted in before Fred could expand yet further on his dilemma. "All of which brings me back to the issue of additional housing in the village. With extra housing, and so more people, we could maybe keep the shops going and increase the number of bus passengers, which would be good. Can anyone see any other good or bad results?"

"Might improve the batting and bowling line-up if we could attract younger families – especially those with older teenagers – some of those youngsters today can get the new ball to swing all over the place. And they'd be quicker fielders. Or maybe if they were older folk they'd join the bowling club. The committee's getting a bit crotchety and….. You were maybe thinking of other kinds of results?" Fred had been getting excited, but managed to haul himself back into the more sombre tones of the discussion.

"Well actually I was, but having said that you do make some useful points there. New people could well support our fine institutions, just so long as they don't just drive off back into town to do everything. But we'll have no control over that – after all most of them will work there."

"Yes, that's one thing we'd have to look out for – there'd be more cars on the road, and depending on where the houses go they could block some of our nice views." Lucinda was pretty sure she was on safe ground this time and broke her vow of silence.

"And we could probably expect some damage to our trees and hedgerows and wildlife." Evadne was an environmentalist at heart.

"Yes, there's that. We'd need to know where the housing would go before we could say whether we agreed with it or not." Eileen Robinson, farmer's wife and award-winning cheesemaker, thought a lot and said little, but within the thinking process much sifting of dross took place, and what was subsequently said was usually relevant and pithy. "Obviously more people will help bring the village back to life, but we don't want to lose what makes it a special place."

"Well said Eileen." Evadne welcomed some supporting input. "So I propose that we take a pro-active approach and, by the time of the next meeting, try to identify some land that could be built on without too much harm and also make out a case for what makes Whimbury special. Then, when we get to see what the Council are thinking we can be ready with our comments and suggestions. Maybe we'll also find out how much the Council believes in this "Communityism" idea?"

"I'm happy to second that." Fred threw his arm in the air with a little too much obvious enthusiasm, but Evadne was now on a roll and was happy to keep the process moving smoothly and without further ado.

"Thank you, Fred. All in favour?"

All hands were raised simultaneously in a further display of exaggerated enthusiasm.

"Good, now can we move on? What is it Fred?" All hands bar one had been dropped.

"Could I suggest that the next meeting does not coincide with the second semi-final of Strictly….." Fred lowered his hand slowly.

****

Will and Miranda walked briskly across Station Road from the bus stop and began to head home up High Street. They stopped opposite the Mission Church and Will jogged across the road to check the notice board once more. He muttered to himself. "Looks like we'll miss the meeting. Never mind, I'm sure Evadne will tell us all about it in the greatest imaginable detail at the very first opportunity."

On walking back he saw Miranda laughing with Milly.

"What's the joke?" The hilarity was infectious.

"While we were waiting for you, Milly looked over to the Royal Oak and said 'Faery Tree!'"

Will knelt on his haunches beside the pushchair. "Well, who's a clever girl then?" He poked her button nose gently.

"She's never said that before. When did you tell her the old story?"

Will looked bemused. "I didn't. I presumed you had."

Chapter Three

BARRY AND ROBIN MEANDERED DOWN the High Street stopping to chat with whomsoever or whatsoever was out and about. It was warm and sunny, and there were noticeably more smiles on the faces of the human population of the village. Kenneth Potts was re-arranging the array of fruit and vegetables in front of his shop ready to chat with each and every passer-by, few of whom in fact bought anything, but he knew what they liked and made sure that he had enough of those things in to tempt them, just in case. He knew them all by name, background, family ties and medical condition. They all knew him and loved him, though that was seldom sufficient to encourage them to cross the threshold and keep him in business. In truth, it was only the post office part of the business that kept him going – that and the joy of providing a personal and sociable service to his clientele.

Barry watched as a young man bought a banana and requested a packet of crisps. Kenneth went inside with the purchase money and returned with the crisps and a paper bag for the banana. A momentary pause to pass the basic minimum of pleasantries and the customer moved on.

"Last of the big spenders, eh?" Robin perched himself on an open sack of potatoes and gestured in the direction of the rapidly disappearing resident.

"In a hurry to get the bus!" Barry clambered up to sit beside his brother and, having decided that was enough exertion for one morning, turned his face to the sun and luxuriated in its warmth. These were good times. The Crossover child was among them, the local faery community was united, village life continued in a relatively untroubled manner, and his brother had finally settled down with a partner bright and sharp enough to keep him in his place, which, he was pleased to say, was Whimbury. Sure, he could never entirely expunge the nagging little thought in his mind that maybe it was all too good, but, hey, so long as he took nothing about the future for granted, it couldn't hurt to enjoy the present, could it?

"What is life if full of stress, we strive for more yet gather less!" Robin broke in to Barry's silent reverie.

"Sorry?" Barry was now one chapter behind the rest of the plot.

"So much in a hurry to get the bus, there's no time to chat, no time to share, no time to eat properly – I mean, those crisps are fine as a crunchy sound effect [3] but whatever happened to real food? Why not get up a bit earlier, make a nice fresh lunch, stop off to talk to neighbours, find out what their hopes and fears are, enjoy the fresh air on your face and, in his case, the sun on your bald patch. Rushing to meet deadlines and failing to experience the joy of living. What's the human world coming to, eh?"

Barry looked askance at his brother.

"Coming from someone who has spent most of his supposedly adult life pursuing pranks with the gusto of a Sprite with his bum on fire, and, what's more, extolling the virtues of such a lifestyle, that last little outburst marks a dramatic change of attitude."

"Maturity bro! Maturity and responsibility! Maturity and responsibility and…"

"And fear of what Trixie might do if she caught you acting the idiot once too often."

"Nothing to do with it, bro!" Robin interrupted a little more hurriedly than was strictly necessary. "I love Trixie to bits, but there's no way she's going to cramp my style. I've still got the clown instinct. Every minute there's a new jape being plotted up here!" He pointed to his head knowingly.

"Checking to see if anything's loose?" Trixie appeared from nowhere and sat in the narrow gap between the two brothers.

"Hello, my precious. We were just talking about you." Robin laughed nervously and gave her a hug. He was a natural joker but useless at covering

---

[3] One used to great effect by the faeries of Whimbury during the Crossover "incident".

his own back, largely because he was in the habit of facing life fully head on. Trixie's ability to confound the principles of time, and be in two places within a millisecond of the same moment, could be seriously disconcerting.

"I was just saying that I love you to bits, wasn't I Barry?" Robin hugged her that little bit tighter.

"He certainly was – he said that you've got a champions style and that it's all down to pure instinct. Oh yes, Trixie! You've got it all taped." Barry stared across the road in a vague, disconnected manner to avoid eye contact with Trixie and Robin, either of which would have broken his resolve to keep a straight face.

"Pity he's not so free with his compliments to my face! Still, I suppose that's males for you[4] – keep their emotions hidden to avoid any possible signs of weakness. Isn't that so, my little prankster?" She gazed into Robin's eyes with a smile that said 'I know you inside out' in all but the words themselves.

"Everything all right at the Royal Oak?" Barry waited for the full embarrassment experienced by Robin to work itself out, and then deftly changed the subject.

"Fine! I've changed a barrel of the 'Innkeeper's Special' and given Junior instructions about cleaning algae from round the taps. Damon is doing a final tidy up in the snug." She paused just long enough to indicate that such matters were insignificant in the current order of things. "But, there's talk of a strange new faery in the village." Her voice quickened. "Everard saw him near the pond and says he looks and sounds important. He asked about the Faery Council and who was in charge. Everard says his voice cut through him like a knife. He was so flummoxed that he forgot to ask the stranger's name."

"We've not had a 'strange' stranger through here since Nefer left, and that was two years ago." Barry felt his heart pound. "Her brief visit was both exhilarating and positively frightening. I can't decide if that's enough of both for one lifetime, or whether I'm ready for another adventure."

"Don't get ahead of yourself, bro," Robin was not renowned for being a steadying influence, and deep in his soul he felt a match being struck under

---

[4] Even fae males.

the kindling of his suppressed daring. "We don't know anything about him yet – he may even have already moved on."

Robin mentally crossed all his digits and touched the whole of Whimbury Wood for luck, in the hope that the stranger had not moved on and was indeed to be the catalyst for another adventure. He daren't say this directly to Trixie – not yet – but the mundane comings and goings of the village could never really hold his entire interest for any significant length of time. In truth she knew this, and had prepared herself to give him a long leash when he needed it. After all, it was his sense of fun and boldness that attracted her in the first place, and village life for the faery community was never going to return to normal anyway, now that the Crossover was in their midst.

****

Evadne and Eileen walked purposefully down the High Street, each clutching a pile of papers.

"Right, if we start at the bottom and work up the street, doing alternate houses each, we can make sure that we stay in sight of one another. Then we can work our way towards Home Farm and back again down the other side of the road. If we're still feeling fit, we can do the houses on Station Road as well. If not, we'll do them tomorrow."

Evadne was in full organising mode, and although most of her sentences terminated in the upward lilt appropriate to a question, they were questions that quite clearly suggested the correct answer and discouraged counter-argument or alternative perspective. Despite this, she respected Eileen and knew that if Eileen expressed concern about any of her ideas or raised questions, there was almost certainly good reason and it would be worth listening. They made a good team, and Evadne was happy to work alongside her. Besides, posting the leaflets took very little time and she had a lovely lemon drizzle cake to share alongside a hot beverage, once they had finished the round.

As a committed devotee of local democracy, Evadne had high hopes of the Parish Council representing the views of the village to the local district council. However, she was also a realist and knew that there were times when the parish councillors needed leadership and guidance – especially when there was something good on the television. A pro-active approach to dealing with the issue of additional housing in the village, as agreed at the last meeting, would not happen unless she made it happen, and Eileen was the most trustworthy and dependable of her fellow councillors when it came to helping with the organisation of any kind of activity. Between them they had designed a simple questionnaire to ascertain the views of the locals on such matters as what they liked most about Whimbury, what they disliked, and what they felt about the possibility of new housing being built within the parish.

So far as Evadne could remember, the only previous time that the opinions of locals had been sought on a serious matter was over 30 years earlier when she was in her final year at school. As inexperienced as she was in the mechanism of local politics at that time, even she could tell a badly designed questionnaire when she saw one. The Council were proposing, as Council's do from time to time, a dual carriageway by-pass around the town of Whimburton that would have involved the demolition of most of Whimbury village and the dissection of Whimbury Woods, along with the loss of a substantial amount of some of the best farmland in the County. A quick skim through the official consultation brochure led the young Evadne to doubt the desire of the Council to hear conflicting views on the proposal.

Such questions as 'Would you prefer that we knock down the village hall or the station?' and 'Explain in up to 12 words why you agree that it would be better to enable traffic flow to flow freely through Whimburton than to preserve a group of very old and ugly buildings in Whimbury', seemed to Evadne to lack a little of the subtlety and impartiality needed to get to grips with the true feelings of local residents on the issue. She persuaded a group of her school friends to write in to the Council complaining about the inadequacy of the consultation exercise, but they were fobbed off with a patronising letter from the Chair of the Transport, Nature Conservation and Childrens' Playgrounds Committee. Fortunately, he, along with many of his colleagues, was resoundingly defeated in the next local elections, and the Committee was re-organised by the new administration into the Environmental Services, School Meals and Highways Sub-Committee. At the same time the roads budget was slashed and the monies provisionally allocated to the by-pass project were instead transferred to a scheme that enabled an increased frequency of emptying the waste bins across the district.

Evadne was nothing if not fair-minded, and she had devised the questionnaire that she and Eileen were now delivering, in a genuine attempt to get local residents to think about their community – what it was and what it meant, along with what it could or might be. They had begun the day with the expectation of a little light stroll before morning coffee, posting leaflets through letterboxes, and then repeating the stroll the next day picking up the completed comments sheet. However, Evadne had failed to factor in the general ignorance of the locals about the Council's proposals for new housing in the district,[5] and she spent an inordinate amount of time explaining the need for the exercise and the importance of their views to everyone they passed on the street or who were working in their front garden.

The two women paused at the bottom of High Street and checked their watches.

"Station Road or lunch?" Evadne posed the rhetorical question whilst turning on her heels and heading for her home. Eileen was happy to defer to Evadne's decisive action and put the remaining leaflets in her bag, ready for another round the next day.

"You're very welcome to stay for lunch!" Evadne lifted the latch on the garden gate and held it open for Eileen, knowing that her offer would not be refused.

****

Will Hope lay on the floor in his living room, watching Milly putting together the small jigsaw and then taking it apart, putting it back in the box, taking the pieces out again, and putting them back together once again. The sequence was repeated time after time, and each time, as the last piece was put in place, she would pronounce proudly, "Milly did it!" Her desire to be able to do everything a grown up could, albeit at a smaller scale, was powerful, as was her sense of independence.

---

[5] Probably due to the lack of any serious attempt to disseminate the necessary information to the people who most needed to know.

Will called Milly his "little diet plan", because he would frequently come home for lunch and spend the whole time watching Milly play. He began his working day at Green's Farm Machinery workshop early in the mornings and often missed his daughter's breakfast time. Not wishing to miss any more of her development than was absolutely necessary, he would frequently pass his lunch hour reading to her or encouraging her to use her imagination with her toys and playthings. Only if her own lunch was ready a little early could he be persuaded to join her and Miranda at the kitchen table and nibble at his sandwiches, or demonstrate to Milly how lovely her mixed vegetable omelette tasted on those days when she chose to be somewhat finicky with her food. Miranda had become used to checking his clothes, and occasionally his hair, for stray eggy or other related deposits when he finally roused himself to go back to work.

For the first few days after Milly was born, Will continued to take his lunch to work and eat with his friends, but since the workshop was so close to home, he soon realised that going home was a practical alternative that enabled him to spend more time with his wife and baby. As Milly grew up, Miranda appreciated more and more the few moments of peace in the middle of the day when there was someone else to keep an eye on things. Milly was getting progressively steadier and faster on her feet, and Miranda would feel exhausted by mid-afternoon just trying to keep up with their "little princess".

This particular day, Milly was repeatedly completing one of her favourite jigsaws. This was a picture of a tree with flowers and fungi underneath, and a little boy sitting against the trunk. There were twelve large pieces and Milly could assemble them correctly in any order with which they came out of the box. She would pick up a piece, hold it hovering over the emerging picture, and state in her most adult voice, "Maybe here?" as she turned it around and around till it was ready to be dropped into place. Will smiled as he recognised his mannerisms being reborn in his daughter.

"Milly's lunch is ready, if you want to come and help." Miranda stuck her head around the door and smiled at the chaos on the floor of the living room.

"OK. Take her through and I'll follow when I've tidied up a bit here." Will stood up and surveyed the carnage, attempting to assess where best to begin.

"Just leave it. I'll sort it later. You only have a few minutes before you're due back. Come and persuade her that beans on toast with grated cheese is exactly what she always wanted." Miranda whisked Milly off, with Will in hot pursuit, tip-toeing as best he could through the toys and books on the floor. By the time he reached the kitchen, Miranda was engaged in a life and death struggle with Milly trying to get her to put on her bib. Will sat down opposite to her, got out his handkerchief, and wrapped it around his throat. He rattled a spoon on the table till he gained Milly's attention. He pointed to his throat dramatically and with great emphasis, and then pointed to Milly, who immediately grabbed her bib from Miranda and made to put it round her own neck.

"Milly do it!" And she did.

Miranda sighed the sigh of a mother who sees the future in terms of herself versus a daddy and a daddy's little girl. Accepting that she was already outnumbered, she laughed inwardly at Will miming the ecstasy of eating beans on toast and Milly copying with the real thing. Once started, she continued eating happily, giving Will the chance to take a bite out of his sandwich.

"What are you having, my darling wife?" Will spat out bits of his part-chewed lunch, as he rushed a conversation before going back to work.

"I'll have my usual. Left over beans on toast and the remains of your sandwiches. Yummy, yummy!" She leaned over the table and held his hand. "Evadne's been round with a questionnaire this morning. Posted us a copy through the letterbox."

"About what?" Will spluttered and picked up a piece of half-masticated bread from the middle of the table, putting it back in his mouth.

"About the Council's plans for more housing in the village. I'll show you." She went to the front door and picked up a letter from the coat-stand. "Here, have a quick look before you go." She handed him the questionnaire and sat back as he glanced through it.

"I thought you might have a word with the lads at the workshop about it? One or two live locally, don't they? They ought to have an opinion. We all need to have an opinion. It's important."

"Important!" Milly repeated Miranda's emphasis on the last word. She had reached the dangerous stage where nothing got past her, and she was able to mimic sounds even when she wasn't sure what they meant. Will lived in dread of visits from Miranda's mother, who was forthright to the verge of being fifthright, and could, on occasion, call a spade something really quite rude. So far, she had been careful with her fruity language around Milly, but there always remained the chance of a mistake, with who knew what repercussions.

"Important, yes." Will leaned towards Milly with pride oozing from every pore. "Clever girl. It's a big word. Important means special. We must decide what's special in the village – the houses, or the pond, or the trees?"

"Faery Tree." Milly spoke precisely and convincingly, and put another spoonful of beans in her mouth.

Will's "proud dad" look metamorphosed instantly into bemusement and wonderment in equal measure.

"You know, I'd swear she understood everything we say." Will turned to Miranda who was laughing silently but hysterically behind her hand. "That's the second time she's referred to the Fairy Tree in as many days. Who told her about it? And do you think she understands what it's all about?"

"Surely not. Though strange things have been going on lately."

"Such as?"

"The way she reacted to Ralph in the park yesterday, for one. They seemed to recognise one another and respond to each other."

"Yes, well that could just be a bit like the way children and dogs get on. Maybe Ralph is a bit child-like and Milly senses a soul-mate?" Will had always referred to Milly as special, but now he was beginning to wonder if he knew barely the half of it.

"Maybe." Miranda pondered.

"Maybe." Milly imitated, and ate her final bean.

****

Evadne picked up the empty coffee cups and walked over to the sink, where she rinsed them out and placed them delicately into the washing up bowl. She wiped her hands on the towel draped over the range door and walked back to the table.

"So we're agreed then, that from our viewpoint, the best place for any houses would be on the old goods yard at the back of the station." She sat down and picked up her pencil, ready to summarise the results of their unofficial meeting.

"Absolutely." Eileen was pleased that they saw eye to eye. In reality it was a bit of a no-brainer, since all other land in and around the village was either farmland, woodland or useful recreational space. "I don't suppose there's too much chance of the line opening up again, but stranger things have happened. Even if it doesn't, the land is very close to the bus stop, and that would encourage greater use of the bus service. Win/win as far as I can see."

"Me too! That's settled then." Evadne firmly, pointedly and definitively crossed the T's and dotted the I's of her report.

"Subject of course to the results of the survey." Eileen wasn't afraid to pin Evadne's feet to the ground, when she felt there was a chance of them running off into the wild blue yonder unencumbered by reality checks and alternative points of view.

"Of course!" Whilst Evadne did not take easily to her plans and decisions being reined in by others, she was secretly glad to have friend such as Eileen who could do just that, in a supportive rather than adversarial way. She didn't mind ruffling feathers in the Parish Council, but she had no desire to pluck the bird totally clean. The rest of the Councillors could not, in all honesty, be called dynamic, but they were wholehearted in their devotion to all things Whimbury, and she had a feeling that she would need every bit of support from them in the coming months.

"Do you think we'll get many questionnaires returned?"

"I doubt it. Most people don't think about what's happening around them until it's too late to influence it. That's why I was happy to talk to as many of the residents as possible, rather than just push things through the letterboxes. I'm confident that most people who respond will think along our lines, though there's bound to be some who can sense a quick and substantial profit to be made by selling their land for housing – wherever it is."

There was a brief silence while both pondered over whom amongst the village folk might be tempted to sell out and sell up. Both spoke as one.

"Hill Farm!"

"Yes! The Johnsons wouldn't think twice about making some easy money out of their land. They've always stuck to the motto of "self first". Evadne had lived in Whimbury almost all of her life, and was utterly devoted to preserving the very soul and character of the village, which she considered, rightly, to be something special. At times her kindliness and selflessness could be put severely to the test by the hard self-interest of others, which threatened the prevailing ethos of looking out for one another. And the Johnsons had more than once tested her better qualities.

"I've never quite understood why they haven't sold their land to Home Farm. I mean, we couldn't afford to take it on at the moment, but the McGregors would have jumped at the chance. They've been wanting to expand for years." Eileen and her family were, in truth, small farmers who specialised in quality products, and on the rare occasions where she had been in civilised conversation with the Johnsons, she had encouraged them to move into that niche market themselves. But they had never seemed to be interested in anything more than taking subsidies where they could and making life as easy as possible.

"It's not worth much as agricultural land, but for a higher value use it's presumably worth their wait - as a bit of a gamble. They've tried to get permission for most alternative uses already – motor cycle scrambling, caravan site, paintball. So next it will be housing. Stands to reason - especially since the Council have thrown down the gauntlet." Evadne had tried over the years to get one of the Johnsons to come to Parish Council meetings or to get involved with local groups and societies, but to no avail. Now she was getting genuinely worried about the future. If Hill Farm went, then who knew what would be developed next. Eileen was effectively her only ally in the attempt to get the other Parish Councillors to see beyond the next semi-final of Strictly Come whatever it was this year, and the next series of whatever it was to become in the future.

"Right. On that happy note, I'd better go." Eileen leaned on the table and from there eased her weary bones over to the sofa, where she had laid her coat. I've some jobs to do around the farm tomorrow, but I'm free the day after if you want to do any more delivering."

"Yes. That suits me fine. Just hope the weather holds." She held Eileen's coat to help her find the sleeves, and lifted and smoothed the collar once it was on. "Thanks for the help today. It's important to have a kindred spirit at times like these."

With a reassuring smile, Eileen left the house and leant over to stroke Spot, who was sitting on the lawn with his mouth open and salivating, and his head cocked at a 45 degree angle. She continued on her way and Spot continued with his surveillance of the activities along the street.

******

Soon after Eileen left, Adrian Potts, returning from school, whistled his way down the High Street. As he neared his home, he heaved his rucksack from off his shoulders and removed from it a half-chewed and mostly-bald tennis ball. He bounced it up and down on the pavement a few times and waited for the expected response from within his front garden. It came in the form of a single deep bark from Spot, whose slobbery face appeared on cue above the wall, followed by his front paws as he pulled himself to his full height, stretched and yawned.

"Nothing wrong with his hearing". Thought Adrian, as he ran the final few steps to the house and lobbed the ball over Spot's head towards the front window. Spot bounded across the front garden to retrieve the ball, giving Adrian the opportunity to open the front gate and carefully shut it again, before being presented with a wet and slimy present from the gleeful dog, dropped carefully at his feet. He picked up the ball and threw it once more, and then once more and once more again. The performance only varied when Spot decided it was time to retain the ball and invite Adrian to take it from his mouth. This resulted in a tug-of-war, as both pulled on the ball in an effort to free it from each other's grasp.

Spot growled as he planted his feet firmly in the grass and refused to be budged. Adrian growled back as the routine was re-enacted from previous days and weeks. The stand-off continued with Adrian twisting the ball from side to side in an effort to dislodge it, while Spot frantically wagged his tail in the pleasure of knowing that this was a battle that he always won.

Up until this day, Adrian had, as a matter of course, continued to play until he got fed up and let go of his grip on the ball, running inside to find a late afternoon snack in the kitchen. Today, however, it was Spot who released his grip, opened his jaws and ran back to the garden wall, standing on his hind legs, as if to keep watch over the activities along the road. Adrian looked bemused, tossed the ball in the air and caught it again. He repeated this a couple of times more until he fully realised the unpleasantness of the feel of the ball in his hands, dropped it and ran inside.

Spot rested his jaw on the top of the wall and tilted his head at a 45 degree angle. His ears pricked up and his tail ceased wagging with the concentration of listening intently to an animated Robin.

"So you need to keep a watchful eye out for any sightings of this new faery. Apparently you can't miss him. Everard says he has a look and feel of authority, and he's at least 10mm taller than anyone else around here. Dresses well, with just a hint of flamboyance, and walks like he has a purpose. No-one's come across him before and there was no word of him having been seen before he just turned up."

Barry motioned to Robin to hold fire for a moment whilst Spot assimilated all the information.

Spot barked twice, followed by a short whine and another bark. Robin and Barry understood this to mean that he hadn't heard or seen anything either, and there was no talk amongst the dogs of the village of any strangers having been sighted. But he would keep all his doggy senses fully open and would report back as soon as something materialised. He'd spread the word round all the others and give them as much information as he himself had. In the meantime, if he saw or met this new faery should he engage in conversation, or just follow at a safe distance. And if he was to communicate with aforesaid faery, should he ask him to pop by the Royal Oak on his travels?

****

It is a well-known fact that time is observer-dependent and perception of time therefore becomes relative. To humans and faeries, with long life spans relative to, say, a butterfly, time moves, albeit in circular fashion, at a relatively slow perceived speed. The butterfly, however, once it has emerged from its cocoon, has a limited amount of human time to undertake its lifetime's activities. Some live for just a few days, and these must wonder at the growing of the light on the first day and the subsequent descent into darkness. Then, just as they begin to get to grips with the repetition of this cycle, it's time to shuffle off this mortal coil. For them it's not so much carpe diem as carpe horam or even carpe minutum. All the survival thoughts and instincts are compressed into a giddy round of activities comprising but a short span to human and faery eyes, but a whole lifetime to the butterfly. It should perhaps, therefore, be no surprise that they can't fly straight – unless of course this is due to problems with their decision-making, in which case they manage to cram a great deal of prevarication into their short everyday lives.

Similarly, Spot, with a much shorter lifespan than humans and faeries - though admittedly much longer than butterflies – could compress a whole paragraph, or even short story, into what might seem like a brief and snappy bark. Humans, with appropriate recording technology and software, could slow down this bark and, with the aid of a good phrase book, understand exactly what he was saying. Faeries do not need such complex technology and this is why Robin and Barry could follow his drift and be grateful that he didn't bark several more times.

****

Armed with a plate of snacks, some healthy, some not, Adrian peered out of the living room window and watched as Spot tilted his head from side to side, occasionally emitting a brief bark or two at no-one and nothing in particular. Adrian cast his eyes up and down the road, as far as he could see, but could make out no pedestrian or cyclist that might potentially have been the target of Spot's vocal exercises. It was turning out to be a strange day with regard to the behaviour of his dog. He began to wonder if there was some extra-sensory perception of the impending "Dog-show" season involved, resulting in a Pavlovian response of barking into the wide blue yonder. True, Spot had been dishonourably discharged from these events by Evadne after the debacle of two years previously, when he had played his crucial role in the "Crossover" by hurling himself into the pond the day before his, as it turned out, final appearance at the County Show. But maybe the trauma of those days had etched themselves into his psyche?

In fact, Spot had suffered no trauma, and was instead the doggy version of ecstatic, not having to suffer the indignity of having his coat washed, permed, knitted and purled each spring, followed by a period of having all privileges cancelled until the event was over. He stood at the garden wall, excited by the prospect of another stranger in the village. He craved something different and perhaps, if he were being honest, something more dramatic than his usual daily fare of morning constitutional and ablution, courtesy of Kenneth; fetch a ball (or stick, or rubber bone, according to what came to hand) with Adrian; and a profoundly embarrassing series of coochie-coos and chin tickling with Evadne (often and most troubling in front of other humans with their canine companions).

He couldn't be too hard on the Potts family. They were, after all, trying to give him a good life, as best as they could understand it. But it could become tedious and repetitive, and he felt obliged to slaver and pant and wag his tail, as if it all were the best thing since dog breath-freshener treats, just to make them feel good about themselves and their care for "dumb" animals.

So this conversation with Barry and Robin was just the tonic he needed. He hadn't been asked to involve himself in any cunning faery plans or japes for far too long, and he had no desire to find himself regressing into a position where even a dog show seemed mildly interesting. Barry explained that as they themselves had no direct knowledge of the "Stranger", it was perhaps as well if he kept a low profile and reported back to anyone from the Faery Council as soon as it was safe to do so.

Spot barked his agreement and tilted his head the opposite way as he followed their progress sauntering down the road.

Chapter Four

Inigo Happling wandered around the public bar in the Royal Oak, handing out pieces of paper and pencils to the quiz teams sat in groups of four around the tables. In a significant break with tradition, since the time of the Crossover, a team from the Families Grump sat in on the quiz, and the Happs were more than content that they should be there. All that was required for a successful evening was to ensure that at least one round should upset the Grumps, either by virtue of "biased" questions or disputable answers. So long as the Grumps didn't win, both sides would go home happy.

"I see that Lancelot's team have poached Eric again." Barry nodded in the direction of Lancelot Happling, sitting contentedly at his table poring over the preliminary picture round with Eric O'Shy. Lancelot had a habit of arriving early for quizzes in the hope of steering Eric towards his table as soon as he came in. The rest of his usual team was somewhat weakened by the presence of his cousin Vladislav, who could only answer questions on Eastern Europe or local matters from the last two years, and Everard Gnappins, who spent a lot of the time imbibing glasses of Innkeeper's Choice, and the rest of it asleep. So no-one begrudged him the services of Eric, who displayed remarkable knowledge on almost all subjects. Eric, for his part was happy to join any team who would ply him with drinks and then willingly share the prizes with him at the end. He seemed to have a knack of drinking continuously throughout the quiz whilst remaining apparently quite sober and totally focussed on the questions. This situation might have proven expensive for Lancelot, were it not for the very high degree of probability that his team would win.

"He's certainly made a lot of friends very quickly." Damon followed Barry's gaze and wiped the froth from the tap of the newly opened barrel of Sprite's Delight, special ale of the week.

"And hardly ever has to buy himself a drink." Barry had to admire how Eric seemed to socialise but little, immersed as he was in his books and papers, and yet never wanted for drinks. It was as if the others had accepted that he was an introvert and yet appreciated his knowledge and intellect. More often than not whilst buying a round, one of the regulars would shout across to Eric and ask if he needed a top-up of his usual, which was the very easy going "Pixie lixir".

"Well, he's certainly not going to be the life and soul of any parties," Damon responded, "but, fair do's, he's got his feet under the table and he's not afraid to be himself,"

"Indeed, and considering there aren't any close relatives from his clan around these parts, he copes pretty well, under the circumstances." Barry took the opportunity of the opening round of the quiz to descend to the vaults and check how Junior was getting on.

The strains of light opera drifted up the staircase, and Barry paused to listen. In truth, he quite enjoyed a little tuneful singing as a counterpoint to the somewhat more raucous variety he was used to upstairs in the public bar.

Junior had a pleasant voice for a woodlouse, and Barry found it hard to accept that Larry disapproved so violently – other than, of course, the affected air of superiority born of his immersion in the higher classics. The young louse had taken easily to his responsibilities and was as precise and thorough as his father. True, he lacked a little of Larry's worldly wisdom, but he made up for it with his youthful energy and enthusiasm. He had been greeted with warm welcomes whenever he had strayed upstairs for instructions or just to sample the atmosphere, and was acquiring the same degree of indispensability that Larry had enjoyed.

"How's it going Junior?" Barry bounced in with a half-shouted greeting designed to grab Junior's attention whilst in full voice.

"Ah, howdo Barry. Fine, fine. All spick and span down here. I've near enough finished the cleaning, so it's just a matter of moving stuff back into its rightful place."

"Looks a bit different from when Larry was in charge – maybe a little more ordered?" Barry was impressed with Junior's initiative in making the job, and the cellar, his own.

"Well, I think I've benefitted from being able to spend a bit of time upstairs. It somehow helps to clarify the relationship between your clientele and my domain down here." He coughed politely and continued hurriedly. "I hope you don't mind me calling it 'my domain'?"

"Not at all. If everything functions efficiently, which it does, then I'm happy for you to take charge." Barry knew when to give a good worker a long leash.

"Goodo!" Junior raised his palm for silence, and Barry felt the presence of Larry in the room. He knew what to expect. Junior launched into song.

"When I went to the Bar as a very young man, (said I to myself, said I), I'll work on a new and original plan, (said I to myself, said I)." He paused, one arm outstretched with fist clenched, and then opened out his fingers, pointing them to the ceiling in the manner of an emerging idea.

After the exactly appropriate moment of silence, Junior smiled across at Barry, who was temporarily bemused as to the correct response.

"Of course, I realise that I have played a little fast and loose with the context, but I expect you get the gist?"

"Absolutely!" Lied Barry. "Excellent. Carry on." He resisted a strangely insistent urge to salute, and leapt back up the stairs before Junior could continue into the next few stanzas. His leaping continued into the bar, where Damon was serving Victor Grumplet.

"How's things, Victor?" Barry instantly dressed himself in his best joie-de-vivre attitude and posture. Victor was not in the same league as Percy when it came to complaining, but since he had now officially taken over Percy's role as Head of Whinging, Whining and Moaning on behalf of the Families Grump, Barry considered it important to help him along with a meaningless opening gambit.

"Too bloody noisy in here!" Victor did his best to sound discontented and un-amused. His best was still relatively low-key, though he was improving with time and practice.

"Dominoes going down well, is it?" Barry threw him another feed line.

"Yes, fine thanks Barry!" He looked up at the ceiling, and then over to Barry, who was tut-tutting and shaking his head slowly. "Dammit. Will I never learn? Don't tell Percy will you?"

"My lips are sealed, Victor. Do you want another try?"

"Yes, I damn well do! We can't concentrate on the dominoes because of the noise, and we've lost our best team member to the bloody quiz. I wouldn't mind but he never wins because the quiz is rigged against us, and even if we did win, the prizes are rubbish."

"Better Victor, better." Barry believed in giving praise where it was due.

"Thanks, Barry! Dammit!" Victor walked off with his tray of drinks, mentally cursing himself for his lack of focus.

Barry put his arm round Damon's shoulders. "Right! I don't think we'll be getting too many more orders till after the first round finishes, so we can relax a bit." He pointed over to the corner of the bar, where Inigo Happling had picked up the microphone and tapped it to check that it was working. A series of booms and crackles indicated that it was, and Inigo announced the first subject. Barry and Damon returned to washing and polishing the glasses.

****

"There's a jumble sale on at the Mission Church later this morning!" Miranda shouted down the hall to Will as he picked up his sandwich box, and took his flask from the kitchen table. "I thought I might take Milly in time for morning coffee. She can look round the stalls with me and I'll take her a snack, to have while I indulge in an antidote to health foods."

"Sounds a good idea – provided, of course, you remember that Mrs Patterson's 'antidotes' are based heavily around the fundamental ingredients of fat and cholesterol. So not too much." Will peeked around the dining room door and smiled.

"Won't you still love me if I put on weight?" Without glancing over her shoulder, she knew that Will would be looking at her from the hallway. She waggled her bottom at him to indicate that she was aware of his presence.

"I promise I will still love you, though it could seriously prejudice my ability to give you a piggy-back, or carry you to bed when you fall asleep on the sofa." Will moon-walked over to Milly and gave her a kiss on the top of her head. She ignored him, concentrating instead on her bowl of Wheatie Bickie cereal. Will knew better than to interrupt her during breakfast, so he moon-walked back out of the room – more for Miranda's benefit than Milly's.

He laced up his work boots on the doormat and took a deep breath as he opened the front door, letting in the aromatic odours of the neighbouring front gardens. He turned back into the hall to deliver one last observation on Miranda's plan for the morning.

"And if the weather holds, you could take her to the Wildlife Garden round the back – she loves running round the paths, in and out of the herb bushes. Last time she came back smelling like the accompaniment to a roast lamb dinner." He meandered down the front path and allowed himself the luxury of a cheerful, if not tuneful, whistle as he shut the front gate and crossed the road to the workshop. He ruminated on his good fortune at living so close to work, such that he could easily pop back home to see his lovely wife and daughter at lunchtime if he so wished - and provided that he didn't happen to have a big-end to repair urgently.

Back in Over Cross View, Miranda was on her hands and knees under the dining room table, wiping up the soggy remains of Wheatie Bickie breakfast cereal that had evaded Milly's bib. She had been planning to do away with the bib altogether for some months, but either Milly had food that she really enjoyed, like Wheatie Bickies, in which case she filled her spoon to overflowing and threw it into her mouth, and elsewhere, with total abandon, or she had food that she hated, in which case the whole bowl went onto the floor. It was not that she was badly behaved as such, it was just that with food she knew her own mind and acted accordingly. Fortunately, thought Miranda, the plasticised cloth under the table and Milly's chair was big enough to catch almost everything that was within normal dropping or throwing range.

She cleared the table and put the dirty crockery and cutlery into the sink while Milly finished off her drink. Then, since it was not washing day, or ironing day, or complicated cooking day, or vacuuming and dusting day – though in truth it was seldom one of such days, because Miranda believed that the life beyond housework was precious – she sat down with Milly and helped her complete her favourite jig-saw. For some reason, which Miranda had never fully worked out, her absolute, all-time favourite was a picture of creatures of the garden, and she always began the jig-saw by putting together the corner pieces that contained the image of a woodlouse.

The first time Milly had attempted the picture, Miranda got her to name the creatures. There was Belinda Butterfly, Willy Wasp, Adam Ant (Miranda had 'helped' her with that one), Bruce Bee, Cyril the Spider (because Miranda thought it would be useful when it was time to differentiate between soft "c" and hard "c"), Robin the Robin (Milly had seemed a little confused by that one), and Henrietta Hedgehog. When it had been the turn of the woodlouse, Milly had screamed defiance at all suggestions such as Woody, Wendy and Wayne, and insisted vehemently that it was called Larry. So, for whatever reason, Larry it remained.

Miranda was justifiably proud of Milly's ability with jig-saws and watched as she searched around for the piece that she wanted and manoeuvred it into place. True, there was none of the scientific approach of beginning with straight-edged pieces, and clearly she remembered what went where, but nevertheless, Milly was adept and had a good eye for colour and shape.

Once the jig-saw was completed, Miranda went off to prepare Milly's picnic and left her talking to the creatures in the picture. On the occasions in the past when she had listened in to the conversations, it seemed to Miranda that Milly always spoke to the other creatures through Larry, creating a fantasy world that somehow also seemed entirely credible. Both the breadth and depth of Milly's imagination never ceased to amaze Miranda. It wasn't just the normal play of mummy, with cuddly toys taking the roles of various offspring. She appeared able to enter into a different world, populated only by animals, in which she knew exactly what was going on and why.

If she had been listening in this time, she would have heard a very serious conversation indeed, as Larry addressed the assembled animals in the best language of a two-year old girl.

"Faery Tree unhappy. Faeries scared. New faery come. Robin find new faery!" This bit was emphasised by Milly putting her finger on the picture of the Robin and directing it over the garden fence.

"Cyril," pronounced correctly, "spin web. Catch faery." She continued, painting a complex spider's web in the air, which immediately flexed in the middle to illustrate that it had achieved its purpose. "Belinda tell Barry." Milly got up and ran around the room in no particular direction waving her arms in the manner of a butterfly's wings.

During Belinda's journey, Miranda returned and watched silently until Milly caught sight of her and stopped.

"OK, little Madame Butterfly, shall we go down the road and look in at the jumble sale?" Milly seemed less than ecstatic, but perked up when Miranda played her ace. "Then we can have a picnic and run around the Wildlife Garden afterwards."

"OK." Milly adopted her matter-of-fact voice, the one she used when she didn't want to seem too eager to accept a bribe.

"Right, I'll get your coat and you put on your blue shoes. They're in the hall." Milly was very independent and resented help putting on footwear. Miranda knew better than to even try, unless of course they ended up on the wrong feet, in which case she felt obliged to intervene. Milly never seemed bothered if left shoe was on right foot and vice versa, but Miranda didn't want the folk of the village thinking that she was a bad mother. No-one ever gave the impression of thinking the worst regarding Milly's food, or eating habits, or the occasional tantrum, which were "normal" for a two-year old girl, but to send one's child out with shoes on the wrong feet was akin to assault.

Today, they were on the correct feet. Miranda held up her coat and offered the sleeves for Milly's attention.

"Good girl. You're getting to be a big girl now, aren't you?" Milly seemed pleased with herself.

"Right, into your buggy." Miranda lifted her up and felt a twinge as she dropped her gently into the seat. "Definitely a big, heavy girl. Unless of course?"

Milly immediately jumped out of the seat and ran back into the dining room, where she had unfinished business.

"Milly going out," She pronounced to the jigsaw. "You stay here. Be good aminals, OK?"

"She gets that upward inflection from me", thought Miranda, making a mental note to be careful about what she said and how she said it. She prepared herself for another attempt at getting Milly into the buggy. Milly ran halfway down the hall, then stopped and returned to the dining room. She stood over the Jigsaw and pointed a finger into her chest.

"I a big girl now, OK?" She ran proudly back down the hall and, much to Miranda's relief, climbed into the buggy by herself, put her arms through the safety straps and fastened the catch.

****

In a quiet corner of Whimbury Woods, a tall elegant faery sat upright on a small, moss-covered stone, whittling a staff from an oak twig. He didn't need a staff, but he did need an opportunity to sit and listen. Sit, listen and watch. Sit, listen, watch and smell. This was a new wood and a new community. He had planned his visit for many months and it was imperative that he gained a full sensory understanding of the place before engaging with the locals. It was dry. He needed some rain to bring out the full scents and flavours of the woodland herbs and plants. But rain didn't come to order. And so he whittled. Whittled and whistled. Whittled, whistled and sang. Whistled and sang tunes from his homeland and from long ago. Tunes that told of battles won – no-one wrote of battles lost – and of fair maidens won – no-one wrote of maidens lost, at least not before they had first been won. Tunes that told of exploits and adventures, and love and bravery. He was not nostalgic, nor was he pining, but it was important for him to remember the times when things were different and problems were dealt with in a myriad of ways, some of which could well still be helpful today, since faeries were still faeries and humans were still humans. Except of course that the Crossover child had arrived and, if the legend were to come to fruition, fae and human folk would be able to live together with a greater bond of understanding. If! The shortest yet potentially most meaningful word in the whole vocabulary.

He sang of the fabled sheep-snatchers at the 'Wild Mutton Time'. He sang "Greenknees", recalling the amorous traditions of early spring in the young wheatfields. As he sang of "Hal's bad toe", a mournful tale of an unfortunate scything accident, he suddenly, and without warning, swung his part-finished staff round behind him with incredible speed. Just as suddenly he stopped in mid-swing, with the staff poised menacingly millimetres from the head of a short, middle-aged, balding faery.

"Not lost your touch, my Lord!" The balding faery wiped an instant outpouring of sweat from his brow. "I approached from downwind, I was silent as a mouse, and I held my breath so as not to disturb the air around you."

"So you did! And very well you executed your plan. It was almost perfect, but there is nothing you can do about your ambient body heat, which, in this case, influenced the path of a mayfly on the wing between the pond on my right and the stream on my left." He rose to his full height as he gestured extravagantly from side to side, and tapped his assistant gently on the top of his head with the tip of the staff.

"Sometimes, I feel that I have learnt so little, my Lord." He gazed up at the imposing figure with a sad, almost resigned look in his eye. "I have absorbed every word that comes from your lips. I have watched your movements in the most minute of detail. I have tried to smell what you smell and leave all my senses open to inspiration. What more must I do?"

The tall stranger sat down again on the mossy stone, and gestured for his companion to accompany him. He pondered for a few moments and finally spoke.

"By all means learn. We all must learn. We cannot stand still and expect the world to continue to revolve around us. But we must learn to develop ourselves, our inner beings – not to become someone else. Of course, you can develop your tactical skills, and become more aware of what your senses can tell you, but you must use all this to be a better and more complete you. You nursed me back to health when I first returned from my travels. You could do that because of your own innate talents and your bedrock of knowledge. Despite whatever you see, and possibly admire, in me, I could not have done that for a fellow faery in the way that you did. You have your own potential, Burr, my friend. Fulfil it and be greater still."

Burr looked straight ahead and sighed. In truth, he didn't want to be himself in whatever version he might be able to attain. He was one of those special people who cannot see or understand their own worth, but will instead always be destined to compare themselves to those they envy or worship. If only he could be clear as to what he was actually good at and enjoyed doing, he felt he would then, and only then, be satisfied with being himself. But at least it seemed that he was appreciated for who he was by someone he respected greatly, and that must count for something.

He continued sitting in the silence, hoping to see more than he was used to seeing, or hearing what he was not used to hearing. He sniffed, this way and that, in an attempt to absorb the palette of aromas that drifted through the woods. Then he sneezed, remembering that this was the start of his hayfever season, and that this was perhaps not the best time to be honing his nasal senses. Sticking a piece of moss up each nostril, he settled back to contemplate his lot and wait upon further communication from beside him.

After a short while, he could contain his curiosity no longer.

"Doh why ecdactly are we here?"

"I beg your pardon?" Came back the bemused response.

"Doh why ecdactly …….. oh dorry!" Burr hastily removed the now moist moss from his nose and started again. "So why exactly are we here?"

The tall stranger paused before giving his fully considered answer. This was standard practice and Burr knew to be patient. His question would be answered clearly and as complete as necessary, but only after having first been thought through fully.

At last, he began.

"Just over two years ago, a momentous event happened in this village. The event has repercussions for both the fae and human worlds, but it is ongoing. There is more to happen or not happen. I need to find out what is the current state of play, so that I can decide what my role will be when the time comes, because I will have a role. I must explore the village and the relationship between the faeries here and the animals and humans. One human in particular."

"Ah." Burr hesitated before adding a supplementary question. The answer had been intended to be full and adequate, but sometimes a follow up question was dealt with if deemed appropriate to the circumstances. "And how long to do you expect to be here, researching the situation?"

"As long as it takes! I have no timetables or deadlines. Can you accommodate that, or must we part?"

"Of course I can accommodate that." Thought Burr to himself. In the relatively short time that he had been travelling with the tall stranger, he had become more and more attracted to the lifestyle. Mysterious, yes. Exciting, definitely. Unnerving, absolutely. But in all of that, the alternative of his previous easy-going existence was never going to satisfy. "Of course, I can accommodate that." came out the thought.

"Good." Came back the reply. "I knew that, of course."

"Oh, yes. I knew that you knew." Thought Burr again to himself. The remaining questions in his mind – where do we stay; what do we say to folk; what do we do for our daily sustenance; what exactly are we looking for; what do we do if we encounter hostility; etc, etc, remained unasked.

Chapter Five

BARRY PERCHED ON RALPH'S SHOULDER and looked up the High Street from outside the old station building. It was a very long time since Ralph had ventured this far from Whimburton, and even longer since he had visited Whimbury itself. Barry pointed out the landmarks that were visible from this spot. The church tower and the war memorial remained the most prominent. Ralph nodded as the memories began to flood back. He turned to right and left and took in the buildings along Station Road, together with the chapel and the Memorial Hall opposite. The tops of the ancient trees of Whimbury Woods provided a green backdrop to the houses and shops along the eastern side of the High Street, whilst the Royal Oak stood the most majestic of all, set back from the road in a broad gap between the buildings. Ralph raised his hands in its direction and smiled.

"Timeless, isn't it?" He mused. "Centuries old. It's seen buildings spring up, and some disappear almost as quickly. It's seen the railway come and fall into disuse. And all that time, your lot have been in there breathing new life into it."

"Not to mention alcohol." Barry felt a surge of pride in amongst the humour and responsibility associated with the fae occupation of the giant tree. It was true. His family had run the Inn for several generations and the legends and subtle activities of the Whimbury faeries over time had lent the tree a notoriety that had spread way beyond the village. It was protected, it was special, and insofar as a tree could be considered thus, it was near as dammit eternal. A lot of liquid stronger than water had flowed under its tables and chairs during its lifetime, while in the last couple of years it had been the scene of one of the momentous events in fae and human history. And that was the reason for Ralph's visit.

"I'm worried, Barry!" To most people Ralph was a harmless eccentric, who talked to himself out loud (without the prompting of a mobile phone), and occasionally railed and shouted at the perceived injustices of the world around him. This perspective was largely accurate. However, Ralph was also one of the very few people still able to relate to the vast world outside of the very narrow experience of the human intellect and imagination. He talked regularly with Barry and any other of the faeries who ventured out of the village, as well as faeries from farther afield. He was a conduit through which faery gossip was transmitted and human activity and rumour relayed back. He looked and listened. He allowed his senses to roam beyond what was accepted knowledge and wisdom into those areas where other, more important, truths lay. Beyond the spiritual, beyond the natural, and beyond the scientific was life rich beyond common understanding, and Ralph was one of the privileged few who understood – at least in part. He knew the significance of the Crossover and had come to check on the progress of Milly Hope.

"What about?"

"There's talk in town about hundreds of new houses to be built over the next few years all over the County. There'll be a lot in Whimbury, mark my words. People will come who don't know about country life – or village life for that matter. People who just want to bring Whimburton with them." His voice broke very slightly as if he was trying to hold back sadness, or anger. Barry wasn't sure which.

"Change is inevitable, Ralph. There's been new houses built in the village many times in the past, and we're all still here, doing what we've always done."

"That's as maybe," Ralph suddenly became agitated and waved his shopping bags in the direction of a car that was travelling at great speed along Station Road. "Twenty's plenty," He screamed, pointlessly, at the fast-disappearing vehicle. "Folk live here, it's home, children play, 4x4 exocet, too big, too fast, spot the braincell." He crashed his bags together in the manner of cymbals and gave a long, protracted wail of anguish. Mr and Mrs Butterworth who, until that outburst, had been approaching Ralph cautiously, chose the moment to make an exaggerated detour across the road.

Barry disentangled himself from Ralph's matted dreadlocks and took up his normal position beneath his right ear once again.

"Sorry Barry, some things just get me so mad."

"I noticed." Barry wiped grease from his fingers onto his shirt, and settled back down. "Anyway, you were saying?"

"I was?"

"You were referring to the concept of change, as applied to Whimbury."

"So I was!" Ralph made a mental note to cool down, with a gentle, hands down movement.

"What I was about to say, Barry, was that, in the past, change was slow. Folk could adjust, and the new houses were for village families to grow, and for others to move in who wanted to fit into village life. This new batch will be too much, too fast – mark my words."

"Oh I will, I will!" Barry always marked Ralph's words, because he understood what really went on in the human world, and could see through the rhetoric and 'weasely words' as he called them. "But in the meantime, I believe you really came here to see Milly again?"

"I did, Barry my friend, I did." Having calmed down, Ralph carried on. "I saw her in the park in Whimburton and my heart skipped a beat. I had no idea what I'd been looking for all those months, and then all became clear. It was the sparkle in her eyes – the innocent acceptance of a stranger who she knew in her heart was a friend. I was someone who'd found the miracle he'd been seeking."

He paused and Barry noticed his lower lip quivering with emotion.

"You're a good friend to us, Ralph." Barry regretted that the significant difference in their relative sizes made it impossible for him to give the dishevelled man a hug, something he almost certainly was never given by anyone else. "There aren't many folk left who care one iota about the world around us. Few really fully use even the first five senses to explore or understand that world, and fewer still use or, more's the point, know about the others. Such a pity."

"A pity indeed. I only want to see her in action – you know, relating to the faeries and animals of Whimbury. Can't get too close or people will call the police. Everyone must have a questionable motive these days – understandable I suppose. But I can keep a watchful eye from a distance can't I? I've a suspicion she's going to need all the support and protection she can get. What do you think Barry?"

"I'm inclined to agree, Ralph! If she starts showing signs of anything that strays from the accepted boundaries of normal, she'll get put away, or given treatment or something to bring her round. No, we've got to be careful in the way we oversee her development. There's less than five years to go now before the Crossover has to be completed and so much to get through. Mustn't rush her, but neither is there time to waste."

"How's she doing?"

"Very well, I think. She's like a sheet of blotting paper. Absorbs everything we tell her – and understands it. She can already hold a primitive conversation with almost all of the animals in the village. Her mother and father put it down to an active imagination at first, but I think they're beginning to wonder if it's something more. They're good folk, and we need to pull them along with us as well, though being adults it's going to be that much harder. Still, we're all up for the challenge and we've got a meeting due in the next few weeks to work out a strategy for dealing with the whole family. It's going to be interesting."

"Think I might stick around in the village for a while." If he was being honest with himself, Ralph was beginning to experience a germ of excitement. There was nothing of great importance to hold him to Whimburton for a while. He could always go back from time to time to pick up the local gossip, which he fervently believed was his primary role in the whole Crossover project. But in the meantime, he would benefit from immersing himself in the life of the village and observing the interaction between Milly, the faeries, the animals, and the adults.

"Where will you stay?"

"Thought I'd just bunk down in the woods somewhere – providing I can find a place out of prying eyes."

"That won't be easy. The woods aren't that big, and everyone uses them – for all sorts of activities." Barry had misgivings regarding Ralph's safety in such a public environment.

"Any suggestions then, Barry?" Ralph was conscious that he hadn't really thought things through in any great depth. It just felt right to be in the thick of things. He'd already missed so much.

"There's one or two places where it's relatively impenetrable. Along with a little bit of faery guile and mischief, I'm sure we can keep you hidden. At least over the summer."

"Excellent. So lead on, my friend. And I shall follow you into the depths of Mother Arbor herself, and make there a home fit for a freeborn travelling man."

And with that, the two of them crossed Station Road, passed the Mission Church building and the Old School House, and turned into the woods beside the Royal Oak. Barry led Ralph towards the foot of Whimbury Hill, where the woods gave way to the sheep pasture beyond. Here there were no footpaths, and the undergrowth was fuller where the light could penetrate beneath the trees.

"Here OK?" Barry pointed to a dense cluster of brambles and young trees.

Ralph looked a little perplexed. "Er fine, Barry, except for the issue of getting in and out thereof with clothes and appendages intact?"

"Round here, Ralph." Barry wandered over to the side of the patch and pointed to a disturbed area of ground beneath a small rocky outcrop. "An old badger run – still used from time to time. You should be able to squeeze along there under that rocky overhang. It's pretty dense and should be cosy. I've never seen anyone walking around here, but I'll get some of the gang to keep an eye out and use fair means, or more probably foul, to divert the attention of any humans that threaten to get too close."

"Well not quite what I had in mind, but I bow to your vastly superior knowledge of the ways of these woods. I had visions of sleeping at night looking up at the stars and rejoicing in the space and openness of the great British countryside. However, I'm sure the warmth and spiky claustrophobia of a bramble bed will prove to be even more romantic…. in time!"

"Good man! It'll be fun having you around."

And with that, Barry strolled nonchalantly back in the general direction of the Royal Oak, leaving Ralph to gingerly and noisily pick his way through the undergrowth.

"Hope he doesn't use that language for too long, or at least not at that volume," muttered Barry under his breath, and allowing himself the luxury of a grin. "He'll be found out. Mind you, I can't see too many folk investigating such noises too clinically. They'll probably just put it down to the faeries and give it a wide berth."

And for a while, he was right.

****

In the Mission Church, Miranda sought out the second-hand book stall and rummaged through the children's book section. The early purchase of a cheap and colourful reading book was, in her experience, the surest way to keep Milly occupied whilst she chatted her way around the other stalls. Milly was happy to look at a book as she walked around, and when she got tired, she'd sit in a corner and make up stories about the characters on the pages. On this occasion, Milly was handed "My Dog's got no Tail", a 'hilarious' story about a dog who couldn't show her happiness because she had no tail. The back cover had a hole for the reader to put his or her finger through and supply the dog with a 'tail' to wag. Miranda spent a few minutes talking her way through the book so that Milly had an idea what the story was about, then she began her walk- and talk-about, while Milly followed on, totally absorbed.

Miranda and Will had little in the way of spare cash, so, aside from Milly's book, Miranda bought only cheap essentials at the jumble sales – keeping just enough money back for one of Lucinda Patterson's excellent cakes to go with her morning coffee. It was a ritual she enjoyed, providing her with both a chance to escape the daily ritual and an opportunity to eat something she hadn't had to make, in the company of fellow villagers. Normally she would sit with Eileen Robinson, who was a little closer in both age and general outlook on life than many of the others, who were, nevertheless, pleasant enough in their own ways. On this occasion, Eileen was sitting with the Butterworths, but had saved Miranda two spare chairs at the trestle table. She sat down next to Eileen and placed Milly on the seat beside her. From her bag she took Milly's drink, some crisps and a few early season strawberries. That was usually enough to keep Milly fed and interested for a few minutes, and the book could then entertain her for a few minutes more.

"She's growing so fast!" Eileen watched as Milly opened her drinking mug and began to slurp through the plastic straw.

"Tell me about it. She's already outgrowing her first spring shoes of the year and she copies absolutely everything we say. We're having to be really careful. And her imagination – well, she makes up complete stories with all her animal friends, and they're quite sophisticated."

"How old is she now?" Betty Butterworth smiled indulgently in the general direction of Milly.

"Two," replied Miranda.

"And a quarter." Added Milly, who to this point had given no indication of listening to any of the conversation, and immediately resumed her slurping.

"Yes, well that's put me in my place. Two and a quarter." Miranda leant over and kissed Milly on the top of the head.

"Well the extra quarter is very important at her age." Betty laughed behind her hand.

"Indeed it is, every quarter marks a major change in the way she looks and acts. Certainly keeps me on my toes. Now what's the gossip?" Miranda looked over to Eileen, since it was unlikely that the Butterworths would have anything to add. However, on this occasion, the response came from an unusual direction.

"Do you know that tramp feller from the town? Always looks in need of a wash and a good meal. Talks to himself – very loud – waves his bags about!" When excited, Fred Butterworth talked in a staccato voice, grinding his false teeth around in his mouth between sentences.

"Yes, Ralph his name is. We often see him on market days in Whimburton." Miranda looked expectantly at Fred and then down at Milly, who handed her a packet of crisps to open.

"Saw him in the village this morning. Just coming back from our morning walk and there he was, talking to himself - as usual, very loud – as usual – and waving his bags at a passing car which, to be fair, was rather speeding along Station Road."

"Did you talk to him?" Eileen was as interested as Miranda. Everyone knew Ralph, or of him, but he was rarely seen in the village.

"Good heavens no!" Betty interjected, to Fred's displeasure, and took over the story. "We crossed over the moment he started waving things about. Who knows what he might have done? He's unstable that one. Give him a wide berth, I say. Isn't that right Fred?"

"Absolutely. But the fascinating thing this time was…."

"…That he seemed to be having a conversation with someone who wasn't there." This was too good a story to let Fred ruin it. Fred sat back and accepted the inevitable. "He often rants and raves – you can hear him going on about all sorts. Licorice we call him, don't we Fred? Anyway," she continued without waiting for affirmation, "as we crossed the road, he started talking much quieter and appeared to be waiting for responses before going on again. Most odd."

"We saw him not long ago in the park at Whimburton." Miranda acted swiftly to get her side of the emerging story into the conversation – and to slow Betty down. "We took a little picnic and Milly was sitting on the grass playing with the daisies. We heard him coming before we saw him – like you said he was loud and talking gibberish, or what seemed like gibberish. Will was ready to interpose himself should Ralph approach Milly, but what happened next was very strange." She paused as she searched for the words to describe the events.

"Come on Miranda, don't stop now!" Eileen was close to clapping her hands. There really was nothing like a good gossipy story – and if she didn't move things along, it would end up nothing like a good gossipy story.

"Well, he stopped dead in his tracks, looked over to Milly, bowed, tugged his forelock and smiled."

"Creepy." Eileen was hooked.

"Yes and no! He didn't try to approach her, or even entice her towards him. He just smiled. Milly smiled back and offered him one of her daisies. He kept his distance and muttered something that I couldn't make out. Then he acknowledged us – warmly - and walked off with what I can only describe as a spring in his step – if he's capable of such a thing." Miranda gazed into the distance as if reliving the situation.

"So I wonder what's brought him to these parts?" Eileen broke into the silence.

"And where is he now?" Miranda had to admit to herself that she was just a tiny bit worried. Ralph had looked anything but dangerous during their encounter in the park, in fact more warm and kindly if anything, but there was still something odd about him, and people can be fearful of oddities. [6]

"We looked back once we felt we were safely in the village, and he was turning off the High Street past the Old School House next door." Betty enlightened them.

"Probably going for a widdle at the old oak tree?" Suggested Eileen.

"Faery Tree." Pronounced Milly, without looking up from her packet of crisps.

"What did she just say?" Eileen sat back on her chair in dismay.

"That's the third time she's referred to the old Royal Oak as the Fairy Tree. We've never told her the legend, so goodness alone knows where she's picked it up from. But she's adamant that it's the Fairy Tree – almost as if she knows more about it than we do."

"You did say she had a vivid imagination. Maybe she's just making things up – a lucky coincidence?" Fred smiled the smile of the elderly, when talking about children, that came across as a combination of condescension and wind.

"I don't think so!" Miranda glanced across at Milly, who showed no outward sign of involvement in the conversation. "She volunteers the information when we're discussing the tree in a totally different context – just making sure that we're aware of the full significance of the tree and haven't missed the point. It's spooky!"

"Will has always told me that she's special, but then, all fathers do, don't they? Nevertheless...." Eileen lowered her voice and gave a knowing nod in the direction of Milly.

"You mean you think she may have some particular gift or other?" Miranda had been wondering that herself over the past few weeks, but not seriously – until now.

"Who can say? I suppose time will tell, eh? She's certainly very sharp –

---

[6] Apart from the ones they inexplicably elect to high office, apparently.

doesn't miss a trick, hears everything and appears to understand more than you might expect.

As the level of speech dropped, so Betty began to lose the thread of the conversation and, therefore, interest in the way that the subject matter had deviated. She motioned to Fred that it was time to move on. Fred, however, had better hearing, and was fascinated by the turn of events. Aware that subtlety was not going to work, Betty yanked Fred by the arm and provided the encouragement necessary to get him to his feet.

"I think we need to have a final look around the stalls before all the good stuff goes." She explained the reason behind her physical manipulation of Fred to Eileen and Miranda and moved away.

"Obviously her idea of good stuff and mine differ somewhat." Eileen laughed. "There's not been any good stuff in here in living memory."

"But hey, we have a good natter and the cakes are amazing, and Milly gets a new book and it gets me out of the house. What's not to like?" Miranda watched as Betty dragged Fred around the stalls and bought a perfumed candle when she realised she was being observed. "I don't think she's especially interested in other people's children – which I suppose is understandable if she can't hear so well".

"She relies on Fred to interpret. She'll be interrogating him for the rest of the morning about Milly."

Miranda smiled and watched as Milly provided the dog with its tail, talking to it as she did so.

"Happy dog." Muttered Milly, as she waggled her finger.

****

Robin and Trixie were animated. Their daily visit to see Spot had today taken on a new and exciting dimension. The value of Spot within the non-human communications network in the parish was based strongly on his central location. Since his retirement from the Dog Show circuit, he rarely ventured beyond his own front garden and, if he did expand his horizons, they tended to stop at the common around the village pond. But all of fae and animal life passed his little empire on the High Street at one time or another on most days, and nothing of any significance failed to stop there and put down roots.

On this occasion, Spot had been able to pass on fully authenticated reports of further sitings of the 'stranger' within the parish. He had it on good authority – via the half-brother of Charlie Brown who had been chasing a rabbit from the second brood of Benjamin and Flop-ear which, when cornered by the dry-stone wall at the edge of Hill Farm, volunteered the information that a tall, officious-looking faery had been seen by his third cousin, once removed (so very close and with impeccable credentials). Such information had been given in return for a safe passage back to the burrow promised by a dog who, in truth, was too knackered to chase it any further anyway.

This then was a story reliable and eminently worthy of repetition, and Spot had been hardly able to wait to repeat it to Robin and Trixie at the earliest opportunity.

"So he's still around!" Robin smiled. Despite settling down happily in Whimbury, he yearned for things to happen. Pretty much anything really but this, this had the potential to herald in a whole new adventure. Trixie smiled back indulgently and mentally sent a memo to herself to prepare for more Goodfellow japes and time-bending messenger errands for herself. She wouldn't be too displeased with this, though the stress of "Crossover Day" itself had taken its toll and she was content that such excitement seemed to be restricting itself to every two years or so. She could cope with that.

Spot barked his response, ostensibly at the Postman on the opposite side of the road. The postman, given the safety of distance, smiled and waved back. This annoyed Spot, who hurrumphed his disgust at the indignities he had to suffer in the cause of conversing with faeries.

"Sorry, didn't quite get the last bit." Robin knew full well the literal translations of the expletive-ridden hurrumphs, but couldn't resist a little fun at Spot's expense.

Spot took his front paws from off the garden wall and lay on the grass, scratching behind his ear in a pointed fit of pique. He followed it up with a contemptuous yawn and waited for Robin to make the next move. Trixie, who knew that to wait for Robin when he was in playful mood would involve wasting much of the rest of the day, stepped in to keep the conversation going.

"So, as I understand it, the stranger has been seen in the last day or so, though we don't know exactly where, or what he was doing. But you're sure we can trust the source of the information." Trixie sat beside Spot and spoke quietly in his recently scratched ear.

Spot hurrumphed a grudging acknowledgement and gave out another half-hearted bark before placing his head between his paws on the ground. Trixie interpreted this, correctly, as an indication that there was more to the story, but it would not be revealed until certain impolite sprites adopted a more conciliatory tone and apologised unreservedly for distress caused.

Trixie hated being the intermediary in these cases, but saw it as part and parcel of the package of her relationship with Robin. It wasn't the first time and it wouldn't be the last that she would have to fulfil this role, and so she had just better become very good at it. At least that way it would speed things up considerably.

"This is very useful information, Spot." Trixie began the ego-boosting, calming- potentially- troubled- waters process. "Barry will be pleased to think that the network is fully operational. It's vital that we have as much detail as possible so that we can protect Milly and maintain her education. You know how important that is for all of us." She placed as much emphasis on the last four words as she dare, without appear gushing.

Spot twitched his nose and yawned again.

Trixie sighed silently to herself. This was going to be hard work.

"So, should I tell Barry to come round here to talk with you about it, or would it be best for him to get it straight from the rabbit's mouth, so to speak? He can't afford to get only half of the story. Maybe it's best he engages the rabbit community directly?"

******

It is a well-known fact in the animal world that dogs and rabbits do not get on. Long before dogs were inbred by humans to within an inch of their lives, they were hunting animals, basically wolves, who preferred eating meat to dying from starvation. Rabbits, by way of contrast, as vegetarians, see themselves as therefore superior to dogs, and better in general for the future of the planet.

When they are too tired to bother running around, dogs will simply hurl insults in the direction of rabbits along the lines of "pellet poohers", and will cast aspersions on their heritage, lineage, and impact on the general overpopulation of the planet. Rabbits meanwhile will counter – usually from the safety of a burrow – that dogs are "smelly, wet-poohers" who live parasitically on the welfare offered by humans. "Get on your paws and find your own food" is a familiar refrain from the rabbit fraternity, while dogs, in return, offer generally rude thoughts on the subject of breeding habits.

Rabbits reluctantly acknowledge that some dogs are faster than them, and that the smaller, yappy ones may be capable of following them into burrows with devastating results. On the other hand, they fail to see how they can treat with respect any dog that can be trained to chase sticks or balls, or even worse to run round and round after pretend rabbits (often confused with pretend hares) constructed out of fur and sawdust. Dogs see rabbits as being jealous, in that relatively few of them get to be cuddled and tickled by humans, or offered an exciting mixed diet of the best varied green leaves that supermarkets can provide.

What Trixie was doing, therefore, was to play along with Spot's baser instincts by threatening to by-pass the usual canine network of spies and routine gossip, in favour of dealing directly with the despised rabbits. She was banking on Spot being unable to allow such an approach on principle, whilst hoping that he would not be so affronted by the suggestion, that he dug his claws in and refused to co-operate any further at all. In truth, she also found the rabbits somewhat sanctimonious and would rather deal with the information that they had at arms' length. But needs must, and she just wanted to know what exactly was going on, and sooner rather than later.

****

To the unaccustomed ear, it might have sounded as though Spot coughed politely before barking his response. "You can tell Barry that I have some important news for him and that if he wishes to hear it, I will be more than happy to divulge it to him in person, as opposed to casting these particular pearls in the direction of Mr 'Oh look at me, aren't I witty' Goodfellow over there. Apologies and condolences to his immediate and unfortunate family, naturally".

Spot was a good friend and Trixie was pleased to have softened his attitude somewhat. She accepted that she may not have supported her life-partner quite as strongly as she should, but there again she often had to accept that, in many peoples' eyes and ears, he could, at times, be a real pain in the bum. Fun, intelligence, wit and inventiveness were his strong points – the ones she loved him for. Sensitivity and diplomacy, however, could be lacking at critical times, which is where the essential teamwork of all close relationships comes into play, and Trixie knew how to de-stress tense situations. Robin, for his part, was self-aware enough to know that he needed Trixie, as well as loved her for accepting him as he was.

"I'll tell Barry." At which point Trixie did just that, and returned before either Spot or Robin had fully realised that she had gone. "He's on his way!" Trixie took a moment for her molecules to re-settle and then sat down next to Robin, whistling aimlessly while waiting for Barry to catch up. Barry arrived just as Trixie was about to repeat the Pixie favourite "Fae-mi-down-dilly" for the seventh time.

"Thank Oberon you've come." Robin removed his hands from his ears. "I like the tune, but there are limits." Trixie smiled the smile of one whose job of keeping Robin from any more potentially aggravating utterances had been successfully completed. The smile drooped slightly when she noticed that Spot was lying on the ground with paws covering both ears but, hey ho, it was job done nevertheless.

Barry stood in front of Spot and poked him gently on the nose. Spot opened his eyes without moving his paws. He barked a long, low growly bark and set his head at a 45 degree angle. Barry smiled and looked up forbearingly at Trixie, who shrugged her slight shoulders. He translated for her.

"I believe he said that he would rather be insulted by Robin again than have to listen to another rendition of "Fae-mi-down-dilly", though I may have lost the odd word in translation."

"Just as well I'm not as sensitive to criticism as he is." Trixie spoke loudly in the direction of Spot, who's paws had now separated from his ears.

"OK. So now that we've cleared the air a little, maybe we can get to the bottom of what's going on in the parish?" Barry was as anxious as anyone to garner as much news and information as possible. This was a critical time in the development of Milly as 'The Crossover child', and Barry needed to ensure that there were no mistakes or negative influences on the process. "As I understand it, the stranger has been seen again. But no-one has actually spoken to him?"

An all-pervading silence filled the air.

"Spot?" Barry furrowed his eyebrows at Spot indicating that enough sulking had by now taken place and that the importance of the situation needed to be recognised and acted upon appropriately.

To the untrained human ear, Spot may have sounded like a dog unexpectedly woken up by the passage of another smaller, and therefore inferior, dog passing his gate, such was the intensity of his barking. In truth he was just glad to be freed from the constraints of pique, and ready to blurt out the full details of his story to a willing, and impartial, listener such as Barry.

The gist of what he was barking was that the stranger had been seen at the edge of the Woods with a shorter, less imposing faery. The stranger appeared to be fashioning a spear and practising combat strategies with his accomplice. They did a lot of sniffing at the air and gesturing before leaving in the direction of Home Farm. What was most surprising, however, was that nothing had been heard or seen of them since, despite the number of animals in the vicinity.

"So no-one knows whether they reached Home Farm or whether they turned away somewhere. Most odd." Barry wasn't sure that he was pleased with the new information. It certainly made him edgy, but also more resolute in his desire to confront this new visitor to the village. He didn't take easily to rumour or half-story and he was determined to get to the bottom of this one, even if he didn't know quite where to begin.

"I have an idea, Barry." Robin had been aware that he wasn't exactly flavour of the month in canine circles, and he could understand why. But that was not going to cause him to change his ways to any great degree. While diplomacy had been taking place around him, he had been listening and thinking. Thinking of jolly wheezes and pranks was, after all, his favourite pastime.

"And what might that be?" Barry was always intrigued by Robin's flair for slightly off the wall ideas and schemes which, despite all rational thoughts to the contrary, often worked amazingly well.

"I'll tell you on the way back to the Oak." Robin was about to jump off the garden wall when Trixie caught his arm before he could head off down the High Street with Barry. She remained silent but merely looked sternly at both Robin and Barry and nodded her head in the direction of Spot. For once they both understood the hint and responded to it, turning back to look at Spot, who was, by now, resting his paws on the wall again.

"Sorry about the little joke, Spot. No offence meant." Robin put on his best contrite face and gave one of his 'so rare that they are almost extinct' attempts at an apology.

"Yes, and thanks for the information. You can't believe how important it is." Barry mopped up the situation with his effusive and, in this case, genuine appreciation.

Spot gave a grudging bark that was intended to indicate that, while offence had been taken, bygones would be considered bygones – just this once. And as for the information, Barry was most welcome to it, and he hoped it would be useful. A final little growl confirmed that Barry would not have had the same co-operation from the rabbits – so there. He watched as the band of faeries, his friends, wandered back to the Royal Oak, then turned his head at a 45 degree angle and pondered over how long it would be till teatime and certain other great mysteries of life.

Chapter Six

THE TALL STRANGER SAT ON a small rocky outcrop at the edge of Whimbury Woods. He motioned silence to his companion and pointed down at a patch of briars with his staff.

In truth, Burr could see nothing and had no idea what he was supposed to be looking at. He was still learning, but knew he had to be absolutely motionless and quiet. He used the time to attempt to acclimatise his senses – slowly and gently sniffing the air – opening his mouth to taste the exhalation of the leaves and flowers of the brambles and the plants and herbs within them – allowing the air to sift through his fingers – and assessing the spirits of the animal life around him.

And then, just for a moment, he felt the presence that the stranger had indicated. He wasn't sure how he knew, just that it touched him somehow. There was a connection and he felt at ease. There was no malice and no sense of impending harm. Whatever was there was friend rather than foe.

Burr smiled with the satisfaction of a useful lesson learned and turned to see the stranger smiling back at him.

"So you sense him too?" The stranger's whisper was as the lightest of breezes.

"Him?"

"Ah! So you sense the presence but not the person. But still it marks a major breakthrough in your education, my friend. There is a human in the briars. Why, I do not know. It is a most unusual habitat for such a being. We must wait for some movement and hope that we can determine his purpose."

"His purpose?"

"It is a male human. That much I can tell. And he is resting and calm."

"I felt no malice!" Burr was anxious for explanations. He was experiencing things that were totally new to him and he needed reassurance that he was correct in his interpretations of what he had sensed.

"Good! Any well-attuned faery should be able to sense a presence, but it takes a clever and patient one to sense the nature of that presence. You will be of much help to me if you continue to learn at this rate."

Burr was cheered. His companion had so many strange and wonderful gifts and, as time progressed, he was beginning to understand, little by little, the power that they possessed. As yet, he still had no inkling of his friend's purposes. And, in all honesty, he was still somewhat at unease in the presence of one who could, at any time, crush him physically, mentally or emotionally should he so wish. But the sense of adventure, in one whose life had thus far lacked any semblance of excitement, was intoxicating, and he had no intention of going back to his earlier secure lifestyle as a fae medical practitioner. He did miss the community spirit of his home village, and had little pangs of conscience from time to time, having left it in the hands of his junior partner, with not so much as a "to-do" list for a farewell present. But something momentous was going to happen, of that he was sure. If only he knew what.

"You have shut down your senses!" The stranger did not look up or to the side, and his whisper was barely audible, yet it startled Burr from his reverie.

"Yes, I have. I'm sorry." Burr was less cheered

"Do not apologise. Just learn and focus."

"I will, I will. I promise."

"I believe you." The stranger appeared to smile in the most subtle of ways, which unnerved Burr more than any rebuke. "The human has stirred. He will wake in just a few minutes. We must observe him in silence and follow him when he moves. There is a smell of faery about him and I suspect strongly that he is, or will be, involved with the Crossover Child."

"Crossover?"

"A human child who has within his or her power the ability to bring together the fae and human communities once and for all. The child lives in this village. I need to find the child and to see for myself what plans the local faeries have to assist the completion of the Crossover. If this human is part of that plan, our discovery of him could be invaluable."

Burr tried to revert to "learn and focus" mode, bur what he had just heard about the "Crossover" child couldn't be filed away for re-consideration another day. From the dark recesses of his memory, he could dimly recall legend or myth about such a being, a part of fae folklore for which a scientist and medical practitioner like himself could not allow much space or time. Much as he would happily use homeopathic magic in his cures and remedies as a last resort, the concept of a human-faery, or maybe faery-human, was too far-fetched to take seriously. He mulled it over, his thoughts churning in the manner of spices in a Christmas wine.

The stranger said that the child was here. Already here, but incomplete. What did that mean? He wished he'd spent more time concentrating on the Fae legend and history lessons at school. But it all seemed like just so much gobbledygook at the time, distant from the realities of everyday life, which he wanted to improve using as much medical knowledge as he could muster. Yet the more he pondered, the more the memories opened up, until he began to appreciate the ways in which human history intertwined with that of the faeries, weaving a tapestry of influence and counter-influence. He'd always assumed that the two strands would continue to bounce off each other for eternity, but if this legend of the Crossover were true, as it now appeared that it might, that changed everything, and all he had previously believed needed a thorough workover.

He was woken out of his reverie by a hand firmly squeezing his lower leg. In truth it was probably squeezing harder than was strictly necessary, and if it weren't for the other hand firmly covering his mouth, he would have given out an involuntary yelp of pain. But the manoeuvre had the desired effect of capturing his attention with little chance of it escaping. Behind him, the stranger leant close to his ear and whispered one word.

"Watch!"

Bearing in mind he had little option, he watched, as the human stretched and yawned, then uttered what Burr assumed was an expletive, given that the man had snagged his arm on a bramble. The snagging swiftly brought the man to his senses and he turned his head to and fro, firstly to assess his whereabouts and then to look anxiously around. After a few moments of silence, the man seemed reassured that he was alone and lay back breathing more slowly.

The stranger gradually released the pressure on Burr's leg and then, satisfied that Burr was calm, took his hand from Burr's mouth. Burr turned his head and gave him a look that confirmed his understanding of the need for silence.

After a while, the human got onto his knees and crawled out of the bramble patch. He stood up, arched his back and flexed his knuckles. He walked over to a nearby tree and stood facing it for a minute or two. Burr watched as the man then gave a satisfied sigh and appeared to waggle his hips in the manner of a static dance. He then pulled a small bottle of water out of his pocket, had a swig, rinsed out his mouth, spat the liquid onto his hands, and then wiped them on a small cloth that projected from his other pocket. Ablutions over, he wandered through the undergrowth to the nearest path and set off in the direction of the Royal Oak.

At a respectable distance, Burr and the stranger followed.

****

Percy and Everard were enjoying (not that Percy would ever admit it) another of their increasingly regular morning tiffin sessions. Percetta had gone out socialising, content in the knowledge that, at last, Percy had someone to take his mind off moaning and grumbling. She was aware, of course, that it was hard to break the habit of a lifetime, especially a lifetime spent as head of the "clan" whose whole ethos was based around being grumpy. Percy had been good at it – too good – and Percetta had feared for his health and welfare if he were to continue that intensity into his retirement.

But the "Crossover" incident had changed all that. Whilst the clans had traditions and lifestyles to maintain, somehow the incident had impressed upon the whole community that even tradition needed to be put in its rightful place when something momentous and deeply meaningful came along. Nothing, not even tradition, could be preserved in aspic for ever. Life moves on and traditions have to adapt, or at least be seen in the context of a new and emerging way of operating.

So now Percy socialised as well, even to the extent of sharing anecdotes and thoughts about life, the universe and all things fae. What's more he was doing that with a member of another clan. Who'd have thought it? A Grumplet and a Gnappins sharing a common bond of friendship, and even, when quite sure no-one would overhear, a laugh. It meant that Percetta had the freedom to go out to meet her own friends and reminisce over past times, including deep discussions about the significance of the pattern she had used in the knitting of the famous Crossover jumper. Where had she got the ideas for the symbols and colours? Was it just good luck, or fate, that had brought just the right human sock into her ownership, for unpicking and use in the knitting? She and her friends never tired of pondering such matters and there were always new directions for the conversation to take, so that it was always fresh.

Percy was explaining to Everard his ideas for developing a "stonery" at the bottom of his garden. In truth it would be more of a "gravellery", but Percy couldn't pronounce it!

"You see, Everard, I want to have some colour all year round, but a lot of the larger shrubs, like bluebells, would just overpower it. I need medium shrubs like primrose, lesser celandine and wood anemone for body and early flower. but what to put amongst them, that's the issue."

"Well, oi knows its dead common, but oi don't thinks you can beat a little bed o' scarlet elf caps – bit o' brightness and you can put it in your salads and it's low growin."

"Obviously, I had thought of that," Percy never had been one to give another faery credit where credit was due, when he could use the occasion to bolster his own position, "but they are a bit commonplace, and they spread so."

"And that's why you needs to keep pickin' 'em fer salads. And Barry used to use 'em in his famous Mushroom Strong'n'off bar meals. Always went down well with the less culinary aware patrons, who chose it fer the excitement – durin' and after – rather than the epicurean experience, shall we say."

"Indeed we shall – I tried one once and thereafter stuck to the toasted sandwiches."

The discussion was cut short by the heavy sounds of extremely large feet crashing along the informal pathway close by. Percy and Everard climbed to the top of the, as yet "naked", stonery and peered over the wild garlic hedge. A few metres away, a large, unkempt male human trudged furtively through the woods, muttering softly to himself.

"Ramble through brambles, ambling, gambling – odds on being seen, evens the rest. Couldn't even take a rest – keep moving, moving, moving – though they're disapproving, keep those faeries moving – raw pride, that's all it is, matter of principle – make a profit. Keep the bankers happy. Bankers? W……. What's here?" Ralph paused and looked around. Percy and Everard ducked their heads

"Faery woods. Faery would live here. Nature all around, minimum interference. Maximum inference. Where are you? No matter. No time. Keep moving, moving, moving….." And Ralph kept moving, moving, moving in the direction of the Royal Oak.

"Oi could swears 'e knew we was 'ere somewhere." After a safe pause, Everard poked his head back up above the hedge and confirmed that the human had indeed moved on.

Had they not returned to their discussion, they might have seen two strange faeries following Ralph at a safe distance.

****

It was coffee break time at Over Cross View. Miranda and Evadne watched as Milly carefully chose a coloured crayon to continue her picture of a unicorn. In truth, only Milly could tell it was a unicorn by just looking at it. Evadne and Miranda had to imagine it through the eyes of the artist and by descriptions provided at regular intervals by said artist. The relationship between the unicorn and the tortoise beside it remained unclear, despite the occasional prompting question from the adults.

"Obviously, you've got your hands full with Milly," Evadne broached a delicate subject with the necessary early caution, "but I'm sure Will wouldn't mind being left with her one evening a week, just for an hour or so – I suppose she might even be in bed by then? What time do you take her up?"

"Depends on whether she has a bath. Usually around 7-ish. On fine days, when she can run around more outside, she gets tired earlier than when she's been indoors with me all day – though she's always on the go doing something, whatever the weather."

"Her drawing's coming on a treat." Evadne had taken a close interest in Milly's development, more especially as she had been present at the birth and been her Godmother since. She had been of relatively advanced years when she had had Adrian, and was anticipating a long wait to grandparenthood, so the arrival of Milly had enlivened her no end. She took her godmothering seriously and, appropriately as it turned out, tended to see the role as akin to a fairy godmother. She was anxious that Miranda should go the ball – only in this case the ball would perhaps be more like a Parish Council meeting, and it would occur more regularly than once every Princely betrothal bash. Besides, Will would be perfectly happy to put Milly to bed by himself and have all the fun of reading her a bedtime story. Evadne had expressed as much to Miranda and put on her best 'godmother knows best' look. Coffee and chit-chat was all part of the softening up process.

"Yes, she's got quite amazing concentration for her age." Miranda never missed an opportunity to express her pride in her daughter's progress. "Though I'm not sure where the unicorn and the tortoise idea came from – she's got books with unicorns and tortoises in but not together so far as I can remember, and having read all her books to her several times each, I'm sure I haven't overlooked that particular conjunction of animals". She smiled as Milly stuck out her tongue while she focussed hard on drawing yet another, largely circular, tortoise in an otherwise empty part of the sheet of paper.

"So, you're not planning on going back to work any time soon?" Evadne's ability to circumnavigate conversations and turn the steering wheel into her preferred direction was legendary in Parish Council circles and beyond. The art lay in the extra finesse that she applied to the relevant question or statement, which in this case involved standing behind Milly and smiling knowingly as if in awe of her artistic talents.

"Not unless we can get Milly into nursery school next year, then I might look for something part-time. But at the moment I'm happy being here with her. There's enough going on in the village or in Whimburton to keep us all occupied, and Will's job can be pretty flexible if needs be!" Miranda picked up one of Milly's crayons and sharpened it. The point broke off as it frequently did, and Miranda made a mental note not to buy cheap drawing materials from the craft stall in future.

"Well, I could co-opt you onto the Council just for a year, and then we could see how it goes after that?" Evadne seamlessly took over the crayon sharpening duties and proceeded to break the points off several in succession, making a mental note not to allow the craft stall into the Parish Rooms for the next Village fete.

"Shouldn't I be nominated and voted for, or something?" Miranda was running out of excuses.

"Only if I invoke the constitution in a literal sense – which I won't. Anyway, I'm sure I must have powers to co-opt if there is a vacancy."

"And is there a vacancy?"

"If there isn't there soon will be if Fred is late for just one more meeting due to a clash with Strictly come whatever, or some TV sports event. You don't follow any quiz programmes, or reality series, or soaps, or...?" Evadne finally sharpened a pink crayon to a firm and secure point and handed it over to Milly, who ignored it in favour of an almost blunt green one, which she considered more suitable for the tortoises.

"No, don't have time on a regular basis for any of those. I could say 'more's the pity', but to be honest, I'm not that interested anyway. Though I must confess to being quite knowledgeable on certain of the Childrens' TV programmes. If quiz questions were solely about Mutant Ninja Tortoises, I'd win easily."

"Don't you mean Mutant Ninja Turtles?" Evadne immediately regretted indicating that she might know something about a TV cartoon series, but she needn't have worried since Miranda did not pick up that particular faux pas.

"Milly prefers tortoises," came back the reply, as if the answer should have been obvious. "If the Parish Council were developing a policy on tortoises, or any garden insects or crustaceans, then I might feel as if I could be really useful. I'm building up quite a body of expertise on such vital matters!"

"Unfortunately, our main concern at the moment is the Council's plan to put a large number of new houses in Whimbury to meet its housing needs. We need to think about what we feel on the matter and produce some sensible suggestions. We don't want to be seen as numpties or whatever…"

"I think the term is nimbys, Evadne." Miranda gently corrected Evadne while treating herself to another biscuit, "though I suspect that we don't want to be considered numpties either!"

"Either way, I need some younger blood at the meetings – someone who understands the modern ways of doing things. And even more important, someone who has opinions based upon the future that they want and not the past that they want back. We are, I must confess, a little short of such people, and we daren't get left behind when decisions get taken at higher levels."

"I have a feeling that creating the future I'd like for Milly is a bit beyond Parish Council level, but I do agree that we've got to try, and use whatever expertise we have to work towards it – no point in complaining afterwards if we haven't even tried to influence things."

"That's exactly why we need you!" Evadne felt as though she had now reached the stage of reeling in her catch. Miranda had her head screwed on, and was well-liked and respected around the village. She could maybe say things and be listened to, in a way that Evadne couldn't. Yes, she already had an ally or two, including Eileen, but they were also of the "older" guard on the whole. The rest were lovely people and well-meaning, but they seemed to find it difficult to see beyond raising money for the long-standing established events, which were great for keeping the community together, or at least most of it, but the time had come when the village had to stand up for itself against greater forces. Change was, after all, inevitable, and better to have an impact on change than have it imposed on you by outsiders with no real interest in your wishes or needs.

"I'll see what Will says!" Miranda had never really seen herself as a stalwart of the Parish Council, but now that Evadne had pushed the door ajar, she perhaps secretly fancied the idea, and one evening out every now and again surely wouldn't hurt. Of course, she would check with Will, but she knew he would agree. He loved having time with Milly, and he wanted Miranda to feel fulfilled. So far, being a full-time mum had sufficed, she had no regrets and wouldn't have gone out of her way to change that, but now she didn't have to go out of her way – the way had come to her.

"Absolutely, I'd expect nothing else." Evadne gushed, as only she could. "Just let me know as soon as you've made your mind up, and I'll make sure you get an invite to the next meeting, along with an agenda and the minutes of the last meeting. All I'd ask is that you don't spend too long agonising over the world-shattering decisions we made – or failed to make, depending on your perspective."

"OK." Miranda had been hooked, reeled in and packed in ice – and she knew it. Maybe it would mark the beginning of a new chapter in her life. Time to carpe a few diems anyway, she thought.

Evadne finished her coffee and made to leave.

"So how's my little god-daughter getting on with her unicorns and tortoises?" She and Miranda turned to check, and saw Milly finish sharpening her green crayon successfully, and get on with drawing yet another tortoise.

****

Later that day, it was another quiz night at the Royal Oak. Damon and Trixie were checking that the glass jugs were clean and dry. They would be seeing a lot of action that evening. Barry had excused himself for a few minutes to go outside and could be found round the back of the tree talking with Ralph.

"So there are two strange faeries lurking around the neighbourhood." Barry passed on his news to Ralph, who leaned back onto a holly bush pensively, and instantly leaned forward again muttering under his breath words that Barry could still hear clearly enough and were largely uncomplimentary to Holly bushes.

"I'll keep my eyes and ears open Barry, but I'm not as perceptive as you, and my senses are still dulled by the usual human frailties. But if they're in the woods, sooner or later I'll find them – or they'll find me, more likely. Just have to hope that they're ready and willing to be found. It'll be important though to know if they are friend or foe!"

"Absolutely. And the sooner we know that, the better. Right, well I'd best get back before the warfare commences. How was your first night in our wood, by the way?" Barry got up and took a deep breath ready for his evening onslaught.

"Not bad. I slept pretty well considering – mind you, I was tired after the walk from town. Once I get into the swing of not standing up immediately when I wake, and thereby avoid the brambles, I'll be even better. Nice talking to you and I hope these guys are benign! See you tomorrow." Barry watched as Ralph quickly disappeared back through the undergrowth, and just for a moment felt that he sensed other movements and sound in the vicinity. He listened carefully, but hearing no more, he turned and made his way round to the entrance. Had he concentrated harder he might just have heard Burr kick himself and whisper "Sorry".

Once back inside the Royal Oak, Barry eased his way past the hubbub of the normal quarrelling between the Happs and Grumps about whatever it was they could find to quarrel about. If they had any difficulties in disagreeing, Barry would always step in to find something to fit the bill – an argumentative Inn was a contented and profitable one. It was a win-win situation.

At the bar, Trixie and Damon were pouring large numbers of jugs of Innkeepers Choice ready for the pre-first-round rush. Robin stood nearby admiring their smooth and efficient styles and looking agitated in a positive, excited way.

"Situation normal?" Barry swept past them into his place, ready for action.

"Normal, fine and dandy." Trixie paused and counted the number of drinks ready and waiting for their eager recipients. "You going to call them to order"

"Not yet, the teams are still setting themselves up and moving chairs. Once everything's sorted and starts quietening down, I'll call them up for final pre-match drink collection, and that should lead to enough hullabaloo and chaos to keep the snug grumbling for a bit longer." Barry nodded towards the quiet area in the snug where the Grumps were sitting morosely waiting for something to happen.

"Good plan, bro." Robin bounced into the conversation keenly. He winked at Trixie and motioned for her and Barry to lean towards him and receive a private and highly secretive message. "The posters are all ready, I just need to get a couple of volunteers to help me put up the boards to attach them to and we're away."

"How many have you got?" Trixie had left Robin painting the posters when she set off for her shift behind the bar. In truth she was amazed at how focussed he was and how hard he was working. It was seldom like this!

"Seven! The perfect number, I just need to decide on seven perfect spots to put them, so that wherever they are in the village they're bound to see one – and once seen, they'll have to respond – guaranteed."

"Would you, by any chance, have a copy with you to show us?" Robin had only provided Barry with the outline of his plan, and Barry was now anxious to see exactly what he had written. The large rolled-up sheet of coloured paper sticking out of the top of Robin's tunic, gave Barry a clue that the finished product may well be available to view.

"Certainly have bro," Robin was about to open up the poster when Barry motioned to him to come behind the bar.

"I don't think we should let any of the regulars in on this little ruse. It would only take one of them to come across our strangers by accident and start talking carelessly, and the whole scheme could be scuppered. We'll discuss it in the cellars." He gesticulated to Trixie who gesticulated back, and then realised that he wanted to communicate with her. "Just going down to the cellar with Robin. Don't let the stampede start till I get back."

"OK boss." Trixie could add just the right amount of mild sarcastic inflexion to the word "boss" when she wanted. Fortunately, their relationship was such that Barry knew it was all in good humour - usually.

Barry led Robin down the steps. In the cellar Junior was lousing about [7], de-fungussing the barrels and pipes in his usual competent and efficient manner.

"Hi Junior, keep up the good work. Robin and I have a somewhat private conversation to have, which is why we are down here."

"Hi Barry, no worries, my antennae are off-signal!" [8] Junior carried on his work, humming to himself loudly.

"Right, let's have a look!" In truth, Barry was very keen to view Robin's

---

[7] Similar to beavering or ferreting but with more legs and antennae.
[8] Similar to "my lips are sealed" but without the lips.

handiwork and get to understand the plan a little better. Robin unrolled the posters and put them down on a table. They read:

Prize Competition
Bring your personal travel stories and win a great prize.
Stories to be read out in person at:
The Royal Oak
Friday night @ 7.30 pm

"That's pretty impressive, Robin. Looks very professional – but do you think they'll be attracted by it?"

"Like a moth to light, bro, like a moth to light. They're strangers, no-one's ever heard of them or seen them before in these parts, so they must have travelled and they're here for a reason. If their intention is to make contact, this will flush them out."

"Might just work. Certainly worth a try – and at least it looks official."

"Took me a long time to get it that neat." Robin was not renowned for taking his time over anything, and was proud of is achievement. "I even measured out all the words."

"And I copied all the letters in a big round hand!" Junior burst into song.

"I thought your antennae were off-signal!" Barry was displeased.

"Sorry Barry, you must have changed frequency inadvertently. People frequently change frequency without realising it!" Junior reverted to humming.

Well, I'll be very grateful if this particular instance of frequency change remains in the cellar and is not repeated anywhere else."

"Message understood Barry. Sorry, but I just seem to pick up links to HMS Pixielore almost by radar, and they elicit snatches of song. Pops is pretty much the same with his classical theatre."

"Yes, I had noticed over the years. No problem, Junior, but please keep all this to yourself. It's most important."

"Righto." Junior returned to his tasks and hid behind his librettos. "A working louse am I, - a thing of moss and fungi – of all things moist and spongy…."

Barry and Robin walked slowly back up the stairs.

"So where were you thinking of placing the posters?" Barry had certain reservations about the likely success of Robin's plan, but as he had no better ideas himself, he was happy to go along with it. After all, it couldn't do any harm could it? That is, other than having to endure a Friday evening listening to less than interesting holiday stories from his regulars, and deciding on an appropriate prize for the best one. Most of the faeries in the village never left the parish even to go on holiday, and his own brother, Morris, who was an inveterate traveller and always had plenty of tales to tell, was Oberon knew where at this point in time. But if it worked – well that could be quite an achievement.

"One outside the Oak, obviously. Then I thought at a couple of the entrances to the wood – by the Grange and at the bottom of the hill – cos that's near where they were last seen. Possibly one at the village pond and then one outside Over Cross View, in case they've heard all about Milly already and are having a nosey around. What do you think?" Under normal circumstances Robin wouldn't have cared less what Barry thought about one of his schemes, but this time it was important rather than just a prank, and he respected Barry's opinions on such things.

"All sounds good to me Robin, that leaves a couple more – how about one near the station and one by the pub. That would cover both main entrances to the village as well."

"Good idea, bro.[9] Now we just need some volunteers to help me put them up – preferably someone with a hammer and some arnica and plasters!"

"I suggest we wait till after the quiz and everyone is in a good mood.[10] Then we'll ask around. How many do you need?"

"Just a couple, bro. One to hold, one to hit, and me there with them to decide whether they're doing it right, and to hold the posts that haven't been put in yet!"

---

[9] Barry couldn't for the life of him remember when Robin had started to call him "bro", but he quite liked it. It seemed to indicate that Robin had settled into village life and it pleased him.

[10] The winners because they had won, the losers because they would have drunk enough to reach the point of not caring, and the Grumps because they'd had a good moan.

"OK. I'll start the ball rolling when the evening's entertainment is all over. Till then, let battle commence."

Chapter Seven

IN THE PLANNING DEPARTMENT AT Whimburton Town Hall, Jessica Huntly-Phillips was having a briefing meeting with two of her staff from the Local Plan section. She had just come out of a meeting with the Chair of the Planning Committee and had a brief window of opportunity to fit in this meeting before travelling to London for the Annual Conference of the Housing Enterprises group of companies (ACHE). Here she was to deliver a paper on the role of Local Plans in delivering Buildings for the Urban Mass Market.

Until the Agenda and Papers for the conference were published and distributed to participants and speakers, no-one in the ACHE team had realised just how disaffected Richard Gwelodd, convenor of the conference, had been, following his failure to secure a promotion at the last company re-shuffle. Only when the conference folder fell through the letterboxes of its members a few days before the event, and the very clear juxtaposition of BUMM and ACHE became evident on the front cover, did the penny drop, by which time of course it was too late to do anything about it. Richard, meanwhile, had taken some belated leave at an isolated cottage in his beloved North Wales where there was no wi-fi signal, and he only returned the day before the conference, whereupon he expressed dismay that only people with a very childish sense of humour could possibly have found any issue with the title of the event in his absence.

Back at Whimburton, Jessica was discussing housing need and supply with Jason Jones and Emily Wilson, two high-flying planners who were destined for great things – Emily because she was bright, perceptive and caring, and

Jason because he could be relied upon to agree with Jessica on all key issues. Jessica needed both – Emily to identify potential problems, flaws in logic, likely local concerns, and political implications of major decisions – and Jason to find a way of overcoming them all with minimum transparency and fuss. Jason and Emily didn't exactly get on, but that didn't matter in the greater scheme of things.

"So the Chair agrees with me that Whimburton can't accommodate all our housing needs and that we need to spread the new developments around the District. From the figures that Jason has produced, it would appear that we need to allocate land for around half of our housing needs in the surrounding parishes, and that Whimbury is our best option for a substantial amount. Any thoughts Emily?"

Basically, Emily thought that the whole idea was rubbish and wouldn't work, certainly not for the residents of the villages concerned and, least of all, for those of Whimbury. But she knew that her thoughts were seldom welcomed wholeheartedly at these meetings and that, if they were to be given any credence at all, they would need to be expressed very carefully. Fortunately, she was blessed with diplomacy and carefulness of expression, along with her other very valuable abilities.

"Well obviously," Emily began with the firm footing element of her arguments, "we have to provide the right amount of housing overall to meet government targets – otherwise we're in real difficulties. So, we need to clarify to the residents of all our settlements that the bottom line is out of our hands. Next, of course, is to be able to justify our decisions on where the houses will go, and for that we need to bring the public on board.[11] At this stage we may have rough ideas about this, but we need to put genuine options out there to encourage local discussion and debate."

Jason interjected, which was his modus operandi of choice. "We've already notified the Parish Councils about the upcoming Local Plan preparation, so they should by now be getting some ideas together."

---

[11] A quaint old-fashioned idea that ordinary people could be involved in the decision-making that surrounded their everyday lives, as opposed to agreeing what had already been decided behind the scenes and presented to them as the best thing since un-sliced bread.

"That was what I was coming onto!" Emily inter-interjected which was her modus operandi of necessity. "I saw the letter that went out, and it ran along the lines of 'We are preparing a really important new Local Plan and we are going to have to put lots of lovely new houses in your village. We need to know where you'd like them to go'. Seems to me that just encourages an 'us and them' mentality. They're bound to have important questions – at least, important to them."

"Like what?" Jason truly believed that Planning could make people's lives better, but he also believed that only planners had the knowledge and understanding to make it happen in the right way.

"Like, what type of houses and for whom? How many and what prices? What else might come along with them?"

"Like what?" Jason enjoyed playing devil's advocate, particularly when the devil might have more senior posts to dole out at some time in the future.

"Like maybe investment in schools, more bus services, childrens' play areas – you know, things that people might need if the population increases?"

"I'm sure the landowners and housebuilders will be more than happy to subsidise such things. The one's I've spoken to have indicated that they would." Jason had many talents, but discretion was not one of them.

"When have you been talking to landowners and housebuilders?" Emily was taken aback – almost so far back as to be to the time before planners – a time that most developers wished they still lived in.

Too late, Jason realised that he had said too much – and to the wrong person. Emily could be tenacious when she wanted, and he sensed that now might just be one of those times. In this he was right, and he twiddled his retractable pencil around his fingers as he searched for the appropriate response, which came after what seemed an eternity.

"I've just had one or two phone calls from people since we sent out the letters – just preliminary expressions of interest should the opportunity arise." He nodded knowingly in the direction of Jessica, and continued, "Nothing concrete – or even brick for that matter!" He laughed self-consciously in the vain hope that a bad joke might diffuse the situation. In this he was wrong, so he twiddled his pencil again whilst waiting for the inevitable next question from Emily.

"Why have you not put that in the file?" Which was exactly the question Jason was dreading. "Or at least you might have told me – we are supposed to be working on this together."

Jason could have answered with, "Because they are friends of at least two of the planning committee members, and/or have potentially embarrassing information about said members, and they requested the whole expression of interest thing be kept strictly off the record." But he chose the more 'self-preservation' version of the answer instead.

"Because I told them nothing would be happening until much later in the process, and that they'd be notified at the appropriate time like everyone else. Didn't seem any need to tell you – it was nothing."

"Funny how I never got any calls!" Emily glanced in the direction of Jessica, who until this time had kept silent while taking the occasional personal note of proceedings and other thoughts.

"Right, so as I see it," Jessica felt it was time to sum up, partly because the discussion could soon turn nasty, and partly because she had a taxi booked to take her to the station, "we have some potential interest in building housing in some of the villages, but we need to keep the locals sweet. I'll leave it to you two to maintain the progress and we can have another update in a week's time. Just make sure you keep talking to each other over the next few days, OK?" She sat back in her chair and Jason and Emily filed out of the room behind her.

As she walked past, Emily cast a furtive glance at Jessica's notepad. The only things she could make out were, 'Whimbury good to go', and 'BUMM'. Emily would spend the rest of the day trying to work out the link between the two.

****

At the village green, on the bank of the pond, Everard sat fishing[12]. He

---

[12] An activity that, in common with most anglers, would be more accurately described as sitting beside water with hands behind head whilst alternating the watching of a piece of string float on the surface with the closing of eyes to give them a well-earned rest.

pondered over how many months it had been since he last caught anything. Not that it mattered, it was getting some 'exercise' in the fresh air that really counted. The sirens were busy flitting in and out of the fountain, which appeared to be having great difficulty sustaining any vertical thrust to the jets that once rivalled an Icelandic geyser. Still, it just about kept the water in the middle of the pond circulating and restricted the worst of the algae to a wide area around the edges.

Behind Everard, on the top of a lamppost that illuminated the graveyard at night, a blackbird sang energetically and continuously. To the faeries and animals of the village, who understood the language, it was saying:

"This is my patch and everything I can see from here out beyond the pond and into the woods, not to mention the graveyard below and the pub car park, is mine, to do with as I please. All the worms and the insects belong to me. All the fatballs and bird seed in the area, including those in the aforesaid graveyard, are mine[13]. Any other blackbird that fancies moving into my territory should be prepared to have its eyes pecked, tail-feathers plucked out painfully one by one, and beak force-filled with more dried mealworms than its bodyweight can physically carry. And if you even think about messing about with the missus, you can double those punishments - and don't think I don't mean it. Anybird fancy giving it a try? Come on. Make my day!" If it hadn't needed its knuckles to hold onto its perch, it would have cracked them loudly.

Nearby in his front garden, Will Hope, who did not understand the language, sat listening to the blackbird and said to Miranda and Milly:

"You know, it almost seems as though that blackbird is singing just for us. It has chosen its most beautiful and melodic song to serenade us with its love and its joy in life and living. Brings tears to the eyes how it can make such wonderful music – and all just for the pleasure of singing."

Meanwhile, at the pond, Everard's reverie was rudely interrupted by Robin barking orders at Mack and Trevor Stout.

---

[13] In truth, this last bit was just bravado, since the bird and its partner alone could not keep a permanent eye on the bird feeders. They therefore had to privately acknowledge that the sparrows and blue-tits, which were only small anyway, could also have grudging access.

"Yes, just there, to the right of where Everard is sleeping and a little way back from the water's edge."

Everard was stirred into a response.

"Oi'm be not sleepin', you cheeky sproite – Oi'm be concentratin' very 'ard on where exactly oi needs to cast moi bait, in order to get the best catch. It be an 'ighly complex and skilled task, it be. And oi'll thank you lot to keep quiet in case you frightens everything off, just when I were near to the catch of a loifetime an' all."

Everard's attempt at playing the role of the ever-alert champion angler fell down somewhat, by the fact that the waking up process did not extend to knowing quite where Robin, Mack and Trevor were standing, which resulted in him pontificating in entirely the wrong direction. The error was compounded when Robin replied from directly behind him, causing him to knock over his entire stock of fruit-fly bait, some of which flew away with the rest beginning to crawl all over and through his lunch box.

"Sorry Everard, could have sworn you were asleep there for a moment."

"Oi could 'ave sworn too, but oi'm too polite." Everard frantically tried to get as many fruit flies back into their jar as he could. "Anyways, what'n you lot be doin' 'ere at this toime o' day?"

"Well, you see Everard," Robin looked around furtively, in a way that only Robin could, and whispered loudly in his ear, "we're putting up the posters to try to attract the strangers to the Royal Oak on Friday – you remember? We discussed it last night after the quiz and asked for volunteers?" He smiled and nodded knowingly at Everard hoping to elicit some form of recognition. "And against our better judgement accepted Mack's offer? Mainly because no-one else offered at all?" He was faced with a completely blank expression.

Everard shook his head. "Nope, must have nodded off at that point!"

"OK, well we'll leave it at that, Everard. Just putting up a poster. It might all come back to you when you read it! If not, you can ask me again this evening in the Oak. I presume you'll be there."

"Oi'll be there, arl roight. Just you be careful to put that thing up with the maximum of quietude. Fishin' be a very delicate activity requirin' patience and silence – though oi don't supposes you youngsters would appreciate that – allus rushin' about and never stoppin' to sit 'n stare, loiks."

Everard wiggled his fishing rod round a bit to get the line to float on a slightly different part of the surface of the water. In reality, Everard didn't have the heart to actually put a fruit fly on a hook at the end to act as bait, so there was little chance of the location of the hook and line making any difference to the eventual outcome of his morning's 'work'.

A little to his right, Robin was showing Mack and Trevor where exactly he wanted the poster board putting.

"Not quite so near to the water, we don't want them falling in trying to read it! Yes, about there will be fine. [14] Now, who wants the hammer?" This was the part of the plan that currently gave him the greatest cause for concern.

"Can I do the hammering?" Trevor was on the verge of quivering with excitement.

"No, I'd better do it," replied Mack, "if you did the hammering and hit me by mistake, you'd feel very sad about it. But if I did the hammering and hit you, then you wouldn't feel sad – in fact you might not feel anything at all till after you came round!"

Mack didn't wait for the logic of his explanation to sink in – mainly because there was very little chance that it ever would. Instead, he gave the post to Trevor, showed him where Robin wanted it positioned and then swung very fast and very hard with the hammer. Trevor held the post and watched innocently, with the supreme confidence of someone incapable of imagining any plan of his father's ever going wrong. The hammer came down with great force, plumb onto the top of the post, which sunk well into the ground. Trevor smiled as his hands, arms, neck, head and teeth continued to vibrate with the sheer violence of the act.

"Great shot, Mack," shouted Robin, a little too loudly for Everard's liking. "That'll probably do it in one. I'll just fix the notice to it." And with that he produced a much smaller hammer and heavy-duty pins and carefully nailed the notice to the board on the top of the post. He stood back and looked with pride at his handiwork. He then took the hammer from Mack [15] and put it back

---

[14] This followed a short "to me, to you" routine between Mack and Trevor, which Robin, for some reason found both funny and familiar.

[15] However benign Mack might have been by this time, it was never a good idea to leave such a dangerous implement in his hands for too long.

in his bag along with his own hammer and pins and the rest of the rolled-up notices. Mack handed the remaining posts back to Trevor to carry as they prepared to move on.

"Well that was a good job well done." Robin believed in giving credit where due. He put his arm round Trevor's shoulders and continued, "So Trevor, all you have to do now is to hope that your luck holds out over the course of the next six posts!"

****

Back in the front garden at Over Cross View, Miranda and Will were each of them reading with one eye, and watching Milly with the other. She was, as usual, laying on the grass with her chin in her hands and feet raised to the sky, absorbed in the activities within the, somewhat overgrown, lawn. She was muttering happily to herself stopping very occasionally to come out with such statements as "Blackbird is very angry" while looking up at the nearby lamppost, and questions such as "What is 'a stage'?" while looking down at a woodlouse on an adjacent log.

"Do you ever listen carefully to what she is saying?" Miranda switched her reading eye from her book to Will.

Will's reading eye appeared over the top of his book and met Miranda's.

"Not that carefully, she seems to have a vivid imagination and makes up stories with the insects and birds around the garden, but I can't usually follow it. So long as she's happy and feels at one with the natural world around her – can't hurt her, can it?"

"Shouldn't think so, so long as she doesn't lose sight of her own world."

"But the natural world is part of her world, isn't it?" Will didn't find conversations verging on, or tending toward, the metaphysical, very comfortable, though if forced to engage, he sometimes found that he had some valid points to make. He just lacked the confidence to make them very often, and usually only in the comfort of his own garden.

"Yes, but the natural world doesn't speak our language, so I'm wondering how she makes up two-way conversations with 'organisms' [16] that couldn't possibly understand her, or her them. Or maybe they can understand each other somehow?"

"It's probably a child thing – you know, like they have a special relationship with dogs – a kind of bond. It might be the same with other 'organisms'. It all certainly seems very real to her. And talking of dogs...." Will pointed over the front wall towards which Kenneth, Adrian and Spot were approaching.

As they reached Over Cross View, Spot suddenly stopped and rose to his full two-legged height with his front paws on the wall. Adrian, who until that moment had been trying to keep Spot in check, also stopped – more suddenly than he had expected – allowing Kenneth to catch up.

"Well, it looks as though Spot has decided to have a break." Kenneth leant on the wall and patted Spot paternally on the head. "Though it's only about 50 metres from when we started. Probably wants to talk to Milly!" He waved to Milly, who got up from her position on the lawn and ran over to Spot, who had paused at exactly the point at which a large block of stone projected a little from the main surface, providing Milly with somewhere to stand at a level equating to Spot's smiley whiskery face.

"Funny you should say that." Will walked over to the wall and gave Spot a coochie-coo moment, which the dog treated with the disdain it felt it deserved. If there's one thing a proud descendant of a wolf can't abide, it's to be coochie-cooed in public. "But we were just saying that she seems to be able to communicate with all sorts of animals and insects - better than with us sometimes."

"It's a child thing, isn't it?[17] A part of growing up maybe?" Kenneth watched as Spot turned his head 45 degrees to the right while Milly did a mirror image movement. Then Spot barked a wide repertoire of barky sounds causing Milly first to look a little surprised and then to laugh loudly

---

[16] For the avoidance of doubt, during the course of this conversation, quotation marks were provided by Miranda and Will using appropriate finger gestures, necessitating putting their books down and then picking them up again in form of synchronised hand-jive.

[17] All grown ups see this as a child thing. Which is why they can't enjoy it themselves.

"See she's doing it now." Will shook his head in bemused fashion. "She always laughs at dogs barking. Somehow, she seems to almost always find a barking dog funny."

In fact, it was not a dog barking, per se, that was funny to Milly, but what the dog said. Which is why in some cases the barking elicited instead a curious look or even a degree of disinterest.[18] She had a good basic, if childlike, understanding of the canine language and could communicate with dogs in exactly the same way as with adult humans. But she also had a basic, if childlike, understanding of the language beyond words used by most non-human beings, and this gave her an advantage over her human family, who knew nothing of this opportunity.

In this instance, Spot was saying to Milly that there were two strangers in the village, one tall faery and one shorter. If she were to see them, and she would of course if they came within vision, she should pass any information onto Spot or any of the other faeries. This had brought on the curious look that Will had failed to notice. What had caused her to laugh, which Will did notice, was when Spot told her about the time he made a cyclist fall off his bike by barking suddenly as he cycled past, though Spot made sure to tell Milly that the cyclist came to no harm – he didn't want to alarm or worry her unnecessarily, obviously.

Just as Spot finished his stories, Milly suddenly looked over the road and then straight back at Spot. She simply said, quietly and unexcitedly, "They over there!" and pointed to the woods beside Green's Farm Machinery workshop. Spot pricked up his ears and followed the direction of Milly's finger. In the fringe of the woods, close to the road, he could make out two figures walking in the general direction of the Royal Oak. He knew enough to realise that he shouldn't make a major fuss over this, but he wondered how he could get the information back to Barry – or whether indeed the faeries were heading to the Royal Oak anyway. There was nothing much he could do whilst attached to his lead, so he filed the details into that part of his canine brain catalogued as 'pending   important'. [19] Having noted, registered and

---

[18] Even dogs can be boring from time to time – especially when they get over-excited comparing, say, dog foods, or the smells from neighbouring dogs' bottoms.
[19] As opposed to "pending until such time as it goes away all by itself".

filed what he had seen, he turned back to Milly, turned his head to the opposite 45 degree angle, and gave a short bark, to which Milly replied "Yes".

Will, Adrian and Kenneth, who had been taking note of this exchange, simply shrugged their shoulders in unison, as if to say, 'What was that all about?' and laughed. Milly rubbed noses with Spot – a gesture that really troubled the public health conscious Will – and returned to her place on the lawn. Spot immediately took his paws off the wall, turned towards the village green and rushed off, pulling Adrian behind him.

"Looks as though the boss has decided it's time to move on. The conversation with Milly is ended and we're simply of use to take him for a walk. Ho hum." Kenneth set off behind a fast-disappearing Adrian and Spot with a cheery wave and a "Maybe see you on the way back!"

****

It was the morning after the night before, as it so often was in the Royal Oak. Trixie was busy in the Lounge Bar clearing up the bent, torn, and wet beermats left after the quiz, along with the bent, torn and wet faeries still sleeping off the effects, while Damon was in the snug picking up the discarded dominoes and trying to put them back into sets. [20] Neither the Happs nor the Grumps were renowned for tidiness or leaving the Royal Oak in the condition in which they found it.

In truth, Barry was just happy that they actually left the Royal Oak in a condition marginally above derelict. Trixie and Damon were expert in restoring the bars to a state that looked welcoming and ready for the next onslaught. At least there wouldn't be another quiz night for 7 days, though the games, faeryoke, ale-tasting, and gourmet nights were not really much quieter. He had tried poetry readings and, with the help of Larry, excerpts from classical theatre, as relaxed and cultural interludes, but they had not gone down well. Eventually, Barry abandoned all hope in these ventures when both bars decided jointly to re-enact the battle scene from Henry V during one of

---

[20] Damon was very willing but found it difficult to remember which dominoes were actually supposed to be missing from each set and which were simply missing without trace.

Larry's monologues. The little louse had got as far as 'For he today that sheds his blood with me shall be my brother', when arguments broke out between the lounge bar and the snug as to the true date of St Crispin's Day, culminating with the Happs charging into a hail of lethally folded crisp packets.

While Trixie and Damon continued with their regular tidying-up session, Barry was testing out the new barrel of Inn-keepers' Choice, ready for the evening's activities. He was complimenting himself on how well he had stored the kegs and kept the lines clean, when there was a sharp and loud rap on the door. Normally, Barry would ignore such matters as someone either trying to get in early, or else to pick up from the floor a sleeping faery who had only been missed when he didn't come down for his lunch. This knock, however, had a more serious and important tone. He couldn't pin it down but it called him to the door. He followed the summons and pulled back the bolts. And his whole body was still, except for his mouth, which dropped.

Standing in front of Barry was the tallest faery he had ever seen - imposing, authoritative, disarming, overwhelming, and big! Beside him stood another faery to whom none of the above adjectives could be applied. There was a prolonged silence, over which the sounds of clearing, cleaning and polishing from inside could be clearly heard. The silence continued as Barry's scrambled brain tried and failed to make sense of the situation. Eventually he moved his hands around in an attempt to create a meaningful gesture that suited the occasion. This also failed. Eventually, the tall stranger spoke.

"Could I perhaps come in?" The voice matched the rest of the appearance and demeanour.

Barry's brain decided that it was necessary to go through the complete list of possible responses in an attempt to decide upon the correct one. This would, in normal circumstances, have happened almost instantaneously. But these were not normal circumstances and his brain was not operating in its normal 'well-oiled machine' manner. In no particular order, the potential responses whirred through the filter mechanism:

"Who are you, and who's your friend? Do you know what time it is?

You're not from round here, are you? We don't need double-glazing.[21] We aren't open yet. We're busy cleaning up. It's just that it's the licensing hours, you know, nothing personal. Can you come back later? We have extremely big security guards and CCTV. Have there been complaints about the noise? Have you come about the new dartboards? Are you the dominoes team from the Whimburton Arms? You're very welcome, please come in."

In the end, the filter mechanism settled on:

"Yes."

And Barry stood aside as the strangers entered, the tall one with a waft of class and status, the smaller one with a waft of disinfectant.

The sound of activity caused Trixie to pause her wiping and polishing.

"Who was it, Ba....?" She gaped at the tall stranger, who stood in the centre of the room looking round and clearly taking everything in – and in this case, everything meant everything. Beside him, his companion stood still with eyes closed, seemingly trying very hard to take everything in. Her eyes initially flitted between the two, but with the passage of time they could not help but continually focus on the tall one, who exerted something of a magnetic attraction.

Eventually, Barry followed them into the room. Trixie unglued her eyes from the tall stranger and looked across to Barry, who was appearing more bemused than she could ever remember. He glanced back at her and simply shook his head slowly.

Trixie was perplexed in terms of words and actions, and Barry was clearly not in a position to enlighten her. In the end, she elected to adopt a part-curtsey and part bow to the taller stranger. She felt like a humble maidservant, which was very unnatural for her, and which probably explained her opening gambit.

"Good day, kind Sir!" was what came out, though how it got there she had no idea. Once out, a whole cataract of verbiage followed. "Have you travelled far? You and your friend must be tired. Please come and take the weight off your feet – any seat and table that you like. We haven't started up the kitchen yet, but I could get you some crisps or beetle-flavour scratchings – they're

[21] Or substitute new roof, cavity wall insulation, upvc roof cladding, tarmac drive, tree pruning, faster broadband, new electricity meter, funeral plan as appropriate.

actually vegetarian. And what would you like to drink, Mr ....? Mr .....?" she looked hopefully at him.

"My name is immaterial." The voice was a strange mix of kindly and terrifying.

"Then please sit down, Mr Material. And your friend? I didn't catch his name?"

"My name is Burr." The voice was a strange mix of confused and subservient.

The two strangers sat down at the most central of the tables, and gazed around the room once again.

Barry waited a moment until he was sure that his brain was back on roughly the right track, and was functioning as normally as he might expect. He re-joined the conversation.

"Well, this is a not totally unexpected surprise!" He paused momentarily, wondering how much information he should divulge at this stage. "Though the poster did say that the travel stories evening wasn't until Friday. But never mind, we're happy have a preview – if you feel like giving us a brief version?" He paused again. Each sentence was something of an emotional roller-coaster.

"Poster?" The tall stranger looked into and through Barry in a way that said 'would you please elucidate' as clearly as if words had been used.

"I presumed that you'd seen one of our posters? About our Friday evening entertainment in the bar here? Travel stories? To be shared?" Each question, with its final flourish on an upward lilt, was greeted with a silence and a look that indicated that elucidation had not taken place.

"No, we've seen nothing. Though the evening sounds as if it could be enlightening. I would like to hear some of the stories from the local faery population – I'm sure they would be fascinating." The tone of the stranger's voice was, if anything, sufficiently more relaxed to make Barry feel just that little bit more at ease. Trixie, meanwhile, sat down and settled in for what she was sure was going to be a most interesting discussion, at which point Damon wandered in from the snug.

"I think I've put all the sets of dominoes back as they should be, but it was quite ....." On seeing that they had company, he stopped, wondered if he should or should not shake hands, and looked at Barry for advice. None came, so Damon settled for "Oh. Company!"

Trixie broke the deadlock. "Damon, this is Mr Material and his friend Mr Burr. They were just saying that they might be interested in the travel evening on Friday. Mr Material, Mr Burr, this is Damon one of our bar staff."

Mr Material stood up and proffered his extremely large hand to Damon, who accepted and did a sterling job of not wincing at the strength of its grip. He flexed his fingers behind his back when the handshake finished.

"Pleased to meet you, Damon. I was hoping to meet you and Trixie whilst we were in the village. And, of course, our most important host, Mr Goodfellow here. In fact, that was one of the main reasons for our visit." He sat down again and smiled a disconcerting smile in Barry's direction.

"But how did you know our names?" Barry added confusion to the mix of unsettling emotions that he was going through at an unprecedented and worrying rate of knots.

"I have studied the Crossover story – very carefully!" The pause before the words 'very carefully' did nothing to put Barry more at ease. "It is an incredible story, and you and your friends have achieved something of a celebrity status amongst those who have an interest in the Crossover Child. There are many faeries, from far and wide, who would like to meet you all – and indeed may well be planning to do so, even as we speak. And I am sure that they would like to meet the child as well!" He sat back and turned his head up towards the ceiling, waiting for his words to have full effect. He did not have to wait long, and the effect was substantial.

Chapter Eight

Miranda and Will stopped the pushchair outside the gate to the Potts' house and Miranda applied the brake. Milly amused herself with one of her books while chatting to various passing butterflies. To humans, butterflies appear scatty and unfocussed but, in reality, they pick up a vast amount of gossip while flitting from flower to flower. Insects with antennae are especially prized as sources of information since they can overhear conversations whilst apparently concentrating their efforts in another direction altogether.

"So, have you had time to think and talk it over between yourselves?" Evadne brushed bread flour from off her hands as she walked down the path to the gate. When Miranda phoned to say that she wanted a quick chat on her way to Whimburton, Evadne was hopeful of good news on the Parish Council front.

"Yes, I've discussed it with Will and he thinks it's a great idea, don't you, sweetheart?" She pinched his cheek lightly and smiled the smile of someone whose smile could melt ice in a freezer.

"I'm not sure I said the idea was great exactly, my little buttercup." Will was a little less than gushing, but had clearly been converted to the proposal, if somewhat begrudgingly. "But so long as it's not every week, and since you obviously want to do it, who am I to stand in your way. I can always give Milly an hour and a half's bedtime story while you're out."

"Yes, you'd like that wouldn't you!" That was exactly the line that Miranda had used to finally reel in her catch when they were discussing Evadne's suggestion.

"I can think of worse things." In truth, Will could think of very few better things. He bent down to pick up Milly's book that she had dropped while talking to an energetic Holly Blue butterfly. He had learnt better than to disturb her when in full "imagination" mode, so he just wedged the book in the pushchair behind her.

"That's wonderful! I'm so glad." Evadne was effusive in her joy. She had long harboured hopes that Eileen Robinson and Miranda might become the next leadership team when she had eventually had enough of her period as chair, and when her sanity had to take precedence over the smooth running of the Council. That, of course, relied on first getting Miranda onto the Council, and that part of the succession plan appeared to be under way. "I've checked the constitution and I can introduce you as a co-opted member this week, with a view to getting you voted on officially next time." Very little gave Evadne more pleasure than a scheme going according to plan.

"This week?" Miranda had either forgotten, or had never been told, that the next Parish Council meeting was so soon.

"Yes! Didn't I tell you?" Evadne feigned mock surprise. "we've fitted in an extra meeting this month because of the District Council's consultation exercise on the housing proposals for the village. I'm sure I told you! Didn't I?" The look on Miranda's face gave Evadne slight cause for worry that maybe she was beginning to put Miranda off the idea.

"What night?" Miranda looked across to Will, who was not paying the slightest attention to the ongoing conversation – so she turned back to Evadne.

"Thursday! Can you make it?"

"I expect so. I was going to check if Will would mind, but as you can see he is more or less permanently engaged in keeping an eye on Milly, so I'm sure whatever night it is, he'll be fine with it. I'll tell him later on the bus – and then keep reminding him at hourly intervals over the next day or so. What time is it? And what did you say the meeting was about?"

"The plan to put more housing in Whimbury – do you remember, we were talking about it while Milly was engaged upon surrealist artwork involving unicorns and tortoises!"

"Oh yes. I confess, I hadn't given it much thought since then – I was under the impression I had more time to get to grips with it. Never mind, if you could maybe give me a briefing before Thursday, I'm sure I can bring myself up to speed before the meeting." Miranda was a community-conscious resident and was already accumulating thoughts and ideas about the future of the village.

"That shouldn't be difficult, given the speed that the rest of the group operates at. But yes, of course, I'll update you before then. So, you're off to Whimburton?" Secure in the knowledge that Miranda was firmly on board, Evadne could relax into general gossip and chit-chat.

"Yes, suits us. There's a bit of something for all of us, and it means we spend a bit of time together away from the house and village. A bit of contact with the outside world and a change of daily routine." Miranda loved living in Whimbury, and was pleased that Milly could grow up with some fresh air and nature around her. But she didn't want to end up isolated without people she knew of her own age who had children that Milly could play with. It was fine at the moment, but that would change when Milly got a bit older – and she was growing up so fast. It was Will who had suggested the weekly trip to town to use the facilities and meet some old friends, and he had been right.

As they wandered down to the bus stop from the Potts' house, she mulled over some preliminary thoughts about new housing in Whimbury. Would they attract some younger people like themselves – or some younger people not like themselves? Would they be people to re-invigorate the community – or people who would isolate themselves and remain immersed in town life? Would they use the local shops or just travel back to Whimburton for all they needed? Would they help in the fight to keep the bus service? Would they support the local pub or the cricket team? Would they even get involved with the Parish Council? At this point, Miranda stopped thinking too much, as the thought of Evadne potentially clashing with in-comers over the future direction of village life didn't bear further consideration – yet! Nevertheless, it would have to be faced, and Miranda wasn't 100% sure which way she would turn if it came to a showdown. All she knew for certain was that change would certainly come in one form or another. Either there could be new ways of doing things initiated by new families, or the traditional village ways could simply fade away as the older residents left or died, or the newcomers might even value the old ethos and keep it alive in their own way. So many imponderables.

****

Everard took a detour back to the Royal Oak via Percy's house. His fishing had been rudely interrupted by the banging in of posts, and that gave him the perfect excuse for his lack of any catch to take home. And he was sure that Percy was exactly the right person with whom to have a good moan about the inconsiderateness of some faeries.

When he arrived, Percy was in his garden laboriously lifting pieces of gravel and carefully placing them onto his new "stonery". Everard waited for some time, watching Percy puff and pant, until he was sure that the job had been finished. At this point he was confident that there was no chance of him having to help out with any chores, and so he announced his presence with a deep and overlong cough.

Percy clutched his heart and swore loudly, then turned to face the origin of the cough.

"I might have known it was you!" Percy was simultaneously peeved and pleased by Everard's appearance, peeved at the shock and pleased at the prospect of company. "I suppose you've come to cadge a drink and a snack at my expense?"

"You'm be spot on there, moy grumpy ole mate. A noice cuppa an' a piece o' cake would go down real well, it would. Oi've 'ad a most frustratin' day down at the pond. Most frustratin' indeed." Everard pulled up a garden stool and sat down, waiting for a response. None came. Percy just picked up his tools and made to go back into the house.

"Well, bain't you a gonna ask me whoy oi've 'ad a frustratin' day?" Everard was desperate to tell his story.

"No!" said Percy as he disappeared into this kitchen.

Everard muttered loudly about impoliteness and lack of consideration for those currently suffering from the selfish acts of others, then sat back on his stool, closed his eyes and fell over backwards. This did nothing for his sense of emotional equilibrium, but did provide amusement for Percy when he returned with a pot of tea and some of Percetta's lavender scones. He was, fortunately, able to maintain his poise and grumpy demeanour as he waddled over to the prostrate Everard. He put the tray with the refreshments down on the garden picnic table, and bent over Everard to pick him up, which feat he achieved with much exaggerated puffing, panting, grumbling and groaning.

"Orl roight, orl roight! You'm be 'ave made your point. Far be it from me to spoil your enjoyment loik, but don't yous think it moight be toim ter get yourself some chairs with backs?" Everard dusted himself down and sat back down gingerly.

"Never thought about it, Everard, my old friend. No-one's ever fallen over backwards off the chairs before. Just a pity I missed it – don't suppose you fancy doing it again, do you? Maybe if I studied it carefully, I could place a cushion on the floor just in the right place to break a fall?" Percy poured the tea rather more jauntily than was strictly necessary.

"Oh, har, har!" Everard was not renowned for seeing the funny side of his own misadventures. "Oi moight 'ave done moiself a grave mischief there. Oi 'opes you'm be proper insured against damage to guests from your lack o' forethought loik! An' any more o' that grinnin', an 'oi'll be tellin 'orl your grumpy relatives that you'm be lettin' the side down by bein' 'appy. An' don't think I won't."

Percy was used to Everard's idle threats by now, and was not, therefore, deflected from his purpose.

"What would you like on your scone, Everard?"

"Oooh, some of your Percetta's 'ome made jam, if'n you don't' moind." Everard was easily distracted, as Percy well knew, and the easiest way to distract him was with scone and home-made jam. He passed the tea and scone over to Everard, who gazed upon them delightedly and sat well forward on his chair to enjoy them.

"So, as oi'm were sayin'," Everard was intent on finishing, or perhaps more accurately starting, his story and was not going to let eating stop him. Consequently, Percy spent most of the ensuing conversation bobbing and weaving around the bits of scone that were being spat at him from across the table.

"I were orl set up at the pond, focussin' 'ard on moi floats and line, when up comes younger Goodfellow wi' them Stouts, and begins an 'ammerin' and thumpin' loik you've never 'eard afore. So oi asks 'em what they be a doin' of, and they shows me a poster that they be intendin' to put up round the village."

Percy wiped a dollop of jam from just above his right eye, by now concentrating on an attempt at balancing scone avoidance with the germ of the beginnings of a mild interest in Everard's story. [22]

"And what was this poster about?" Percy held his handkerchief close to his face, ready to repel the next salvo of crumbs.

"Well, they said it were an attempt to attract the strangers into the Royal Oak on Froiday, but it seemed to me more loik an advert for an evenin' of 'oliday reminiscences. We'm all s'posed to bring travel stories, an' it says there be a proize – but it don't say what the proize is." He paused briefly, looked across at Percy, and then resumed. "Oi thinks you should praps get that hankie washed, Percy moy ole mate, it looks filthy from where I be sittin'."

"Thanks for that observation, Everard. I might just do that, later." Since Everard had now finished his scone, Percy felt safe to fold his sticky handkerchief and put it back in his pocket. "And as for holiday stories, that lets me out. P and I haven't been on holiday for years – it's much more difficult having a good moan when you're relaxing somewhere nice, and that just means that we're on edge and can't really enjoy it."

"But, if'n you be comin' 'ome orl on edge loik, don't that mean you got an excuse to 'ave a reet good session o' grumpin' when you finally does get back?" Everard knew from experience that Percy was one of nature's most natural complainers, and that such situations as he had just described would normally be meat and drink for him.

"Well there is that of course, but it doesn't make for interesting travel stories. And in any case, there's plenty to moan about here without having to go away for more. Since when have I ever needed an excuse!"

"Fair point, Perce!" Now that Everard had eaten and drunk, he was ready

---

[22] All of Percy's interests began with a 'germ'. No-one ever called him spontaneous.

for his afternoon nap and effectively deemed the conversation now ended by closing his eyes.

"Still, I dare say it might be worth turning up Friday night anyway, just to see what boring tales come to light. Should be good for a mind-numbing evening in the snug followed by a good family whinge. I presume you'll be going, Everard, since you always ……."

Percy looked up just in time to whip a cushion onto the table top as Everard's head dropped into it.

"I just knew that would come in handy one day." Percy congratulated himself on his foresight and then began to tidy up the remains of the afternoon tea onto his tray.

****

Robin, Mack and Trevor ambled their way back to the Royal Oak.

"A good job, well done. Thanks lads, for helping out. Much appreciated."

Robin swung his sack of tools jauntily, as they followed a well-worn[23] footpath through the woods behind Green's Farm Machinery workshop. Secretly he was longing for Friday evening, convinced that his plan would deliver the strangers into their midst.

"And I'm sure Barry will have some ice in the cellar, Trevor, so we can plunge your hand into some cold water when we get back. That should ease the pain a bit."

Trevor grimaced his thanks, while gripping the red and throbbing knuckles of his right hand with his left hand, and periodically wafting both of them around to let the air get at them. Mack slapped him on the back in a pointless gesture of support.

"I reckon we did pretty well to get to the last post before my slight miscalculation, eh? Now you're almost ready for the last post too, eh?" Mack found his joke more hilarious that Trevor did. "And remember, like I said before, that you won't have to feel guilty about hitting me with the big

---

[23] In fairy terms! Though humans would have experience of its presence, if only unawares, through the sudden pause of their dogs, followed by incessant sniffing and head turning, whilst on their early morning or evening walk.

hammer, now. You should be very grateful that it won't be hanging over you, troubling you at night."

"It definitely won't be that that troubles me at night, that's for sure." Trevor kept unclenching his fingers and counting them, to make certain that they were all present, even if not correct. Although he wasn't completely confident about counting as far as ten, he did know that there should be five on each hand and that gave him a fighting chance of getting it right in stages.

"So, what's the prize for the best travel story, Robin?" Mack had been itching to find this out since the first post was hammered in, and now was the time to scratch. "Not that I have much chance of winning of course, if those two strangers turn up."

"You don't know that, Mack. None of us know what tales, if any, they might come up with – if they arrive. And if they don't, then any stories you might have could well be as good, if not better, than anyone else's." Robin was hoping that he could deflect the conversation away from the prize, since neither he nor anyone else knew, at that precise moment in time, what it was going to be. He hadn't actually discussed that with Barry, though he was sure that Barry could always magic a bottle or two[24] of some special brew from the cellars if needs be. And if it turned out that they were even stranger than anticipated, and happened to be teetotal, then one of the spare quiz trophies that Barry kept behind the bar would have to suffice.

"Well, as it happens, I do have one or two tales up my sleeve, that might just give me the edge. Not that I need an edge mind, cos no-one else around this village does anything much." Mack swaggered, just a little.

"True, Mack. True. Unless my brother Morris turns up unexpectedly. He's got some pretty impressive experiences to share!" Robin, enjoyed winding people up, though he was always very careful not to go too far in the case of Mack, who could be somewhat unpredictable and more than somewhat irrational from time to time.

"If he does, I'm presuming you'd do the decent thing and disqualify him, on account of him being a professional traveller, and all that."

"Absolutely, Mack. You know me, fair's fair and everything above board.

---

[24] Or six.

Since Barry and I won't be entering, for obvious reasons, we could always give him the job of choosing the winner – he'd be good at recognising a good story when he hears one!" Robin, began to wish he'd never mentioned Morris in the first place. Fortunately for him, Trevor was beginning to catch up with the general flow of the discussion and, being only a few items behind, felt able to join in.

"You could tell them all what happened when you disappeared the day of the Crossover!" Trevor felt sure that there must be a winning tale in amongst the goings on of that auspicious occasion[25].

"Well I could, but I doubt anyone would believe it." Mack puffed himself up to his full, self-enhancing stature and strode off with a full, self-enhancing strut.

Robin and Trevor followed Mack in silence, Robin because he was lost in thought, and Trevor because he couldn't blow on his throbbing fingers and talk at the same time. They continued along the path until Robin, who had had his head down most of the way, came to a sudden realisation of what he had unknowingly been looking at since they had entered the woods.

"There's something or things, or someone, very big been walking along here since we set out. This path has been trampled, and twigs broken and berries picked, and...." He looked around. They were very close to the Royal Oak, and none of this made much sense. Animals never used the path and the local faeries couldn't leave such an extravagant impact. He was going to ask his companions if they had any thoughts on the matter, but then he realised with whom he was walking. The one in front, oblivious to anything but his attempt to look important, and the other behind, oblivious to anything but his attempt to cool down his fingers. He ran forward to Mack.

"Hold it right here!" He shook Mack out of his reverie. Mack, in turn, transposed automatically into a kung fu stance and waved his hands and legs into what he supposed, wrongly as it happens, was a threat and warning not to mess with the star of Crossover Day or else something very bad would

---

[25] Mack had somewhat recklessly entered the conflict with the Nixies and been propelled by them "into the middle of next week". He had never before tried to explain what happened in the time between then and when he "re-materialised" on the next Wednesday.

happen. The fact that his transformation had involved spinning around until he was facing away from Robin, and thus culminating in a bemused look when he finally settled into his pose and saw no-one, did not uphold his credibility as a superhero one little bit.

"I'm here, Mack! Behind you!" Robin stepped back to avoid the anticipated flailing arm of Mack as he swung round sharply with a 'Faaaaiijiiing Shaaaaaooooow" scream and threw himself into the shrubbery at the side of the path.

"Impressive Mack!" Robin leant into the shrubbery to help Mack extricate himself. "we might be needing those skills soon - though perhaps with a degree more accuracy?"

Mack brushed himself down and jerked all his joints back into their correct alignment and juxtaposition.

"Not lost any of my speed, eh Robin?" He breathed noisily in through his teeth and performed small-scale and gentle hand manoeuvres to prove that he was still in control of his martial arts skills.

"Not one bit, Mack! Awesome, quite awesome!" Robin was unsurpassed in the use of flattery to achieve his aims – never so effusive as to appear sarcastic, or so matter of fact as to appear disinterested. "Now the thing is," he continued, "that there is something a bit odd going on around here, and I'm going to let Barry know. While I pop in to the Oak, I need you and Trevor to keep your eyes and ears open out here, till I call you in. Is that OK?"

"Our eyes and ears are fully open, Robin. Aren't they Trev?" Mack shouted back along the path.

"Pardon?" Trevor paused in his finger waving and cool air blowing

"I said…..Never mind!" Mack turned back to Robin. "My eyes and ears will do the work of two sets. You can rely on me as ever!"

"Good man!" Robin tapped him on the shoulder in a gesture of solidarity and wandered into the Royal Oak.

****

Ralph sat himself down on a pile of dry leaves close to the edge of Whimbury Woods. From here he could see Over Cross View, the Rectory and the Parish

Church. He noted with interest that the Parish Church was dedicated to St Vitus[26].

"When the Saints, go dancing in." He sang quietly to himself, as he often did. He did most things by himself, since no-one else was particularly interested in encouraging him to join in with their activities. He was as clean as he could reasonably keep himself, and his clothes were barely thirty years out of fashion. Indeed, his trousers, with their holes around the knees, could have been considered back in fashion where they not for the frayed turn-ups and the string belt that held them up. Nevertheless, he did not look or behave in what passed as normal for that part of the world.

When he first dropped out of modern society[27], he had comforted himself in the knowledge that if hair was not washed for long enough, it would eventually keep itself naturally healthy – though not necessarily stylish. He kept his woolly hat clean by washing it in rivers or streams or public toilets from time to time, and in the summer when it was too hot, he simply added it to the rest of his soft belongings as stuffing for his "pillow". And if it rained, a plastic bag would keep his head dry, although he was environmentally aware enough to keep re-using the same single bag for as many purposes as possible. In this way he minimised plastic pollution but, depending on its previous use, occasionally it also maximised strange sensations on his scalp.

Since taking up residence in the woods, Ralph had seen very little of Milly, apart from the occasional walk to the shop or the village green with her parents. He smiled as he remembered the defensive posturing adopted by her father when he saw Ralph in Whimburton Park – totally understandable, and maybe even appropriate for the circumstances. But he also knew that it precluded him from ever talking to the child directly, except possibly in the most desperate of situations. And so, he settled down to watch and listen and sense her actions, speech, thoughts and emotions from afar. He could learn

---

[26] In fact, the only church in England to be so dedicated. It has a history of close ties with a community of emigres from Central Europe and was frequently visited by Vladislav Happ while staying with the extended family in Whimbury, to remind him of home.

[27] No-one has ever been able - or willing - to ascertain whether he dropped out or was pushed; at least no-one in the somewhat disinterested human community around Whimburton.

from her interactions with the local animal and fae communities, and judge her progress toward full Crossover status from a human perspective, - that would be useful to the faeries.

While he sat and waited, his brain was working overtime, as it so often did when he had several things on his mind at once. That had been the cause of his problems so many years ago when he had failed to conform to the established norms of society by allowing his mouth to utter whatever was going through his mind at the time. Most, if not all, of it made absolute sense if you knew him well enough and understood his background. But few did, and they were usually too embarrassed by his utterances to admit to knowing him or why he was as he was. And so he left his neighbourhood and his work and began to wander, often through the countryside, but always coming back to Whimburton and its surroundings, for everyone needs some place to call home

This day, his brain was focussing on Whimbury and the new things he had noticed since his arrival, including the Parish Church.

"I danced in the morning – led them a merry dance. Waltzes and Two-steps. Two-steps to heaven, halfway to paradise. Ladies excuse me – excuse me ladies. May I have the pleasure? May I have pleasure? I'll sit this one out, sit just here, enjoy the view, pleasant view – Over Cross View. Pleasant cottage, pheasant cottage, peasant cottage, crossover cottage – get cross over cottage. Never get cross, never a cross word. Crossword – always a puzzle, life's a puzzle – pick up the pieces – Jig-saw. Jigs or reels. Real or unreal? How do we tell? Who do we tell? Say what you see, what do I see? What DO I see?"

Ralph's brain paused as Will and Miranda wandered back home up the High Street after their day in Whimbuton. It re-focussed itself onto Milly, sat in her buggy and chatting away apparently to the back of her hand. As they approached the gate to Over Cross View, Ralph saw a ladybird fly off Milly's hand across the road and over his head further into the woods. Once inside the garden, Miranda and Will left Milly in the buggy as they went to the fence to chat with the vicar, who was weeding at the front of the Rectory. Milly amused herself by "talking" to a sparrow that landed on the front wall beside her[28]. A few moments later, she uttered a single note to the sparrow which took off urgently and flew at speed across the neighbouring front gardens, as a sparrowhawk aborted its attack at the last moment and diverted to the top of a tree above Ralph's head.

"Well-spotted, little one!" Ralph mentally congratulated Milly on her vision and communication skills. "You won't always be able to intervene in nature, but you don't want to be interrupted in mid-conversation now do you?" He smiled and lay back in the undergrowth as a sparrowhawk dropping splatted on the bush beside him.

"Don't go blaming me", said Ralph quietly up to the canopy of the woods, "You must know what she's capable of by now!"

****

"Your Milly seems a very contented child." The vicar leaned on his spade, secretly glad of an opportunity to rest for a moment. The Rectory had a large garden and, although the church committee organised working parties every now and again, there was always the routine maintenance to carry out. Will and Miranda weren't regular attenders at the church, but they did try to support special occasions and Will frequently helped the vicar with odd jobs and repairs. The vicar in turn had pulled out all the stops to conduct a very special baptism service for Milly as his newest and nearest neighbour.

"Yes, I think she is!" Miranda turned back to check on Milly just as the sparrowhawk incident unfolded. "Goodness," she exclaimed, "What on earth was that?"

"That, I think you will find, was a sparrowhawk narrowly missing out on obtaining lunch for the family. I often see it around here – quite an impressive bird when in hunting mode, swift and deadly, yet elegant and a symbol of the natural order of things. Must be a sermon in there somewhere!" The vicar, though getting on years, was constantly trying to find new material for his reflections and sermons from the life of the village and the political situations of the day. He was a believer that religion was of little use unless the heavenly

---

[28] Since Sparrows only chirp it can be difficult to follow the subtle nuances of their language, although Milly appeared capable of maintaining a simple conversation.

promise was firmly rooted in both the practical realities of human existence, and the issues that could be influenced by the application of principles and actions by each individual. Sometimes he even felt that his message might just have got through.

"It can't have missed Milly by very much. It was really moving!" Will hurried over to the buggy to ensure that his little princess was unharmed.

"If I didn't know better," continued the vicar to Miranda, "I could swear that your daughter warned a sparrow to get out of the way. I was watching her while we were chatting away, and she seemed to make a chirping noise and pointed her finger down the road." He smiled knowingly and awaited a response.

"She's always talking to the animals, insects and birds. Has an amazing imagination that one. If there are no animals or birds around, she'll happily talk to herself for hours. We tell ourselves she's away with the fairies." Miranda giggled with just the slightest hint of embarrassment.

The vicar pondered, as only vicars can[29]. "You might be nearer the truth there than you could possibly know." He raised himself up from his supporting spade until he acquired his full height. This took a considerable amount of time and lot of creaking, clicking and groaning. After a long, wide grimace, he elaborated. "This village has always had a reputation as a veritable hub of fay activity, and a lot of strange things have gone on in recent times!"

"Well I never thought I'd hear a vicar say things like that!" Miranda was momentarily flummoxed. "Do your parishioners follow you on that particular road to enlightenment?"

"Not in so many words! But there are many ways to try to explain the unexplainable and to explore our faith in what we do not know for sure – or indeed understand. My parishioners believe in Angels, though few claim to have seen one, and even those that do claim it have difficulty in describing what they've actually seen, or how they knew that it represented an Angel! Others believe they've experienced the activity of Angels just because they can't explain that activity any other way. Angels? Fairies? What's in a name?

---

[29] At the time when the vicar underwent his theological training, there was an optional unit in "Creative Pondering", for which he was awarded a distinction and the year prize.

When the villagers in earlier times told fairy stories about the Royal Oak, who's to say what prompted those tales? And in the end, as we vicars and our flocks are wont to say – 'God works in mysterious ways'. Maybe your Milly has a key to some of those mysteries, eh? As we also say, 'out of the mouths of babies comes forth strength', eh?"

Before he had the chance to utter another quote ending in 'eh?' Miranda butted in. She was now thoroughly confused about Milly's behaviour. Yes, she had always been told that Milly was special, but then didn't nearly everyone believe that about their children. Yet there was the undeniable way that Milly was different, and as she grew older, so new and more unusual forms of behaviour were becoming apparent. Miranda used the opportunity to quiz the vicar further.

"So, do you believe in fairies, Vicar? Yourself personally, I mean"

"I believe that there are all sorts of things around us that are beyond our senses. I believe in God, and I believe in angels, and I'm not sure that I was expected to find the answers to everything that is beyond my understanding in the Bible alone. We've discovered so much about ourselves and our world since the Bible was written – some of that helps us by explaining things that we never knew before, and some of it tells us that we can't explain them, and maybe never will. I have an open mind on fairies, whatever they may be called in different cultures. And I happen to think that children may have a key to such matters until we end up forcing it out of them with 'adult' logic, and restricting them to the current limits of our 'adult' knowledge. It could well be that your Milly is more finely attuned to the true extent and nature of the world around her than we are. That's all."

"Certainly food for thought, Vicar". Miranda turned back to see Will and Milly in earnest conversation about she knew not what – only that the conversation involved Milly in pointing in lots of different directions and Will nodding sagely in agreement. She passed on her thoughts to the Vicar. "And maybe some adults haven't altogether lost their fine attunement?"

"Maybe not, Miranda. Maybe not!" The Vicar leaned back onto his spade and joined Miranda as she happily watched her 'children' communicating in the best possible way.

****

Robin burst into the Royal Oak in a state of obvious anxiety. He immediately saw Barry in conversation with two strange faeries, one of whom, with nothing more than a passing glance, managed to turn Robin's obvious anxiety into obvious panic. Robin was rarely speechless and seldom without an immediate response to whatever circumstance he found himself in. In the midst of this rarely experienced situation, the strangers stood up. One was of decidedly average size and demeanour, while the other was distinctly taller and had piercing eyes that burrowed themselves into Robin's psyche, had a good rummage around, re-arranged one or two errant synapses, and left again with the equivalent of a paternal pat on the head on the way out. The tall stranger smiled a smile that did nothing to re-assure Robin that all was, in fact, well.

"And this must be the famous Robin Goodfellow." The stranger spoke in a voice that matched his gaze.

Robin instinctively looked behind him, but seeing no-one there assumed that he must indeed be the famous version of himself referred to by the stranger.

"I suppose it must be," said Robin in as brave a voice as he could muster which, in truth, would not have fooled anybody. "But I don't think I know you – either of you."

"You don't." The tall stranger continued to speak for both of them, while the shorter one appeared to be absorbing everything in the manner of a student in the presence of his mentor. "We have only recently arrived in the village. We came to find out more of the Crossover story and to meet the faefolk involved. We assumed that the Royal Oak, being the hub of the community, would be a good place to begin. And lo and behold, already we have come across some of the key players in the drama. But forgive me, you rushed in here, and so you must have something urgent to discuss with your brother. Please don't let us interrupt, we have plenty of time to talk afterwards." He sat down and once again looked up at the ceiling. His companion followed suit.

Barry looked at Robin, who looked at Trixie, who looked at Damon, who looked at Barry, no-one willing to break the ice. As publican and elder brother, Barry eventually and reluctantly accepted the role of ice-breaker.

"What did you have to say that brought you in so hurriedly?" The words came out in somewhat staccato fashion as he half-stared at Robin and half-glanced at the tall stranger.

Robin looked over at Trixie, who by now was staring back at him – as was Damon, and as indeed was the smaller stranger. In fact, all eyes were on him apart from those of the taller stranger, who still gave the impression of watching him intently with his right ear as he continued to look upwards.

"I just came in to say that….that….do you know what, I've forgotten what I came in for. I was walking along back through the woods with Mack and Trevor – we'd finished putting up the posters – and I noticed something that I wanted to tell you – urgently – and…it'll come back to me in a minute." He paused, with nary a jest or a quip to rescue him from his desperate situation.

Trixie was perhaps the only faery to appreciate that Robin had a sensitive side that was almost permanently hidden by his jokey demeanour. She recognised his insecurity and hurried over to where he stood alone, putting her arms around him and leading him to the nearest table.

"I'm sure it will come back any minute now. It can't have been all that important if it's got temporarily lost. Sit down, I'll get you a drink of water and perhaps Mr Material here will tell us a bit more about why he's here and how we can help him?" She glanced over at Mr Material, prepared to repeat her request more loudly if he was still gazing at the ceiling. She was surprised to see that he was now looking straight at her, with no malevolence, authority or condescension, but with a smile and a more relaxed attitude. She was amazed at how much she could seemingly interpret from his look. If she didn't know better, he was effectively saying that he had been quietly assessing the relationships of the personnel around him and had now realised who it was that exhibited the most strength and understanding. It was vaguely unsettling, though she couldn't put her finger on the reason why. Nevertheless, she was emboldened enough to press home her attempt at getting him to open up a little.

"This is Mr Material, Robin, and his friend Mr Burr. I think you might find that what Mr Material has to say will be very interesting – if he would be so kind as to enlighten us?"

Mr Material waited long enough to ensure that his audience was well and truly listening, but not so long that they fell asleep. Then he began to speak.

"We have travelled for a long time and over a great distance to get here. I planned the journey very soon after the news of the Crossover child reached me. I had to find out for myself the truth of the story – for as you know, the truth can often be mislaid in the telling and re-telling. So I needed to hear it from those who were part of it, before the myth overtook the reality, as it were. My friend Mr Burr here has accompanied me on my journey, and though he knows little of the story, other than what is written in the Chronicles and Legends, he has developed an interest of his own. We have yet to see the child since we arrived, but would very much like to do so: to see for ourselves how she differs from other humans and how her special powers are beginning to manifest themselves. She must, after all use her powers before her seventh birthday. That is not far away, and it beholds you all to teach her those powers quickly, and to judge when she is strong enough to put them into practice, otherwise it is for nothing."

The last sentence brought Barry out in a cold sweat. He had always taken seriously his responsibility for Milly's fae education, and attempted to co-ordinate the efforts of the other faeries and animals in and around the village in that direction. But somehow, coming from the mouth of Mr Material, it all seemed heavier and more urgent. Surely another 5 years, give or take, would be enough to complete her training – and yet? Perhaps, just perhaps, Mr Material knew more than he was letting on. He certainly knew the basics of the Crossover Legend, but maybe he had personal reasons for getting involved himself. Life had just begun to get back to some kind of new normal since the Crossover episode and he liked it that way - where he could generally keep things under control and let nature take its course. To be fair to the tall stranger, Barry had never really allowed himself to consider any other scenario than that of communicating as much faery and animal wisdom to Milly as possible, until around the time of her seventh birthday, and then seeing what happened. He had no idea what to expect at that time, but was sure that it would all work out fine. Now, it felt as though all the coins had been flipped into the air at once and they had all come down on their side.

Trixie broke the awkward silence.

"We're doing our best, Mr Material. All of the animals are talking to her and we give her little introductory lessons in magic and communication whenever we can get her on her own, but that's not easy. She's only two and is rarely on her own long enough for us to get messages across to her. Maybe, once she starts school, we will have more time with her, and we can catch up with what else she needs before her seventh birthday?" Trixie sounded more hopeful than convinced by her own response.

"What do you think, Mr Burr?" Robin jumped in with a degree of urgency. He instinctively felt that Mr Burr was an easier touch, and hoped beyond hope that he would back them up in their vision for the future.

"I think that you are all facing the most difficult and critical time in your lives, and that you will need all of your wits and resourcefulness to see it through to a satisfactory conclusion. It will not be straightforward, and success cannot be guaranteed." Mr Burr spoke hurriedly and looked across at Mr Material for moral support, which he found in the form of the slightest upturn in his lips and an almost imperceptible nod of his head.

The answer was not what Robin, or any of the others wanted to hear.

"Can you give us any clues as to what can be considered a satisfactory or successful conclusion?" Barry was beginning to perspire. "And what do we need to do to get there?"

Mr Material placed his fingers and palms together in a gesture similar to prayer. He looked at his hands all the while that he spoke.

"Success will be the achievement of the full Crossover. For this, a satisfactory conclusion will need to be one in which the child knows enough about Fae life and powers to be able to transform herself into Faery, knowing that she is doing so, knowing the risks of doing so, and knowing the rewards for doing so. She has to understand why and how she is undertaking this hazardous transition, and how to transform back again as and when she wishes or needs. She has to understand that this will not be a one-off occurrence but may be necessary many times in her life. She has to appreciate her significance without dwelling excessively on her role or allowing it to lead her into a sense of arrogance or self-importance. She will have to love the idea of being both human and faery, and seek always to do what is best in the interests of both, in whatever form she finds herself at any particular time.

Finally, she must learn never to abuse her powers once she realises what they are and what she can do with them. You have to guide and lead her to this position. Each of you has a special gift that you need to help her assimilate. Are there enough clues there for you?" He looked up directly at Barry, and then around the room at each of the faeries in turn, including Mr Burr, who appeared as shocked as the local residents.

"So, like I said before, no pressure there then?" All eyes swivelled as one to the main door, where Mack and Trevor stood side by side just inside the bar; Mack with arms folded impassively, and Trevor still waving his hand around searching out cooling air streams.

"It was good to notice you creep in earlier, Messrs Stout." Said Mr Material, rising from his seat. "You were another pair of local heroes that I was hoping to meet. I applaud your confidence and optimism, which I know has stood you in good stead over the years, but I do, unfortunately, have to disagree with your current interpretation of what I revealed as you came in. There will be a great deal of pressure for you all to deal with, and it will be intriguing to see how you do indeed deal with it."

"It would appear," said Barry, desperate for any further enlightenment that he could glean from the strangers, "that you know an awful lot about what might or might not happen, but that you intend to watch all this unfold from the sidelines. And we have to do all these preparations for the Crossover child, which you have summarised most eloquently, by the time of her seventh birthday?" A degree of incredulity was creeping up on him.[30]

"The faeries of Whimbury have clearly been chosen for this most important task, and it is not my role or purpose to interfere in that process. It is up to you, all of you, and you alone. One thing that I will, however, tell you is that it would be wrong of you to believe that you have until her seventh birthday to complete the preparations. The circumstances that generate the need for the actual Crossover may come sooner than you think, and the child must be ready to do what is necessary earlier than anticipated. You must not be afraid to let her fulfil her hoped-for destiny at the right time, whenever that time may be."

---

[30] Which, when it settled on his shoulder, manifested itself in a nervous tic.

Barry was becoming increasingly agitated.

"But the weight of responsibility on the child would be almost unbearable at the ripe old age of seven, let alone earlier than that. How can she be expected to deal with it with the level of understanding typical of a seven-year- old human, or a six-year-old, or even......" He paused, startled at what he was about to say, and what he was implying by saying it. But he said it anyway. "five-year-old???[31]"

"The completion of the Crossover is essential for the effective continued co-existence of humans and faeries. She must be ready. You have to be prepared for any eventuality at any time." Mr Material stressed every syllable of every word. "At that time, she will know that she has to cross over. The situation will force her into action – to protect faeries and humans alike."

"And if she is forced into action before she is ready?" Trixie already loved the little girl with all her heart, and the cool, calculated manner of the tall stranger's speech was deeply upsetting.

"Better you don't think about it." Mr Material gestured to his companion that the time to take their leave had come. "I'm very glad to have been able to spend some time with you all at last. But there are others that I have yet to meet, and perhaps I will come across them before we leave. Until my return to this historic place, may I bid you good day."

With which, Mr Material strode to the door, followed with rather less charisma by Mr Burr. As he strode, he passed in close proximity to Mack and Trevor and paused just long enough to unnerve Mack completely with a subtle wink of the eye. He then took hold of Trevor's throbbing hand and shook it farewell. Both strangers left the building without a backward glance.

In the bar, five pairs of eyes were focussed on the main door in an attempt to make sense of what they had just witnessed. A sixth pair of eyes sparkled in wonder and, at last, Trevor broke the silence.

"Hey, everyone," he shouted, happily, "My hand doesn't hurt any more!"

---

[31] It is difficult to know how many question marks are needed to indicate the level of Barry's disbelief at the very thought of what he was uttering.

Chapter Nine

PERCY AND PERCETTA GRUMPLET WADDLED down the garden path and met Everard Gnappins by the garden gate. Everard doffed his hat in deference to female company, and greeted them both as they prepared to set off for the Royal Oak in an unlikely threesome.

In the months after the Crossover 'incident', the bond between Percy and Everard had strengthened, and since Percy had retired from his post as 'Grump-in-Chief' of the tribe, he felt less in need of keeping up appearances.[32] Percetta had always been fiercely, if grumpily, supportive of Percy, but age had mellowed them both to the point where they could now tolerate what passed in most faery circles for normal enjoyment and relaxation. This exhibited itself most clearly in the friendship that they had grown to appreciate with Everard, though to be fair to their erstwhile long-established traditions, that friendship was helped by the fact that Everard had a tendency to fall asleep at very regular intervals. He, therefore, seldom interfered to any great extent with their natural tribal patterns of behaviour, which in turn avoided any unnecessary embarrassment.

On this occasion, they were off to the Friday Quiz Night at the Oak, and the topic of conversation quickly turned to the extra spice afforded to the occasion by the "travellers' tales" competition.

"Oi thort oi moight regale the hassembled masses with moy tale of

---

[32] Outside of semi-official occasions, such as those that took place in the snug at the Oak, of course. There are always limits!

travellin' to the next Parish for the annual fishin' competition a few year back." Everard seemed unusually lively and verbal until the last phrase when he was overtaken by a sudden sleepiness.

"And?" Percetta waited a decent amount of time before finally becoming convinced that the train of thought had long since pulled into its terminus and was going nowhere else for the foreseeable future.

"And what?" Everard sparked back into life. "What were oi sayin'?"

"You were going to regale the "hassembled" masses with a no doubt fascinating tale from the Upper Whimstead Fishing Competition of a few years ago, though the potential for fascination escapes me at the moment, possibly due to the story being curtailed suddenly, or possibly for some other reason." Percetta was caught in the, for her, unsettling position somewhere between routine grumpiness, which came naturally, and a new forbearance of demeanour, which did not.

"Were oi? Why on earth were I be a doin' that?" Everard was one of those talented people who could not only sleepwalk when awake, but transition seamlessly into wakewalk when asleep.

"Something to do with the 'travellers' tales' competition at the Oak this evening?" Percy attempted to prod Everard's memory in a fairly direct manner, which was the preferred method at times such as this.

"Aar, that's roight, oi remembers now! Oi managed to stay awake the whole toime that the competition were on. And oi caught summat an' all, even if it were later disqualifoied. Pretty spectac'lar day orl round, as oi recalls." Everard was puffed up with pride at the memory, though Percy and Percetta were expecting a little more information.

"What did you catch, Everard – and why was it disqualified? The judges will want to know all that." In truth, even Percy was beginning to develop an interest in what it was that Everard had caught that might have resulted in disqualification.

"Ooh, oi couldn't be a tellin' you that, Percy, moy old friend. Not for the ears of polite company, it be not." Everard touched the side of his nose to indicate secrecy.

"I think I may be able to guess," responded Percy with a twinkle in his eye, "let me have a go! Does it involve water-nymphs and items of clothing?"

Percy leaned over to Everard in a pose suggesting an element of subterfuge, and which elicited an equally knowing look from Everard, at which point he received a not entirely friendly clip round the ear from Percetta.

"I think we'll have less of that, Percy Grumplet. In fact, I know we will. And I would suggest, Mr Gnappins, that if you intend to relate the fully story later this evening, then you should be very careful as to what information you divulge and how you divulge it." Percetta was impressive when in full flow. Those who had experienced the force of that flow had been known to describe it less in terms of a rabbit caught in a car's headlights but more as a human standing in front of a charging rhino and having feet stuck in quick-drying cement.

"But I said nothing untoward, my precious diamond." Percy was pushing his luck with a desperately poor defence facing a rampant attack.

"It's not what you said, my little piece of Zirconia[33]," Her look would have withered an air plant, "but the way that you said it - alongside the accompanying gestures. Don't play mind games with me!" Percetta strode off ahead of the others in a march of defiance. Percy and Everard followed slowly until they were separated by what they considered a safe distance. This was the point which was just within visual range but just outside of hearing range. The precise point at which this occurred left little room for error, and they had only worked it out accurately after a prolonged trial period of having been numerous times out of favour with Percetta while still having a long walk ahead of them.

"She be quite a one, your Percetta!" Everard was himself quite a one at encapsulating the obvious neatly and succinctly.

"She certainly be!" Percy loved Percetta deeply and was genuinely proud of all her many achievements and abilities. He was also often taken on a rocky ride with her, but that was a key part of the attraction, as was the thrill of trying to find the 'safe distance' point whenever he was in trouble.

"So, does you think oi should mebbe not tell moi travel story tonight? Pity, oi thought it moight be a real winner, that one."

---

[33] Percetta had had previous experience of Percy's attempts to cut corners and expense during their long marriage – most notably at their third diamond wedding anniversary. She had since become an expert on fakery.

"Not at all. You should definitely tell it. Just be a bit careful how you tell it – don't get carried away or you might get carried out. My Percetta has a keen moral stance on the kind of issues you often inadvertently raise, and she has a very powerful way of expressing that stance. If she can't immediately get to the perpetrator, she'll find someone else to be the recipient of her strong opinion, and that's often me - when we get home. I could do without that tonight, thank you very much."

"Orl roight then, my friend. Discretion it is. You know me!"

"Yes, I do, and I don't recognise the reference to discretion as being applicable to you in any shape or form."

"Well that bain't very noice!" Everard put on his most affected mock-hurt attitude and tone of voice.

"Maybe not, but the urge for self-preservation knows few bounds. I wonder if those posters will have done the trick?" By this time, they were approaching the Royal Oak, and Percy's thoughts were turning to other aspects of the evening – in truth the main attraction of the evening, if the strangers in fact made an appearance.

"I were beginnin' to wonder that moiself. Could be a very hinterestin' evenin' if'n them there strange faeries decides to come and treat us to some tales of far off places. Could be very hinterestin' indeed – though it moight, on reflection, endanger the chances of moi own reminiscences winnin' a proize!"

"Ah well, nothing ventured eh? If they do come and if it looks like they could have a good story to tell, you can always elaborate on the items of siren clothing that you accidentally bagged – and then run like fury away from Percetta! I'll pick up your prize for you, and if it happens to be Innkeepers Choice, I'll let you know how good it was."

"Can't say fairer than that, Percy! You'm be a good friend." Everard put his arm round Percy's shoulders and they wandered into the Royal Oak some distance behind Percetta.

****

Junior had finished his work for the day. The cellar at the Royal Oak was as clean as he could make it, the pipes were spotless and the barrels free of algae.

He whistled a medley of light operatic tunes as he made his way homewards along the gutter of High Street. As he whistled, he pondered over the events of the day. Barry had seemed more agitated than normal, and had been down in the cellar much longer before opening time, taking extra care with his routine checks. He had not been communicative in the slightest, but just kept muttering to himself. Junior had not been able to follow most of these internal conversations, though he did note that most of the sentences tended to start with 'what happens if....' before trailing off into incoherence as Barry's head disappeared into the mass of pipes and connections between the barrels and the bar upstairs. At the time, Junior had been very taken up with the old woodlouse favourite, 'I am the very model of an isopod crustacean', from one of the most popular operettas, and sang it almost incessantly, giving each rendition slight variations in inflection until he was happy with the end result. As Barry set off back to the bar from his extended inspection, Junior heard him start to sing 'I am the very model.....' 'B****r it Junior, you've got me singing it now!' was the last he heard before Barry disappeared and it was time for him to get home.

He had just reached Over Cross View, when he heard a familiar voice.

"So yer sees, Milly, there was a lot a' faery folk ararnd 'ere, when you was born, wot was very bovvered abart what 'appened to yer next! You're a very special little girl, you are, and we've all – that's the faeries and us animals – have got ter look after yer, an' see that yer learns all the fings that a special girl needs ter know if she's gonna get even more special. Yer mum an' dad are good people and luv yer ter bits, an' they can teach yer the knowledge of human beins, which is wot you are, but there's lots of uvver stuff wot they can't teach yer, cos they ain't faeries or animals like. So, if there's anyfink you ever need ter know, just ask me, right?"

Junior cringed at the cockney accent of his father assaulting Milly's ears, and he wondered how on earth she would manage to understand the language spoken in such a way. He needn't have worried. Milly was indeed special, and her degree of specialness extended to understanding 'louse' English in its many different guises, just as, of course, she was being brought up to understand the many different varieties of human English as used in the day-to-day life of Whimbury village.

"Who lives in Faery Tree?" Milly looked up from her nature study of the front garden, and pointed down the High Street at the majestic oak that stood between the back gardens of Arnold Lane and the Old School House.

"What did you say, Princess? Fairy Tree again?" Will called over from the other side of the garden, where he was dead-heading the early flowers and roses, one of the few jobs he quite enjoyed – mainly because it took very little time and involved a limited amount of bending right over. He received no reply because Milly was listening intently to Larry the louse as he attempted to explain the complexity of life at the Royal Oak. He continued dead-heading while shaking his head ruefully. "Sometimes I wonder about that girl. Is 'special' another word for 'weird'?"

"Only Barry accherly lives in the Oak," Larry was grappling how to explain the goings on in and around an Inn to a two-and-a-quarter year old girl. "but all the uvver faeries in the village come and visit 'im most nights, cos 'e gives 'em drinks and organises games for 'em."

"He's funny!" Milly liked the idea of drinks and games since it reminded her of her last birthday party. Miranda had invited some of her closest friends and provided party food and drinks, which went down very well with all concerned, while Will was in charge of games, which were carried out in the most chaotic and uncoordinated fashion, and which consequently resulted in huge hilarity and also went down very well with all concerned.

"Yes, he is!" Junior came into the garden and joined the conversation. "I've just come from the Faery Tree, and there's going to be a special party there tonight. If your bedroom window is open, I think you may hear all the faeries singing and laughing."

"Birthday party?" Milly was now sitting with her chin in her hands pondering over what she was being told, and trying to relate it to her own little world and her knowledge of it. Will stopped dead-heading yet again, and was about to ask Milly who she was talking to, but then thought the better of it. He valued his sanity and, as she was obviously happy in her garden and imaginary community, he decided to leave her to it. He could ask her later over her tea. She would tell him – she always did, and he was never really much the wiser for it. But her answers made him and Miranda smile, and a little fun and jollity over a meal is never a bad thing.

"No, not a birthday party. It's a different kind of party. People will come and tell interesting and exciting stories about special places where they've been and what they have done and seen there. You know Barry and Robin and Trixie?" Although Junior only worked in the cellars at the Oak, he was fully aware of how significant Milly was in the life, present and future, of the village and beyond. Barry had made a point of explaining to Junior exactly who Milly was, and he had grown up listening entranced to the bedtime stories that Larry told him about the Crossover story and part that Larry and his relatives from London had played in it - the magic that had been used and the cunning and bravery of everyone involved. And so, along with all the other animals in the village, he knew to take very seriously his role in the education of Milly into the ways of faery and animal life, a role that he played very well.

"Robin and Trixie! They like mummy and daddy!" Barry had long felt that Robin and Trixie were the ideal Fae couple to take charge of Milly's upbringing in the ways and senses of the non-human community in Whimbury. They had complementary skills and attributes, and both were outgoing and fundamentally caring. So it was that, out of the whole village of faeries, Milly had the most contact with them, and so it was that she was learning how to listen with her fingers and eyes, how to run with her eyes closed and not trip over, how to see with her nose, and other clever tricks, such as how to move so quickly that time had hard work keeping up[34]. Being only two, everything was possible without question. All she had to do was to believe and trust in her tutors. She did this with Will and Miranda (most of the time), and it came naturally with Robin and Trixie also.

"Yes, they are. That's right!" Junior winked at Larry, who was secretly pleased that the responsibility for explaining the workings of the local Fae hierarchy and its interrelationships had been lifted from his shoulders. He was getting old and easily tired, and his brain wasn't working as sharply as it once did. "They are what we call 'Faery Godparents'. Every child has them, but

---

[34] This was Trixie's responsibility, and though Milly was an excellent and quick pupil, she still hadn't mastered this trick entirely, which was why she was still always where Will and Miranda had left her whenever they looked. This was not always to be the case!

there are very few like you who talk with them- it makes them very happy when you talk with them."

"They happy, I happy!" Milly clapped her hands because she was happy and she knew it.

Junior and Larry smiled and waved to her as they left the garden. Will smiled as he watched and listened to his little princess playing 'imaginary' games on the grass. He thought no more of it until he put her to bed and she asked for the window to be left open so that she could hear the faeries.

****

Behind the Royal Oak, Barry sat himself down on the dry leaves next to Ralph. These were troubling times – Ralph sensed it, which was why he left Whimburton to camp out in Whimbury for a while, and Barry sensed it too. He knew that the fae community in the village had a huge responsibility with regard to preparing Milly for the final act in the Crossover. He had assumed that they had a few years left to deal with it, but Messrs Material and Burr had somewhat scuppered that idea, by instilling a sense of urgency where there had previously been none. The thought that Milly might have to undertake her ultimate test whilst still relatively young sent shivers up his spine. He had full faith and trust in the capacity of his helpers, fae and animal, to handle the training, but in a potentially reduced time frame, that was a big ask. The girl was still only two, and while she showed quite amazing aptitude for the fae life-skills that she was learning, she had, through no fault of her own, only limited life experience, which made communication that little bit more difficult.

Barry and Ralph sat in silence for several minutes attuning themselves to the colours, movement and sounds of the woods behind them, and blanking out the background sounds and movement of the High Street on the other side of the tree. All that needed to be said between them required them both to be focussed and in touch with the natural environment around them. And somehow, the Oak itself imprinted its aura increasingly on their consciousness. It was Barry who spoke first.

"This side of the tree is ours – the other side is fully in the human domain.

Their activity is concentrated along the road. They see the tree, but they don't sense anything other than a tree. That's good for us in some ways because they leave us alone, but if they can't see within and beyond the tree, how are we to communicate with them?"

Ralph only spoke quickly and profusely when he was agitated. On this occasion, he thought hard and Barry watched and waited as the veins of his temples tensed with thought and the ordered sequencing of ideas.

"It's not for you to communicate with them – that's where the girl comes in. At the moment she's like me – well, not much like me obviously – but she's human, and thinks and acts like a human, if only a very small and relatively unpolluted one. But she could be like you, if we get things right, and she could communicate both ways – properly I mean, not like the way I communicate with you – properly I mean, with proper fae thoughts and understanding," he paused before ending with a flourish, "AND the ability to BECOME like you when she needs to – literally like you. People like me can't go that far: she's the only one that can – if we get things right!"

Barry did not visibly cheer up. The weight on his mind had not lifted, though everything that Ralph had said was true.

"You said that twice – IF we get things right! Most ifs are big ifs, but this one has gargantuan overtones, and pity help us if we get things wrong. Who knows what's going to happen then?" Barry exhaled loudly and meaningfully, and there began another period of silence, eventually broken this time by Ralph.

"You can only do your best, Barry. Somewhere in the mists of time past, some Fate or other decreed that the Crossover child would be born here, and that the responsibility for looking after her welfare and development should rest with you and your mates[35]. I reckon that Fate knew a good solid community when it saw one, and it saw one right here – all that time ago, it could foresee you and what you could achieve. Trust me Barry, you can do this, I sense it."

"Thanks Ralph," Barry looked up, way up, to see Ralph smiling gently

---

[35] As suggested in Book Seven of the legendary Fae folk poem "Paradise Mislaid", which amplified the history of Faedom as laid down in much earlier times in the Fae Chronicles.

way above him, "I don't know if you mean any of that, but it's appreciated anyway. What's really bothering me though, is how we are going to know when is the right time for the girl to cross the great divide? She only gets one chance, and if we don't spot it at just the precise moment, that's it – end of story. And what if we haven't prepared her in the way she needs for that moment? Oh, Nodding Donkeys!"

Barry had always prided himself on his ability to coax out the answers to all of the problems that cropped up in his own little world at the Royal Oak; to find the right person to call upon at the right time and in the right place. He ran a tight and effective ship keeping potentially warring factions of gnomes, sprites, pixies and others on speaking, as opposed to punching, terms. He brought joy and social bonding to the community – not to mention one of the most lethal varieties of Innkeeper's Choice to the taps at his bar.[36] But now he was worried. He'd been worried before, of course, but this was a panicky kind of worriedness that was all new to him. It had been pervading his thoughts ever since the strangers left the bar – and left him with a headache. Had they really come just to meet the "heroes" of Whimbury? Why did Mr Material go on so about the responsibilities of the local fae community? He still didn't know if Mr Material would ever be seen again, him and his companion, the enigmatic and largely silent, Mr Burr. Questions, questions, questions locked up and revolving inside his head. If only he had the key to release them and share the burden. At that moment, all he had to support him was an itinerant and homeless human, but he was thankful for Ralph more than he could say. He might not fully understand all of Barry's concerns, but he could give a human perspective and Barry needed that if he were to make sense of the situation.

"I think," said Ralph after another ponder, "that the right time will come clear when it needs to, and I've a strong suspicion that if it involves a "crossover" between human and faery, then the issue will be something that affects both humans and faeries. Forgive me if I'm stating the obvious, but maybe it's going to take both of us to work out what it is. I don't know what may or may not be of great significance to you, but I should be able to find out what's of great significance to the humans around here, and if something

---

[36] Because after a couple of glasses of Barry's Innkeeper's Choice, very few faeries were in any position to mention anything at all.

crops up that seems to both you and me to combine the two, we might just be on to the answer?"

"What would we do without you!" Barry had a rare 'light-bulb illuminating the murky realms of human and fae intrigue' moments. "Suddenly, it all starts to make sense. I've been thinking 'us and them' all along when it should have been just 'us'. We're all in this together, aren't we? You're absolutely right – something with the potential to unite us is what we're looking for. We still don't know what it is, but hopefully it will be obvious when the time comes. Brilliant Ralph, you're a star!"

Barry looked up at Ralph, and through the careworn, lined and sun-dried face that gazed back down at him, he thought he could detect just the merest hint of an embarrassed blush.

"Well, I'm glad if I can be of assistance – lord knows you've got enough to be worrying about, so if I can help to enlighten….." he paused, as another thought passed rapidly across his eyes and he tried to read it before it disappeared into the ether. He took his time to assimilate the messages that it contained, while Barry watched as his lips moved and head swayed in rhythm with the internal re-filing processes. At last, his lips went still and his head found a satisfactory rest position. Barry waited.

"There could be one little problem!" Ralph was finally in a position to share his conclusions.

"Which is what?" Barry was getting nervous again.

"As you may have noticed, I am not readily welcomed anywhere by the human community. I don't fit in. People are wary at best, and aggressive at worst." He paused.

"And?" Barry didn't like pauses.

"So how am I going to find out what troubles the humans, if I can't get near them?"

"Good point!" Barry turned to ponder, and ponder he did. He pondered long and he pondered hard until a suggestion wormed its way into his mind.[37]

"I think, though this may not sound a very attractive proposition the way

_____

[37] It could be said that he pandered to his pondering until it was no longer pending, but it probably shouldn't be.

things stand, that you will need to break cover here in the village and establish a contact with the child and her family. They are the ones most likely to accept you and give you access to the village gossip."

Barry had never before seen the face of a human transmute from "ruddy" to "pale and gaunt" so quickly or so vividly. He watched enthralled as the colour drained rapidly and inexorably from the top of Ralph's head to his chin without pausing for so much as a breather at his nose.

"You all right, Ralph?" Barry wasn't quite sure what he was seeing, and so resorted to the standard pointless question adopted by so many when faced with obvious distress but not knowing whether it required an urgent trip to hospital.

"Absolutely fine, Barry," croaked Ralph, "or at least I was till you uttered the words 'break cover' and 'establish contact', at which point I developed a nervous sweat and a hot flush. You really don't fully understand the nature of my relationship with the local human community, do you?"

"Can't be that bad, can it? You all speak the same language, and most of the people I've come across seem basically OK."

"Most are! It's the few that aren't that worry me. Some of them can be aggressive for the sake of it, and then take out their aggression on anyone who differs from their idea of the norm. To be fair, most of the folk here seem pretty reasonable, and even if some of them aren't overflowing with tolerance, I suspect they will at least be non-violent types. It's just that I'm used to Whimburton, and things aren't quite the same there. Things can turn nasty at the drop of a hat, and I've developed a strategy that involves avoiding certain places at certain times of day – that's one of the reasons I've still got most of my teeth!"

"Fair enough, Ralph. I quite understand if you can't get involved with us. It is your health and welfare after all." Barry prepared to return to pondering mode, but Ralph responded quickly.

"Oh no, I'll do it all right, but I just need you to know that it might not be as straightforward as you think. I can't say for certain that I'll be accepted – they might all run away screaming or, even worse, run at me screaming. But if it needs doing – and I think you're right – then I'll give it a go! Though I wish it to be put on record that it goes against all my long-established practices of self-preservation." Ralph took a deep breath and then slumped just a little.

"Ralph, you are a marvel. And I think I can say quite safely, even without any council meeting, discussion or vote, that we all love you and would be lost without you as a friend!" There was just the faintest of pauses for effect, then Barry seamlessly moved onto the matter in hand. "So now we just need to find a way to get you to meet the child and her family officially. Any ideas?"

"Well the thing is, they only know me as a semi-itinerant, partially sane, homeless beggar, so I can't really introduce myself in any other way, particularly as they don't know I'm here. I'll just have to hope that my suddenly turning up doesn't just freak them out completely." He lay back on his elbows and stared up at the tree canopy above him, deep in thought.

At this point it became unclear whether the conversation was short staccato bursts interspersed with deep pondering, or deep pondering interspersed with snatches of conversation.[38] At last Ralph had an idea.

"The village notice board!" He seemed pleased with himself.

"Yes, absolutely!" Barry prompted progress.

"On one of my rare furtive forays outside of the wood yesterday, I read the notices on the board. The Parish Council is having a meeting tomorrow night. There's an emergency item on housing proposals and there will be tea and biscuits afterwards. I could murder a nice cup of tea and a biscuit. If I could gate-crash the meeting, I might get both information and refreshments." Ralph sat up again, the colour returning to his cheeks and a self-satisfied grin covering his face.

"That's brilliant." Barry was enthused and highly impressed by Ralph's plan. "What will you do – just turn up at the village hall?"

"No, previous experiences tell me that creating a sudden 'me versus the group' scenario never works out to my advantage. If I just turn up out of the blue, they'll just slam the door on me. No, I'll try to highjack someone who's on the way there and see if I can get them to let me have a cup of tea and a biscuit. In a one-to-one situation, most people show a degree of decency and sympathy, and if I choose a place that's open and nearby and unthreatening, I

---

[38] See previous reference

should be able to manage a bit of friendly persuasion! I'll give it a go anyway. The only problem is that if the whole plan fails miserably, they'll all know that I'm around and I'll probably get hounded out of the village and forced back to town." Ralph appeared to be debating with himself the pros and cons of his scheme. Barry decided he couldn't risk the cons wheedling their way into the debate and so he intervened hurriedly.

"Well, if you're prepared to take that risk, we'd all be indebted to you. And if it's any help, I'd say that the people round here are more than likely to spare you a cup of tea, so long as they can remain in control of the situation."

"Yes, you're probably right – and the chance of a cup of tea is very appealing. OK, onwards and ever upwards, eh Barry?"

Decision made, Ralph got up and walked back into the woods. Barry called out his farewell greetings and retired back into the Royal Oak.

****

Evadne and Kenneth shut the front gate behind them as they set off for their regular early evening walk with Spot around the village.

"Clockwise or anti-clockwise?" Kenneth paused as Spot strained at the leash, eager to get into the woods opposite.

"Clockwise today, I think." Evadne strode off in the direction of the village green. "And keep that dog tight on the lead until we get near the church, otherwise he'll be all over everywhere – you know what he's like."

"I certainly do!" Kenneth tugged at Spot's lead to direct him up the High Street, at which the dog launched himself along the footpath to catch up with Evadne. Kenneth performed heroics to rein Spot in before he got pulled over by the ferocity of the acceleration. This happened every day, and every day Kenneth vowed he would never let it happen again. However, there is a very clear dividing line between well-intentioned bluster and actual achievement, and even Kenneth knew that, in this matter, he was all bluster.[39]

On this occasion, almost as soon as he got into the rhythm of a fast hobble immediately behind Spot, he was pulled up suddenly as both Evadne and Spot

---

[39] And in this respect, with the exception of the 'well-intentioned' bit, Kenneth could have been mistaken for a high-ranking politician.

paused outside Over Cross View. At the upstairs window, Will and Milly were leaning out, looking up and down the street and waving in all directions. Despite all the attention given to the street and its immediate surroundings, Will was not aware of the presence of the Potts family group until Spot starting barking excitedly, paws on the front wall in traditional pose.

"Oh, hi!" Will's wave suddenly turned from an enthusiastic one into a highly embarrassed one. "We were just waving to the fairies on their way to the Fairy Tree! Milly wanted the window open so that we could see and hear them."

"Of course!" shouted Evadne in a loud whisper, "I thought it was quite noisy tonight." She waved to Milly as she spoke and Milly waved back. At the same time Spot turned his head at a 45-degree angle and Milly did the same.

"Yes indeed." Will was glad of the moral support and maintained his pretence. He put his hand across his mouth to indicate secrecy. "Apparently, there's going to be a party tonight, or so Milly tells me." He nodded his head in Milly's direction, but she was still engaged in an eye-to-eye conversation with Spot.

"Really? Well I hope they aren't too noisy." Evadne made a point of addressing Milly directly, who eventually caught her eye. "Last time I didn't get a wink of sleep all night."

Milly shouted back for all the street to hear. "Party – drinks and games! Happy party!"

"Right, now off to bed my little princess." Will put on the best authoritative voice he could muster, which in truth was a substantial distance from its intended tone. And as Milly showed no inclination to leave the window, he added, "wave goodnight to Auntie Ev and Uncle Ken."

Milly complied happily, and then turned her head to 45 degrees as a farewell greeting to Spot, who replied in kind but with an added loud bark.

"Well, that should please the neighbours!" Will waved goodbye to the Potts and gently ushered Milly to bed, closing the window as he did so. Moments later he opened it again, and the Potts could just make out "Alright, alright – if you insist!"

The window stayed open and the Potts carried on up the High Street.

"She rules the roost, that little one!" Kenneth laughed as he took hold of Evadne's hand and escorted her across the road to the village green while attempting to restrain Spot, who had a considerable amount of energy to run off.

"She's certainly one of a kind. I don't think there can be too many like her around, that's for sure. Mind you, there always was something a bit strange, a bit special, about her birth and immediately after." Evadne's mind was taken back to the day when she had to act as emergency midwife to Miranda. A privileged moment certainly, and not one she would readily forget for a number of reasons. In amongst all the routine mess and noise, there was an underlying calm that she had never been quite able to put a satisfactory finger on. And a kind of glow…..

She was brought back into the moment by Spot jumping up at her as he was finally allowed off his lead.

"You were miles away then, my lovely – muttering about the day that Milly was born. It certainly was a crazy day, wasn't it!" Kenneth threw a ball for Spot to chase - in the opposite direction to the village pond. Ever since Spot had jumped into the pond, just after Milly was born and, more pertinently, just before the dog show that he had been groomed for, Kenneth had been given responsibility for bathing the dog should it come back from a walk in a bad visual and malodourous condition. He had rarely been required to fulfil that responsibility due to the policy of extreme care that he always followed when in the vicinity of the pond.

"It certainly was." Evadne threw her head back in an attempt to keep her face away from the slobbering kiss that Spot aspired to give her. "Now if you'd kindly throw the ball so that I can extricate myself from this monster – albeit a loveable monster, to give him his dues – then he can have a bit of exercise before we need to put him back on the lead." She brushed herself down and laughed as Spot chased, jumped at and missed the bouncing ball. Having waited till the ball stopped bouncing and assumes a static pose, Spot then 'caught' it and brought it back.

"Stupid dog," said Kenneth in a mildly exasperated tone.

"It might be interpreted as intelligent – waiting till the ball stops before

~ 147 ~

picking it up. Perhaps his idea of fun is not quite the same as ours? Though we do need to tire him out before we get back near the wood – we don't want him running off into the trees again." She watched as Kenneth carefully picked up the saliva-laden ball between two fingertips and placed it back into the dog ball thrower.

"This is true." Kenneth propelled the ball into the middle distance and smiled as Spot once again ran, jumped, missed and waited. "I wonder what he sees or hears in there. He's certainly very agitated of late. There must be something not quite right."

"Well, whatever it is, we don't want him finding it or, even worse, bringing it home as a present. Whatever's suddenly arrived in there is better off left in there – at least, that's my opinion."

"I agree. What say we sit on the bench? I reckon I've got quite a few more throws in me before one or other of us gives up, and if we're sitting down it's more likely to be the dog!"

At which point, they sat down on the bench and prepared for a long session of trying to exhaust Spot.

Chapter Ten

IN THE PUBLIC BAR AT the Royal Oak, there was a buzz of excitement. A few of the regulars were poring over sheets of notes, preparing to tell their travel tale, and making last minute adjustments to increase the scale of their escapades. Rumours that the prize for the best story might involve an amount of Innkeepers Choice, galvanised the faery population to enhance their stories, just an iota, in an attempt to outdo any possible competition.

Meanwhile, in one corner, a loud group of pixies, who appeared indifferent to anything that might disturb serious drinking time, were getting into their stride of exhausting the canon of raucous faery folk songs.......

Blow the wind southerly, southerly, southerly

Blow the breeze south which is downwind from here.

Blow the wind southerly, southerly, southerly,

Leave no reminder of my pints of beer.

In another corner, the one furthest away from the songsters, Eric O'Shy was deep in research with his Encyclopedia of Fae History and Legend and other reference books[40] in preparation for the next quiz night. Whilst he had little in the way of a sense of humour, and was never going to be the most popular of the faeries in the hostelry, everyone had come to appreciate that every solitary minute spent by Eric in study, meant one minute less that they had to do the same. This equated to one extra minute of drinking time instead,

---

[40] Including his book of Fae remedies for common back problems, otherwise known as the Encyclopaedia Sciatica.

and so Eric was indulged to the point where exceptions were made for his relative isolation and lack of bonhomie.

They told me last night there were drinks in the offing
So I hurried down to the old hostelry.
I furnished myself with a pint of the special,
And before that I knew it, I'd had two or three, so.
Blow the wind... ...

In the third corner[41] were gathered the regulars who never joined in with any of the formal activities, but enjoyed them nevertheless – their presence guaranteed on a nightly basis by their desire to get out of the house and meet up with friends and neighbours for a good natter, and a laugh at the antics of the increasingly inebriated quizzers and singers. Tonight, they were particularly excited by the prospect of a new form of entertainment provided by the story-telling competition.

It is not sweet to breathe in near the hostelry
After an evening with excess of beer.
For in amongst laughter, and ribald exchanges,
There's much to expel, and malodourous I fear, so
Blow the wind....

Barry was on edge. Under normal circumstances he would have been more than happy to see the bar full, with numerous groups of contented faeries, drinking and laughing and generally in good cheer. But tonight was different. Part of him was hopeful that Mr Material and his friend would arrive and perhaps provide more information about his background and why he was in the village – the earlier conversation had left more questions than answers. The other part of him was worried about how the other faeries in the community would respond to what the new strangers had to say, if they did indeed turn up. He busied himself cleaning and recleaning the same glass over and over, looking through it from all angles to check for smudges. After several passes through the routine, he lifted the glass to his eye and saw what

---

[41] For those remotely interested, the fourth corner was taken up with the opening into the "snug".

he was dreading through its 'magnifier' bottom. An already huge Mr Material, along with his friend Mr Burr, appeared even larger than life in the doorway to the bar. Even if Barry had not seen them, he would have known of their arrival by the sudden eerie silence that overtook the room. He lowered the glass, gave them a somewhat pathetic wave of welcome, and gestured to them to join him at the bar. As they walked over, Mack Stout gave them the nonchalant wave of an old friend. Mr Material nodded his head ever so slightly in Mack's direction, while Mr Burr gave him a smile. Mack looked around to ensure that as many people as possible had seen the exchange, and so appreciated his close relationship to the strangers.

The eerie silence gave way to a communal whisper as the various groups scattered around the room tried to make sense of what was happening. Meanwhile, news of the goings-on was being relayed around the families Grump in the snug by Victor, who had positioned himself near the entrance when all had fallen silent in a strange and unprecedented manner.

Barry engaged the newcomers in preliminary conversation.

"Glad you could make it! I had hoped that your earlier visit wouldn't be the last. I've a suspicion that you have some interesting stories to tell, and the folk here would, I'm sure, benefit from hearing them." Barry hated embarrassing gaps in conversation and so he continued until he could get round to the question he really wanted to ask. "So will you be telling us your traveler's tale – and if so, do you want to go first or wait till later."

"I will tell a tale," said Mr Material, "And it is indeed one that your friends should hear. Perhaps I could go first?"

"Of course," Barry moved effortlessly over to the pump with the Innkeepers Choice logo garishly emblazoned on the shield. "Would you like a drink?"

"Not for me, thankyou." Mr Material looked around the room at the sea of faces hiding behind beer mats, with just the eyes looking over – each pair looking directly at him.[42] He turned towards the snug, to see the doorway fully blocked by grumpy-looking faeries all similarly part-concealed by beer mats. He gave a knowing look at Barry and continued. "But perhaps a soft drink for my friend Mr Burr?"

---

[42] Except for Trevor, whose eyes were focussed on Mack in order to try to judge where he should be looking.

"Of course," repeated Barry and turned his attention to the smaller stranger. "What can I get you?"

Mr Burr pondered for a while before deciding on a Sarsaparilla. Barry looked momentarily confused, then like a good bartender went to the back shelf, dusted off an ancient earthenware bottle, and muttered to himself as he flipped open the sealed lid. "I hope this is still OK."

Barry poured out the Sarsaparilla and gave out a silent sigh of relief when it came out clear and still slightly fizzy. He made a mental note to order another bottle to cover himself for the next ten years. Mr Burr took a sip of his drink as he followed his mentor to an empty couple of seats against the far wall of the room. Momentarily breathless from the experience, he gave a discreet cough into his hand, slapped the back of his head and sat down. Mr Material smiled at Trixie's mum and dad as he sat beside them, then drew himself up to his full seated height and settled down to await the evening's proceedings. A veritable 'ceiling' of beer mats[43] slowly descended from the faces of the patrons, with nervous grins and 'good health' gestures with beer mugs to follow. Mr Burr, still coughing, returned the gesture while Mr Material adopted a relatively benign look in an attempt to put folk at their ease.

Once the hum of mass whispers had died down, and the clatter of replaced beer mats had ended, and the Grumps had taken back their seats, Barry took command of the situation and prepared to make a pronouncement. In order to get silence, he rang the last orders bell which simultaneously resulted in half of the room picking up their coats and the other half supping up unfinished drinks as quickly as they could. In the ensuing gap in the conversation, Barry began to speak – very loudly!

"Friends. Friends." He shouted. "Welcome to the very first of our travelers' tales evenings." He paused while half of the room took off their coats again, and the other half wiped large quantities of spilt ale from their clothing. "We are very pleased to welcome a special guest visitor, Mr

---

[43] A "ceiling" is the correct collective term for a number of beer mats. No-one is quite sure whether it is because so many inns have an official collection pinned to the ceiling above the bar, or because that is where so many wet ones end up stuck after a raucous evening.

Material," He pointed with a totally unnecessary gesture of identification, "who, along with his friend Mr Burr, will begin our evening's entertainment in just a few moments. And I'm sure I don't need to remind you that there will be a prize for the best story at the end of the evening. So, after Mr Material has finished his story, I'd be grateful if the others with tales to tell would put up their hands so that I can invite them to take their turn."

There were one or two half-hearted murmurs of 'what's the prize?' but within seconds Barry had the attention he craved.

"Without further ado, I ask Messrs Material and Burr to begin their story." At which point, he sat down in eager expectation, along with everyone else in the Royal Oak that evening.

******

Miranda was sitting at the kitchen table reading the minutes of the last Parish Council meeting when Will came back downstairs.

"You took your time! You were only supposed to read her two short stories. Has she gone off now?" Miranda wiped her eyes in an attempt to ease the itchy strain resulting from reading a far too detailed account of the proceedings of the meeting.

"Yes, flat out. I only had time to read one story before she fell asleep. Probably spent too much time watching the world go by and waving to the fairies. You know, I could swear that she sees them. She called out to each of them by name and shouted something about a party. Do you think her imagination is a little over-ripe for her age?" Will picked up the kettle from the work surface behind Miranda, walked over to the sink and filled it with water.

"Well it certainly seems very vivid – and the vicar did say that he thought there might be something supernatural going on – or at least he didn't rule it out, which surprised me. What names did she give them?"

"Can't remember them all but I think there was a Robin and a Trixie – she seemed particularly animated by them – and maybe a Mac and an Ivor or something like it. I don't remember any of those names from stories that we've read her. Anyone from the village fetes or bring-and-buys that you go to who have those names?" Will poured two cups of tea and brought them over to the table, looking over Miranda's shoulder as he did so.

"Don't think so, but then she picks up so much – and never forgets anything. We're going to have to be very careful what we say in her hearing before too long!"

"True. Though Robin and Trixie aren't the sort of names I associated with fairies. I would have expected more along the lines of Alfric or Ethelwynd or something – or at the very worst Rosepetal or Tinkerbelle - or Puck even. What's that you're reading?"

"Minutes of the last Parish Council meeting. Or more like a complete record of every word spoken and gesture made. And I still can't tell who was supposed to do what! And, thinking about it, wasn't Puck Shakespeare's name for Robin Goodfellow? Maybe Milly is friends with him? Almost makes sense." Miranda sat back on her seat and thought hard.[44]

"Whoa, just a minute there!" Will dreaded getting into discussions like this, where he might be required to think about matters beyond his normal sensual experiences. "I can just about cope with her calling woodlice Larry and Junior....." He was interrupted by a Miranda fully into interrupting her own cogitations.

"Junior? I knew all about Larry[45], and that's weird enough, but where did Junior come from – that's a new one?"

"Oh, she was talking to him earlier in the garden – along with Larry."

"The same one?"

"How should I know?" Will was getting flummoxed. "They don't have name tags, and I'm not yet an expert on differentiating between woodlice. Surprising as it may sound, they all look alike to me – except of course the one with the rather sweet way of wiggling its antennae! She's cute." At times, Will could exercise the beginnings of a nice line in sarcasm, though he needed to be extremely agitated for it to become employed.

"Oh, ha ha!"

"Well all I know is that she talks to woodlice, and spiders, and beetles, and

---

[44] Which is very much like pondering – a very common pastime apparently at this point in time in Whimbury.

[45] See "A faery merry Christmas to one and all" about Milly's first Christmas.

bees and butterflies." He emphasised each example with his fingers. "They all have names, and the conversations give every appearance of being more intellectual than any she ever has with us, even at age 2 and a bit. It would seem that we are far down the conversational pecking order when compared with insects, lepidoptera and arachnids – who are clearly much more engaging – and have more legs!" He paused to dunk a biscuit into his tea and then swore to himself when the bulk of it collapsed and fell back into the cup. "Changing the subject – anything interesting on the Parish Council Agenda? Tomorrow's the meeting, isn't it? Excited about your foray into the wild and unpredictable machinations of village business?"

"Yes and no, yes, and yes and no – in that order!" Miranda was in two minds about her new adventure into local politics.

"Sorry?" Will had failed to keep up with the conversation by virtue of using his spoon very carefully to get as many soggy bits of slightly stale digestive biscuit out of his cup of tea as possible.

"Anything interesting on the agenda – yes and no! Yes, the meeting is tomorrow! And am I excited – yes and no! I waver between morbid interest and overcome with indifference. The main item," she continued, "is this issue of the Council's new plan and the likelihood of more housing in Whimbury." She handed the Agenda over to Will and pointed to the relevant item.

"Hmm! Don't know what I think about that. I suppose I ought to have an opinion, but it's quite complicated isn't it? Pros and cons to weigh up!" He used his hands as a none too convincing impression of weighing scales. "Any indication from the minutes as what the local dignitaries think?"

"From what I can make out,…" Miranda attempted to refresh her memory from the wodge of papers but found it difficult to find the right page. Eventually she reached the section she was looking for. "Ah yes! The person who had been allocated to find out all about it missed the Committee Meeting and so had nothing to report. But they did have a discussion about the principle of the whole thing and it would appear that the 'pros' included more people to support the local shops and bus services - and to provide a fast bowler for the cricket team, while the 'cons' were more traffic and possible dilution of local traditions – though I may have paraphrased that wrongly."

"Sounds like they could do with a new secretary!"

"Quite possibly. I think it's Fred Butterworth, so he may not be the most efficient that they could find. But I have no intention of mentioning such things at my first meeting. Find my feet first, before I risk upsetting anyone – or indeed the whole applecart!"

"Probably wise!" In truth, while Will was happy for Miranda to get involved in local affairs, he did not relish her having a significant role. She always gave everything she did her fullest attention and made sure it was done well. It was an admirable trait, but one that could end up with a large part of her time being taken up with organising less capable people.

Will drained the residue of his tea and biscuit and took the cup over to the sink. As he rinsed it, he glanced out of the window over the back garden to the open countryside beyond. To his right he could see the nave and side-chapel at St Vitus' church, with the small inter-war housing estate just visible through the trees beyond. He considered himself lucky to be living in such a beautiful and quiet place. True, it was only possible because Miranda had inherited her parents' house – they would never have been able to afford to live there otherwise – and it was sad that they had not lived to meet Milly, but the important thing was to make the most of the present and try to create as good a future for their child as possible. Nothing stays the same for ever, but all change should be for the better, and he wasn't sure what he felt about new housing in the village. Would it make things better for existing residents and in-comers, or would it just generate profit for nameless and faceless people who had no personal interest in or commitment to the village? There was no reason, of course, why they had to be mutually exclusive end results, but his limited experience of the ways of the commercial world led to a degree of scepticism about the promises and motives that usually enveloped property deals and developments.

"Perhaps we ought to have a talk about the planning proposals when you get back from the meeting? Sort out our own views? That is if anyone knows any more than they did last time." Will walked past Miranda and into the hallway to listen out for any noises from Milly upstairs. There were none.

"Yes, I think perhaps we should. It might be good for us to get more involved in local affairs now that Milly is growing up. It's her future as much as ours after all."

"I suddenly feel a weight of responsibility." Will shuffled back and laid his hands gently on Miranda's shoulders.

****

At the edge of the woods, out of sight of the rest of the village, Ralph poked around in one of his plastic supermarket 'bags-for-life'[46]. He was getting short of provisions because he hadn't expected to be away from Whimburton for so long, and in the village he didn't have the same sources of food available to him.[47] He identified a couple of apples that still had a day or two of life in them; a tin of tuna that he was confident would continue to last way beyond its official best-before date; a bagel, well-wrapped and tied; a small piece of blue cheese that he hoped had already been blue when he first picked it up; a few nutty, raisiny, seedy bars donated by a thoughtful well-wisher, which always came in handy when he was desperate – though in truth he found the recyclable cardboard wrapping almost as tasty; a packet of long-life milk which he had not yet opened; a stick of celery that always gave him hours of fun pulling off the stringy bits; the inevitable tin of baked beans; and a bottle of water taken from the drinking fountain in the market square. He took from his pocket the combined spoon, knife, fork, and bottle/can opener that was so often his lifeline, and planned out his evening menu.

"Eat the nearly fresh food first, Ralph – no point in letting it go off altogether. Tuna would be nice, but that's only 6 months out of date so will keep a bit longer. Has to be cheese, I think – maybe half a bagel with it? Piece of celery? Yes, why not? Live a little, that's what I always say – actually it IS what I always say – ah well, one day maybe I can say live a lot and mean it. Till then, 'live a little' it remains. And 'a little remains' is what I live off

---

[46] Ralph was very particular about not polluting the planet with plastic if he could possibly avoid it. In his current circumstances a relatively solid and long-lasting bag seemed to be the best option.
[47] Chiefly throw-aways from the local supermarket where kindly blind eyes were turned whenever he came to filter through the bins and pallets in the service area.

mostly. Ha." He chortled at his own jest and held up the apples to check which was nearest to disintegration. He put back in the bag the one that could just about be made to last another day, and rubbed the other one vigorously on his trousers in much the same way as a fast bowler would attempt to shine a cricket ball. "Afters!" He exclaimed to himself, and placed the apple carefully on a pile of moss that he used as his tablecloth.

Ralph sat back against a grassy tussock with a cheese-covered, half bagel in one hand and a freshly de-strung piece of celery in the other. He looked up through the canopy to the blue sky above and gave thanks to whoever was in control for the joy of enough food to keep him going and a dry warm day. Unlike Whimburton, it was quiet and the air smelt fresh. In due course he would miss the bustle of town – the overheard conversations, the shop windows, the fresh food smells of the cafes and bars, the newspapers in the library, and the kindness of the few who engaged with him and helped him through the days in whatever practical way they could. But for now, it was important that he was in the village. He had felt drawn there by snippets of news that he had picked up in town and, having talked with Barry, both his hopes and fears had been confirmed.

Now he needed a plan. Much as a fresh, hot cup of tea and a biscuit would be welcome, it had to be the secondary consideration – secondary to the ultimate goal of discovering what major issues were facing the village and who thought what about them. More especially, he would need to find the link between the affairs of the villagers and the affairs of the faeries. He would have to be very careful and attentive - that is on the assumption that he could get invited in. It was pretty much a one-off opportunity, since it would not be wise for him to loiter around Whimbury for much longer, and he almost certainly couldn't come back again before a reasonable period had elapsed. In any case, once the crucial matter had been identified, he'd have to go back to Whimburton to keep his eyes and ears open for clues as to future events.

Ralph chewed on his celery and tried to visualise himself getting invited into the Parish Hall for refreshments. He'd never previously directly come across anyone in the village apart from Milly's parents, and he didn't know if they were involved in the meeting. From what he had felt in the park at

Whimburton, when he first saw Milly, he was sure they would be kind, but what of the other villagers? If he had to rely on one of them, what were his chances? And what should be his opening gambit?

'Please help an old war veteran?' No, honesty was always the best policy and 'Please help an old pacifist' was unlikely to have the same impact. 'Could you spare me the cost of the bus fare back to Whimburton?' That might work, but it might work too well and he might end up with his bus fare but no entry to the Parish Hall. Eventually, and having eliminated certain other less plausible opening gambits, including a range of health and amputation problems that he didn't have, and a starving pet that he didn't have either, he decided on the straightforward and simple approach of asking for help to get a drink and a little something to eat, to tide him over till the next day.

He knew that the meeting was due to start at 7.30, and he guessed that someone would be there early to open up and get things ready. So the ideal time for him to be around would probably be enough past seven so as not to interfere with preliminary setting up, but not so much past seven as to be when most of the members would be arriving. Catch any early-comer on their way in was probably best - pot-luck and hope that the fates were in a good mood. It perhaps wasn't the most cunning and complex of plans, but then sometimes simple is best.

Ralph picked some of the remaining celery string from his teeth and prepared to peel and core his apple. In better times he would eat the apple whole, but these weren't among the better times and even Ralph had difficulty enjoying the soggy bruised bits, which in this case formed the greater part. Still, he counted himself lucky to be eating at all and as he tucked in to what was left, he cheered himself with visions of a nice cup of tea and a biscuit. They may be secondary matters in the greater scheme of things, but they were good and sustaining dreams to have in the efforts to while away the hours.

****

Mr Material stood up and, with one sweeping glance, took in every faery in the bar and snug. Even those who thought that they were safely out of view, could feel the glance through the walls and furniture. It was clear to all that he was used to having the undivided attention of his audience.

"Mr Burr and I have a tale to tell. My tale is long and complex." There was a shuffle of bottoms on seats as those in the room who had not had time to refill their glasses looked anxiously at the dregs left behind and wondered if it would be acceptable, or even safe, to go to the bar. Listening to a long and complex tale with no Innkeepers Choice for company filled many of them with dread, and it seemed unlikely that any one of them would be prepared to be the first one to risk getting up and becoming a distraction or interruption. Mr Material continued, while slowly sitting down again,

"And so, if anyone needs to refill their glasses, now might be a good time to do it."

Satisfied murmurings swiftly gave way to noisy clatterings of chairs being moved and grunts of faeries being elbowed as a long queue formed at the bar. Barry, Trixie and Damon worked hurriedly to meet the sudden demand and within a few minutes the room was settled and silent again. Barry had been impressed by the gravitas and authority that naturally exuded from Mr Material. To that he now added diplomacy. 'Clever move, Mr Material!' he mouthed silently to himself looking over at the two strangers. To his dismay and discomfort he saw Mr Material silently mouth 'I know' back in Barry's direction. Barry came out in a cold sweat and leant on the bar for support as the stranger stood up once again.

"My story begins a long way back in time and place. Mr Burr has been with me for the last, most important part of it, and he it is who will now take over from me to put you in the picture." He sat down again and gestured to his companion to get up and continue. His companion had clearly not expected this turn of events, and rose slowly in a confused manner, looking at Mr Material for some form of guidance and support. But Mr Material was looking round at the faces of the assembled faeries, taking in the manner of their response and feeling the vibrations of their emotions. His eyes met those of Eric O'Shy and there was the slightest of pauses before his gaze moved on further round the room.

Mr Burr realised that this was another test of his ability to deal with the kind of unexpected situation for which his travelling companion had been training him. He knew enough to clear all thoughts of inability or negativity from his mind and let the moment lead him along the correct path with the right words.

"Friends!" he began, "I hope we can call you friends, even so soon after first meeting you, because we have come in friendship." He paused for a moment while he gathered his thoughts. "We have been travelling for a long time, though I should add that my companion has been travelling for far longer than I. I will have to leave him to tell you his stories from before we met, but I can tell you of the time that we have been making our way here from across the country. We have an important reason for being here with you – one that I have only just realised the significance of. But first I must tell you where I come from and how I came to visit you."

Barry noted that Mr Burr had his eyes closed from after his first sentence. It was almost as if he were in a trance, or willing himself to be so. What he also noted was that, although Mr Burr was not the main attraction, everyone, without exception, was hanging on his words.

"By trade, I am a doctor. I studied hard in the decades of my youth to understand the world around me and the way that fae folk interacted with it. I believed that the way to help my fellow gnomes and other faeries was through medicine. Don't get me wrong, magic is fine in its place, but it doesn't work for ever, and when it wears off it just leaves you weak and beyond help. Too much magic is bad for your overall health. I joined a local group of medics and became a member of the NES[48]. I was contented there and had no desires to leave. It was my home and vocation. Then one day, a tall stranger walked in looking pale and weak. No-one knew him or anything about him. He told us that he had travelled a long way on an important journey, and that he did not have much further to go, but had contracted a fever and needed help. He said that it had come on recently and was getting worse very quickly. My colleagues suspected magic, but I felt sure there was a more natural explanation – and in any case, magic is merely the manipulation of natural processes for other purposes."

---

[48] The National Elf Service, obviously, though Burr was also affiliated to Gnome Help, Pixielixir, Sprite Welfare and numerous other medical agencies that were also non-exclusive and free at the point of delivery.

Robin and Trixie, who had been known to resort to using magical powers, though only when absolutely necessary, looked at each other and nodded agreement.

"I carried out many tests and gave him a full examination. During this time, he got weaker and weaker until I felt sure that some kind of poison was in his system. I gave him a common antidote and it calmed the fever to the extent that I could let him sleep. I stayed with him for many days, and when he was sufficiently rested, I gave him fluids and food. When he was strong enough and in control of all his faculties, he told me his story – which perhaps he will share with you later. He then asked me to accompany him on the rest of his journey. He didn't tell me where he was going or how long it would take, and until that moment I had had no desire to leave my home and friends, or my work. But somehow, I knew I had to join him, and we left that very night. I'd never before slept anywhere but in a comfortable bed. Since we left my home, I've slept under the stars, or clouds – in the open, under trees, beside streams, in barns and old buildings. I've had no bed and sometimes I've got very wet. We've walked everywhere and seen many places. I didn't know our destination or our purpose until we arrived in Whimbury – and I've never felt more alive or in tune with my surroundings. I know that we have a mission here, and I know that some folk that we have met along the way have been willing to help us get here – others have been suspicious and less helpful."

"Can we ask questions?" A less than confident hand was raised from a table in the snug, as Percy shouted out across the floor.

Mr Burr seemed to be shaken out of his train of thought and once again looked across to Mr Material for confirmation, or otherwise. Mr Material smiled and made to stand. Mr Burr breathed a sigh of relief and made to sit.

"Of course you may!" His voice was now silky smooth and most reassuring in its gentleness. Mr Material could lay on the charm when it was necessary, and as his turn to amplify the story had arrived, he deemed it necessary. "And what is your question, Mr Grumplet?"

Percy was disconcerted, dismayed, disturbed and several other disses all at once.

"Ah! Well! I haven't got one as yet, or at least I hadn't, it was more about whether we could ask questions as a general principle, but as it happens, I do have one now." Percy felt a cold sweat coming on, which was unfamiliar territory for him.

"Which is?" Mr Material exuded patience.

"Which is…. How did you know my name? Have we met?"

"That is two questions, Mr Grumplet, but I will answer both. The answer to your second question is no, we have never met. The answer to your first question is that we are here because this village is the home of the Crossover child, and the story of the birth of the child has been spread to many, many parts over the past two years. Your part in the story is well chronicled and since Mr Burr and I arrived in the village a few days ago, I have been watching and listening to what has been going on, and I was extremely keen to try to find out who you were. And I did."

Lancelot Happling raised his hand. Immediately, Mr Material looked in his direction and gestured for him to ask his question.

"So is your visit all to do with the Crossover child?" Lancelot was more comfortable in his role as quizmaster, but he felt a compulsive urge to discover more about the strangers.

"Yes, it is. It is vital that you all understand the value of the child here in this village at this point in time – not just for yourselves but for all faekind. My travels began long before I met Mr Burr in the circumstances he outlined to you. This part of my journey ends here, but your journey into the unknown future of faeries and humans the world over, is just beginning. I am here to set you on your way."

Trevor Stout raised his hand urgently and waved it wildly in the direction of Messrs Burr and Material. Mr Material recognised Trevor and invited his question.

"Please may I go to the toilet?" Trevor was nothing if not polite.

"Indeed you may." Messrs Material and Burr watched as Trevor ambled at top speed with a legs-crossed gait. As he passed their table, Mr Material called out, "And how is your hand?"

Trevor halted momentarily and waved his hand in free and easy fashion. "It's absolutely fine, thankyou. Oh dear." He smiled and grimaced in quick succession and then ran smartly to the toilet.

"Before I met Mr Burr," Mr Material continued, "I had travelled all around the world to hear the stories of the birth of the Crossover child. I was preparing for the time when I would meet her myself. You'd be surprised at how far the stories had reached and how varied they had become in the detail of the events of that day. But one thing remained constant. There was a hope for the future. One day, before her seventh birthday, a situation will arise that will have major implications for both faeries and humans. It will be here in this village and it will need the child to complete the Crossover in order to deal with it. If not, the lives of the fae and human communities in this place will change irrevocably and separate for all time. And not only in this place, for the child is that hope for the future across the world as we know it. She must be ready – that situation, that moment could come at any time. She and you must be fully prepared for that moment, even if it is in the next few days or months. Yes?" Mr Material looked over to Eric O'Shy who sat in his corner with his hand raised high in the air.

"I have a question." There was an element of surprise around the room. Eric was normally diffident and said little.

"Then ask it, by all means." Responded Mr Material, who remained standing.

"Perhaps not so much a question as a concern." Eric stood up and looked straight at Mr Material, giving him a stare the like of which that no-one had seen from Eric before. "I've read the Fae chronicles and histories a lot over the last couple of years – it's come in useful for the weekly quizzes here." He smiled around the room and he received many smiles in return from grateful quiz team members, and others who recognised and respected his knowledge. "All the writings seem to indicate that the event you talk about will come about close to her seventh birthday. If she is put under pressure to reach her full potential too early, surely there is a danger that she will not be ready, and that to try to fulfil her Crossover destiny could be fraught with danger, and a high risk of failure. Where would we be then? Where would she be? And how will we know which situation is the right one for us to call upon her to act in the way that only she can? I'm sorry, I've ended up with three questions, but I would like answers please, because your story and vision of the future could lead to disaster if the girl is asked to do too much too soon."

Mr Material did not change his expression all the while that Eric was speaking. He replied only after a long pause during which he appeared to be considering very carefully the points made by Eric. There had been a degree of head nodding while Eric spoke and Mr Material was clearly aware of the need for a measured response. At last he spoke.

"Your concerns are interesting and valid." If it were possible, his tone was even more serious that it had been earlier. "And you deserve answers to your final questions – you shall have them. I am familiar with the Chronicles, myths and legends of our peoples. They tell me that if the Crossover were to fail then we will be in a position whereby the chance of any kind of partnership between faeries and humans to ensure the future of this planet will have gone forever. That would be nothing short of a catastrophe. If it fails, the child will be left with a number of supernatural powers that she can use from time to time, but she will have an unending sense of a lack of fulfilment, and who knows how that will affect her through her developing years. And how will you know what is the right situation and time for the event to take place? All I can say is that you will know. You will see something that affects both yourselves and the humans in a way that is both intimate and life changing, and which will only be resolved by an action that is unprecedented. Those are my answers." Mr Material sat down, leaving the floor to Eric.

"Thank you for your answers, Mr Material. But it seems to me that we are in danger of risking everything if we act too early. That is all I am saying. As I understand it, the Crossover ceremony was only completed at the last possible moment, but it was completed successfully. I believe the same will happen when her time finally comes, and we should not be sidetracked by "red minnow"[49] events in the meantime." Eric sat, picked up his reading matter and settled back into his corner with a deep breath.

There was a prolonged silence as the two rooms took in the significance of what Mr Material had said along with the implications of the final exchange of views. No-one seemed prepared to be the first to make a move. Eventually, Mack Stout rose and strode purposefully across the floor. He pronounced loudly to the whole audience.

---

[49] Similar to 'red herring', but more faery-sized.

"Well, that gives us something to think about. Now I'm off to check on Trevor to see if he's OK. Barry, another Innkeeper's Choice for me please, and the usual for Trev." He continued his strut towards the toilets, and allowed himself the luxury of a swift wink to Barry as he passed the bar. Barry smiled. There were times, increasingly more often as it happened, when he was grateful to have Mack around. He was unquestionably the best 'embarrassed-bubble burster' in the village, and every village needed one.

Chapter Eleven

MIRANDA GOT UP FROM THE table and walked to the front door. Outside Evadne stood with a bag containing tea bags, a jar of coffee, a bottle of milk, a carton of non-dairy 'milk', and a selection of biscuits. It also contained pencils, ballpoint pens and a large notepad. Evadne was nothing if not organised, and she recognised and accepted the limitations of her fellow committee members. None could be trusted to remember refreshments and no-one had ever offered to take on the role of secretary on an official basis. The position tended to rotate on a meeting-by-meeting basis with varying degrees of competence, legibility and clarity. Miranda was still, after three attempts over two days, trying to make sense of the last couple of items from the previous minutes as set down by Fred Butterworth.

"Just checking that you're still OK for this evening?" Evadne was greatly looking forward to having a relatively young and very intelligent companion on the committee. Secretly she was hoping for good things from Miranda – including, at some time in the future, maybe the secretary role. Also secretly, Miranda knew what Evadne was thinking and, mindful of her family commitments and Will's concerns, had no intention of taking on any further responsibilities just yet.

"Yes, I'm fine. Just ploughing through the last of the minutes that Fred wrote up. It's a bit of a struggle I'm afraid – not knowing all the background."

"It would be a bit of a struggle even if you did know it all. Fred is not the most succinct or precise of note-takers, in case you hadn't already noticed. But don't let it put you off, all will be revealed later tonight when we get round to matters arising – which is usually much later than I would like. They're a very willing bunch, but easily distracted. See you in a few minutes?" Evadne walked back to the garden gate, followed closely by Miranda who enjoyed taking the early evening air.

"Yes, give me about 10 minutes and I'll be setting off – all raring to go." Miranda ambled back to the house, taking in the smell of the early roses and lavender. Neither she nor Evadne had noticed Ralph leaning against a tree at the edge of the woods opposite. He was just close enough to hear their exchange and was now fully prepared to carry out his plan. He waited a few minutes and then crossed the road, grateful that all was quiet and that no other Parish Council committee members were yet on their way. He sat on the pavement close to the wall of Over Cross View and waited, hoping that, to Miranda, 10 minutes actually meant 10 minutes. He was not disappointed. Just two or three minutes after he had sat down, he heard the door to the cottage open and then shut again. He rested his head on his raised knees and went over the planned opening gambit in his head one final time.

Miranda wandered slowly down the front path, taking in the plants, shrubs and weeds resplendent in the early evening sunlight. She dead-headed an early rose and threw the ex-bloom expertly into the rockery, behind the succulents, before opening the front gate. As she closed it behind herself, she turned and stopped suddenly. Ralph sat on the floor a few metres away, looking up at her with his arms wrapped around his knees in an attempt to make himself appear as small, insignificant and harmless as possible. He gave her a mixed toothy and toothless smile, and spoke while he still had the element of surprise.

"Don't suppose you could spare the price of a cup of tea, could you?" Over the years he had perfected a look that managed to combine a potent mix of serenity and gentle pleading. Few outside of the naturally aggressive and self-interested in society could refuse it, and Miranda was one of the many, not the few. Ralph continued.

"I've only had water for the last few days, and I could murder a nice warm, milky cup of tea – with a bit of sugar to keep the energy levels up." Ralph managed to talk whilst still smiling, almost certainly aided by the gap in his teeth.

Miranda paused while her brain computed the mixed messages that were feeding it. After a few error codes and lost connection moments, she placed Ralph firmly in Whimburton and conjured up an image of him walking through the park and bowing to Milly. But what was he doing in the village? How did he know where they lived? Did he know where they lived – or was it a total coincidence? Part of the same coincidence maybe that placed him right outside her gate? And if she gave him the price of a cup of tea, where would he get one? Not in the village certainly, and it was much too late for him to get back to town. She paused again, engaging him in eye contact. She saw a harmless, needy human. He saw a kind, caring human. Phase one of his plan was working out quite perfectly, and Miranda was finally ready to break into conversation.

"I'm afraid there's nowhere to buy a cup of tea in Whimbury and I'm on my way out, but if you don't mind sitting through part of a boring Parish Council meeting, I'm sure we could make you a cuppa - and throw in a biscuit too, I shouldn't wonder. Would that do for now?" Miranda turned her head to a 45 degree angle, a habit she seemed to have picked up from Milly.

Ralph, who had maintained his fixed smile until this point, allowed his eyes to sparkle to emphasise his pleasure at the offer. He made to get up and was surprised to find Miranda offering her hand to help him. He wiped his own hand on the cleanest part of his clothing that he could find and gratefully accepted the assistance. In truth, he was stiff from huddling up against the wall and needed support. Once on his feet, he let go of her hand and stretched. In mid-stretch a fascinating thought came into his head – one that made him smile in a much more natural manner. Miranda noticed.

"What are you smiling about, Ralph? It is Ralph isn't it? I think that's what people have been calling you in town."

"That is indeed my name." Ralph looked her in the eye. "And I owe you thanks on two grounds. Firstly, for taking notice of me and my name in the metropolis we know as Whimburton." He paused.

"And the second?" Miranda started walking towards the Village Hall, conscious of the need not to be late for her first meeting. Ralph hobbled alongside.

"And the second is for helping me up. I was smiling because I remembered the last time any human being actually touched me. It was two years ago and it was contact considerably less gentle than yours. I can barely remember the last kind touch. You know, it's really rather pleasant – I shall treasure the moment." They strolled the final few metres in silence.

****

Barry, Trixie and Damon flitted around the bars picking up towers of empty beer glasses and returning them to the bar, where Robin made himself useful rinsing them through in the sink. Ever since the last patron had left the Royal Oak, not a word had been spoken. Each knew his and her role, and the well-oiled bar-staff machine had slipped effortlessly and quietly into gear. Beer-soaked table mats were thrown expertly into the recycling bin[50] from all corners of the bar. Each of them had damp cloths attached to their shoes by elastic straps that give the floor a preliminary wipe-over as they glided between tables. From the cellar, Junior could be heard checking the barrels, numerous feet clattering rhythmically over the metal bands interspersed with occasional rasping sounds that signified the hoovering up of algae.

As she brought the final few glasses back to the bar, Trixie at last broke the silence.

"So what did you all make of the discussion this evening?" As she tossed her opening gambit into the room, she ambled off behind the bar to collect a mop and bucket.

The ensuing lack of response was accompanied by a collective re-grouping of the remaining assembled minds each waiting for one of the others to come up with a sensible reply – or indeed any reply. In the end, it fell to the eldest and therefore, by default, most senior of the group to set the conversation in motion.

"Not sure really!" Barry paused in the vain hope that someone else would take up the baton. As he himself had expected, he was forced to continue.

"I don't know if I'm more worried about the responsibility that Mr

---

[50] Employment opportunities in workplaces that recycled materials collected from Inns and Hostelries were greatly sought after, involving as they did extracting the alcohol before processing the resultant base substances. Recycling the alcohol itself was not a problem experienced in fae circles.

Material has placed upon us, or the doubt that Eric threw onto the whole process. Mr Material and his friend seem authoritative and generally aware of stuff going on around us that we haven't even noticed. But Eric is very knowledgeable and clearly understands the Crossover legend much better than anyone else in the Parish. I just don't know who to believe." Barry was genuinely perplexed and, for once, could not see the way forward. Damon leapt in with uncharacteristic assurance.

"Mr Material said we'd know the right time to intervene and help Milly with whatever it is that she needs to do. That sounds a bit easier said than done!"

Damon, for all his relatively simplicity, was a good listener and thought more carefully about things than he was generally given credit for. Robin threw his tea-towel over his shoulder and weighed in with a carefully measured response.

"I agree!"

"Agree with what, exactly?" Barry sat at a table and raised his feet so that Trixie could mop the floor under him.

"I agree that we might well know the right time to intervene, and that it sounds easier said than done." Robin reverted to drying the last glass for a second time, in order to be seen to be doing something productive and to try to gather some thoughts together.

"Thanks Robin, that pretty much clears everything up nicely. Do you have anything to add Trixie?" Barry knew his most reliable and bright bar staff member would not have raised the subject without having something worthwhile to say about it.

"For some reason I kind of trust Mr Material, and Mr Burr seems harmless and honest. I can't explain why, but I think they are right to encourage us to prepare Milly as early as we can just in case she needs to be ready sooner rather than later. It can't do any harm can it? I mean for her to be ready, even if she's not needed till near her seventh birthday as Eric suggests. Eric may well be right of course, as you say, he is very knowledgeable, but why risk waiting when we don't need to? Just saying!" Trixie said all this without looking up or ceasing to mop the floor – until the very end, when she very pointedly gazed in turn at each of her colleagues in the bar. She learned this disarming tactic from her mother, who said little but made each word count.

Suitably disarmed, the others tried to pull together a rational answer to her very reasonable question. Damon was first to respond.

"I know I'm not likely to be asked to be in the group that will train Milly for her important role here – in fact, I still haven't met her." He paused in case his last point was taken as disqualifying him from speaking further. He took the following silence to mean that he should continue. "But what I do know from my experience here at the Royal Oak is that it is always better to be ready for something that may not happen than not to be ready for something that does. Whether that be opening a new barrel of Innkeeper's Choice before the old one runs out, or washing up some dirty glasses towards the end of the evening in case of a late charge to the bar, or standing well away from the door to the toilet at the end of a quiz round, or…."

"Yes, I get the picture Damon." Barry cut him off kindly. "And I think you're right. What Eric says may well come to pass, but we really should start preparing Milly now. There's no excuse for delay and, in fact, no reason to put it off. It must happen one day, and we – and Milly – must be ready to seize that day when it comes. I know that Robin and Trixie have gained her trust, and that she already appreciates a lot of what we do here, but now we have to move on to a different level of understanding altogether. So, we must decide how we start this next stage off, and who is to do what."

A decision having been made, Robin felt in more secure territory. He was essentially an 'ideas' sprite and once his brain had set off in a familiar direction, he was difficult to stop.

"Right!" He began. "Firstly, the girl knows all about us, who we are, what is special about the Royal Oak, and how we interact with the animals around here. She sees us clearly, and she can already follow fae language and engage in basic animal conversations. That's pretty impressive for one so young. Her parents suspect that she is unusual, though I doubt they yet know exactly why. They are kind and decent folk, so she'll know the concepts of right and wrong – we need to build on that. It's going to take something pretty dramatic to propel her to the actual Crossover itself, so she'll also need to understand what's important and what's not, and how to identify when a magical intervention is needed. That's asking a lot of a seven-year-old human."

"Or a five- or six-year old even." Trixie leant on her mop. "Whilst I would like to hope that Eric has the right and sensible approach, if Mr Material is right we might have to prepare for the event to take place much earlier. We've already agreed that. So, hard as it is to imagine such a situation, we have to plan to get a five-year old child ready for probably the most momentous event in both fae and human history since…" She hesitated in order to regroup her rapidly developing thoughts, "… since…since… Gaia created our universe".[51]

Trixie became aware of three sets of eyes focused very intently upon her, and resumed mopping in a highly agitated and exaggerated manner.

"Well that just about wraps up the discussion, I think." Barry felt inclined to reach an executive decision. "We need to get started on an accelerated training programme. But it needs to be done in a gentle and thoughtful way. We don't want to lose her trust by bombarding her with too much, too soon. We'll need to decide what are the key matters for her to understand first and what could be left till the end – in case the end turns out to be, in actual fact, before the end, as it were. I trust I make myself clear."

"Crystal clear, Baz". Robin sounded a little less than certain. "Apart that is from that bit at the end about the end not being the end. That was just a teeny bit obscure."

"Right, well to put it another way, we don't know when the end will be so we need to make sure that she is ready to do what is required in the end."

"Which end, Baz?" Robin was genuinely confused. As was Damon, who deemed it best to keep quiet, especially as it was he who had started the discussion off.

"The very end – which may come earlier than the end we had originally planned for. Anyway, the sooner we start the better, and if we end up ending the training before the eventual end, so much the better. So, who do we think is the best person to be in charge of all this?"

Seeing a way out of the conversation all three of his friends responded instantaneously.

"You", "You", and "Percy", came back the responses. The latter came from Trixie and threw Barry off his guard. He and the other two turned to face

---

[51] For more background on this consult the "Reader in Fae Chronicles, Theology and Folklore".

Trixie, still nonchalantly mopping the floor in the snug, with a combination of quizzical, astonished and confused expressions. In the case of Barry, all three were on the same face – his. Faced with three open and silent mouths, Trixie began to explain.

"I don't want to upset you Barry," she began, "but I think Robin and I are getting on well with her, and to have you alongside would just be another voice saying basically the same things. Percy is older and has a different perspective – or percyspective even?"

She giggled to herself and paused to see if she had managed to create a somewhat more relaxed atmosphere. She hadn't, and so she continued.

"I just think that Percy is reliable and, underneath the dour exterior, has a common sense and a genuine concern that would be a helpful counterpoint to the rest of us. Maybe add something a bit different – something she might need one day?"

The silence continued as Robin and Damon turned their gaze towards Barry.

"Much as I find myself surprised to say this," he began, "I think you may have hit upon something very profound there. I'm not in the slightest upset, just wondering how we might persuade Percy. It's quite a responsibility."

"Leave that to me," said Trixie, "I have an idea – unless anyone else would rather take it on."

The other three all began whistling softly and made themselves useful launching into unnecessary jobs around the bar.

Trixie put down her mop and moved to the door. "Right, I'll get started."

******

On the fast train from London to Whimburton[52], Jessica Huntly-Phillips had two piles of papers on the table in front of her. She had sifted out some of the more enlightening offerings from the conference, which were contained in the smaller of the two piles. The much larger pile was destined for the nearest recycling bin at Whimburton station. Her presentation had gone down well,

---

[52] Or more accurately, the slightly faster than the slow train, given that Whimburton was not a major metropolitan hub.

she felt. There had been some interesting questions following her paper on the effects of the latest government housing forecasting method, and the rapid response of her District Council to its implications.

She had also spent an 'interesting' lunch break talking to Robert Hancock, one of the delegates who, in addition to being a director of one of the larger housebuilders in the region was also a resident of Whimingham, neighbouring village to Whimbury. He had stressed to her the rationale behind avoiding the allocation of any more housing in Whimingham, on account of it being already fully built up, and also that the local Bridge Club had a number of very influential members who, coincidentally, were heavily involved in the village conservation group.

Jessica was making copious notes in advance of her next meeting with Jason and Emily. Her networking with housing developers from around the country had always proved fruitful, which is why she persisted with attending the meetings and being noticed. Some of her contemporaries conscientiously avoided any contact with them, while others were transparently hostile. She, however, felt that she was gleaning essential background knowledge and was seen as someone sensitive to their needs and aspirations. It was a tightrope that she walked expertly.

She enjoyed the periodic train rides to and from London. They gave her precious time to herself to think things through, mull over reports, and prepare for meetings. And she could avoid annoying phone calls by claiming that the train must have been going through an area with no signal, or a tunnel, or that her pre-booked ticket was, for some unaccountable reason, in the 'quiet' carriage.

Today, there was no-one sitting on the opposite side of her table and she had the luxury of being able to spread out her paperwork. She had a map of the District open in front of her with a number of circles and arrows, and scribbled notes linking the two. Had there been anyone sat in close proximity who was both interested in her map and able to decipher her appalling handwriting, they would have perhaps noticed the large circle around the village of Whimbury, the arrow between Whimbury and Whimburton, and the words "strong connection" and "high potential" written either side of the arrow.

******

A startled and cavernously deep silence enveloped the village hall as Miranda walked in with Ralph. All talk of last night's TV, tonight's TV, tomorrow's TV, and the next episodes of each programme the following week, instantly halted. This was nothing less than what Miranda had expected and she was ready to explain while she took off her coat.

"This is Ralph, he's homeless and spends most of his time in town, but he's here now and in need of something to eat and drink, so I promised him a cuppa and a biscuit. Hope that's OK – he won't interfere, he can just sit in the corner and I'll sort him out afterwards." She motioned to Ralph to follow her into the kitchen.

"That's if he can cope with the level of excitement of a Parish Council meeting enough to stay till the end." Evadne spoke out. She had long since ceased to be surprised by anything that Miranda could conjure up, and smiled at the thought of the effect the presence of Ralph might have on the proceedings.

"I'm sure he will have suffered worse in his time – isn't that true Ralph?" She glanced at the assembled group and continued into the kitchen.

Ralph also glanced at the assembled group and then muttered softly as he pursued Miranda. She thought he said "I doubt it very much", but she couldn't be sure. The kettle had only recently boiled and she hurriedly made a cup of tea for herself and Ralph.

"Milk, sugar?" She looked across the kitchen at Ralph with a bottle of milk in one hand and a bowl of sugar in the other.

"Both, please." Ralph had not been a position to say 'no' to anything at all offered in the way of edible substances for some time.

Miranda turned back to the teapot and smiled at his politeness. As she did so, she remembered once again the way that he had greeted Milly from afar with a deferential touch of his forelock. There was something in his manner that pointed very clearly to an interesting back-story.

"I'm afraid we only appear to have either digestive or custard cream biscuits – not very exciting I'm afraid. What would you like?" Miranda handed him the cup of tea and pushed a plate of biscuits in his direction.

"I really can't decide." Ralph waved his hand over the plate, first over one type of biscuit and then over the other. "Do you think anyone would mind if I tried one of each?"

Miranda laughed. "I'll tell you what. You take one of each for now and hide another couple in your pocket for later. I won't tell anyone, and there's plenty here. If anyone's counted them it will be Evadne and she won't care one little bit who eats what."

Ralph eagerly accepted Miranda's invitation and then carefully held his cup of tea as he meandered back over into the corner of the room and sat on one of the spare chairs, watched all the way by the rest of the Parish Council members. As he sat, he became aware of the number of pairs of eyes trained upon him. He raised his cup with a clear and grateful "Cheers – and thankyou everyone", and then took a very delicate bite out of his custard cream. Miranda placed the plate of remaining biscuits in the middle of the table and sat down on the seat reserved for her next to Evadne. She noticed the other Council members looking awkwardly at the plate and each other, so she pointedly leaned over and picked up a biscuit, popping it straight into her mouth and biting into it as noisily as she could without appearing common.

As Miranda continued her provocative display of indelicate eating habits by dunking the rest of the biscuit into her tea, Evadne called the meeting to order. And when Evadne called to order, order was what she got.

"Right, we are all here, so there will be no apologies. Minutes of the last meeting anyone? Correct record? That is if anyone has been able to decipher Fred's 'summary' of the proceedings." All hands immediately rose in agreement, except for Fred's, who wasn't at all sure he'd got everything right.

"Minutes approved, with one abstention." Evadne was nothing if not speedily efficient, and hurriedly moved on to introduce Miranda.

"You will, of course, all know Miranda Hope from Over Cross View. I've invited her to join us as a co-opted member to give us a different dimension on village matters, especially that of the proposed housing, which is the main topic for discussion this evening. She has also, valiantly, offered to take minutes on this occasion so that she can listen in and get the feel of our meetings, and who's who and who thinks what. And she can lob a few hand-grenades into the proceedings to keep us on our toes. So, a warm welcome to you, Miranda."

A brief smile later and Evadne was ready to plunge into the main topic. Miranda had heard a few rumours about the Council's plan to allocate some land in Whimbury – and other villages – for housing, but in truth, she knew very little of the actual proposals or procedures. And so she listened, and took copious notes of those relevant parts of the discussion that took place between the analysis of TV programmes, and the topping up of cups of tea. She was pleased that Evadne and Eileen included Ralph in the top-ups, and that occasionally one or other of the committee would glance over to him while making a point, as if to include him in the proceedings, even though such moments were often regarding televisual moments that he would not have seen. But it showed her that, deep down, they were all basically kindly people who just needed time to overcome their long-standing pre-conceptions about what constituted an acceptable appearance and standard of cleanliness. Ralph, for his own part, kept quiet and listened carefully for any information that he could profitably feed back to Barry and the others.

What Miranda and Ralph gleaned from the meeting in their own separate ways was that the Council had previously sent round to all residents a newsletter explaining that it had to find land for a lot more housing around the District, and that Whimbury was currently looking like a prime candidate to take a large amount of that housing. The committee had little to say on the matter, despite Evadne's promptings, but Miranda did manage to take time off from jotting notes to say that she hoped the council would ensure plenty of cheaper houses to attract new young families. Eileen agreed that that would be far preferable to having fewer big houses just for the relatively well-off, who might not actually live in the village all the time anyway, or even if they did, who tended not to have much interest in the existing community anyway. Evadne said that the main thing to avoid was turning Whimbury into another Whimingham, and that Miranda's and Eileen's point was well made. It was minuted, unlike some of the other comments, which often strayed off the point into issues that related more closely to TV schedules.

At the end of the meeting, when the rest of the committee had raced home to catch up on the latest episodes of whatever it was that took their fancy,

Miranda helped Evadne and Eileen to wash up the cups while Ralph stacked the chairs in order to make himself useful. He also helped to finish off the few surplus biscuits by adding a couple more to the stash in his pocket. He worked slowly and quietly so that he could hear what was being discussed in the kitchen.

"If they need as many houses as they say they do, it's highly likely that part of Hill Farm will be a prime site." Eileen had been following events very closely. "But to get to the land, they'd need to go through our farm, and I'm not having that. I'll do everything in my power to stop them using our lane. Andrew, my brother, is a lawyer and I'll enlist his help if needs be."

"Well, I don't know what they can and can't do on that score, but if they can't get through your farm, the only alternative would be to go through the wood, and the council would never allow that, would they?" Evadne didn't have a great deal of faith in the council at the best of times, and she betrayed her lack of trust with a hesitancy that was uncharacteristic.

"Surely not," Miranda had not yet had Evadne's depth of experience of the ways of the council, and found such possibilities to be almost unimaginable. "The only ways through would be to the side of Will's workshop, which would be a very long way round, or by chopping down the Royal Oak?"

"Anything is possible in this day and age, Miranda. It is up to us to try to ensure that such things are not allowed to happen. That's why I'm so glad you've come along to the Committee. The others have their heart in the right place, but they nearly all still believe in the inherent trustworthiness of politics and big business. I've tried to encourage them to always ask questions and dig beneath the surface, but it's an uphill struggle. We could be in this struggle for a long time." Evadne put the wet tea towels in her bag to take home and wash.

The three women walked through to the main hall where Ralph was busy looking round the notice boards.

"Anything interesting Ralph?" Miranda put her hand on his shoulder.

"I see you have a chess club that meets here. I used to play chess once, when I had people to play with. Quite enjoyed it."

"All a bit intense for me!" Evadne moved in to find out a bit more about him.

"And me in the end." Ralph gave a rueful smile. "I got expelled when instead of shaking hands when I lost, I upset the board. I was only annoyed with myself, but it's not the done thing." He changed the subject expertly. "I couldn't help hearing about the housing thing. And I see there's an exhibition of the new plans in Whimburton – I don't recollect seeing it, and I wander round quite a lot."

"We got a letter about it – as an interested local group. But I think there are plans and display boards in the foyer at the Council offices." Evadne motioned subtly to Miranda that it was time to encourage Ralph to leave and allow her to lock up.

"Oh, right! I'll perhaps have a look when I get back to town. And now I suppose you'll be needing to lock up. Thank you very much for the tea and biscuits – and the interesting discussions. Makes a nice change." He started to move towards the door.

"It's a pleasure. Maybe we'll see you again?" Evadne was genuine. He had been no bother and anyone who showed an interest in the affairs of the village couldn't be all bad.

Miranda followed Ralph to the door. As he went out, she stopped him.

"Have you anywhere to stay tonight? I'm sorry if its rude to ask, but just being nosy! If not, I'm sure we could find room for you." She looked him squarely in the eye.

"That's uncommonly kind you, and I really mean uncommon. But I'm fixed up tonight, thank you. I don't want to be a nuisance to anyone, because I might need another cup of tea and biscuit sometime. So, thank you very much and I hope I may catch up with you again soon. I think there may be some interesting things going on around here before very long. I'll keep my eyes and ears peeled for you all." And with that he gave a wave and disappeared down the road.

"Well, that was strange!" Miranda talked over her shoulder to Evadne and Eileen as they locked the door. She continued watching Ralph as he disappeared down the Hight Street.

"What was?" Evadne put the keys in her pocket and picked up her bags.

"He turned up my offer of accommodation and then said he thought some interesting things would be happening around here – and he appeared to offer to keep us informed of whatever he could find out. I may be wrong, but I have the feeling there's more to our Ralph than meets the eye."

The three women walked together down the road, discussing what had turned out to be a very unusual Parish Council meeting indeed.

****

The tall stranger and his friend Mr Burr sat on the edge of Whimbury Woods, close to where they had first encountered Ralph. As usual, the stranger was silent and Mr Burr was trying his utmost to train his senses to take in every experience offered by the environment around him. He looked and sniffed and listened. He sat with his hands raised to feel the wind and his mouth open to taste the atmosphere. All responses were fed into his other sensory perceptions. After a short while, he swallowed a large insect and spent the next few minutes trying desperately not to make a sound while going redder and redder in the face. The moment he felt ready to burst, a flask of water suddenly appeared in front of his face and he thankfully grabbed it. After a long slow gulp, the insect was washed down into his stomach and he could breathe again.

"When tasting the environment, it is important to keep your tongue up against the roof of your mouth. It opens the taste sensory buds and keeps unwanted organisms out." The stranger smiled at Mr Burr and took back his flask of water. "And you will learn that you don't need to keep your mouth open at all times – regular repeated testing will suffice, not unlike reptiles."

Mr Burr's breathing eased and he felt able to speak.

"I have so far still to go. Sometimes I worry that I will never get the hang of all this. Just when I think that I understand the mechanisms of sensing my surroundings, I end up with a coughing fit or some other embarrassing interlude." He lay back and sighed wistfully.

"You are doing very well. Don't be hard on yourself. You could practice these things for decades and at the last there will still be more to learn. I have been working on such matters for far, far longer than you, and I still pick up new techniques and abilities every day. Persevere my friend and you will progress, I promise you." He gave Mr Burr a brief, gentle and somewhat uncharacteristic touch on the shoulder as a gesture of support.

"How long are we staying here?" Mr Burr sat up again and ran his fingers roughly through his hair to fully wake himself up.

"Just until the human returns here. I know now that he is working closely with the local fae community and I think we have done all we can do at this time to mobilise them all in readiness for the final act of the Crossover process. Once I know he is back here, in his rather unusual home, and still playing his part, we can leave - for now. We will need to return nearer the time. Until then, I just have a few places to visit round the parish, to check on the human personnel and their homes and workplaces. Things here are very complex, and I need to understand the workings of the community clearly. When we come back, I must be prepared to do exactly what is necessary as quickly as possible." He paused, and his head raised imperceptibly as all his senses were instantly engaged.

"He is coming. We should go!" The stranger stood up and began to stride away. Mr Burr looked around, listened, sniffed, and opened his mouth – being careful to place his tongue up in the roof. He then shook his head sadly, and moved off to follow his friend across the fields in the direction of Hill Farm.

Chapter Twelve

TRIXIE WAITED UNTIL PERCY HAD disappeared in the direction of the Royal Oak before she walked to the front door of his cottage, took a deep breath and rang the bell. Suddenly, she began to question the belief that she had earlier had in her ability to persuade Percy to take on the training of Milly. Her plan depended very much on getting Percetta to agree that he was indeed the ideal person to do it, and then for the both of them to trap him in a pincer movement to crush any possible resistance. She had discounted the obvious tactic of asking Percy directly, but now, faced with the prospect of discussing it with Percetta, it was beginning to seem like the easier option. Percetta could, especially in public, be quite intimidating, though she could also, especially in private, be kind and charming. This was why Trixie had chosen to confront her in the comfort of her own home, in the hope of meeting with the kind and charming version.

The door opened and Percetta filled the doorway. She looked quizzically at Trixie and waited for an opening gambit. The opening, when it came, took the form of a couple of 'erms' followed by an 'ah', a 'right then', and a pause.

"Well out with it, girl." To activate the kind and charming Percetta, it was necessary to work hard at breaking down the historic bad-tempered traditions revered by all members of the Grumplet tribe. She continued to give Trixie the kind of look that made it impossible to 'get it out' without a monumental effort of will. Trixie mentally gave herself a slap on each cheek and stood tall, maximising her self-belief and willpower.

"There is something very important that I need to discuss with you." She focused extremely hard on looking Percetta squarely in the eye, and was surprised to see her momentarily confused.

"With me or Percy?" Percetta had grown used to being the partner of the unofficial head of the Grumplet tribe[53], and therefore normally something of a background figure – at least in the Royal Oak, where pecking orders remained important. Percy had to be seen to be authoritative in public, and she was content to encourage this scenario just as long as he knew his place in the home – which he did, and to which he acquiesced quite happily.

"With you, Mrs Grumplet. It's about Mr Grumplet, you see. We all believe he has a crucial role to play – another crucial role, I mean, of course, - in the Crossover process. You both did so much when Milly was born, and we think Mr Grumplet has more to do, but we need you to support us in getting him to agree. It really is most important, and you're just the person to start the ball rolling – as it were?" Trixie had blurted it all out in an attempt to let speed prevent the erosion of confidence. The tailing off of her story into a statement that required a concluding question mark might have undermined this, but Percetta was still processing the information.

Having done so, and been impressed by Trixie's sincerity, she stood aside and ushered her in.

"Then I suppose we'd better discuss this." She shut the door behind her and gestured to Trixie to move into the living room. Trixie walked ahead of Percetta and waited to be shown which chair to sit in. One chair was well-worn and 'comfortable' with a small table beside it, on which was a large pipe and smoking paraphernalia. Another chair was well-worn and 'comfortable' with a small table beside it, on which was knitting paraphernalia. Trixie guessed, correctly, that the third chair, looking little-used and purely functional, would be where she would sit, and she headed in that direction even as Percetta pointed to it. She sat and glanced around the cosy room, taking in the paintings, pottery and general bric-a-brac that made it a home.

"The last person to sit there, looking around as you're doing, was

---

[53] Until his recent retirement of course, in favour of Victor. However, transition of 'power' always takes time and involves teething problems, even in fae circles, and to many faeries in Whimbury Percy remained, de facto, the 'Godfather' – or more accurately, 'Gaiaparent'.

Egyptian[54], and she had an interesting proposition for Percy as well." Percetta made herself comfortable in her chair and was about to pick up her knitting when she paused, sensing that the subject matter of Trixie's visit might demand her full attention.

"I wouldn't have troubled you if it wasn't really important, Mrs Grumplet."

"Call me Percetta!" Trixie allowed herself an inward sigh of relief as it became clear that she had gained Percetta's confidence.

"Thank you, Percetta." She emphasised the name. "Barry, Robin and I were talking about Milly, and the need to prepare her for whatever is needed for fulfilment of the Crossover prophecy. We've been getting to know her and introducing her to the animal fraternity around here, but we felt someone with a different approach and long-standing experience of the parish would be more able to take her to the next level of understanding. She's only young, of course, but she learns very fast, and we were hoping Mr Grumplet might help out in the wise-head department. We weren't sure how to approach him so I thought I'd run it past you first – see if you could offer any advice."

Percetta was silent, looking down at the floor and twiddling her thumbs. Trixie watched and waited. She focused on a picture, sitting proudly on the sideboard. It looked like a very old wedding portrait. The couple, whom she assumed to be Percy and Percetta,[55] seemed very happy. Eventually, Percetta spoke.

"Deep down he would be thrilled. The events around the child's birth were hair-raising for him, but he was proud of what he managed to achieve, and he learnt so much from the experience. Then again, it took a lot out him and he's not as young as he used to be, so he needs to be careful not to take on too much. What exactly would be expected of him?"

"Well, we've already established contact with Milly, as you know, but she needs to know so much more about Fae history and the ways that we operate.

---

[54] This was, of course, Nefer, the mid-wife fairy who assisted the beginnings of the Crossover process over two years previously. Everard was never allowed further into the cottage than the kitchen

[55] Though, in truth, with young gnomes it was difficult to tell the genders apart since roles – and appearances -, did not become fully formed until after relationships had been established for many decades and they were beginning to settle down.

I'm sure Mr Grumplet would be great with that. And she'd need to be prepared ready to cross over into being Fae when the situation first arose. That's a bit more complex, of course."

Percetta smiled. "A bit? Rather more than a bit I'd say, and rather more than Percy would normally be prepared to commit to. But, like you, I think he could do it, and would be good at it – though he'd never admit to that. It would seem too self-congratulatory and unbecoming of the Grumplet clan if it ever got out that he was enjoying it."

"I understand that, Mrs.....Percetta." Trixie corrected herself, and began to feel an unexpected bond with the older gnome. "And that was why I thought you might be the best person to raise the issue with him, in a tactful way shall we say."

"Yes, let's say that. It means a lot to me that you've come here with your proposition and, handled in the proper manner, it will mean a lot to Percy as well. Now let me know exactly what I need to do – I've a suspicion this is becoming rather urgent."

******

In the front room of the Potts' home, Kenneth was playing chess with Adrian when Evadne returned from the Parish Council meeting. Spot rushed to the door to greet her, and Adrian followed to check on whether she had brought back any left-over biscuits. Kenneth took the opportunity to remove one of Adrian's pieces from the board to see if he'd notice.

Evadne took Spot's face into her hands and stroked his chin with the accompanying coochie coos sounds that he hated so much. Still, it was a small price to pay for the strokes - and the treats that usually came soon after.

"Who's a lovely boy then?" Evadne patted the dog's head.

"Me!" said Adrian, "though I'd prefer a biscuit to a pat on the head."

"Sorry no spare biscuits today. It's been a rather unusual meeting – to say the least. All the biscuits were either eaten or taken away by this homeless person that Miranda brought in with her." Evadne spoke to Adrian, but loudly enough for Kenneth to hear also. She then walked down the hall followed by an excited Spot and a disappointed Adrian.

"Homeless person?" Kenneth rose from his chair and joined Evadne in the kitchen.

"Yes. Ralph his name was. Miranda said she had seen him before in town, but not around here at any time. Seemed very polite if a little odd. He was no trouble – just drank a cup of tea and ate a biscuit or two."

"Or three or four – or more?" Adrian was still disappointed.

"Well, we turned a blind eye to him having finished them off at the end of the meeting. He looked hungry. And like I said, he was very polite, and had quite a gentle voice. Miranda believes there's more to him than we might think. He picked up on the housing issue and seemed to offer to become our local Whimburton secret agent – or so Miranda thought." She pondered for a moment, letting the events of the evening sink in a little further, then got some treats for Spot, and some cheese out of the fridge for their supper.

"Even so, I'm not sure it's a good idea letting somewhat 'odd' folk just walk into the meeting like that. You've no idea what his intentions might be." Kenneth was more circumspect than his wife and less sanguine regarding Ralph merely being a bit 'odd'.

"If his intentions were dishonourable, I'm sure we would have got an inkling tonight. In any case, we've got Fred to look after us." She smiled at the thought. Kenneth did not.

"Fred? He's a bit frail for unarmed combat, and I don't have him down as a secret martial arts expert, nor would I expect him to do much damage with a table-tennis bat and ball, which I believe are the only weapons at his disposal." Kenneth cut a piece of mature cheddar and placed it carefully on a cheese cracker. Adrian sighed and went back to the living room.

"So, any more news on the housing issue?" Kenneth paused between bites to check on the progress of the main item on the night's agenda.

"Nothing concrete, though Eileen still thinks that Hill Farm will be put forward as housing land. We've suggested the land around the old station yard to try to be positive, but I suppose it depends on how much land they want. It's all actually quite worrying. I think there's a council meeting in the next couple of weeks to discuss the results of these consultations, so maybe we'll know a little more after that?"

Kenneth looked across the table at Evadne and could see that she was more concerned than she perhaps made herself out to be. And that made him concerned too. He sat back, savouring his cheese and not knowing quite what to say to make things better.

"I suppose it's all anyone's guess." Evadne feigned stoicism. "What do you think, Spot?" She handed him another treat.

Spot turned his head to a 45 degree angle and gave one of his most quizzical looks, as if contemplating the answer. From the living room, Adrian called out, "Who's pinched my knight?"

****

Ralph sat beside his bramble home, thinking and planning. He was waiting for Barry and needed to have clear in his mind what he was going to say. The information gained from the Parish Council was complex in its implications, and he didn't want this pre-arranged feedback meeting to go on any further into the night than it had to. Maybe he should have arranged it for the morning but if he had to leave early, which is what he suspected, it was better to have the next stage in the proceedings already agreed. He knew in his own mind what he had to do, and he would need faery help to achieve it. Whether Barry would go along with his scheme was another matter, so he had to present it in the appropriate way. Barry was a good and special friend, but at the end of the day he was a faery and Ralph was human. He couldn't take their bond for granted. So, he thought and planned.

By the time Barry arrived, Ralph had been through several versions of his script and had settled upon his preferred approach. Barry sensed his apprehension even before he sat down beside him. He smiled and watched as Ralph played with his fingers and displayed a slight twitch in his right shoulder.

"Problem Ralph?" Barry put on his most reassuring voice.

"I sense something big Bazza." He avoided Barry's gaze so as not to be deflected from his intended rendition. "The big item on the agenda of the meeting was proposals for more housing in the villages around the District, including this one – in fact, quite possibly, mainly this one. Apparently, there's been an exhibition in the Council Offices, which I haven't seen –

obviously, given that my general appearance and demeanour tends to debar me from such places. But if these rumours are true, it's going to mean big changes in Whimbury, and what that will mean for you and your faery community I can't say at the moment. But I will find out, I promise you. Don't want them developers messing about with your homes and business if we can stop it. So, I'll investigate, search, research – search again, all for gain, profit, not fit and proper, selfish not elfish, help one's elf, I'll help alright, got to make it right ….." Ralph was going seriously off script and Barry recognised the signs of stress. He climbed onto Ralph's shoulder and rode out the twitches while trying to calm him down.

"It's OK Ralph, take it easy. We love you for caring about us and for being one of the very few people who communicate with us. You're special to us, but we don't want you making yourself ill with worry. So, let's talk this through and try to get to bottom of what's happening and what might happen. OK?" Barry had had many experiences of Ralph going into meltdown when agitated, and he knew that it could be eased by gentle and supporting words.

Ralph shivered and twitched a little more and then began to breathe more slowly, deeply and deliberately, as Barry's words began to take effect. In a world where fellow humans rarely showed him kindness, or even simple acknowledgement of his presence or worth, his relationship with the faeries of Whimbury was of maximum importance. Constantly thinking through the major issues of life, which he did, without the ability to discuss them with anyone except himself, took its toll. Barry was a sounding board and a lifeline. A rare chance to find conclusions to his questions and soothe his troubled soul.

"Sorry, Bazza!" Ralph regained control. "I had all my words planned out, but I got a bit worked up, didn't I?"

"Just a bit, Ralph. But carry on now, we need to get this sorted – it's obviously important. Just remember that we're all with you and not against you."

"That's the point, Bazza. That's why I want to help you, but it's not going to be easy, and I think I'm going to need some faery assistance if I'm to play my part effectively. I have a plan – I think." Ralph was now calm enough to realise that he had to be quiet. Although it was highly unlikely that any humans would be out in the woods at this time of night, there was always the chance, and Ralph also knew that malevolent faeries existed and that they could be anywhere.[56]

"Tell me, Ralph. And tell me what you think you need us to do. If there's any way we can help we will – and in the event of a problem, there's always magic, though you know we can only use that in an emergency."

"Yes, I know that Bazza, and I've a horrible feeling that this could end as an emergency. I might just need that magic, or at the very least tricks and japes, because it's not easy for me to go anywhere I want, and even if I can, I can't easily merge into the background and be inconspicuous." Ralph threw up his hands for emphasis. "Hard though that may be to believe." He smiled a smile of greater security and confidence in himself and his friend.

Potential crisis averted, Barry climbed down from Ralph's shoulder and sat down beside him again.

"I do believe it, Ralph. Sorry, but I genuinely do. I've seen a good number of these humans, and listened to them and observed their habits, and I can honestly say, that I do believe you may have just the teensiest problem in being inconspicuous. I hope that doesn't offend you?"

"You're only re-stating the obvious Barry – it's the way of the world. Distrust the unfamiliar and anything not 'normal'. And that's me – not normal. I know it and I've got used to it. I'm 'away with the faeries' and thank – who is it? Oberon and Titania? – that I am."

"The very ones, Ralph. Not that we come across them very often – at least we don't think so. They have a habit of turning up somewhere when you're not expecting them and, very often, in a form you're not expecting either. So be careful what you say, and to whom. They'll know you've got a special relationship with us, and they could well choose to check you out."

"No problem, Bazza. I've nothing but gratitude to offer them if they do communicate with me. I'd be totally lost without my fae friends."

"Excellent. Now where were we?" Barry had become used over the years to losing the thread of a conversation with Ralph. Ralph could easily get

---

[56] Barry had told him all about the Nixies and the way that they had tried to sabotage the first stage of the Crossover process. Ralph had had the willies scared out of him.

sidetracked or over-emotional and lapse into an internal stream of consciousness. Fortunately, he could also generally be relied on to know where he was when he came back to where he had left himself.

"I've got a plan – I think!" Ralph focused his mind.

"Oh yes! So you have."

"I need to get to see what's in that exhibition, and if I can't get in, I might need someone else's eyes and ears. If they can pop in and out and get messages to me while I wait outside, I could tell them what to take note of. A human couldn't keep jumping around between inside and outside without someone being suspicious – or at least escorting them to the toilet, but a faery could. And, depending on what we find, I might also need someone to do a bit of jiggery pokery with their communications systems – only if absolutely necessary of course – I wouldn't want to involve your lot in anything bad, not without good reason."

"Perish the thought!" Barry was glad to see Ralph back on track and back in control of himself. Ralph was bright and very sharp – sometimes too sharp, but when he was clear in his mind, he knew exactly what he was doing and why he was doing it, and how it should be done best. "So, depending on when you need help, I should be able to spare Trixie for a while. She's pretty quick[57] and reliable."

"I don't know how long the exhibition goes on for, so I thought I'd go back tomorrow and find out. Any chance Trixie could come with me – and maybe Robin too? He's always got a trick up his sleeve." Ralph was very good at putting on an irresistible pleading face.

"Bit short notice Ralph, but I'm sure we can manage that. I'd like them back for evening opening time if possible." Barry was not very good at resisting irresistible pleading faces.

"You're on. Thanks, Bazza. I'll aim to leave around dawn before anyone is about to see me. Can you get a message to them before then? I can meet them at the Royal Oak if that's easiest."

"It probably is. Leave it with me and I'll make sure they're there. I doubt Robin will be very keen, but Trixie'll get him moving." And with that Barry

---

[57] In terms of the theory of relativity, she was relatively quick.

patted Ralph reassuringly on the finger and hurriedly left the bramble patch in the direction of Robin and Trixie's home on the edge of the wood.

****

In a small meeting room at the Council Offices, Jessica Huntly-Phillips sat down opposite Jason Jones and Emily Wilson to update them on her recent trip to London, and to let them update her on the progress of the Local Plan. As a way of leading the discussion from one topic into the other, she recounted her conversation with Robert Hancock.

"He made it clear that Whimingham village should not be burdened with any more housing because it was full." She looked up over the top of her glasses and her furrowed brow invited a response.

"Would I be far wrong if he also mentioned the local conservation group and the highly influential residents who run it?" Emily was not one to hide her true feelings, especially with regard to "The Hancock Gang" as they were known, unofficially, amongst many of her peer group. She braced herself for a somewhat unpleasant debate regarding the housing provision in the settlements surrounding Whimburton.

"Less far wrong, more adjacently correct." Jessica reverted back to her notes. Jason interjected.

"But you can see their point of view. It is a very pretty village and ….." Emily inter-interjected as so often was the case when the three of them sat down in meetings.

"Pretty, and expensive, and elitist, and privileged – but maybe that means they should be above the normal planning considerations that affect the rest of us mere mortals?" She looked over at Jessica, who was perhaps displaying just the slightest hint of a smile while checking over her notes. "There's no justification for treating Whimingham any differently from any other 'pretty' village around here – of which there are many…." She paused to stop herself from getting really angry. "Surely?" Emily hoped that she'd saved herself from crossing the line between righteous indignity and the unprofessional. Fortunately for her, Jason hadn't finished with his own point.

"As I was going to say, they do have a flourishing group of very active people who support a wide range of conservation measures that benefit the local community. They deserve some recognition, do they not?" He looked at a point in between Emily and Jessica to ensure that both knew that they were expected to take full account of his thoughts on the matter.

"Recognition, yes! Special favours, no!" Emily concluded her case for the prosecution and sat back.

"So are we changing our minds at all about more houses for Whimingham?" Jason had friends in the village and often met them at the Fox and Hounds for a drink or two. He would never knowingly try to give Whimingham preferential treatment because of that, but he didn't exactly relish being one of 'the planners' who would be responsible for upsetting their idyll, and if that could be avoided by quite legitimate means he would be happy.

Jessica, removed her glasses – a sign that an important utterance was imminent – and looked across at both of them.[58]

"Absolutely not! Hancock is an odious man and, even if he wasn't, there is no way I'd prejudice my position by appearing to be swayed by his threats and innuendos. No, unless you've had any new information or comments or objections in the last few days, I see no reason to change our original recommendations. Whimingham gets its share of the new housing, but Whimbury still offers the best opportunity for substantial development – particularly if the owners of Hill farm can find a suitable means of access, which shouldn't be beyond them.

"Even so," Emily re-entered the fray, "Whimingham already has a few shops and a school, so it stands to reason that it should be able to take more houses."

Jessica was fond of Emily and her love of the common-sense approach to life in general and planning in particular. However, common-sense can often be viewed from different angles and Jessica had to find the path that bisected those angles in the most widely accepted way. Sometimes the answer was obtuse, sometimes acute, but rarely did it end up with an equilateral.

---

[58] A sign recognised, and feared, by all in her department

"But I expect the locals in Whimbury would be happy if their shops had a few more customers? And the bus service from here could easily be improved." Jessica passed the ball to Jason with a sideways glance.

"Well actually, they were a couple of the main points I got from the consultation replies – support for shops, better bus service – oh and a suggestion that the old station goods yard might make a good housing site."

"Indeed it might." Jessica bisected another angle. "If we could guarantee that the owners were prepared to sell. But it's not a big site, and we would still need more if we're to meet our targets."

"So Hill Farm is still our main hope?" Emily still had doubts about the direction the planning proposals were going in, but she couldn't pin down why. In any case she had no realistic alternatives to throw into the debate and so, for the time being she was prepared to defer to greater experience.

"That's going to be my recommendation to committee." Jessica turned her attention back to Jason, who could be relied on for a relatively unquestioning agreement to her suggestion. "Though I could do with you keeping your finger on the pulse regarding the access issue, Jason. Once we get this housing matter sorted, the draft plan will be pretty much ready to go on to the next stage."

With that, Jessica rose from her seat, checked her watch, placed her documents back in their file, and walked briskly out.

******

By coincidence, at the very moment that Jessica Huntly-Phillips left the room, a large car pulled up outside Hill Farm House. Mr Material and Mr Burr watched silently from across the farmyard as a besuited man stepped out of the car and then swore audibly. The man then leaned back into the car and re-emerged with a piece of newspaper, which he used to clean a cake of fresh cowpat from his otherwise spotless shoe. As he did so, a middle-aged woman, in wellington boots, walked across to greet him.

"Mr Hancock, I presume!" She shook his hand vigorously. "Diana Johnson – I see you've finally found a useful purpose for the Gazette! Terrible rag – we only get it for the public notices - you know, check for what's going on and what might be of interest to the small but growing businessperson." For the benefit of Mr Hancock, she led him towards the house in zig-zag fashion, avoiding obvious pitfalls and other animal deposits. Neither of them was aware of being followed very closely by two faeries who were listening in carefully to the ongoing conversation.

"Good of you to come." Diana Johnson continued. "Hopefully, we won't be needing to carry on with this line of work much longer." She guided him round a particularly unpleasant dark green puddle. "Richard never did really like it much – part of the drawback of marrying into an old farming family, I suppose. I found it all very romantic at first, having my own small farm, but the novelty soon wore off, and Richard can't wait to be rid of the whole thing." She pointed Mr Hancock to the safety of the front door. "If we can sell up for housing, that should see us able to buy something really nice in the countryside that won't come with its own inimitable smell. That's what Richard really couldn't adjust to."

As she shut the door behind them, and Mr Hancock gave his shoes an extra wipe on the somewhat unsavoury-looking doormat, Messrs Material and Burr eased their way into the dining room and secreted themselves beside the log basket. Diana Johnson and Mr Hancock sat themselves down either side of the dining room table. Mr Hancock took some plans from his briefcase and began to spread them out, while Diana called for her husband to come and join them.

"He's in the office," she said, "doing the accounts. Will that affect the price we get, do you think?"

"I doubt it." Robert Hancock smiled the smile of a long-established profit maximiser. "However good or bad the farming business, it's the price of housing land that is key here. Ah! I take it this is Mr Richard Johnson?" He stood as Richard entered the room and shook his hand warmly, and for rather longer than was strictly necessary, speaking as he did so. "I was just talking with Mrs Johnson about business and the price of land."

Once disengaged, Richard sat next to Diana, and Robert Hancock resumed his position on the other side of the table. From beside the log basket, Mr Material gestured silently to Mr Burr in what was clearly meant as a sign that they should both listen and observe very carefully. For perhaps the first time,

Mr Burr felt that he was sensing exactly what he needed to focus upon. Maybe all the time spent with Mr Material was now paying off and he was becoming attuned to the needs of the moment. He concentrated as the conversation between the humans continued.

From what he could gather, in between the ebb and flow of chat and finger-waving over the plans, Mr Hancock was a great friend and confidant to the planners at Whimburton. As a result of this privileged position, he had managed to lobby the planners to divert their attention as regard housing land away from Whimingham and towards Whimbury. Moreover, he was sure that Hill Farm would be one of the first sites to be allocated for housing in the new Local Plan and, fortuitously, he had a close link to a major housing developer who would be willing to pay a good price for the land. Said developer would be more than happy to take an option to buy the farm, subject to planning permission being granted, to save the Johnsons the cost of selling through an agent on the open market.

Mr Burr, who had followed the gist of the conversation, without necessarily fully understanding the ways and ground-rules of human interaction of this type, was impressed that Mr Hancock had already prepared appropriate documentation for the Johnsons to sign. He felt it showed great forethought, even if Richard Johnson said he'd need to look through everything before committing pen to paper. Mr Hancock seemed a little disappointed but managed to smile throughout, although Mr Burr thought he detected a little annoyance as well. He looked across at Mr Material and saw that he was deep in thought, clearly filing away what he had learned ready for when it would be needed.

"So, I'll love you and leave you." Mr Hancock put the plans and other papers back into his case. He rose from the seat with his hand already extended in handshake mode. First Richard Johnson, then Diana gave their farewell greetings and Mr Hancock moved towards the door. He turned as if to add something important to his closing greetings, at which point Messrs Material and Burr hurried to the front door.

"I'll see myself out." Mr Hancock had quite forgotten what he meant to say – obviously it can't have been too crucial. "I'm sure I can safely retrace my steps to the car." He opened the door and exited, accompanied by two unseeable faeries. Mr Burr wondered why Mr Material picked up a small twig from under a bush outside of the Farmhouse and then hurried to get in front of the property agent. Mr Hancock walked gingerly towards the car watching very carefully where he put his feet. When he reached the middle of the yard, Mr Material very deliberately placed his foot on the twig and pulled it violently towards himself. At the sound of the crack, Mr Hancock stopped suddenly and looked around. Satisfied that he was alone, he absent-mindedly turned and stepped into a cowpat.

Mr Material beckoned Mr Burr to follow him out of the farmyard. As they walked away, they paused to listen happily to the curses emanating from Mr Hancock as he tore another page from The Gazette. Mr Burr had never before seen such a mischievous smile on the face of his companion. He clearly still had a lot to learn about the tall faery behind his stony exterior.

****

"They want me to do what?" Percy sat down urgently, his heart racing. Percetta handed him the cup of herbal tea that she had prepared ready for the moment she was going to reveal the substance of her conversation with Trixie.

"They want you to prepare the Crossover girl for the moment she meets her destiny." Percetta put on her best matter-of-fact voice, though the choice of words that came out might, on reflection, have been more carefully and subtly chosen. She passed him a plate of real faery cakes and, for good measure, also waved one of his favourite biscuits under his nose. This unusual and uncharacteristic show of generosity of spirit and unhealthy food, only served to disturb Percy even more.

"Oh! Is that all? I thought it was something important." Percy took a large bite out of a faery cake, working on the basis that the longer he spun out his obvious discomfort, the more edible treats he could enjoy. "And was it explained to you exactly what this involved?"

"Not exactly, no!" Percetta put rather too much emphasis on the word 'exactly' for Percy's liking.

"So how much 'inexact' information did they pass on?" Percy was reaching the stage in his consumption of faery cakes and sweet biscuits where he was mellowing, and developing a genuine interest in the project the Percetta was laying before him. Since his unexpected prominent role at the beginning of the Crossover process, he had grown to rather enjoy his newfound celebrity status – not that he would ever display this in public. After all he had a reputation to keep up and, in any case, showing a positive interest in something almost always led to becoming invaluable, with consequences often beyond one's control. But faery cakes – now they could break through even the hardest resolve, especially those containing Percetta's secret ingredient – which varied according to circumstances.

"Only that they needed someone respected and wise to train up the girl in the ways of faedom so that she can be ready to fulfil the Crossover as soon as it becomes necessary – and that could be sooner rather than later. They thought that they might be too young and inexperienced to give her all the knowledge and advice that she needed.[59] I'm only repeating what Trixie said which was that they believe you to be the ideal person to lead the training programme. Obviously, they'll be around to provide any physical and moral support that you need." She smiled reassuringly.

"Ah well, that's different. I feel so much better knowing that she and her mates will be hanging around in the background in case I need them." Percy snorted gently and took another bite of cake.

Percetta smiled to herself as he began to revert to type, which was an indication that he was coming round from the initial shock. One or two pointers in the right direction and she was sure he would agree to what was being asked. He would have done so anyway, she knew that, but the process of coaxing and gentle cajoling, mixed with a bit of flattery and praise, could be guaranteed to speed the process up, as well as propelling him forward with greater self-belief.

"So, I'll tell them you'd be proud to accept the offer?"

"Proud? Offer?" Percy was getting into his stride. "The offer appears to involve me in dedicating months of my life…"

---

[59] Trixie and Robin were barely into their second century, and Fae history, legend and folklore took a long time to assimilate.

"Years of your life, my sweetness!" Percetta interrupted smoothly and efficiently.

"Dedicating years of my life," Percy picked up where he left off. "to teaching a human child all of our history and customs and powers so that one day, maybe, she can use all of my hard acquired knowledge in a manner, we know not what, to achieve a purpose, we know not what, that may or may not be harmful to her and possibly even ourselves?" Percy effortlessly switched his attention from cake to biscuit as if to add emphasis to his point.

"Yes, that about sums it up nicely." Percetta sensed just the tiniest element of pride in the tone of his voice, pride that he was being entrusted with this scheme. "So, I'll tell them you'll do it?"

"You'll do no such thing!" Percy was on a roll. "I'll take myself down to the Royal Oak immediately and have it out with them all. This needs a full discussion before I can possibly come to any conclusion. There are implications and details that need coming out into the open. Procedures and strategies to be worked out. I can't just drop everything and devote my time to training up a very small human on how to become fae! This is complex; this needs wider commitment. I don't know if I can handle such a situation. I will need assurances, resources – and I don't know if they can give any guarantees." By now Percy was striding around the room on a route that regularly brought him into touching distance of the plate of biscuits.

"They probably can't! That's why they need a wise and understanding head to keep control. It's an honour, Percy. That's why you have every right to be proud that they are asking you, over and above everyone else, to do this."

Percy drew himself up to his full height.[60] Pausing only for one last exaggerated snap of his biscuit, he launched into his 'coup-de-grace'.

"Right, I will be back later when I've added some flesh to the bare bones of the draft scheme that they have cobbled together. And if I'm not satisfied, they can look elsewhere for inspiration." He picked up his hat from the hall table and opened the front door, at which point he stopped and turned back to Percetta.

---

[60] Which even in fae terms was only modest

"YEARS of my life, you said? YEARS – plural?" He looked at her quizzically.

"Indeed, I did!" She smiled innocently.

"Oh, right!" Percy stared vaguely in her general direction. "Years, right!" And he disappeared down the garden path lost in thought.

Chapter Thirteen

OUTSIDE THE ROYAL OAK, RALPH hopped from one foot to another and blew into his fingers. The early morning chill was forcing its way through his slightly incomplete and well-ventilated coat, fuelled by a sudden northerly breeze that had developed during the course of the night, and which ran unchecked down the High Street.

"Cold front! Wind from the Arctic." He muttered quietly to himself. "The north wind doth blow – from the northern regions! Currently it doth blow around my nether regions. Never trust it. Cast ne'er a clout till May be out – not that I've got any spare clouts to cast anyway. Cast away, sail south, warmer climes, happier times, sight of beaches – 'we shall fight them on the beaches' – fight them in the beeches. Save the trees, save the woods, Nature would – human nature? Short term, instant return – devil take the hindmost, devils take the most hinds. Spare the deer. Dear oh dear......"

"Sorry we're a bit late." Barry nudged Ralph back into the moment. "Robin's not the best at getting up in full bright'n'breezy mode." He pointed behind him to where Trixie was holding Robin in as near to a vertical position as she could, whilst slapping his face in an attempt to keep his eyes open.

"So I see." Ralph smiled. "And this is my crack back-up team?"

"So long as you don't need back-up too early in the morning, it's about as crack as we can muster." Barry joined Trixie in the early morning slap ritual, only using a little more force. "It takes a lot out of him being as dynamic as he is the rest of the day."

"So I see!" Ralph knew better than to doubt the willingness and

~ 201 ~

capabilities of his fae friends, and besides, he was unlikely to be out and about spying in the Whimburton community this early of a morning – even under abnormal circumstances. But he did want to get moving urgently on this particular morning, so that he could be out of the village before anyone was likely to see or hear him go. "Would it help if I carried him?"

"Unfortunately not!" Barry paused from the slapping routine momentarily. "Aside from the fact that he wouldn't like it, faeries are not supposed to allow humans to have any sort of control over their physical movements, and as he's not currently in a position to make that kind of decision for himself, I'd better not make it for him. Once he's fully awake he'll be fine – and a few more well-placed slaps should do the trick."

Barry continued while Trixie gave an embarrassed look in Ralph's direction, accompanied by a knowing shrug of the shoulders and a grimace as Robin made what she hoped was a waking-up shudder that almost broke him free from her support. Ralph instinctively looked at his wrist to check the time, then remembered that he hadn't had a watch for several years.[61]

As Ralph continued to look around him in agitated fashion, Robin began making utterances that almost made sense.

"I've had a terrible dream!" He separated himself from Trixie and stretched each of his extremities in turn. "I was being dragged into a fridge and beaten about the head, then the back of the fridge opened up into a forest full of human beings all trying to catch me. It was weird – and somewhat disconcerting to say the least." He yawned, sat down on a very cold stone and immediately stood up again.

"Well, I 've no idea what all that can have been about," lied Barry, "but I do know that Ralph is the only human being up and about in these parts at the moment, and that you will be leaving with him and Trixie to go to Whimburton any minute now. So, nothing to worry about." Barry gave his brother a reassuring clap on the shoulders and turned him towards Trixie in an attempt to get him moving before he had completely come round. He considered this the safest option, in that it would get Robin out of the village and well on his way before he could ask too many questions. He had been less

---

[61] Then immediately forgot again. It's what a lot of humans do!

than enthusiastic the night before when Barry had briefly outlined the situation to him, and only the intervention of Trixie had finally persuaded him to agree to 'go along for the fun of it', as she carefully put it.

"Oh, hi Ralph! Didn't see you there." Robin looked up at the towering figure of Ralph, who by this time was kneeling down in an attempt to hear what was being said.

"I pride myself on being able to blend into the background." Ralph was an expert in the art of irony and self-deprecation. "I'm sorry if I startled you."

"No worries. It was just that I wasn't sure where I was for a minute there, and you weren't part of the scene I expected to unfold. Barry did say we'd be meeting you today, and that you had a job for us, but it was all left a bit vague and it obviously never really sank into my sub-conscious. So, is it breakfast time or what? I'm feeling peckish."

Still slightly dazed, Robin looked round in the misapprehension that there might be a breakfast buffet bar lying around somewhere in the vicinity of the Royal Oak. Slowly and disappointingly, he became aware of the reality of the situation, while a little more of the substance of the previous night's conversation eased its way out of its nightwear and settled down in its rightful place on the day's agenda.

"I made up some snacks for our journey to the town while I was waiting for you to wake up. We need to get going before the village gets moving." Trixie decided it was time to take full control and drag Robin into the next phase of the journey before he settled too comfortably into the current phase. She patted her rucksack to indicate where the goodies were stashed and gestured to Robin that he should think about moving.

"What does it matter if the village gets moving?" Robin remained hesitant.

"To us it doesn't – to Ralph it does. He needs to be out of here before anyone sees him." She glanced up at Ralph and noticed him looking at his wrist and tapping it, trying to get an invisible pair of hands on an invisible dial to tell him the time.

"OK! Then remind me why we're going with him again?" Robin found properly waking up quite a complex and troublesome procedure. He had a tendency to hover in the vortex that revolved around the edges of the conscious, and then would suddenly escape into action, upon which he was a livewire for the rest of the day. Trixie tried to get all her personal jobs and interests sorted out during this period, knowing that the rest of the day was going to be one long blast of action.

"I'll tell you as we go along – now please can we just get started. It'll soon be sun-up and we need to be well on the way before it is." She attracted Ralph's attention by flying up to eye-level and coughing discreetly. This was followed by further coughing – progressively less and less discreetly – until Ralph stopped tapping his wrist and took note of Trixies's gestures, which indicated that they were finally ready to leave. At least, he hoped that was what they meant.

Trixie descended back to Robin's side and gave him a gentle push in the direction of the High Street. She smiled at Barry who mouthed 'good luck' silently and set off noisily cajoling Robin. Barry grinned inwardly as he watched the three of them disappearing and catching the last few snippets of conversation between Trixie and Robin.

"Can't we just fly – it'd be quicker?"

"Ralph can't fly, don't be so ridiculous."

"And what are we going to be doing in town?"

"I told you, Ralph has a mission and may need our pranks and powers to help him succeed."

"I didn't know he was a missionary!"

Barry lost the response from Trixie as they wandered down the road, but he could see that it involved Trixie giving Robin a playful cuff round the ear.

****

Evadne, Kenneth and Adrian were walking along the High Street at a pace set by Spot, which was considerably faster than any of them were happy with. But none of them complained. It was a brisk morning and a gentle stroll would not have succeeded in keeping them warm. Nevertheless, a brief pause every now and again, allowing Spot to sniff out the opposition and establish his own territory, was a welcome respite in amongst the otherwise relentless exercise.

Kenneth and Adrian took it in turns to hold the lead – Evadne claiming that she couldn't hold the dog back when he was straining at the leash like that.

Since he was nearly always straining at the leash like that, she rarely took over, which suited her just fine. It meant that she could stop for a chat with whoever was passing without holding anybody, or any dog, up. But this morning, few people seemed to have taken the effort to brave the cold wind, so Evadne walked along with the other two, happy in her own thoughts and laughing occasionally when Kenneth and Adrian, in turns, got tangled up in the lead.

The normal morning route took them past the church, along the footpath between the graveyard and the Whimbury Arms, through the new 'estate'[62], across to the cricket field and round the pitch, past the village pond – where Evadne always made absolutely sure that Spot's lead was held very firmly – and then, depending on the weather, either a short detour through the woods or straight home past Green's Agricultural Machinery workshop and the entrance to Arnold Lane[63].

As they left the 'estate' and crossed Whimingham Lane into the cricket field, Spot stopped abruptly, wagged his tail vigorously, and began to bark excitedly, jumping up and down as he did so. Across the field and heading in their direction was Fred Butterworth with his dog, Fred. Fred had called the dog Fred deliberately, despite the protestations of his wife Dorene who had a tendency to shout to him from a long distance away and then carry on a long, loud conversation, usually berating him for some misdemeanour. Fred reckoned that by calling the dog Fred he could pretend to all and sundry in hearing range that Dorene was complaining about the dog rather than he. And it had worked more times than not, though many of the village folk never really worked out why the dog had to be back before its dinner went cold, or why it might have failed to tidy away the plates after breakfast, or not put its underpants in the washing pile.

Both Freds were by now somewhat slow of movement, but the Potts family knew better than to let Spot off the lead so near to the cricket square and within relatively easy reach of the pond. So they waited as the Freds

---

[62] 'New' insofar as it was post-war (which war no-one seemed to bother about) and 'estate' in that it contained over 6 houses – in this case 8.

[63] Which was only about 20 metres from the far end of Arnold Lane – a cul-de-sac that didn't quite qualify as an 'estate'.

walked over to them and broke into conversation as the dogs sniffed each other in the way that dogs do. By this time Spot had ceased to bark and Fred the dog was too old to bother anyway. So it was now possible for a civilised conversation between the Potts and Fred the human in such a way that Fred could actually hear what was being said.

"Hi Fred!" Evadne put on the most cheerful voice that she could muster at that time of an unseasonably cold morning. Both Freds immediately looked up at her[64], the one wagging its tail slowly and panting and salivating, the other just panting and salivating.

"Evadne! So glad I've met you. I've some news that might interest you and might get me a few bonus points before the next Parish Council meeting." Fred wheezed in excitement. Adrian and Kenneth knew that this could be a long interval in the dog-walking project and so they made a dangerous executive decision to risk taking Spot off the lead in the hope that 'chase the ball' would restrict his movements to those safe areas where the ball was to be thrown.

"Tell me more, Fred, tell me more – this sounds intriguing." Evadne was unused to Fred having anything of great significance to say and could tell it was important by the way that Fred (the human) was not watching when Fred (the dog) made to cock his leg up against Fred (the human's) ankles. Fortunately, just at that point Adrian threw his old tennis ball towards the boundary of the cricket pitch, upon which Spot set off in hot pursuit, followed by a newly energised Fred (the dog) who got to within 50 yards of where the ball landed before meeting Spot coming back with it, upon which he turned round and ambled back just in time for the ball to be thrown again. This continued throughout the conversation.

"Well, I don't know if I've mentioned it before, but my cousin is a councillor in Whimburton, and he happens to be on the Planning, Economic Development and Localism Committee – PEDAL.[65] I was talking to him......" Evadne interrupted.

---

[64] Fred (the human) was quite small and stooped. He blamed his stoop on too much leaning over the table-tennis table.

[65] Getting the use of this acronym first, before the Highways, Environment, and Landscape Protection Committee (HELP) could gain control of it - and rename itself somehow -, was seen as a feather in the cap of the Chair of Planning.

"You mean you've got a cousin on the very committee that is dealing with the Local Plan and you've never mentioned it before? We've been struggling to find out what's going on and all along you've had access to inside information? I'm speechless."

"I thought you'd be pleased." Fred hadn't really been listening, he was far too wrapped up in his story to be deflected from its content. "As I was saying, I was talking to him yesterday over the phone – we chat every couple of months or so – and for some reason the subject turned to Whimbury and the housing that they're going to locate here. He wanted to know what I thought about Hill Farm being allocated as a major site. I told him I didn't think he was allowed to discuss such things with me, especially before the committee meeting, but he just said he trusted me to forget what we'd been talking about as soon as we put the phone down, like I always do anyway. He was only making small talk and thought it might fill a rather long pause in the conversation."

"So let me get this right! Your cousin says that the council is going to allocate Hill Farm for housing in the Local Plan? You're quite sure that's what he said?" Evadne was almost speechless, an unusual condition for her to find herself in.

"Quite sure. I made an effort to remember it this time, because he's right, I do usually forget, so I wrote it down to tell you next time I saw you – which by happy coincidence was today. Here's the piece of paper." He handed over a scrap of paper that had been screwed up, then folded carefully in an attempt to make it seem neater and more important. Evadne perused it and raised her eyebrows as she confirmed to herself the accuracy of what Fred had just told her. She folded the paper up once again and handed it back to Fred.

"Eileen and I had talked about the possibility of Hill Farm going for housing, so it's no great surprise, but I didn't think they'd be making a decision so soon. The consultation period hasn't actually ended just yet." Evadne shook her head as if to check that she was fully understanding what was going on.

"Well, of course, they don't actually make the decision till the committee meeting, but I don't think my cousin would have mentioned it to me unless it was near enough certain. He said that there had been a lot of discussion behind the scenes, and a lot of toing and froing of well-connected people, and that's why he was confident that what he had told me was the likely outcome." At this point Fred became aware that his dog had grown tired of chasing balls and was more interested in the relatively gentle pursuit of biting Fred's trouser turnups. The state of Fred's turnups was testament to the regularity of this situation arising.

"Ah! Fred has decided it's time to move on, and if I want these trousers to last any longer, I'd better agree." Fred bent down to replace Fred's lead and, on the basis that he didn't want to have to bend down too often, he did up his shoe laces at the same time. It would have been a shame to waste the opportunity while he was already down there. He slowly reverted to vertical with a mix of groans and creaks. Once back upright, he gave a rotating smile to each of the Potts' family in turn and doffed his non-existent cap in a somewhat unnecessary show of deference.

"So, good morning one and all." The Freds moved off slowly. Evadne turned to call after them.

"Well done, Fred!" Both Freds stopped momentarily to look back in pride. "That's very useful information, if a bit surprising. Have a good day." The Freds continued on their way, the human Fred appearing to have just a little more of a spring in his step than normal.

Kenneth, relieved that Spot hadn't decided to run off in unacceptable directions, put him back on the lead and handed the lead to Adrian. Spot pulled Adrian around the cricket field while Kenneth and Evadne followed a short distance behind. Kenneth had heard what Fred had been saying and wanted to hear Evadne's take on it.

"It obviously doesn't surprise me on one level, though I'm a bit concerned about the way that decisions seem be taken by our beloved council. Still, it appears we may now have two spies in their camp, which can only be useful."

"Two?" Kenneth wasn't quite keeping up with her train of thought.

"Ralph and Fred's cousin – one a social outcast and the other who doesn't even realise what it is that he's doing. It doesn't seem much when compared to MI5, but we need to take all help that we can from whatever source. I feel I can trust Ralph, though heaven knows what, in reality, he can do – and Fred's cousin will be a useful source of information all the while he continues to have no sense of diplomacy and can't keep his mouth shut."

Then let battle commence!" Kenneth took hold of Evadne's hand in a gesture of solidarity and they speeded up to catch Adrian and Spot.

****

Percy sat on the front wall of Over Cross View, waiting for Barry to arrive. He was still bemused by how easy it had been for Barry and the others to persuade him to take on this project. He had gone into the Royal Oak the previous evening with no intention of surrendering YEARS of his life to the training of a small human child – or at least he thought he had – but the longer the conversation went on the more he felt a pride in being chosen for the honour. Somehow it had turned from being a chore to being an honour without him noticing. Or maybe it was that Percetta's words kept coming back to him during the course of the session. Or maybe it was the last glass of Innkeepers Choice that had sealed his fate.

But it was too late now for retrospective analysis. He was sat on the wall of Milly's home, wating for moral support from Barry, and for the little girl to come out to play. Up until that point, it had been Robin and Trixie who had taken on most of the responsibility for pointing her in the direction of becoming fae when the right time would arrive. Barry had also helped, which was why he was coming to introduce Percy to Milly officially. Whilst they had seen each other from time to time, they had never really had a conversation of any kind – not that it was easy to have a deep and meaningful conversation with a two-year old in any case. Nevertheless, she was clearly bright and learnt fast and could already communicate with faeries in ways that almost all other humans could not, whatever their age and gifts. And communicate with animals too, thought Percy. He had seen her converse with Spot and the various birds that visited the feeders in the gardens around. The more he thought about it, the more he began to look forward to getting to know her – not that he would ever let on of course. He still had some standards.

A sudden cheery pat on the back, that almost propelled him into the hydrangea below, brought him back to reality. Barry sat himself down next to Percy and welcomed him to his new position in the 'Crossover' team, reiterating the honour that had been granted him and the importance of the next few YEARS. In truth, Percy would have been happier if Barry had ceased his congratulations before he'd got to the point of reminding him how long the whole process was likely to last. But it was too late now. He was sitting on the wall waiting to meet the child he was going to be seeing a lot of over the next few YEARS. And he had no idea what to say to her or how to begin her training – or even what to train her in.

Then there she was, trailing her father down the path and waving goodbye to him as he crossed the road to his place of work. She stood on the gate and watched till he entered the building and then returned to her favourite log in the middle of the overgrown lawn and began looking for insects to play with and talk to. Percy looked on entranced, noticing perhaps for the first time just how vulnerable and innocent she appeared. But he could also sense the inner strength that she possessed and felt her spirit connecting with him. At which point she lifted her head and looked right at him. Percy was never able to fully explain what he experienced at that moment but it was something he hadn't experienced ever before and it quite took his breath away. Here in front of him was the Crossover child, and she was definitely and unarguably special. The importance of the task ahead seared itself into his very being.

"Hi Barry." She looked at Percy's companion and then returned her eyes to Percy himself. "Hi....?" She turned her head to a 45 degree angle and waited for the inevitable introduction. Percy was speechless and so Barry answered on his behalf.

"Hi Milly. This is Percy, he is one of our oldest and wisest faeries. He's going to teach you all he knows about us and how one day you can become just like us. Robin and Trixie will still be around, but you'll be seeing a lot more of Percy from now on." Percy gave her an embarrassed and over-enthusiastic wave which caused his hat to fall over his eyes. Milly laughed.

"I like Percy – he's funny." She sat straight-backed with her hands on her knees. "Will you play with me?"

Barry gestured to Percy that they should get down from the wall and join Milly on the log. When they got there, they sat either side of her. Percy noticed that she was already talking to someone, and looked down to her feet, where he could just make out Larry, part-hidden in the grass. For the first time, Percy realised how old and frail Larry was sounding. [66] He could just make out Larry's parting words.

"Well, I'll luv yer and leave yer. Yer've got some important chats ter 'ave wiv these mates o' mine. Hope ter sees yer agen termorrer, unless by that time I've already gone to the great decaying log-pile in the sky, of course." With that and a jaunty wave of his antennae in the direction of Barry and Percy he wandered off, Milly waving to him as he went.

"Larry very old." She proclaimed as he disappeared from view. "Even older than me! I like Larry – he tells me stories." Then she switched her attention to her new friend. "Will you tell me a story?" She motioned to Percy to sit on her knee and then, to make sure that he wasn't left out, pointed out the other knee as being vacant for the use of Barry. Both faeries obliged.

Percy looked pleadingly across to Barry who gestured, unhelpfully, that he should get started. Percy for his part had not expected his role to commence quite so soon and with such little preparation time. Barry could see that he was struggling and stepped in to give him an introduction.

"You remember what Robin and Trixie were saying about humans – like you -, and faeries – like us -, having to live together in the same place, but that most humans can't see or hear us?" Milly nodded. "But you can see us and hear us, can't you, and you talk with us, don't you?" She nodded again. "Well that's because you're special and Percy is going to tell you all about why you are special and how we can all help each other when you get older. Percy is much older than Robin and Trixie and me, so he has lots more stories."

"Will he go to the great log-pile in the sky?" Milly missed nothing and remembered everything. She also understood far more than might have been expected from a two-year old. Percy was rather taken aback by her forthright question. Again, Barry came to his rescue with an answer that gave Percy a foothold in the conversation.

"I think faeries go to a special, very big Royal Oak in the sky when they get too old to stay down here. It needs a lot of faeries to fill it up and make it

---

[66] Not so much how old he was 'looking', because it is very difficult for any non-woodlouse to spot the physical effects of the louse ageing process.

work. But Percy isn't quite old enough for that yet – and anyway, we need him here, so he'll be coming to see you a lot from now on." Barry knew this version of Fae theology was somewhat distant from the formally accepted interpretation, but he was pretty sure he'd got the basic thrust of it right.

"Yes! I'll be coming here a lot from now on – sometimes with Robin and Trixie and sometimes on my own. We can talk and we can play, though I'm not very quick at running any more." Percy wasn't sure how much, if at all, he should talk down to the level of a two-year old. It was something he would have to work out as they went along.

"I faster than faeries – if they don't fly, but flying is cheating." Milly was looking directly at Percy now and the bond was ready to be forged. Percy was amazed at the twinkle in her eye, and her ability to joke about the differences between humans and faeries. Whilst it might be difficult to know what to talk to her about, it certainly wouldn't be difficult to engage with her and enjoy her company.

"Yes, flying is cheating." Percy nodded and gestured in agreement. "But let me tell you a secret." He beckoned to Milly to bend towards him so that he could speak softly. He turned his face away from Barry to indicate total secrecy was in order, and began to whisper in Milly's ear – just loud enough for Barry to get the main points. "I don't fly. Not all faeries can fly, and my kind of faery – the gnome kind – doesn't fly. So I will always play fair with you. No cheating – I promise." Percy tapped the side of his nose to show Milly that this was a true secret that she could safely believe. In true Milly style, she also tapped her nose in the same way, and smiled acceptance.

"Percy not cheat. Percy good." Milly directed her conclusion at Barry. At that point Miranda came to the front door and called Milly back inside. "Milly go for breakfast. We play later?"

"Yes, we'll play later. And I can tell you some stories." Percy climbed down from her knee and he and Barry waved as she got up from the log and wandered slowly back to the house.

"Come on, little Miss Dreamer. Your egg is waiting and will go cold." Miranda waited patiently – she knew better than to try to hurry Milly in from the garden. "And who have you been talking with today?"

"Percy. He old, but not going to great log-pile in the sky. He not cheat."

Milly eased past Miranda, who shut the door behind them, shaking her head in wonderment at her special little princess.

Percy and Barry wandered back towards the Royal Oak for a de-briefing, Percy almost giggling to himself in disbelief at the thought of what he had just said and done.

****

Outside of the Council Offices in Whimburton, Ralph sat on his small pile of spare clothes,[67] watching the passers-by suddenly find that they knew someone on the other side of the road as they neared him. His re-cycled cardboard cup [68] sat beside him, empty of any loose change, while Robin and Trixie sat either side of the cup.

Over the course of a day, provided it wasn't raining, he could generally guarantee getting enough coins of the realm to buy himself at least a drink and a sandwich, which he supplemented by picking up the out-of-date throw-aways from one of the supermarkets. Over the years he had struck up relationships with some of the shelf-stackers, who ensured that anything still reasonably edible was thrown away in his direction. It wasn't always as tasty or healthy as he would have chosen for himself – but beggars can't be choosers and he was, essentially, a beggar.

Occasionally, a passer-by would ask him what he would like from a shop and get it for him as part of their shopping – but that was rare. He always took care not to offend by virtue of asking for something ridiculously expensive, but at least it could be a snack or meal of his own choice, and it had the added bonus of tasting better because of the side order of kindness that came with it.

But today he had an ulterior motive for choosing this particular spot to set up his temporary home. He needed inside information on the current plans for housing in Whimbury, and he couldn't get inside – the meeters and greeters at the door and at the reception desk would see to that. Robin and Trixie, on the other hand, could come and go as they pleased and bring back whatever

---

[67] Spare in the sense that they were only really needed for wearing in the winter. They were never spare with regard to being out of use for sitting or sleeping on at any time.
[68] Ralph would never dream of using a plastic one. He'd rather starve – and often did.

snippets of gossip and more concrete proposals that they could. Ralph had briefed them on what he wanted, and they were now just waiting for an unsuspecting visitor to get the doors open for them so that they could sneak in. Before too long, just such an opportunity arose and they set about their exploration of the corridors of power.

"So, remind me again. Where are we supposed to be going?" Robin was an expert at setting up japes and wheezes, but not so good at listening to other peoples' schemes and taking them in fully. For that he relied on Trixie. Living on his wits was his speciality, and that was highly likely to come in handy while ferreting around in the Council Offices.

"Somewhere called PEDAL – though Ralph said that if we heard anyone asking for Planning we should just follow them." Trixie looked around the large entrance hall for any helpful signs. Seeing none, she levitated herself to around human eye level and had another look. A brass plaque on the wall beside the stairs gave her the information she needed. She dropped back down to floor level and dragged Robin by the sleeve. "Third Floor," she said as they headed for the grand staircase, and then half-walked, half flew up the six flights necessary. As they reached the Third Floor, Trixie was gratified to see a large notice with the word PEDAL and an arrow pointing down the corridor to the left. There was a great deal of activity in this part of the building, and they were able to enter the PEDAL offices without any meaningful delay. Robin noticed the way that the humans used a large green button on the wall to open the doors and filed the information away for future reference.

"Right, we're in!" Robin sounded triumphant, then looked around. "Now what?" He sounded less triumphant as all around him desks with computers and telephones were occupied by humans, some seemingly engrossed in what was on their screens, others engaged in conversations over their phones, some apparently doing both. Trixie made an executive decision.

"I'll flit round them all and see if anyone mentions anything about Whimbury or housing or both." With that she disappeared momentarily and then reappeared very slightly out of breath.[69] She paused for a second and

---

[69] Using her 'theory of relatives', passed down through generations of her family, Trixie had the ability to visit multiple destinations at once and return at virtually the same time as she left – but it was tiring and only to be used in special circumstances.

then motioned to Robin to follow her – at a respectable but more modest speed.

"We need to check in here!" Trixie led Robin into a small meeting room where Jason was putting the finishing touches to a report on the potential housing developments across the District, watched intently by Emily in a half-bored/half upset manner.

"So, Hill Farm remains our prime target for Whimbury?" Emily seemed to sigh a resigned sort of sigh.

"Best and biggest one we've got!" Jason smiled a successful sort of smile and continued typing without breaking rhythm. "I've added the old Station Yard as well, as a back-up – or we can use both if we need to. OK! Concluding sentence." He raised his hands above his head and cracked his knuckles – a habit that he knew really irritated Emily. Shaking his hands to loosen his wrists for the final few phrases, he exhaled deeply and positioned his fingers over the keyboard as if it were a grand piano. Emily rolled her eyes and left the room. Robin and Trixie took her place beside Jason and waited for him to resume. As he did so, Robin took careful note of all of his actions – for future reference.

"In conclusion, on balance, and taking into account all considerations," Jason began, talking himself through the sentence as he did so, "it is recommended that Hill Farm, Whimbury is added to the existing list of housing sites within the Local Plan." He applauded himself. "Done!" He exclaimed proudly, and then closed the file and logged off the computer. With a hop and a skip he made his way out of the room and down the corridor to the coffee machine, unaware that he was being followed by two faeries. At the coffee machine he queued behind Emily. With a sickly smile he informed her that their report was finished.

"All over, bar the shouting!" He proclaimed loudly. "Unless we get a visit from some gremlin or malevolent software fairy, it's off to the committee clerk tomorrow." He made what he imagined to be a grisly, gremlin or malevolent software fairy type of face, and pressed the button for cappuccino. If he had looked down, and had eyes capable of seeing, he might have noticed the true face of a 'gremlin' gazing back up at him, with a decidedly malevolent grin. Robin and Trixie then made their way back to Ralph.

Ralph's paper cup was still empty when they returned, but he was more interested in their report back than in the contents of his 'begging bowl'.

"Any luck?" Passers-by smiled as they heard him talking to himself as usual. One of them took pity and dropped a small denomination coin into the cup. Ralph muttered a slightly incoherent 'Thankyou' and touched his forelock, while maintaining full concentration on his fae accomplices.

"Yes and no and yes!" Trixie outlined the results of their mission – yes, they had luck in tracing the relevant human and ascertaining his intentions - no, in that his intentions were probably not good news for Whimbury – yes, in that Robin had a cunning plan, one that even Trixie was enthused by. Robin took over.

"I think we can throw a dandelion into the lawn seed!" [70] Robin looked highly self-satisfied. "All we need is a gremlin or software faery to help us out as quickly as possible. I'm not bad at the gremlin impersonations, but I don't have the technical understanding to carry out the particular software necessaries. However, I know just the person who does, and if we can get hold of him before tomorrow, we could cause a bit of havoc – and a bit of havoc wouldn't go amiss right now."

Ralph laughed out loud and shouted his appreciation of their assistance. Another passer-by dropped a coin into his cup with a sympathetic smile.

"I'll stay here for a while, and listen out for any useful conversations from folk coming out of the building." Ralph was feeling upbeat for the first time in a long while. He had great confidence in Robin and Trixie and was sure that if anyone could cause the necessary havoc it was them – along with Robin's mysterious friend, whom he was looking forward to meet. "And I'll come back and sit here again tomorrow to wait for you – hopefully when the building opens – I suspect that we can't afford to leave things too long."

Robin and Trixie rose to leave as yet another passing human dropped money into Ralph's cup.

"Pity you can't stay longer, I've had more donations while I've been

---

[70] The human equivalent would involve a spanner and works, but this had no relevance to faeries. Ralph understood, thanks to his long association with the fae community, and his knowledge of their colloquialisms.

talking to you both than I've had in many a week." He waved them off, with a jaunty 'Farewell my friends', and smiled happily as another coin clinked into his growing collection.

Chapter Fourteen

MIRANDA CLEARED THE TABLE OF the empty dinner plates and took them into the kitchen. Milly rushed off to watch Childrens' television, followed closely by Will. One brief episode of Tinkerbelle and the Pirates while she was being changed into her bedclothes was the established routine. Also part of the routine was Milly announcing to Will and Miranda all the contextual and factual errors in the plot as it progressed.

"Faeries not fly like that!" was a common complaint. "Pirates not see faeries," was another.

Will would reply with "But it's only pretend, just a story!" And Milly would curl up between her parents to watch and listen and occasionally point out another inaccuracy.

After taking her to bed, reading her a story, and trying to stay awake till she went to sleep,[71] Will went back downstairs to relax on the sofa. He yawned as he sat beside Miranda, who placed a cushion against her ear and laid it on Will's shoulder. It was time for her to tell Will the stories from the day – stories that generally revolved around Milly, but occasionally, on more exciting days, involved other people. It wasn't that a day with only Milly for company was not lovely, it was just that other peoples' news livened things up a bit, and gave them something different to discuss. Today she had both.

"Milly has a new friend." Miranda exclaimed.

---

[71] Which was more often than not, touch and go.

"Really! What's her name?" Will was excited. They had often dreamt of teaming up with some other parents from the area and for Milly to be able to play with other children in their houses. She met others occasionally at events in the Parish Hall, or at the monthly toddlers' group in Whimburton, but there was no-one special and local.

"His name is Percy, he's old but he isn't going to the great log-pile in the sky – at least not yet." She had to giggle. Milly always found ways to make her giggle, even if she wasn't aware of the effect she had on her mother.

"Ah! Another fairy I presume. And what exactly is the great log-pile in the sky?" Will was a little disappointed, but somehow Milly's sayings and escapades always managed to overcome the initial disappointment that the tale did not involve a human friend or acquaintance.

"Fairy, yes! Apparently, he is going to tell her stories and play with her – along with Robin and Trixie. As for the great log-pile in the sky, that I'm afraid eludes me, though from what I've been able to piece together it may involve Larry the woodlouse."

"Well that would make sense, that's where woodlice hang out isn't it – have their parties and banquets? Recycling all the nutrients and putting goodness back into the soil?" Will paused as he realised that he may have displayed too much knowledge of crustaceans for his own good. Miranda raised her head from the pillow.

"Aren't we the clever naturalist all of a sudden? Where did you dig that bit of information up from?" She looked at him in a way that made him turn just a slight shade of red.

"I searched for it on the internet. What with Milly going on about woodlice, I thought maybe I should know a bit more than I did, so that I could converse with her on the subject – you know, show a bit of interest and maybe add to her education." Will tried to remain matter-of-fact about the issue.

"And have you talked with her about it?"

"Yes, a few days ago I started to tell her all about the role of woodlice in the wider scheme of things and the food cycle and other cycles of life."

"What did she say?"

"She said – 'yes, I know', and that was the end of that." Will laughed as he remembered the easy-going way that Milly accepted his scientific explanations, and was ready and willing to carry on the conversation with tales of Larry and his family.

"Do you think she actually understood what you were saying to her?" Part of Miranda was amazed by the way Milly seemed to be developing her own education in some of the basic ways of the world. Another part of her happily accepted it as just another example of how Milly was unusual and special. Yet another part remembered what the vicar had said about her and how it increasingly fitted the way that Milly was developing. [72]

"I genuinely believe that she did! But there again, nothing surprises me any more."

"Same here!" They both went quiet as they pondered the meaning of life, natural processes and Milly. Will pondered for just a few moments before resting his eyes and ears and exercising his nose and throat. Miranda elbowed him back into the there and then.

"Oh, sorry, my beloved. Was I dozing off?"

"That was the impression I was getting. I thought for one moment you were working out something deep and meaningful about our existence and Milly's part in it, but it was too noisy to be that."

"Snoring too?" Will didn't like falling asleep so early, partly because it was anti-social, and partly because he was afraid that he would stay awake in the night instead.

"Indeed! Let's change the subject – did I tell you that I bumped into Evadne earlier?"

"Don't think so, though you do that so regularly I can't be sure whether you told me today or yesterday or some other day. She seems to be omnipresent." Will slapped himself around the cheeks in order to stay awake while Miranda recounted her tale.

"Well, this afternoon I was in the garden when Evadne came past and told me that she'd seen Fred on the cricket field earlier this morning – and in the course of their conversation, Fred told her that his cousin was on the very planning committee that was going to make a decision on housing across the district – including in Whimbury, and what's more….."

---

[72] You needed lots of parts to even begin to unpick Milly's relationship with the natural and supernatural worlds.

Will placed his hand gently over her mouth and uttered one simple word - "Breathe!" – followed by other words – "slow down, and tell me the story in short sentences so that my brain can keep up." He removed his hand.

"Sorry. Short sentences, right!" Miranda took a slow breath and continued. "So it appears that the Council are likely to allocate Hill Farm for housing, as we suspected. Evadne said that Fred's cousin was quite certain. You could get a lot of houses on that land. Although, as Evadne said, the only access to the land, other than somewhere in the village, would be across Eileen Robinson's land, and that she'd never sell. So that's going to be interesting, isn't it?"

"Very! Though everyone has their price!" Will mulled the information over in his mind. "And if she didn't sell, what would the Council do? They're obviously desperate for housing land."

"Well, if they were intent on getting housing built there, they'd have to find another access. Evadne reckoned it would have to be from beside your workshop or through the gap where the Royal Oak is. Neither seems like a good option." Silence reasserted itself as they both considered the likely scenarios resulting from large amounts of new housing being built on the land at Hill Farm. In itself, it wouldn't necessarily be a bad thing, but nevertheless both of them, in their own ways felt a great sense of unease; an unease that was, as it happened, shared by large numbers of both the human and fae communities of Whimbury.

****

In the Royal Oak, Barry was changing barrels down in the cellars. Junior was singing and Barry, wearing ear plugs, was lost in his own thoughts. He was in almost meditative mode, working through the meaning of Messrs Material and Burr and the conflicting views between the two strangers and Eric. All of them seemed to have a deep-seated knowledge of the legend of the Crossover, and what needed to happen, but there couldn't be two different interpretations of the stories that were both right. The strangers sounded authoritative while Eric just knew stuff. Could Mr Material be authoritative without a depth of knowledge? Could Eric have knowledge but a wrong interpretation? Could one of them have both knowledge and authority – and if so, which one?

Getting this wrong could lead to Milly failing to complete the Crossover, and all their efforts around the time of her birth would effectively be wasted.

But the most immediate issue revolved around the humans and their urgent need for more houses in Whimbury. He was expecting Robin and Trixie to arrive at any time with their mystery comrade. He had been intrigued by the story of their time inside the Council Offices at Whimburton, and had his curiosity whetted by Robin's plan to create havoc there. He had been discussing with Junior who the unknown co-conspirator was to be. From what Robin had said, It had to be someone with complex technical know-how, and that pointed to a Goblin. He had his suspicions but now he just had to be patient and wait. Barry found waiting and being patient hard enough at the best of times, but being patient, waiting, and listening to Junior rattle through his repertoire of light opera was a bit too much. Hence the ear plugs.

Barry felt a tug at his boot. He looked down and saw Junior waving his antennae urgently. Removing his ear plugs, he became aware that Junior had stopped singing and had been talking to him for some time with no response.

"Sorry Junior! I've had a bit of earache and put these soothing ear plugs in my ears to see it they would help. Were you saying something?" If he were being honest, which he was most of the time, he was unsure whether he preferred Larry's classical soliloquies or Junior's light 'arias' – if indeed preferred was the right word. Either way, silence was very definitely the better option, especially when he had serious matters on his mind.

"Sorry about the ears, Barry!" Barry was sure that he'd never really discerned mild sarcasm in a woodlouse before. Maybe he was just imagining it. "I was just saying that there appears to be a noise from upstairs. Perhaps Robin and Trixie are back?"

"Perhaps they are indeed. Do you want to come and see who our mystery guest is?" Barry knelt down to let Junior climb onto him, and the two of them ascended to the bar. There to greet them were Robin and Trixie with Clive, goblin inventor and technical wizard extraordinaire.[73]

"Good to see you again, Clive!" Barry was effusive with his greeting. "I

---

[73] Clive had been instrumental in making a microphone, an amplifier/speaker, and a packet of potato crisps sound like an army of fae-folk on the march, at the time of the birth of Milly Hope.

said Clive was my best guess at the mystery accomplice, didn't I Junior?" Barry avoided giving Clive a welcome handshake on the basis that the last time he did so he received a nasty electric shock.

"Nice to know that my fame precedes me!" Clive was serious – not that he had an oversized ego[74], just that he was serious.

"Indeed it does. And it's good that you've agreed to help us in this very important matter. Have Robin and Trixie filled you in?" Barry was happy to accept that Clive was not the most cheery or light-hearted individual in normal times, but these weren't normal times, and Clive could certainly get enthusiastic enough and more outgoing when he had a project on the go.

"They have. It shouldn't be too taxing a task, so long as they can get me to the site of the relevant equipment. I've been studying the modern methods of human communication and, whilst complex, they are largely logical and predictable – despite their efforts to hide important elements behind security systems that any self-respecting goblin could deal with in moments." Again, Clive was just being serious and, in his own way, merely stating the obvious. He was the very epitome of the self-respecting goblin.

"Great, great." Barry was pleased that Clive seemed ready, willing and able to get cracking with his task. "We already owe you so much from when the Crossover child was born."

"Actually, I really quite enjoyed that challenge. It taxed my brain and, most satisfactory of all, it seemed to work out well. In truth, while I'm generally happy with my research and experimentation, having a live project to get stuck into can't be beaten. So, let battle commence!" Clive was ready to exit the bar and head off into the wild outdoors, but there was no point in getting to Whimburton before morning and so Barry stalled for time.

"First we need to discuss your plan, so that Robin and Trixie can brief our human 'undercover' agent as to what must be done and when. He won't be in place until early morning – you know what humans are like about working at night. But at least he's reliable." Barry half-pointed and half-led Clive to a table near the bar and motioned to Damon to pour out some glasses of Innkeeper's Choice. It seemed like the best way to get Clive into a more

---

[74] Which would have marked him out as potentially more politician material than scientist.

relaxed frame of mind, in preparation for what appeared likely to be a long and confusing night.

"Don't mind if I do!" Clive accepted his drink with what could almost have passed for a smile. Getting Clive interested in a project was one thing, but slowing him down when the bit was between his teeth but a little patience necessary was quite another.

Trixie glanced up at the clock. It was one minute to opening time.

"I'd better get the door open." She stated, dashing from the table. They'll be turning disgruntled." As she approached the front door, sounds of disgruntlement became instantly evident. Unlike humans, who tend to queue under sufferance and with growing impatience, the fae community stood quite still and silent until the very second that a key event was due to happen – in this case, the opening of a door – at which point all hell broke loose. If said event then happened bang on time, the loosened hell stopped as suddenly as it started and the queue progressed in an orderly fashion until all the queue members were in their desired and/or allotted places. Faery logic proclaimed that being disgruntled too early and for too long was just tiring and weakened the resolve[75]. Furthermore, disorderly pushing and barging was more time-consuming, and consequently less drink-consuming, than staying in line and progressing steadily. Faeries would often spend large amounts of time on days off, or on holidays, just watching human queues forming and then disintegrating, as a form of popular entertainment.

Barry and Robin watched as the regular patrons made their way to their usual tables in the bar or the snug as appropriate. Percy ambled and grumbled his way into the snug with the merest hint of a wink to Barry and no-one else. The Happling quiz teams sat themselves down, while Eric, on his own as was the norm, sat in the corner with a satchel full of books, waiting to be invited to join a team. Families and groups of friends settled into the established routine, with the designated first orderers making their way to the crowded bar and elbowing Grumps as a way of creating the right kind of atmosphere.

Clive was not a big drinker, so a couple of glasses of the powerful 'Choice' was enough to render him sleepy and incapable of further scientific

---

[75] And, in the case of Inn opening times, hampered their ability to drink consistently over the period of an evening.

thought and scheming. With luck he would be out cold on one of the long, padded seats before the end of the evening and ready to pick up on the project early in the morning.

In the far corner, the Royal Oak songsters soon got into their stride.

We're all going to Whimbury Fair
Pasties, pies and Innkeeper's Choice;
We'll eat and drink till we've had our fill,
Then we'll make a very rude noise.

Barry and Robin visibly relaxed and chatted their way through the plans for the next day.

****

In the Potts' household, Adrian and Kenneth were in the front room engaged in their nightly game of speed chess. Spot was gazing out of the front room window in somewhat excitable fashion, and Evadne was putting away the crockery and cutlery that the 'menfolk' had earlier washed and dried after dinner. As she did so, she smiled to herself at the regular cries coming from Adrian of 'cheat'. Kenneth always cheated, because he couldn't take the game seriously enough to practice and was not, therefore, as good as Adrian. His cheating consisted most commonly of failing to use his time clock or moving a piece while Adrian was distracted. Adrian was not only better than Kenneth, but he was one of the rising stars of the school chess club. He could play blindfold chess and was perfectly capable of memorising the positions of all the pieces after each move. As a consequence, Kenneth's attempts to disrupt the game invariably failed.

This night, Kenneth was able to use Adrian's pre-occupation with Spot's unusually agitated behaviour as a screen for his diversionary tactics. Evadne came into the front room as Adrian was opening the window in an attempt to see what Spot was growling at.

"What's got the dog so worked up?" Evadne called over to Adrian while making exaggerated faces towards Kenneth in an attempt to persuade him to stop cheating.

"Don't know! It's weird!" Adrian poked his head out of the window. "It's not that he's barking – just growling defensively." He peered from left to right, and failed to see Messrs Material and Burr climb into the living room, at which point Spot stopped growling and just turned his head to a 45 degree angle while stepping away from them. Mr Material looked directly at him and gestured that he should remain silent. Spot was nonplussed and couldn't make head or tail of who these faeries were or what they might be doing, but Mr Material had gravitas, so Spot adopted the precautionary principle and lay down quietly.

"Stupid dog!" Adrian came back into the room leaving the window open. He sat down back at the table and replaced his queen to the square it occupied before he had moved away, giving a deep and meaningful sigh as he did so. Kenneth smiled. His son was not going to be one who would be easy to manipulate when he grew up, and that was pleasing.

Evadne stood at the window and looked down the street in the direction of the Royal Oak. She tried to put her thoughts into some kind of order and work out how they all fitted together. Why was Ralph so interested in the housing issue, and why did he offer to be the local spy? Why were the Johnson's so intent upon selling their land when they must have known that Eileen would never let them buy the access route they needed? Was Fred's cousin aware of how sensitive was the information that he was giving away in advance of important decisions being made? And why did she have the distinct feeling that the Royal Oak was going to be a crucial factor in the whole ongoing saga? She sighed. Kenneth heard her sign and, without looking up from the board, sought enlightenment.

"A very heavy sigh, my lovely?" His fingers wavered over a chess piece as he mulled over the wisdom of a move.

"Just thinking. What will happen to Whimbury if all this new development goes ahead? Will it make things better or worse – because they will obviously change, and all change benefits some people but not others? What do you think?" She placed her hands on the window sill and took in the evening air.

"Just a minute my precious, I think I may be onto a winner here. Ho ho ho." He cackled evilly as he finally put his hand onto a bishop and moved it forcefully along a diagonal, finishing with a flourish. "Get out of that!"

"OK. Whenever you're ready – I'd hate to interfere with something so unimportant, when you're clearly on a roll. You are on a roll, aren't you?" Evadne found the concept of Kenneth being on a roll somewhat difficult to deal with.

"Checkmate!" Adrian moved a pawn and thrust his hand out to accept a handshake gesture from his father.

"Obviously not on a roll after all!" Evadne continued. "So, as I was saying...."

"I remember quite clearly what you were saying, and it had the desired effect of distracting me, fatally, from my game. Completely disrupted my chain of thought, just at the crucial moment, when I had a rare win in my sights." Kenneth feigned disgust, heartbreak and misadventure in equal measure.

"Actually, you were always going to lose from move three onwards." Adrian replaced the pieces in their rightful places on the board. "Another game?"

"Just one more. I'm too upset to concentrate fully now, but I know how much you appreciate some tough warm-up games before a school tournament, so I won't disappoint you."

"Before you start," Evadne turned back into the room while she had the opportunity to get Kenneth's full attention, "I was asking you what you thought about this housing situation in the village – will it be beneficial or not? What do you think?"

"If you ask me, which you have, I'd say it had the potential to really liven up the village, but it's too much too soon. A little at a time, I'd say. Give the newcomers time to adjust and assimilate rather than just take over. There's the makings of a good expanded community here, but it needs time to bed in. Will we have that time? Do you know?" Kenneth absent-mindedly went through the first few moves of the new game, without thinking too much. Had he not been talking to Evadne he might have noticed Adrian scratching his head and acting a little bemused – if not confused.

"Who can say? But I think you're right – it's too much all in one go. But if they're having to buy land to get to the farm, it'll need a lot of houses to recoup the outlay. Would it be cheaper, do you think, to use the land where the Royal Oak is – and who actually owns it?" She gazed back out of the window to where the Royal Oak stood majestically above the rooftops of the houses on Arnold Lane and to the Old School House beyond.

"It might be cheaper, but it's protected – and they'd have to take some of the wood with it just to reach the first field. I can't seem them getting away with that." Kenneth played his next move without looking, and wandered over to Evadne to admire the Royal Oak from their open window. As he did so, Messrs Material and Burr made their exit after seemingly having heard enough. Spot lifted his head as they went and turned it forty-five degrees first to the left and then to the right as if unsure of how to respond to their presence and eventual departure. He growled softly under his breath as he wondered how to pass on his experience of the two strangers to Barry, Robin and Trixie. It somehow seemed important – and urgent!

"What on earth are you grumbling at, silly dog." Kenneth left Evadne to close the window and gave Spot a tickle under the chin followed by a stroke behind the ears. As he did so, he noticed Adrian sitting at the dining-room table with his hand outstretched in his father's direction. He walked over.

"What's this then?" Kenneth glanced at the board but could make little sense of the configuration of the pieces.

"I resign." Adrian was crestfallen. "I used the Morphy Defence to your opening Ruy Lopez, but you countered with something, I've never come across before. Very clever – you've never done it before, how did you work it out?"

Kenneth shook Adrian's hand and silently tapped his nose with his finger knowingly. "Sudden burst of inspiration," he lied.

"Yeah, right." Said Adrian, as dismissively as he could, while still pondering over how he had managed to lose while using his favourite defence. "Well, I've written it all down, so I'll head off up to bed and analyse it, if that's OK."

"Absolutely fine. Sleep well – as I'm sure you will if you focus on the Morphine Defence or whatever." Kenneth put the pieces back in the box and folded up the board. "Shall I leave these on the table ready for tomorrow?"

"I suppose so – I'll smash you next time." Adrian managed a smile as he left the room.

"I suspect he will." Kenneth sat down on the sofa and motioned for

Evadne to join him. "Well, what do you know?" He began, as they snuggled up together. "I not only know an opening, but I can break down Murphys's response – or law or whatever. There's hope for me yet. All I need to do is to stop thinking and let my natural talent express itself." He gestured expansively and theatrically.

Evadne expressed herself with a somewhat unexpansive, "Hmmm". Spot expressed himself by standing up, moving over to join Kenneth and Evadne at the sofa, laying his head on Kenneth's lap, and breaking wind.

******

All around your hat
There are flies of every colour,
And all around your hat
There are flies of every hue
And if anyone should ask you
The reason why it's happening;
It's all from the magpie
That passed over you.
You walk through the woodlands
And through the fields so gay;
You watch............
the lambs....................
.... a'gambolling......

The Royal Oak choir stuttered and stopped as one by one they noticed what everyone else had noticed a few moments earlier. Messrs Material and Burr were standing in the doorway surveying the merry scene. As the last notes flattened and faded away, Mr Material strode to the bar addressing the assembled masses as he did so.

"Please don't stop anything on our account. I merely wish a brief word with your esteemed innkeeper." He and Mr Burr waited respectfully as the conversation slowly and quietly resumed. A lone choir member picked up where they left off and was soon joined by other hesitant voices.

.........You watch the kids at play.....

Oh, nature is a wonder .....
And nature is a joy, ...
But beware the passing magpie
And its power to annoy.
Oh, All around your hat...

As the chorus began to swell, Mr Material leaned over the bar and spoke quietly but purposefully to Barry, who listened intently.

"I am beginning to understand more fully, the issues affecting this village. I have heard all about the plans for housing from the owner of the land, and I have been listening to gossip from the dog's home."

"Battersea?" Barry looked puzzled, and Mr Material was momentarily pushed off course. Amid the hiatus, the normal hubbub continued and the choir were getting back near to full volume.

You gaze to the heavens,
You stare at the azure sky,
You follow the magpies
As above your head they fly.
But nature has its patterns
And what goes in comes out again;
The birds drop a present
On your hat like falling rain.
That's why, All around your hat
There are flies ....

"I don't follow." Mr Material, having failed to follow the logic of Barry's question, at last responded.

"The Dog's Home?" Two unrelated strands of thought were wandering around the bar searching for a connection.

"The dog that helps you communicate with the Crossover Girl? His home?" Mr Burr interjected in an attempt to prod the conversation back on course. It worked.

"Ah, Spot! The dog who lives at the Potts' house. The one who keeps an eye on things for us. The one who chats with Milly Hope. That dog!" Pennies were dropping as if from heaven. Barry instantly felt more confident with the direction in which the discussion was heading. "So, what is the gossip?"

"More human housing is coming, and to build the housing the humans will need to take more land." He paused, not for effect because he had no need of effect, but to measure his words carefully. "And, in certain circumstances, it may mean the loss of the Royal Oak."

"Yes! We heard that as well. We have a crack team on the case as we speak – a human 'spy' in Whimburton, and specialist fae undercover agents about to meet him tomorrow."

"I'm glad to hear it. I suspect you will need all of your talents to win this battle." He paused again, for similar reason. "And I suggest that you make sure that the Crossover child is ready to step into her destiny at a moment's notice, and as soon as possible."

"But she's only a little over two years old – surely we have till she's seven – or maybe a bit before that if absolutely necessary. We're doing all we can as quickly as we can. Besides, as Eric over there said when you were here before, it would be dangerous to rush the legend, for the child as well as ourselves. What might premature action do to the poor girl?" Barry was just a little panicky and also a little unsure of how to relate to the two strangers.

"All important points to take into consideration. I can only advise. You must do whatever you think best, but the girl must make the transition at some time, and if this matter brings you all to the right time, then she must be ready. Of course, whenever the time does come, she herself will have to make the decision to fulfil her role. No-one can make it for her. If she has been well prepared, then all will be well – not just for the fae folk of Whimbury and around about, but for the future of fae- and human-kind for all generations. If not, then yes, there may be dire and long-lasting consequences." Mr Material glanced over to the far corner of the room where he met the gaze of Eric O'Shy. Each stared at the other long enough for Barry to realise the frostiness of the relationship and to feel the tension for himself. Mr Material pointed Mr Burr to the door and raised himself for a parting word.

"I'm sure Mr Eric over there is well versed in Fae folklore and legend, and I'm sure he speaks with some[76] authority." He looked Barry in the eye so hard that it physically hurt. "We will meet again before too long, Mr Innkeeper.

---

[76] Barry could sense the mutual distrust between Mr Material and Eric just from the intonation of the word 'Some' – which had a distinct barb to it.

Until then, focus very hard on the child. She is going to need all the support and preparation you can devote to her. She must make the Crossover before she is seven – how long before, only time will tell."

And the two strangers walked out of the door, taking an aura, an atmosphere, and a whole lot of tension with them.

Chapter Fifteen

OUTSIDE OF THE WHIMBURTON COUNCIL Offices, Ralph was already installed at the back of the pavement. It was much earlier than he would usually be up and about and there remained a slight chill in the air following a clear night. But the sun was up and would soon reach his side of the street, then he would be able to fold his blanket beneath himself, and sitting would be that much more comfortable. With his donations cup in front of him he began talking to Robin and Trixie as if they were beside him, which they weren't. He was working on the basis that he got a record sum[77] the day before while he was deep in conversation with them, and so it couldn't hurt to try it again. Passers-by wouldn't know he was on his own and he was experienced in talking with and to himself. He concentrated on giving his imagination some rein.

"Making money - take the silver, take the plastic, plastic litter, litter the countryside; on the side of the country, support nature; homes for wildlife, homes for life, homes not units, you nits! Parasites, housing sites, sights for sore eyes; polarise, rich there, poor nowhere; where? No! Pull up the drawbridge, retreat to the keep, keep out, keep away, private, major-general, general malaise......"

"Morning Ralph!" Trixie gently interposed herself into Ralph's psyche. He jumped suddenly back into that part of the reality that surrounded him at that particular point in time.

---

[77] More than enough for a cup of tea.

"Ah! Morning Trixie! Robin! And er?" Ralph had never been in close proximity to a Goblin before and, whilst he had been told about them, he hadn't known what to expect. On seeing Clive, he still didn't know quite what to expect, although as he was clearly a friend of Robin and Trixie, Ralph was happy to embrace him into the fold.

"This is Clive, otherwise sometimes known as the software faery but at present known as Mr Havoc, or at least we hope so." Robin presented Ralph with Clive who, not used to being sociable with strangers, and especially human strangers, gave a combined bow, wave and wink.

"Pleased to meet you Clive." Ralph waited until Clive was back into a physical position where he could see that Ralph was genuinely pleased to make his acquaintance. "And I sincerely hope that I also can refer to you as Mr Havoc in the not-too-distant future. I think this situation that we've found ourselves in is indeed one that will need a dose of havoc to resolve it."

"Unfortunately, it appears that I have something of a reputation to keep up. I try not to create havoc with everything I do, but it seems to have a habit of following me around. I just hope that there is a positive outcome, otherwise the havoc will have been in vain." Clive was itching to get started. He prided himself on always having a detailed and fully thought-out plan well before the designated commencement time. He had been briefed by Robin long before he had been given his first glass of Innkeeper's Choice in the Royal Oak and, fortunately, he had already finalised the whole scheme in advance of the drink taking its full effect. He now stood before Ralph with a clear idea in his head as to how the scheme was going to pan out, and if havoc was the correct term to describe it, then so be it.

"Excellent!" Ralph was excited by Robin' and Trixie's new friend, who seemed just the right kind of 'gremlin', with the right kind of expertise and enthusiasm, to deal with their problem. Even as he spoke, the sound of tinkling loose change could be heard in his cup, and with his customary 'thankyou', he leaned over to check the result, and found that it was almost full. He turned back to Robin and smiled. "You know, part of me is excited enough to want you all to get to work immediately, and another part wants you to stay here at my side because, at the rate things are going, I shall soon be in the next level up on the not having to pay income tax bracket – which I believe is the 'still nowhere near, but potentially upwardly mobile' level." Chink! "Thank you!" He emptied out half of the coins into his trouser pocket and rammed an old handkerchief in after them to keep his hoard safe.

"Sorry, but we'll have to leave you to count your fortune, Ralph. Time waits for no faery, as they say[78]. I presume the building is fully open?" Robin jerked his thumb back towards the main doors.

"It is! But be careful, it's always very busy early in the morning – judging by the number of comings and goings." Chink. "Thank you!"

"Of course. 'Careful', as you will know is my middle name." Robin winked and jumped up, ready to get started.

Ralph watched as they ferreted their way into the building in and around the legs and feet of the humans entering and leaving the building.

"Unless 'careful' is spelt very differently from how it sounds, I doubt very much that that is your middle name my friend." He laughed out loud. Chink! "Thank you very much."

****

Eric O'Shy sat silently reading in a clearing within Whimbury Woods. Other than when he took part in the Royal Oak quizzes, no-one had ever seen him do anything other than read. He would answer questions and speak when spoken to, but unless it might have been construed as impolite or rude not to do so, he would not readily join in other faeries' conversations. Whether or not that was just a family trait, no-one had become close enough to him to find out. He had no obvious friends, but there again he had no enemies either. He was knowledgeable, and therefore useful in a number of ways and situations, but seldom, if ever, displayed a sense of humour. When he had first arrived in Whimbury, the sociable Happs had tried to engage him in their fun and activities but with no success. Eventually, without any rancour on either side, they gave up and restricted their contact to quiz nights and when they were faced with difficult crossword clues. This suited everyone.

Eric was absorbed in his book. So absorbed that, for a while, he failed to

---

[78] 'They' being other faeries, obviously. Humans have their own non-inclusive version.

notice the presence of two other faeries immediately behind him. But then his sixth and seventh senses kicked in and without taking his eyes off the page, he responded quietly and calmly.

"As you do not appear to have any aggressive intentions, I presume you want to talk?" He looked up from the page but did not turn around.

Messrs Material and Burr stepped into his line of vision and found a suitable large twig to sit on.

"Indeed we do, Mr Eric. We were just wondering what your interest in the Crossover Child might be? You have a wealth of information at your disposal, and I believe it would be useful to discuss the matter further, with none of the Royal Oak patrons present." Mr Material sat bolt upright as if he was in a business meeting, which in a sense he was.

"What information I have, has been gleaned from reading through all the books of fae legends and history that I have been able to acquire. They are readily available and seem quite clear and consistent. I'm surprised that you don't come to the same conclusion. The child must complete the Crossover before her seventh birthday. If she doesn't, then it will never happen. If she tries, but is not fully prepared, it could be worse for her than if she if had never tried at all. Yet you appear to be prepared to throw her into the ritual whatever the consequences and however unprepared she might be." As he was speaking, Eric pointed to various books that he carried around with him, as if to emphasise his points.

"Insofar as what you have said is correct, then I have to agree with you." Mr Material gave something approaching a wry smile. Mr Burr shuffled uncomfortably on his twig. "But it is what you have not said that is most important. Nowhere in the Histories does it specify when, during her first seven years, the Crossover itself must take place. What they do say is that there will be a time and an occasion where only the Child can act to resolve a critical issue between humans and the fae world. That time and that occasion will be clear to the Child, and she must enact the Crossover then, for they will never occur again. The fae community here must have her ready, or ready enough, such that she can make the decision herself. It is not for us to control her destiny. It is in her hands, and her hands alone – only if they fail to do all they can to prepare her properly, will it be their responsibility."

"They? Their?" Eric became more animated than anyone had ever seen him, and if they saw him now, they would be shocked. "What right have you to come here and dictate what this community has to do, and what responsibility it has. If they push her too hard and too soon, it will be your responsibility, not theirs. Consider that, Mr Material – or whatever your name is".

"I already have, Mr Eric. I already have." Messrs Material and Burr rose as one. Mr Material focussed his gaze on Eric O'Shy and stated, very deliberately. "Perhaps you and we are on the same side, but see things from a different angle. Or perhaps we are on different sides. The important thing is that the Child is prepared as thoroughly as the fae community is able. We should at least be able to agree on that."

Eric avoided Mr Material's eyes – they bothered him more than he was prepared to admit. He re-immersed himself in his book as the two strangers walked slowly out of the clearing.

Once well away and out of earshot, Mr Burr spoke.

"Why did he call the local faeries 'They'? And why did he question your name?"

"Two excellent questions, my friend. Your thought processes are becoming very highly attuned. Excellent questions! 'Why' Indeed? I think that is something we should discuss in the coming days and weeks, but for the moment we need to leave the local fae community to come to their own conclusions and decisions about what should happen next. We have said what we need to say and now we must keep our distance,"

And with that, the two strangers made their way out of Whimbury

****

Barry sat with Percy on the wall outside of the Potts' house. They had been on their way to Over Cross View, but paused when they saw Spot standing up at the gate, watching the world go by, albeit very slowly and intermittently. On the occasions that Spot was alone in the front garden, conversations could be carried out freely with frequent opportunities for apparently random barking at nothing in particular. Barry was glad of the chance to question Spot on the visit of the two strangers the day before.

"Did you notice anything especially odd about them? Did they talk to you?"

In the absence of any obvious reason for barking anywhere along the road, Spot responded with a series of barks in staccato fashion so as not to arouse any suspicion, and waved his paws around for emphasis where necessary.

"There was nothing really odd – *pause* – The tall one seemed extremely authoritative and masterful – *paws* – the smaller one seemed to be somewhat in awe, but thoughtful – *paws* – the taller one just came straight in through the window – *pause* – and gestured to me to keep quiet – *pause* – and to be honest, it never occurred to me to disobey as it were. – *paws* – It felt natural just to do what he said – *pause* – as if it must be right." Spot hadn't thought about it before, but now he did so, he realised that he had never questioned the gesture from Mr Material that he should remain silent throughout their time in his house. He wasn't normally so compliant.

"So they never asked you any questions?"

"Not one word! – *paws* – But they listened intently to everything the humans said." Spot barked a series of threats and insults to an innocent bystander across the road. "Then just as quickly as they arrived, they left. I was going to find a way to get a message to you – *pause* – but it looks like you know all about it already."

"They came right round to the Royal Oak. Caused a bit of a stir, and had another set to with Eric. Don't know what it is between them, but they have different ideas about how to look after Milly and prepare her for what she will have to do. Percy here is going to give her as much help as he can, as quickly as he can, but there's a lot to get through. Fortunately, she seems bright as a button and already has a good understanding."

"And we got on quite well on first meeting, I believe." Percy took over the narrative. "I wasn't sure what to expect, but she relates to us very well by the feel of things. Against all my better instincts, I think I might even enjoy spending time with her – not that the family must ever find out."

"May I never sniff another dog's bottom if I ever let slip your secret! – *paws*." Spot used the opportunity presented by Charlie Brown being taken for a walk to bark out the rest of his conclusions without interruption. Charlie Brown initially looked quizzical to be told that Milly Hope was indeed a special child who already spoke fluent, if simple, canine, and showed great awareness of her natural and fae environments. He understood the situation better when Spot tilted his head in the direction of Barry and Percy, and so responded with a ritual scratching behind his right ear and a brief bark of good wishes before being dragged along on his lead once again down the road.

"Indeed! Keep up the good work my furry friend. Milly should be out for her morning play in the garden by now so we'd better get on and let Percy make a start on lesson two." With a satisfied wave, Barry got down from the wall, gave Percy a helping hand, and moved off with him towards the Hope's home.

"Any ideas what you're going to regale her with today?" Barry was looking forward to watching Percy interact with Milly and, given that Percy was older and had greater knowledge, he thought he might even learn something.

"Well, she's only young and I don't want to bore her or put her off, so I thought I'd concentrate on things in her garden, what they represent and how they all interconnect. Of course, I'll tell her all about Gaia and where faeries and humans fit in to the overall picture, but I don't want it to get too heavy, so I might just stick to stories of Oberon and Titania to lighten it a bit."

Barry chuckled to himself as he realised how seriously Percy was taking his responsibility and how wise he was in his approach. He was definitely an inspired choice. As they slid through the gaps in the wrought-iron work of the front gate, Milly saw them immediately and her face lit up. She knew better than to rush to greet them, but she beckoned them over with her eyes.

Percy ambled over to the log that Milly was sitting upon and took up his allotted place beside her. Barry watched from a respectful distance as Percy began to engage the child in conversation. He experienced a sense of contentment as he saw Milly smile and laugh at a story, expansively told in words and gestures by Percy. From time to time, Percy would point to something in the garden and both he and Milly would crawl slowly and quietly across the unmown lawn, acting out some part of a story and searching out some examples of the natural world from various parts of the garden.

"A whole life perfecting grumpiness," thought Barry silently, "and now look at him. The years have dropped off and a lost youth regained. The child is working her own version of magic already." He felt good. The world felt a little bit better, and he allowed himself just a tiny portion of optimism about the work his little community had taken upon itself.

******

Trixie led Robin and Clive up the stairs and along the corridor towards the room where they had first seen Jason prepare his committee report. At the first door, Robin leapt effortlessly and threw himself at the green button on the wall. He then fell effortlessly and inelegantly back to the floor, where he landed in a heap. Rubbing his shoulder, he slowly stood up again and pretended not to notice Trixie and Clive somewhat cruelly giggling behind their hands.

"Quite firm, that button!" Robin grudgingly accepted the reality of the situation. "But I think it is necessary to press it to the wall in order to get the door to open – at least, that's what I noticed the humans doing."

"Then maybe we just need to wait for a human to come along and press the button?" Trixie had visions of Robin making further attempts repeatedly until he did himself some serious damage.

"I was hoping that we could get in before the humans started taking the room over. It might make it easier for Clive to do whatever he needs to do!" Robin rotated his arms to convince himself that he still had a full range of movement.

"Right! Let me take a look." Clive was the next to levitate himself to the green button. He looked carefully at the button, then at the door, then back to the button. He then took out of one of his many pockets[79] a screwdriver with a light on the end, a piece of wire, and a small hammer. With a dexterity that filled Robin and Trixie with admiration, he managed to manipulate these three items with two hands and the space between his chin and shoulder. Within just a couple of seconds of tinkering with the button, the door opened and the three faeries processed hurriedly through, before it closed again behind them.

"Nice one Clive! That was pretty impressive." Robin believed in giving

---

[79] Like those humans who gain enjoyment from a variety of outdoor pursuits, Clive was a faery who adhered to the principle of "you can never have too many pockets".

praise where praise is due, but he also knew not to ask Clive how he had done it, because time was precious and Clive had a tendency to give the full scientific and technological reasoning behind his decisions and innovations.

Trixie led them into the room with the computers, and was gratified to see that they were alone. All of the screens on the large table in the centre of the room were black and lifeless. She was about to point out the machine that Jason had used and query the fact that it was not turned on, when she noticed that Clive had already wandered over to a bank of plugs and switches underneath the table. He jumped up and stamped down heavily on the red switch at the end of the bank, at which point all of the machines hummed into life and the screens became illuminated with pictures and symbols.

"I'm not sure I can remember which machine he used, can you Robin?" Trixie followed Robin and Clive up onto the table.

"Doesn't matter." Clive walked up to the nearest screen and stood beside the keyboard that was attached to it, waiting for the changing pictures and symbols to settle down. When they finally did so, Clive put his head in his hands and concentrated – hard. So hard that Robin and Trixie were concerned for his welfare. His face turned red and his nostrils flared. Most alarmingly, his hair stood on end and the tips of his fingers started smoking. Robin became anxious.

"You OK?" He went to touch Clive, but Clive lifted a smoking finger in his direction to indicate that he was not to approach.

"Everything is under control," hissed Clive, steamily. "I just need to work out how to get started. Nearly there, no more interruptions please!" He returned to his pose and near-flammable demeanour. Robin happily stepped back and stood beside Trixie as both watched entranced at Clive's efforts.

Suddenly, and as if nothing had happened, Clive lifted his head and began to dance up and down on the keyboard in a jitterbug meets capoeira fashion. As he swung over some keys and bounced off and on others, a series of words and random letters appeared on the screen. With a final flourish on two adjacent keys, the screen changed to a drop-down menu which Clive activated, and selected one of the choices available.

"OK! So if we search for 'housing, Whimbury' that should take us to the right place". A few tap-dancing moves later and the screen came up with the option to enter the Whimburton District Plan – Draft Version for Committee. "Right! Now we're cooking with dry tinder." [80]

Robin and Trixie looked on with raw amazement as Clive manipulated his way around the District Plan until he found the section on housing and the sub-section relating to Whimbury. He pirouetted on the computer touch pad and performed a gentle tap with his extended toe, which had the effect of bringing up the proposals for new housing sites in the villages around Whimburton. A snap of the fingers (now not smoking) and a delicate hop from one foot to the other and the sites in Whimbury itself came up on the screen.

"Now which of these sites are we interested in again?" Clive turned back to Robin and Trixie with a triumphant look on his beaming face.

"I am overcome with awe, Clive." Trixie mimed a worshipful bow which Clive accepted with an acceptable level of arrogance mixed with grace. "The site we are looking for is Hill Farm."

Clive turned away and manipulated the keys on the computer until a summary of the recommendations regarding Hill Farm was visible.

"So, let me get this right," he said, displaying the caution and precision of an expert in his field. "We don't want to have this farm developed for housing, is that right?"

"Right!" Robin and Trixie spoke in unison.

"Then we need to change this report somehow?" Clive pondered the options available to him.

"Right!" Robin and Trixie spoke in unison again.

"And we don't want the author of this document to know that we've done anything until the committee meeting itself?"

"Right!" Robin left it to Trixie on this occasion.

"Then I think this should do it." Clive was, by now, in full gremlin mode and, moreover, a gremlin with a significant amount of the software faery about him, which was exactly what was needed. A mildly acrobatic samba on the keyboard later, and Clive was happy with what he had done. He closed down the computer and the three of them dropped back to the floor, upon

---

[80] Faeries never got into the coal/oil/gas way of life, having never seen the point of using anything other than sustainable renewable energy sources.

which Clive switched off the power to the whole table, just as the first of the council employees entered the room for a morning session on the machines.

"Nicely timed, Clive!" Robin congratulated Clive with an arm around the shoulder. Clive flicked it off again as if affronted by the implication that the whole episode could have been timed any other way other than 'nicely'. They waited a few moments for another human to enter and used the opportunity to leave the room while the door was still open.

Outside, Ralph sat back against the council offices wall with his eyes closed, basking in the late spring sunshine. The three faeries sat themselves around him and waited for an opportune moment to report back on their mission. A few polite coughs later and Ralph opened his eyes and smiled as he saw Robin looking down at him from a few centimetres above. He turned his head to see Trixie and Clive either side of him, and the contented look on their faces gave him assurance that their work had been completed successfully.

"You look pleased with yourselves!" Ralph grinned. Chink! "Thank you!"

"We've done what we set out to do – or at least Clive has! We think. In all honesty we have no idea what exactly he's done, but it all sounds promising. Can you explain what you did, Clive?" Trixie passed the commentary over to the expert, hoping that Ralph might understand more than she did.

"I just needed to make certain adjustments to what the human had written. But I couldn't allow it to happen until it was actually sent out to the 'councillor-type' humans in case somebody noticed. Fortunately, the humans have built-in calendars of dates and times, and these can be manipulated – or 'gremlinised' to use their own terminology. So I hope that what I've done is to time my alterations to come into effect a few minutes before the document is due to be circulated. It should work – the humans use a very simple form of logic in their systems. They try to stop other humans from interfering, but their methods can't deal with the use of sixth and seventh senses. I am quietly confident." Clive exuded quiet confidence and an air of satisfaction.

"And if Clive is confident, so are we!" Robin winked at Clive, who immediately passed him some eye drops on the basis that he must have some kind of infection.[81]

---

[81] There were times, indeed quite frequent times, when Clive displayed a greater

"With that, it's back home to report to Barry." Trixie got up and made to travel back to the Royal Oak. "Come on guys, our work here is done – at least for now. Good to see you Ralph, we'll no doubt be seeing you again very soon, hopefully to celebrate a successful outcome."

"Indeed. Stay safe my friends, and a pleasure to meet you Clive. I don't know what we'd have done without you." Ralph waved them off. Chink. "Thank you."

As they left the confines of Whimburton and wandered through the surrounding countryside, the three faeries began to sing. In a rare display of bonhomie and calm, non-technological socialising, Clive started them off.

I'm a gremlin, I'm a gremlin from Whimbury way....

****

Twelve Days Later

Outside Committee Room A in the Council Offices, Jessica Huntly-Phillips was going through her final briefing session with Jason and Emily. Her department had spent several years preparing its new Development Plan and tonight was the night when it should finally be adopted. Jessica had done all her groundwork and, so she hoped, covered all the bases. All the key issues had been discussed with the Committee Chair, and she knew she had his backing. Despite their frequent differences of opinion and approach, Emily and Jason were a good team in terms of getting things done thoroughly and on time. What's more she trusted them to attend to all the necessary detail – essential when preparing for heavy debate on weighty matters affecting the whole of the district.

"I'm expecting some argument and dissent on protecting the environment and on transport issues, but I think we've anticipated the main issues and got them sorted. Housing is always a problem, but now that we can show we've got enough land in total – just – that should deflect attention away from the detail. You presented the information in the way we discussed?" She looked across at Jason, who sometimes walked a tightrope between efficient and

---

awareness of the emotions and symbolism of his beloved technology than those of fellow faeries.

smug. Emily tutted quietly as, on this occasion, he veered towards toppling into the smug.

"Yes. I did a proof read before it got sent out to members, and everything should be fine. I don't think our beloved councillors will find much to disagree about on that score!" He sat back with his hands behind his head in a manner even Jessica could, from time to time, find annoying.

"Let's hope not!" Jessica gave him one of her famous withering looks. "I have enough fronts that need defending without discovering more! I'll call on you if I need you, so make sure you keep up." As she stood up and moved off, she was sure she heard a 'Yes boss, will do boss,' muttered in the direction of the opposite wall, and stifled a grin as she entered the committee room followed by her team. Emily and Jason took their seats in the corner of the room, while Jessica walked round the table to sit next to the committee chair, who was already in place and in discussion with the committee secretary. She waited patiently until he turned to look at her, and then gave him what she hoped was a confident and assured smile back.

The meeting progressed in the manner expected by Jessica, with the occasional need to ask for information from Emily or Jason, but not with any great doubt that the main substance of the discussion had been successfully steered in the right direction. She held her breath for a few moments when the chair noted that the proposed housing land supply was running close to the minimum level set by the government, but there was no response from the other committee members, not even from the member for Whimingham – though he looked as though he may have been asleep and she had no intention of doing or saying anything to disturb him. Fred's cousin made not one comment throughout the meeting, which confused Jessica just a little, but she passed it off as accepting the inevitable.

As each part of the plan was examined and accepted, including that relating to housing, she breathed yet another sigh of relief, and as the end of the meeting drew nigh, she made a note to herself to warn Jason about his 'I told you so' posture in the corner, which was fine in the office, but not in committee.

With the meeting closed and all important decisions made, Jessica picked up her papers and walked out of the room with Emily and Jason. As she was about to reprove Jason for his body language, she passed Fred's cousin, who was clearly waiting to talk with her.

"I was a bit surprised that the Hill Farm site didn't make it onto the housing land register. I've been telling people that it would be, and that the access problem would be solved somehow." He was not only left a little short-changed when the diplomacy genes had been given out, but he was also very easily confused. In truth he was only still a councillor because he had been around for over a generation and because most people in his ward had always voted for his party regardless of whether it had any relevant policies or proposals – or indeed irrelevant ones.

"How do you mean?" Jessica was as confused as Fred's cousin.

"Hill Farm? You know? The site in Whimbury that we were told was going to be allocated for housing? I looked for it in the documents, but it wasn't included, was it! Just surprised me a bit, that's all. Still, there'll be quite a lot of locals pleased about that – especially with the probability that there would have to be an access off the High Street." Jessica cut him off before his ramblings took him off to pastures new and unrelated, a feature of his nature that she had experienced before, many times.

"Not included?" She looked accusingly at Jason, and then quizzically at Fred's cousin, making sure that her question was framed not so much as an element of surprise but more as a need for elucidation.

"No! Not as far as I could see."

"Yes, well," Jessica played for time as she searched for the right answer to a question that had left her totally flummoxed. Like any good council officer, she hit upon a fictional though entirely reasonable-sounding response almost seamlessly. "We often have to make rather late decisions on matters of detail, especially when taking into account consultation responses. Now that the decision has been made you can go back and tell your local community what the situation now is, as opposed to what you said it would be before the meeting had discussed it." And with the barbed final comment left to find the way to its mark,[82] she moved on back towards

---

[82] And failing to do so, as is usually the case with those persons who happen to remain wholly unaware of the realities and protocols of the political life that they have inhabited for a good portion of their lives.

her office, followed by Emily and Jason who were silently mouthing questions to each other.

Back in the office, Jessica sat, perplexed and pondering the implications of what she had just discovered. Emily and Jason sat perplexed and pondering the implications for them of what she had just discovered.

"Right! Let's just have a look, shall we?" Jessica opened the document and flicked her way to the section of housing. Emily and Jason did the same. When all had stopped flicking, Jessica spoke again.

"What I am reading - and please interrupt if it does not correspond to what you are reading – is as follows: 'In conclusion, on balance, and taking into account all considerations, it is recommended that Hill Farm, Whimbury is NOT added to the existing list of housing sites within the Local Plan.' And when I look over the page at said list...." They all, in unison, flicked over to the next page. ".... lo and behold there the site is, indeed, not to be seen. Any comments, anyone?" The atmosphere was too thick to be cut with a mere knife.

"But that's not what I wrote!" Jason was mortified. "I checked everything in detail the morning before the document was sent out in the afternoon. I double-checked even. It's been nobbled somehow – sabotaged by someone." Jason read the sentence over again and double-checked the list of housing sites, but he couldn't change what was undoubtedly and inextricably there.

"Nobbled or sabotaged by whom would you suggest?" Jessica sat back and removed her glasses, then twiddled her thumbs. Jason wondered if mediaeval torturers and executioners did that before starting work, but hoped that they didn't, both for his sake and also that of the mediaeval criminals and heretics.

"I have no idea – disgruntled Whimbury residents? Whimbury witches? Poltergeists? Gremlins?"

Jessica packed her things and stormed out of the room with a parting "We'll discuss this in the morning!"

Emily and Jason followed at a safe distance, accompanied by Robin, Trixie and Clive, who had been following events in the committee room and Jessica's office, and who now were in fully exuberant mood.

"I'd say he was closest when he blamed gremlins. What do you say Clive?" There was a spring in Robin's step as the three faeries skipped along the corridors of power.

"Gremlins definitely the closest." Clive was proud and satisfied in equal measure. "Though, I think software faery is the more accurate description. And the moral of the story is 'Never underestimate the powers of the software faery'." He laughed. They all laughed.

******

The next evening in the village hall, a special Parish Council meeting was taking place. There was only one item on the agenda – the Whimburton Development Plan. Fred had persuaded his cousin to come and report to the meeting what had happened with regard to the housing proposals for Whimbury. He considered this the best course of action, since there was little chance of him remembering what his cousin might have told him earlier that same day.

"It was a bit of a strange meeting actually." His cousin stood behind the desk and addressed the rest of the group who sat in a semi-circle around him, eager to hear the news. "I told Fred here – which I shouldn't have done at all really, but he promised me he wouldn't spread a word of it, and he assures me that he didn't….." At which point Evadne avoided looking at Miranda in case they both laughed.

"Not a word!" Fred interrupted, and seeing Evadne holding her hand over her mouth, leaned over to whisper in all seriousness, "Not a lie. It was several words!"

"…. Anyway, I told him that Hill Farm was going to be allocated for housing in the new plan – so imagine my surprise when it didn't appear anywhere at all in the housing site list. The Old Station Yard was there, which I believe was a suggestion from this meeting?" There were nods of agreement. "But no Hill Farm. I checked with our planning chief and she just said that the decision was taken late, and I gather it may have been due to local representations. So that's the current state of affairs. The Plan was approved with no housing on Hill Farm."

"I wonder what the Johnsons will make of that?" Eileen was the first to speak. "They seemed pretty confident last time I spoke to them."

"Well that's their problem now, not ours." Miranda was as shocked as anyone, but saw it as one less issue for the Parish Council, and indeed most of the village, to have to worry about.

By this time, Evadne had settled down from her fit of the giggles and was looking more pensive. She realised that the rest of the group was waiting for her to pronounce on the matter, but she was in no hurry to make a statement before thinking it through carefully. Eventually she stood up and walked to the desk, standing beside Fred's cousin.

"Thank you for coming here this evening councillor to give us the up-to-date news on the Development Plan. It is indeed something of a surprise. And I'm not yet sure whether it is a pleasant one or not. All I can say at this stage is that these matters have a habit of not going away quietly, so while we can now carry on with other village matters over the next few weeks and months, I have a suspicion that the whole issue of housing in Whimbury will rear its head again at some time in the future. But for the time being, who's going to offer to make the tea?"

****

At around the same time in the Royal Oak, Robin and Trixie were providing Barry with a full run-through of the events at the Whimburton Planning Committee meeting. Clive had already been given a complimentary glass of innkeeper's Choice and was happily regaling a table full of fascinated[83] Happs with tales of how he had infiltrated the computer systems of the humans in the council offices, and of the results of his efforts. As the raucous cheering of his audience grew with the telling, so more gathered around the table to hear the tale, including even Eric, who had been drawn away from his reading to join the proceedings.

"So we followed the leader and her officers into their war room. She was very confused and very unhappy about it, but we got the impression there was nothing they could do – and they had no idea how it could have happened." Trixie was effusive about their success.

---

[83] Fascinated, though bemused, since, even without the aid of Innkeeper's Choice, Clive had a habit of overestimating the levels of scientific and technological understanding owned by his listeners.

"And they put it down to witchcraft or gremlins." Robin took up the story. "Though no-one mentioned faeries specifically – they really do need to develop their additional senses more fully. That is, of course, once they get the hang of making the most of the first five." He laughed at the limitations of the humans and their inability to discover the true extent and nature of the world in their immediate proximity. A frequent topic of conversation in fae circles related to how much humans concentrated their activities on studying the outer edges of the universe, and yet almost totally ignored the wonders of what was around them all in their everyday lives.

"So round one to us then?" Barry seemed slightly less enthusiastic than the others.

"I'd say more game, set, match and tournament.[84]" Robin gave a confident grin. "No?" His grin displayed a little less confidence as he realised that Barry did not share it.

"It would be great if it were indeed so, but these things, unfortunately have a habit of re-inventing themselves and popping up again in a different guise before too much time has passed. The issue obviously means a lot to some humans, and I doubt very much they will just give up and go elsewhere – even assuming they could go elsewhere. So, let's celebrate for now, but let's also keep our eyes and ears open for what might happen next, eh?"

---

[84] Though faeries used the same general phrase as humans, in faery circles it referred to dominoes, where rivalry was intense.

Chapter Sixteen

Three Years Later

"AS I SAID, ALL THAT time ago, I always had a suspicion that the whole issue of housing in Whimbury would rear its head again at some time in the future." Evadne addressed the Parish Councillors - now officially including Miranda - and Ralph who, not for the first time in the last three years, 'just happened to be in the neighbourhood' and 'just happened to have been noticed by Miranda on her way to the village rooms'. "And that time in the future would appear to be now – if somewhat sooner than expected."

There were murmurings of discontent from all around the floor, with the exception of Ralph, who was busy eating digestive biscuits and slurping tea in the corner – though he was also listening very carefully.

"As you know," Evadne continued in a higher register in order to make herself heard above the ongoing muttering. "The government increased the requirement for housing land in the district a few months ago, and that meant that the provisions in the Development Plan are now inadequate. And that has put pressure once again on Whimbury in general, and Hill Farm in particular. The Johnsons were very upset when their farm was unexpectedly omitted from the approved plan, and now they're trying again to get permission. Eileen here is still holding out on selling land for access, but we don't know how long that will be possible. In the meantime, we think that the developers who are interested in the site, are exploring other ways to reach the land. We don't know for definite where these are, but very credible rumours are suggesting that they could be from here on the High Street."

"But that's not possible surely?" Fred spoke for the rest of the group. "There's only a couple of gaps they could use, and both would mean cutting through the woods. They wouldn't be allowed to do that would they?"

The progress of the Development Plan three years earlier, and indeed what had been happening since, had left a lasting impression on the Parish Council, whose members were now much more aware of the potential impact of local politics on their community. True, a degree of naivety had been lost, which might in some circumstances be considered sad, but in others, including greater effectiveness at standing up for local interests, was to be welcomed. Fred, in particular, now took a keen interest in all matters planning, despite the fact that his cousin was no longer on the committee[85]. The almost miraculous scale of his transformation could possibly be measured by the fact that had never missed a meeting due to televisual conflicts since the night of the special meeting three years previously[86].

"It would be nice to think that it was not possible," Evadne managed to blend cynicism with realism in just the right measures, "but I suspect that all things are possible with politics and planning. We just need to remail vigilant and keep as many people as possible fully aware of events as and when they happen. Then, it's a matter of mobilising supporters as quickly as we can."

"Sounds like we're on a war footing?" Eileen had been showing signs of getting worn down as a result of continued pressure from the Johnsons and their developer friends. She appreciated the moral support of the rest of the community, but there was only so far that moral support could take you, especially when the tactics of property developers gave the appearance of taking on a slightly nastier dimension.

"Much as I hate to say it, I do believe we are." Evadne had reached the reluctant though inevitable conclusion that it was necessary to have a Plan B, in the event of Plan A - namely the democratic processes of local politics - failing to protect the village and its woodlands. The village had character.

---

[85] He had been 'removed' from the committee immediately after the meeting that had adopted the Development Plan – though he claimed to have no idea why that should have been.
[86] Though it might also have had something to do with the fact that he had learned how to use the catch-up facility on his set.

Yes, it had to accept change, there was always change, but it was the character that made it different from the next village, which had its own character, and so on. A large development on Hill Farm just felt wrong, too dominant. And if it meant losing parts of the woods and bringing traffic onto the narrow High Street, then maybe it was indeed time to be on a war footing. The council had tried once before to promote development on Hill Farm, or so Fred's cousin maintained, and still no-one knew how it had come to be omitted. So, it could happen again, now that the pressure was back on. Evadne was on a mission to get Plan B sorted out in readiness.

"But the thing is, who are we at war against?" Miranda stepped out of her secretarial role for a moment. She had learned a lot from her experiences in Parish Council meetings, and she wanted to be sure about what she was minuting. She was as worried as the next person[87] regarding possible dangers to the village, especially now that Milly was really enjoying little nature walks in the woods with her and Will. For a 5-year old, she seemed to know so much more than she could possibly have learned from her parents or at the local nursery, and was at that time in her life when everything was absorbed and processed. To Miranda, it was important that her daughter had the freedom and quietude of the woods to grow up in, especially given the way she had readily assumed the responsibility of an elder sister to teach her sibling all she could about the environment around her.[88]

"A very good question!" Evadne had to think hard. "On the one hand, I'd like to think that the council would be on our side when it comes to protecting local communities, although...." She was thinking on her feet, "...they always have the requirement to meet whatever targets are put in front of them. Then on the other hand, we have to have more houses somewhere, and not all developers are just in it solely for the profit, although....." more thinking about choice of words, "...most of them are, because that's what their business is all about, when all's said and done. What I'm trying to say, I think, is that we perhaps need to be prepared to see both as potential enemies – sad though that may seem."

---

[87] Who just happened to be Eileen, and who was indeed very worried.
[88] But more of little Daisy later.

"A war on two fronts, eh?" Fred drifted into a wavy line moment[89]. "I can remember my father telling me about how, in wars, changes in alliances could lead to one of the groups having to fight on two fronts. We don't really want to drift into that kind of situation. As he told me, that splits your resources and leaves you at a grave disadvantage. I can remember at school...."

"Yes, thank you Fred. A point well made." From experience, Evadne knew at what point Fred had actually finished saying what he originally meant to say and when, therefore, it was time to move on.

"Two fronts, no back..." All eyes turned to Ralph who, without warning, spoke out loud in a meeting for the first time. "Watch your back, back to the future, what does the future hold, hold on to what you hold dear, dear heart, close to your heart, make it heartfelt, feel it inside, follow your feelings, feeling your way, finding your road, road to nowhere, news from nowhere, no pain, no hurt, no tyranny, no surrender." He stopped as suddenly as he began, aware of eyes upon him. He waved his hand apologetically and went back to his biscuit. Miranda glanced round the room, put her fingers to her lips, and stepped over to Ralph where she engaged him in hushed tones.

"You've been listening to all this Ralph, we all know that. What are you thinking?" Miranda had talked several times with Ralph since the first time he had come to the Parish Council meeting, and she knew that he usually had relevant and important things to say. It was just that, more often than not, there was no-one around who was prepared to engage him in conversation. Once, she herself had asked him to explain what happened on the occasion when he first saw Milly in the park in Whimburton, but he simply replied 'Later!'. She had increasingly had the feeling that 'Later' was becoming 'Sooner'. But for now, she genuinely wanted to get him to focus his thoughts.

"What was I saying?"

"Your journey began with 'Two fronts, no back' and ended with 'no surrender', passing several busy stations on route." We were discussing the housing issue here in the village. Do you remember?"

"Yes! Yes!" Ralph's mining of his memory was open-cast, in that it

---

[89] This was what Fred called those times in the visual media when a wavy line gradually transforms the picture from one place to another, or from dream to reality. In meetings he often spent much of his time in the wavy line zone.

required only minimal excavation to reveal what was just below the surface. "The old feller over there is absolutely right. You don't have the resources to fight on both fronts, so you need to listen to everything that is said in the village, and beyond, to decide which front will take priority. Listen, hear, consider and follow your feelings as to who is true friend and who is the real foe. But, above all, listen!"

As Ralph picked up another biscuit, Miranda returned to the group and reported on what he had said. Ralph looked in the opposite direction, but nodded agreement as Miranda expanded on the approach that he had recommended.

"It all sounds eminently sensible to me!" Evadne was happy to endorse Ralph's analysis. "Maybe we should appoint Ralph as an ex-officio Chief Advisor to the Parish Council? He obviously knows what's going on here and in Whimburton, and understands the seriousness of the situation – what do you say Ralph?" She hated the idea of talking about someone as if they weren't in the room when, in reality, they were. And so, she brought him into the conversation.

"I accept!" Ralph replied without making eye contact. "You could pay me in biscuits!"

Evadne smiled. "And the cups of tea can act as a productivity bonus."

"Agreed." A rare glimmer of a smile appeared on Ralph's face. "No need for a contract, I trust you all."

"Thank you for that vote of confidence, Ralph." Evadne deftly swung back to the immediacy of the matter in hand. "Now we must get to work on the plan."

******

"Her level of understanding is really quite amazing!" Percy placed a cup of hot herb tea on the table in front of Everard. The weekly afternoon chat in the garden with his friend had become something of a highlight – a session of meaningful discussion mixed with meaningless gossip. In short, the perfect combination of the significant and the banal that makes for a truly relaxed moment in stressful times. Everard was viewed by many in the local fae community as something of a loveable and harmless buffoon, and while there was a side to him that warranted that perspective, he was also decent, honest and capable of great insight[90]. Percy greatly valued his friendship and had discussed with him many of the issues about his times with Milly, in attempts to clarify how he should be developing her preparation.

"Understandin' be one thing," Everard pronounced as he picked up his drink. "but ….. b*****r that be 'ot, it do really be, phew." He waved his hand in front of his burning mouth. "Will oi never learn to wait till it do cool down a bit? Now, where were oi?"

"You said, 'but'." Percy helped him out.

"But what?" Percy's help was insufficient.

"You said the understanding was one thing, but …." Percy expanded on his level of help.

"Yes, roight, exactly!" Everard resumed from where he left off, having first placed his cup well out of easy reach, to avoid another careless moment. "Understandin' be one thing, but knowin' how to 'be' a faery – well that be quoight another thing. And knowin' how to switch from one to the other and when to do it, they be even more things that she need to fathom out." Everard reached out for his cup and then withdrew his hand quickly.

Percy pondered. At length, he pronounced on the result of his pondering. "The way I see it, I need to make sure she understands enough so that if and when she makes the Crossover, she'll recognise things from the faery angle, and won't get frightened by those things not being the way they were before it happened. And she'll know how to behave in that moment. That's another thing I've learned over the past three years. If I'm to help her recognise places and people and circumstances from the faery angle, then I've got to recognise how she experiences those things from the human angle – and it's been quite a journey, I can tell you. When you're limited to the five basic senses, it's a real handicap. When she finally completes the Crossover, and becomes fully aware of the other senses, it's going to be a big shock to her. I just hope I've prepared her for that."

---

[90] Much of his insight came from meditation whilst fishing in the village pond - the moments when less perceptive faeries might have assumed he was just resting his eyes!

"Sounds to me like you been doin' a good job. I wouldn't even 'ave thought of them things, let alone know how to teach 'em. Oi've said it afore, and I'll no doubt be sayin' it again, that oi think's you'm be the best faery that could've been picked for this lark."

"Well, thank you, Everard, that means a lot to me. I've got more enjoyment out of my time with the child than I could ever have imagined, she's quite a character, I'll tell you, but there are times when the weight of responsibility hangs heavy. Percetta will tell you that I'm sometimes at a complete loss as to what to do next – but I've got support. Robin and Trixie back me up, and the animals are really pulling their weight. Spot talks to her regularly. And Junior has stepped into Larry's role with barely a ripple.[91] The birds bring in snippets of gossip, and she's been learning a lot from her walks in the woods with her parents, who seem good sorts."

"Does they know about the child, d'yer think?" Everard had often wondered, in his moments of meditation by the pond, what Will and Miranda made of their daughter talking with faeries, animals and insects in the garden. He had frequently heard them speaking of how special she was to all and sundry in the village, but did they have any idea at all just how special, and in what way her special nature was being played out?

"They definitely know that she's not like other children, but I don't think they have any notion as to why that should be. The important thing is that they support her and are bringing her up in ways that are helpful to us – encouraging her imagination and finding the answers to all her questions – well most of them. I'm sure it wasn't just the child that was chosen, but the parents too!"

"So, what 'ave you got lined up for her next?" Everard picked up his cup and very carefully blew into it to cool it down.

"I thought I might advise her to listen to the crows when they suggest something. I know they fancy themselves as the 'academics' of the avian

---

[91] In the intervening period, Larry's joints had finally given up and he made his way to the great log-pile in the sky. Milly was upset at what was, for her, the first really close experience of a loved companion moving on. But it was all part of the learning experience and she enjoyed being with Junior in a different way – and Will and Miranda had become used to being serenaded with extracts from Gilbert and Sullivan light opera, even if they couldn't understand why.

world, but the fact is that they are bright and they do learn from experience. And on a similar theme, on the odd occasion when she meets up with a hawk, it is as well to engage the bird in conversation about the 'other' world. It may well come in useful at some stage in the future. Other than that, it's much the same – chat about the fae inhabitants of the area and how they might all react differently in different circumstances. If she is to become fae, for however long and however frequently, she'll need to know which type of fae it would be best to identify with most at the time."

"You bain't not be wrong there, Perce." Despite the misplaced double negative, Everard was able to convey how impressed he was with Percy's logical approach. "Oi just 'opes that you've still got toime to finish off the preparations. The way things 'ave been goin' lately, anythin' moight happen, and she could be needed urgent like."

They both considered this possibility carefully as the herbal tea cooled.

****

"Rumour has it," Robin began, "that the people from Hill Farm are going to try again to get permission for their housing scheme. And from the same source it would appear that they are still having trouble getting the rights to access, which was their problem before."

Barry sighed the sigh of someone who had been reluctantly expecting something like this for some considerable time.

"I did say, did I not, that these things have a habit of re-inventing themselves and popping up again in a different guise before too much time has passed." Barry was not saying this in an 'I told you so' tone of voice, but as one who had accepted from the beginning that his troubles, and by extension those of the whole community, had only been temporarily halted by the intervention of the software fairy some three years previous. "So, who is your source – as if I can't guess – and what else did he or she say?"

"I couldn't possibly divulge his or her identity, so for the sake of anonymity we shall simply call him or her, ….. Ralph." Robin whispered the name behind the back of his hand, which was technically unnecessary since there was only the two of them in the bar at the time.

"OK, so what else did this …. Ralph, have to say?" Barry maintained the façade of secrecy, since not to do so could have delayed the retelling of the story by a considerable amount of time. Robin continued'

"He said '…"

"Or she said …." Barry tapped the side of his nose and knowingly corrected Robin's confidentiality error.

"He or she said …." Robin was having difficulty keeping a straight face. "Wait a minute, you know he's called Ralph, I just told you. Where does the 'she' come in?"

"Front door like everyone else – come on Robin, we haven't got all day. Enough meaningless frivolity and let's get on with the story."

"Right. He said, just before disappearing into the woods – from whence he will come later tomorrow to meet you outside and discuss matters further – he said, that there was a distinct possibility that the developers might try to get permission for a new road off the High Street through the woods to Hill Farm." Robin waited for this to sink in and then continued. "And one further piece of news – this time from a reliable dog, whose identity, as a secret agent, we must also protect ….. "

"Yes, yes, Spot. Carry on for Gaia's sake." There were times when his brother's sense of humour frustrated Barry more than he let on. This was not one of those times. This time he let on!

"All right, all right, calm down Bro. As I was just about to say, the dog, whom for the purpose of this tale we will call Spot[92], is sure that he saw the two strangers again today, hovering at the edge of the woods and then following the character, known to us only as Ralph, into said woods. Bit of a coincidence wouldn't you say – we haven't seen anything of them for three years or so, and now, just at this precise moment, they turn up again?"

"Yes! A bit of a coincidence is very much what I would say. Almost as if they knew something was about to happen, or even happening, before we did. That is indeed most odd, disturbing even. If it isn't just a coincidence, then how did they come to know about this latest development, and why are they here anyway?" Barry felt nervous, and as he very seldom felt nervous, that

---

[92] There were very few things in his life that he enjoyed more than winding Barry up mercilessly.

made him even more nervous. He had to pull himself together before he got sucked into a vicious whirlpool of worrisome activity and thought patterns. "But no use speculating, let's wait for the person known only as Ralph to come round later and fill us in on what he knows."

"He, or she, knows!" Robin noticed Barry's disquiet and did his best to divert his attention back onto something trivial.

"Indeed, he or she! Now let's get moving to help Trixie and Damon tidy the Bar area ready for tomorrow's business." Barry launched himself into bustle mode, while all the while still entertaining worrying thoughts about what might be to come.

****

In a field, on the edge of Hill Farm, Robert Hancock, along with Diana and Richard Johnson, was looking at Whimbury Woods and making notes, taking care every time that he moved to notice where he was putting his feet. He made a rough sketch of the field boundary, the degree of slope, and the height of the trees at various points. As he progressed methodically from north to south, he was convinced that he heard sounds from just inside the wood.

"Did you hear that?" He looked up from his clipboard and attempted to co-ordinate his gaze and his hearing in order to identify where the sound was coming from. The Johnsons who had been chatting happily, and totally ignoring what Robert Hancock was doing, protested ignorance of having heard any sound at all.

"Do you get badgers or anything like that in the woods?" Hancock strained to pick up any aural clues.

"Not seen any in years." Diana replied. "There was a cull a while back, to protect cattle like ours, and we haven't noticed any at all since then, have we?" She turned for confirmation to Richard, who nodded in agreement. "Not sure how exactly they went about it, and I didn't feel inclined to ask too many questions. Personally, I was never sure how necessary it was, but the men from the ministry insisted and so we just had to go along with it."

"I could have sworn I heard something quite big from just in the trees and undergrowth there." Still in his suit and nearly best shoes, Robert Hancock had no intention of straying any nearer the barbed wire fence than he had to, and so, after a short while continuing to listen carefully, he moved on.

Making a note to be more careful where and how he walked in future, Ralph followed the threesome from inside the wood, also continuing to listen carefully. He had a feeling that what was being said might prove to be useful, and he didn't want to miss anything.

Hancock now moved quickly along the boundary since he wanted to make sure that he finished his task before lunch. He had a working lunch meeting planned with his project manager in order to pass on the information he would have gained from his morning's survey, and he needed to progress matters as swiftly as possible. At the southern end of the field, he made his last note and put away his pen.

"Penny for your thoughts, Robert." Richard Johnson was finally interested enough in proceedings to want some preliminary feedback.

"You don't get much for a penny in this day and age, Richard." Robert Hancock smiled the greasily artificial smile of a confirmed businessman, for whom real humour is only shared at a realistic price. "But I assure you, I'll send you a bill at the earliest opportunity. But for what it's worth at this stage, and subject to what my project manager has to say, I'd suggest that it would be easiest and cheapest to build the access road nearer to this southern end. The slope is less and it appears on the face of it that there are fewer really large trees, which should make the area simpler to clear."

"Whatever you say Robert! Easy and cheap seems to fit the bill nicely." Richard knew little or nothing about the building trades, but he knew how to make money for as little outlay of effort as possible. After all, the basic principles had to apply to all industries, surely? What couldn't be paid for directly could almost always be paid for indirectly, given the right amounts and the right kind of contacts in the right places.

"Just one little issue comes to mind!" Diana hesitated to raise the little issue, but felt that considering it at an early stage might make dealing with it more straightforward in the longer term.

"Fire away!" Robert smiled the smile of one who could always find access to the right amount of cash, and who had intimate contact with the right people in the right places.

"That southernmost access point to the woods and this field would involve removing the old Royal Oak tree, would it not? And isn't that tree protected by some Order or other? And the locals love it – it has some kind of historical connections that they find important and characterful[93]. I'm not sure that we want to add any further complications to the ones we already have?" Diana had a pragmatic side to her nature, and while she was not in least bit bothered about a few trees out of a whole wood-full, she could often be relied on to spot potential pitfalls in the best laid schemes of mice and men.[94]

"That may well be the case." Robert had a way of minimising the influence of potential pitfalls, by minimising the significance of truth and reality to anyone other than those who made real money. "But we mustn't let sentimentality get in the way of providing new housing for those in desperate need of a roof over their heads.[95] One tree against dozens, if not hundreds, of families? I think we can get over that hurdle. And as for protection and Orders and the like, I've never let things such as that get in the way of schemes before, and I have no intention of starting now. No! No worries on that score, we can deal with it – we have the ways and means."

"Such as?" Diana retained just a modicum of conscience, though it had never before been quite enough to fully support the adoption of a principled approach to decision-making.

"Such as a chain saw!" Robert laughed. "Do you know how much money you could make from this development?"

"Yes, you told us!" Diana couldn't remember the exact amount but she remembered being impressed.

"A lot," confirmed Robert. "And do you know how much you can get fined for chopping down a protected tree?"

"No!" replied Diana, suspecting that the answer was going to be revealing.

"Very little – relatively. So don't worry about it – I know who to contact in Whimburton in order to sort out that particular issue, should the need arise."

---

[93] Having apparently once been widdled on by none other than George III himself, whilst caught short on one of his journeys to visit the more rural parts of the kingdom.
[94] And they usually were men – very few in practice involved mice.
[95] Who were not the same group of people as those who would eventually live in the houses he intended to build, but it was a good line.

"So, we can leave it in your capable hands?" Richard was generally happy to leave anything in anyone else's capable hands if it appeared likely to be to his advantage. That left him to concentrate on those aspects of business that he knew more about.

"Absolutely!" Robert Hancock pointedly looked at his watch. "Now if you'll excuse me, I have an important lunch meeting relevant to our situation here, and, once I've packed these papers away, I must be off." Diana and Richard set off slowly across the field, waiting for Hancock to follow.

Robert Hancock fitted his drawings and notes back into his case and was about to follow the Johnson's when he was sure he heard another sound from inside the wood. A cracked twig maybe, but what about the accompanying deep sigh? He turned to where they were standing.

"Are you sure there are no sizeable animals in the wood?" At which point he set off hurriedly in their direction and immediately stood in a cowpat. "Damnation." He started to wipe his shoe on some clean grass.

"What was that, Robert?" Diana put her hand to her ear.

"Oh nothing! Keep going, I'll catch you up in a moment." Robert Hancock continued walking up through the field, stopping every few metres to utilise another clean area of grass.

In the woods behind him. Ralph set off as silently as he could in the direction of the Royal Oak, sighing deeply every time he cracked a twig. From a safe distance away, Messrs Material and Burr tracked his every move.

****

In the front garden of Over Cross View, Miranda was sitting with Milly and asking her what she had done in class that day. The nearest school was in Whimingham, well over a mile away, but Miranda, with Daisy in her buggy, always walked to pick Milly up, unless it was really pouring with rain, in which case she could usually leave Daisy with Evadne and cadge a lift with one of the other Parish Council members, with many of whom she had now struck up a close friendship.

Milly had lots of school friends, and was never short of a story to tell about who had done what that day. But none of her friends lived close by in

Whimbury, and so at regular intervals Miranda arranged a joint pick up so that Milly could visit a friend's house, or vice versa, and then Will or the parent of the other child would collect their child after tea. Today they were on their own, which Miranda enjoyed. She loved to talk with Milly. Apart from finding out bits of gossip, she could also probe Milly about her relationship with all things nature and fairy. She still wasn't sure that she was completely happy with Milly's vivid imagination, but it didn't seem to be upsetting her schooling and she clearly had both feet planted in the realities of the Whimbury world around her, at least those realities that Miranda could also relate to.

While she was in the garden, Milly always seemed to have one ear and eye open to the natural world and the other of each pair focussed on what her mother was saying or showing her. She could be talking to a ladybird or woodlouse and still manage to answer questions from Miranda, without losing track of either conversation. Miranda told her friends it was as if Milly was already multi-lingual, where one of her languages belonged to a different world altogether – spoken in English but heard in who knew what other medium. As far as Miranda was concerned, she was party to only half of the conversation whenever Milly was speaking with one of her non-human contacts.

On this afternoon, with Daisy dozing off in her buggy, Miranda asked Milly what she had done at school that day, and was told that the class had spent the last part of the afternoon on a nature walk around the edge of the school field. Her school, St.Julian's, was very progressive for a small infant school, and managed its limited space in such a way that there remained room for wildlife around the perimeter.

"And what did you see?" Miranda always enjoyed asking questions such as this because the answers never failed to be unexpected. On occasions she could also learn something new herself.

"We saw lots of flowers – poppies, cornflowers, cranesbill, daisies." Milly counted her fingers as she tried to recall the various plants she had seen. "But bigger daisies than these. And there were bees and two butterflies – but they didn't talk much, they were too busy and, anyway, I had to listen to what Miss was saying because she told us she was going to ask us questions after. I had a little chat with a woodlouse who knew one of Larry's cousins, but she didn't have much interesting to say."

Miranda often wondered what Milly's teachers thought of her vivid imagination, but neither of them had brought it up at parents' night or even in informal chat at the school gates, though one of them had said that she was very good at joining in at story time, and took particular interest in stories that involved animals. She also mentioned that at times Milly gave quizzical looks at some of the antics of the animals in the stories, as if she were saying 'they'd never do that!', but otherwise she was very attentive and bright and made friends easily, which was good to hear.

"So do woodlice often have interesting things to say?" Miranda probed, as she often did.

"Yes! Lots of fun things happen under logs and stones that we don't usually see. Junior tells me about that, and Larry used to tell me about what happens in the Faery Tree."

"And what does happen?"

"They have parties, and play games, and Larry had to tidy up." Milly smiled as she recalled the more detailed accounts of what went on at the Royal Oak.

"What games?" Miranda kept digging away into Milly's other world.

"Percy says they play donimoes, but I'm not sure what that is. And some of them play darts with pointy arrow things - that sounds dangerous[96]! And some of them sing and dance on tables." She laughed and jumped up onto the large tree stump in the garden and performed an exaggerated dance on it.

"You be careful now!" Miranda put up a protective hand to help Milly down. Milly took hold and jumped down again.

"Percy says that I can come to one of their parties when I'm ready." Milly resumed poking around in amongst the lawn clover.

"When you're ready? Whatever did he mean by that?" This was a new direction, one with which Miranda was totally unfamiliar.

"Don't know. He said we'd both know when I was ready, but it could be soon."

---

[96] Little did she know – at this stage – quite how dangerous faery darts could be.

Miranda took time out to consider this latest revelation. In truth, over the course of Milly's short life thus far, she had herself begun to think that there might be some validity to the idea that fairies existed, if only because Milly seemed so sure, and no-one else had put the idea into head. She and Will had often discussed just what 'special' might mean in the context of their own daughter. There was 'special' in the sense of saintly; 'special' in the sense of gifted; 'special' in the context of intellect; 'special' in the context of worthy of being doted upon[97]; and then 'special' in the context of Milly.[98]

What Miranda could not get out of her head was how Ralph fitted in to the jigsaw that was their lives at the present time. The first true encounter in the park where Ralph had bowed to Milly; the subsequent coincidental encounter on the way to her first Parish Council meeting; subsequent meetings – also always involving Parish Council meetings; and the sudden interest that Ralph had taken in the life of the village. Somehow, and she couldn't quite put her finger on it, Milly seemed to be involved in the whole business. She decided that now was the time to broach the subject with Milly herself.

"Milly darling, do you remember the strange man who we met in the park in Whimburton a long time ago and sometimes comes here as well? I think you saw him out on the street through our front window a couple of days ago?"

"Yes!" This was not new interesting conversation to Milly and so she remained more engaged with life on the overgrown lawn.

"Have you heard any of the local animals talking about him? Do they know anything about him?" Miranda accepted that the only way to get information from Milly was via her 'imaginary' world.

"Spot say he on our side. Barry, Robin and Trixie like him. They talk to him a lot. He helps faeries."

The reply was much as Miranda expected, but it didn't help her to understand the links between Milly and Ralph, and why he treated her, or indeed Miranda, with so much respect and consideration.

---

[97] Strictly speaking this is not really special at all, merely what nearly all parents feel about their offspring, with or without any justification.
[98] Which is more what special should mean – no-one else quite like her, whatever the context!

Milly had finished rummaging around in the garden and walked into the house shouting, "Can I watch TV now?". Miranda followed her.

"Yes! But only for a few minutes mind, while I get tea ready. What do you want to watch?" Miranda put the plug into the socket and switched on.

"Snow White and the Seven Gnomes!"

"Seven Dwarfs! Again?" Miranda wondered if it had been a good idea to buy a job lot of classic childrens' cartoons at the recent jumble sale. Still, Snow White seemed pretty harmless, apart from the unexpected and slightly worrying delight that Milly took in Grumpy, for whom she displayed a strange but definite affection. This regularly left Miranda perplexed. "OK, princess, one last time!"

Miranda set the film off and walked off without hearing Milly mouth silently and absent-mindedly to herself, 'you said that before'.

Chapter Seventeen

OUTSIDE OF THE ROYAL OAK, Ralph was explaining to Barry what he had heard a little earlier.

"So, it seems we'll have to deal with the worst-case scenario!" Barry was deeply disturbed. "And they definitely talked of taking a chainsaw to the tree?"

"That's what the guy with the clipboard said, and he seemed to be in control of the whole thing. The other two were just happy to let him get on with it – though, to be fair, the woman was less happy than the man, who simply washed his hands of the matter. I didn't much like the way Mr Clipboard – Hancock I think his name is – claimed to know the very people to sort the matter out without going through the correct channels. This could become a worryingly imminent issue, and I think we need to have a plan in place as quickly as possible, in case it does." Ralph was showing signs of nerves and stress once again, and Barry felt the need to appear calm in order to prevent Ralph from having one of his 'bad dos'.

"Right! Well, I think this is the time for the Whimbury faeries to take control of their own destiny. Thank you, Ralph for being our eyes and ears in and around the village, but I think now we are going to need you more in the town. Would you recognise this Mr Clipboard again if you saw him?" Barry was putting on his best 'we can handle this' persona, and was hoping that his attempt to get Ralph out of the firing line would work.

"Definitely! I'd remember his face, and his voice, anywhere. He looked – and sounded - as if he'd just crawled out of the village pond covered in algae.

And I know where he'll most likely go! First to the council and then to arrange his own dirty work. I'll keep track of him, don't worry about that." Ralph was secretly enjoying the subterfuge of being a secret agent. It was the kind of undercover work that had little pressure attached. No-one really noticed him around Whimburton and, if they did, they passed him off as somehow mentally deficient and basically harmless. This was tension he felt he could handle, and Barry was relieved to send him on his way with a mission that was tailor-made for his talents.

"Excellent!" Barry gave Ralph the nearest equivalent of a hug that a small faery could give a large human[99]. "We'll send Trixie over from time to time to give and take messages. She's by far the quickest amongst us. If you need reinforcements just let us know."

"I think it may be yourselves that will need the reinforcements." Both Barry and Ralph were temporarily stunned by the imperious voice behind them. They both jumped up with a start and turned to face Messrs Material and Burr.

"Sorry to startle you, but we couldn't help overhearing your conversation and, while we agree with all that had been said up until that last point, I think you will find that the final act of this drama will be played out here at the tree and not in Whimburton. Your human friend here will certainly have his part to play, but the whole community here will need to be prepared for what is to come. And by whole community, I mean the whole community." Mr Material looked stern with a slightly unnatural kindly manner thrown in. Mr Burr looked, as ever, deferential but clearly in agreement.

"Have you been following me?" Ralph had never seen a faery such as Mr Material before, and he wasn't sure if the usual rules of engagement applied.

"We have, on more than one occasion, in the past and just now. You clearly have special gifts of insight with regard to the fae world, and you exercise them in a friendly and honest way. I have never before seen such a connection - it is interesting and most enlightening. One day you must tell me how it took place, but now is not the time. I have things to discuss with Mr Goodfellow here, and I believe you may have urgent business to attend to in

---

[99] Which was more symbolic gesture than physical envelope.

town?" Mr Material stood up in a manner that was clearly a gesture of farewell.

"I believe I have!" Ralph knew when he wasn't wanted, he'd had plenty of experience in that regard and recognised the signs. "It may or may not have been a pleasure to meet you Mr....?"

"Mr Material." Barry blurted out.

"My name is different in different parts of the world." Mr Material opened up to Ralph in a way that he hadn't previously done with any of the faeries in Whimbury. "I was most recently in France, where they called me Daniel. Perhaps I will explain on the next occasion that our paths cross. And this is my Doctor friend, Mr Burr. From our perspective, meeting you has indeed been a pleasure. I look forward to seeing you again soon. Now, Mr Innkeeper, I have matters to discuss with you inside." And with a parting gesture to Ralph, he and Mr Burr headed off to the front door, followed by Barry who simply shrugged goodbye in Ralph's general direction.

Ralph watched them all enter the Royal Oak and moved off down the High Street in the direction of Whimburton, with a gently whispered 'goodbye, then. or should I say au revoir, Mr Daniel Material'?.

****

Over a steak lunch in the dining room area of the Fox and Hounds in Whimingham, Robert Hancock was chatting with his project manager, Derek Garner. Hancock was a busy wheeler and dealer, and these lunchtime work meetings were a frequent occurrence. He had a finger in a number of development pies, and needed reliable allies to smooth over cracks, or plaster over crevices, when bureaucracy or local democracy threatened to delay or otherwise hinder the progress of his projects. DIG construction[100] was one of these essential allies, and Derek was the partner that had a number of useful contacts who were happy to operate around the fringes of what was and was not acceptable in the world of construction.

Between mouthfuls, Robert explained the potential problem surrounding

---

[100] Named, unimaginatively, after Derek and his brother Ian.

the Hill Farm scheme, and flagged up the kind of 'specialist' he felt that he might need in order to rectify it.

"I've already got the informal support of the planners in Whimburton, because they thought the proposal was OK three years ago. No-one seems to know how it got missed off the housing site list when the local plan was adopted. The only issue remaining is that of getting access. The planners want us to use the existing track, but we're getting nowhere with the woman from the other farm that it goes through. They couldn't support the most promising other option, which is through the woods, because it would involve chopping down a protected tree. I can get a tree condition report to show that it needs 'selective pruning' because its unsafe, that's easy. But if that tree weren't there at all.....?" Hancock left a none-too-subtle pregnant pause while he constructed another forkful.

"If the tree weren't there...." Derek Garner picked up the familiar theme while filling his mouth with a large number of tomato-sauce covered chips. "... If the tree weren't there.... " he repeated while spraying out fragments of food, "... then access wouldn't be a problem. Am I right?"

"Exactly!" Hancock wiped a fragment of chip from his lapel and reminded himself to book his suit in for dry-cleaning the next day.[101] "Once the tree is down, we have a clear run into the woods and beyond into the bottom field at Hill Farm. But it will have to be done quickly and irrevocably. It's not the kind of thing that can be done secretly and quietly, so it has to be completely down before there can be any response from the powers that be. Is your 'Vancouver Chainsaw Massacre' man still around?"

"Tyler? He certainly is. British Columbia Logging champion for three years in a row before he came over here to spread his knowledge and experience."

"All I want is for him to spread the tree over the ground in as few pieces as necessary. Misunderstanding over the scale of pruning necessary etc etc... safety of local residents etc etc ..... There will of course be legal implications." Hancock wiped his lips with his napkin and pushed his plate

---

[101] Which he could, in fact, have done in advance had he remembered the last meal he had with Derek Garner in the Fox and Hounds – or indeed any previous meal with him.

into the middle of the table, in order to set up his laptop and make the necessary calculations.

"Of course. There always are. But if you can cover the financial aspects of that – with the emphasis on fine – as you have in the past, then I see no practical problems."

"Leave it with me!" Hancock began tapping out 'memos to self' and entering figures into his financial appraisal. "Just before you arrived, I set up a meeting with the planners for later this afternoon, and I've warned my tree man to have ready a draft report on the danger to the public of leaving the Royal Oak unmanaged. It's an old tree, there must be bits about to fall off. He'll find something. You and your tame lumberjack just need to be ready at a few hours' notice to perform the necessaries. There! The usual arrangements and remunerations?" Hancock swung his laptop round for Derek Garner to see. For his part, Derek Garner was disappointed to see that the remunerations were exactly the same as on his previous contract, but as the risks to Hancock were greater this time round, he didn't feel it appropriate to haggle.

"Ok by me! Any idea as to how soon we need to be ready?" For the amount of money resting on this project, Derek Garner was prepared to make himself ready by working all night if necessary, but a rough idea would be helpful.

"I think we are talking about a day or so. I don't want the opposition to have time to organise if we can avoid it. A lightning strike is what we're after. And if God won't give us a bolt of lightning, then your lumberjacky man will have to provide it himself. And now if you'll excuse me, I have to go and see an official about a tree." Hancock allowed himself the luxury of a smile.[102]

"Do your worst, Robert, do your worst." Derek Garner was quite prepared to finish his drink at the table in peaceful solitude. "Just remember to pay the bill on the way out!"

Hancock placed his hands over his heart in a faux 'as if I could possibly do anything else' gesture, and made for the bar. As he paid the bill, Derek Garner called him over and whispered a farewell shot across his bows.

"If I were you, and this is just advice from a friend to a friend, you

---

[102] Which, in common with the smiles of similarly ruthless businessmen, was little short of nausea inducing.

understand, I wouldn't refer to our champion logger as a 'tame lumberjack' or 'lumberjacky man' to his face. It wouldn't go down too well – and have you seen the Chainsaw Massacre film? He was the technical advisor! Just saying."

****

Eileen Robinson sat with Evadne in the Potts' front room drinking a de-caffeinated tea. It was late in the evening and she wouldn't normally have been out and about at that time, but she had been disturbed by what she had seen that morning on the field at Hill Farm, and had to discuss it with Evadne before the day was over. She was agitated and didn't want to be kept awake by a combination of adrenaline, stress and caffeine. Evadne had been busy earlier that evening and so this late heart-to heart was the only chance she would have to air her concerns and share her thoughts on the matter.

"I was out in my north field, which as you know is immediately next to the south field at Hill Farm[103]. I saw Diana and Richard Johnson with another man, who had a clipboard. This other man was walking along the bottom end of the field by the fence, looking around and staring into the woods, and then writing notes on his clipboard. Then, when they got near to my field they stopped and the man with the clipboard pointed first to the far end of the field and then into the woods at the near end. He was, I think, indicating where the access to Hill Farm could go."

"What makes you think that?" Evadne tried to calm Eileen down. Eileen was not known for being over-dramatic or inventing conspiracies, but she was clearly in need of getting what she knew off her chest.

"I was using my binoculars and lip-reading! Anyway, that's not important. They were definitely discussing access, and it definitely involved taking a road through the woods – and from where they were standing it had to be at the gap where the Royal Oak is, off the High Street. But the tree is protected,

---

[103] Farmers around Whimbury had a fairly pragmatic approach when it came to naming fields. Those who had more than 4 fields had been known to spend many agonising hours deciding how best to name field No 5 and beyond – intermediate points of the compass being considered a little over the top.

isn't it?" Eileen was calming herself down with the process of talking things through with someone else who was on the same wavelength.

"Yes, it is. So, any rational, reasonable and decent human being would leave it alone to continue its long and eventful life. Unfortunately, I don't think we're dealing with rational, reasonable and decent human beings here. There's big money involved and these people have powerful connections. Personally, I think you're a saint for resisting their offers to buy you out. It could set you and the family up for many years to come." Evadne offered Eileen a biscuit, which she refused on the grounds that the sugar would make her hyperactive, considering the mood she was in! Spot, who had no problem with hyperactivity at that time of night, smelt the biscuit, sat up and put his head on Evadne's knee. He got half a biscuit for his trouble, and he lay down again licking his lips to collect stray crumbs.

"I couldn't live with myself, if I did that!" Eileen sighed the sigh of someone with principles and a sense of community spirit who had fought the mental fight of maintaining those virtues over her own security. "It's too big. It would swamp the village. Too much, too quickly – don't they consider these things when they make their decisions?"

"I think it rather depends on who 'they' are. Sometimes, in fact often, decisions aren't in the hands of the people who have to suffer the consequences, or even those who are supposed to represent their interests. This may be one of those occasions. But it doesn't necessarily mean there is nothing we can do – it doesn't invalidate the plan we put in place at the last meeting, but it may need us to put it into action sooner than we'd intended. Do you think we could get the banners and placards ready tomorrow?"

"It should be possible." Eileen at last felt energised and ready to go on the offensive. Evadne had that effect on people. "We already have the materials and, so long as no-one has other pressing engagements tomorrow, I'm sure we can mobilise everyone first thing in the morning. With the skills at our disposal, it shouldn't be difficult to get it done during the day. Then what do you suggest – a march on the Council Offices?"

"Exactly that. We'll need to decide where and when to start – most of our retired members can't march very far and some can't march at all. We need to make sure that we can all reach the offices, and that the more absent-minded among us can still remember what we're marching for when we finally get there." Evadne grinned as she considered the motley group of activists at their disposal. They all had their heart in the right place, but some of their other organs, not to mention limbs, were more questionable.

"What about media coverage? It won't be of much use if hardly anyone sees or hears us, or even knows what on earth we're all about. I'm not very good on these things." Eileen tempered her new-found enthusiasm with a dose of realism and a recognition of the need for a well-thought through strategy.

"I think I can handle that side of things. I know one or two people in the local press from previous Parish Council issues and events. This is a bit different, but I'm sure they'd be prepared to cover it. For heaven's sake, there's precious little else happens around here of any genuine interest, and it would save them having to make things up, like they often do. If you're happy to leave the media to me, can you sort out the practicalities? We just need to liaise on progress and, hopefully, call out the troops at a moment's notice."

"I'm on it!" Eileen was relieved that she could concentrate on those aspects of the plan that she felt were within her comfort zone, and even more relieved that she could rely on Evadne to deal with those that were not. "I feel so much better about it now. It was all bottled up – the responsibility of knowing what I knew and knowing that no-one else knew what I knew."

"I know!" Evadne stepped in before Eileen tied herself in knots. "But remember, although being active is good, it doesn't guarantee success. We just have to do what we can and hope it makes a difference. At least then we won't look back on the next few days with regret at never even having tried to stick up for ourselves, and allowing other folk to walk all over us without so much as a whimper."

"Right, I'd better go." Eileen skipped to the front door, then turned. "What do you think should go on the placards and banner? Save our woods, Save our tree?"

"Good enough – short and snappy. Though I think I'd think I'd use 'Save the Royal Oak', rather than 'Save our tree'. Makes it sound a bit more personal and special. After all, it's not just any old tree, and it might get people asking a few questions about it."

"Brilliant Evadne." Eileen wandered down the path to the front gate and waved as she shut it behind her. "I'll ring you tomorrow with regular progress reports."

"Fine!" Evadne walked pensively back into the front room, broke a biscuit in half, put one half in her mouth and held the other half out for a Spot who had sniffed it out from his somnolent state and was already sitting beside her with mouth open. She tickled under his chin as she remarked, partly to him and partly to herself, "so, it's aux barricades, mes amis. Who'd have thought that it would come to this – that WE would come to this, eh?"

Spot knowingly turned his head to a jaunty 45 degree angle.

****

In the Royal Oak, an unprecedented argument was taking place, which involved both bars and all of the patrons.[104] The argument took the form chiefly of a verbal tennis contest between Messrs Material and Burr at one end of the bar, and Eric at the other end. All of the other faery patrons cheered loudly and shouted out support and/or matters of relevant and irrelevant significance to each of the protagonists in turn, twisting their heads from side to side in unison as they did so. Barry, Trixie and Damon were bemused by the lack of drinks orders, despite the closeness to closing time. Junior had come up to the bar just to find out what the noise was all about, and was discovering the delights of sampling the content of the bar towels.

The argument had begun much earlier in the evening as Mr Material was holding court and pronouncing on the dangers of allowing the humans to use the Royal Oak as a weapon in their quest for access to Hill Farm. He clearly saw the issue as something of great significance to both the fae and human communities, and he doubted the ability of the faeries of Whimbury to protect the Royal Oak and all it stood for. Whilst the patrons of the Royal Oak agreed whole-heartedly with his concerns, it was when he outlined his idea for a solution that things immediately became heated.

"I cannot make decisions for you," he had said, "but I believe that this is

---

[104] Unprecedented in that it involved much more than just trading of mutual insults between the Happs and the Grumps, and in that it couldn't be settled by a drunken darts match.

the time for the Crossover Child to fulfil her destiny. I cannot see the humans in this village, fair and just and kind as most of them are, succeeding in preventing the outsiders from destroying the basis of the fae community in this place. They can only see the threat from their own perspective, and they will, I am sure, do their best to divert it. But it also affects you, us, and it will take a crossover human/faery to win this particular battle. You have defeated Nixies, but you have never been in direct combat with humans. This will be different; this will be nasty; and this will need something very, very unusual if your way of life – our way of life – is to be protected." He paused in an eerie silence, a silence in which no faery picked up his or her glass, his or her domino - a silence that could only be broken by Mr Material's next utterance.

"Do you believe the child is ready?" Messrs Material and Burr between them took in the scene with a joint sweep of the eyes. As one, all eyes turned away from their gaze, with the exception of those belonging to Eric O'Shy, who gave every appearance of carefully composing a response.

"She still has a lot to learn." Barry eventually broke the silence as Mr Material's gaze ceased wandering and instead focussed entirely upon him. "She is willing and caring and interested, but she is only 5 years old, and these humans are wily and experienced. What do you think Percy?" Barry was keen to pass the buck.

Percy was not keen to receive the buck, whatever it was.[105] But he had taken his responsibility seriously for over three years and was not about to back away now. He thought for a moment and then spoke.

"There is certainly a lot more for her to learn, but it would probably take a lifetime, in her terms, for her to learn it. Whether she has enough knowledge and insight now, I can't say, because I don't know what kinds of actions will be required of her. But I do know she is strong, intelligent and devoted to our cause. If she were put in the position of having to make the Crossover, I believe that she would – and without hesitation. What effect it could have upon her, I couldn't predict – and that's the one thing that worries me. We now have less than 2 years for the event to take place, and I'm not at all sure

---

[105] There is no direct equivalent in the fae vocabulary, since faeries do not play poker. Pass the double-six is close, but doesn't sound so dramatic.

that continuing her preparation over that period of time would make all the difference. It might not do."

It was at this point that Eric joined in the discussion. His contribution was measured and, initially, calm. He stood up to make his point.

"But there again, it might! Whilst we have a long-standing affinity and devotion to the Royal Oak, who's to say that the impending problem that we face is of such fae and human significance that we should risk the girl's entire future on this one issue? If it proves to be the wrong time and the wrong battle, not only her future, but also that of all of us, could be seriously threatened. Surely, there will be another occasion within the next two years when we will need her to complete the Crossover, and every day that Percy and others are preparing her, must make her more likely to succeed. We only have the opinion of two strangers that this is the time. Why is it of such interest to them – and indeed, who are they? How trustworthy are they? No offence Mr Material, but I must disagree with your analysis. The girl's condition, present and future, is too important to be played games with."

"Your point is well made!" Mr Material stared at Eric with a somewhat less than friendly eye.[106] "But your perspective, I would suggest, is one borne more from book-learning and less from experience. In my experience, the times when human and fae interests collide in the way that we now see are very rare. This is one of those times, and the community here needs to think about what the Royal Oak means to it, and what it is prepared to do to protect it. And remember, this community was chosen by Gaia to be the one where the child should be born, and where she should be prepared. You have all been through traumas as a result of this – and now is surely the time to bring the legend to its fruition?"

Already, by this time, the Grumps and Happs had assembled as one in the main bar and, as time went on, were becoming totally flummoxed by the arguments being traded to and fro by Mr Material and Eric. Both sides seemed equally plausible and reasonable, but only one of them could be right. If indeed there was a right or wrong side.

---

[106] The other one was also pretty antagonistic.

At last, to everyone's surprise, including his own, Mr Burr found a gap in the debate in which to interject his own thoughts.

"If I may say something?" He began diffidently. "I have only been travelling with my companion here for a relatively short while. But in that time, I have learnt so much. Some things make me feel better about the world and myself, and some make me feel worse. But all are important, because they help me make sense of the fae and human condition. I have put my trust in him and, so far, it has proved well worth it. Like yourselves, I cannot say for certain that now is the time for the Crossover to happen, because no-one can. It is, and always will be, - at least until the child reaches the age of seven - a leap of faith. After that it will forever be too late. From where I stand – and with no disrespect to Mr O'Shy intended – now seems to be that moment. With help from all of us, and the co-operation of the humans in the village, I believe the child can succeed." Mr Burr suddenly became aware of his situation and his historic lack of self-confidence once more took over. "Just saying!" He concluded.

"Thank you, my friend!" Mr Material seemed genuinely touched by this unexpected speech. "I think that, between us, we have made our point as well as we can. Now it is up to you. There is no more to be said, and we must now leave you to make your decision." He bowed very slightly as a gesture of respect and turned to the door. Eric O Shy, however, had one final question on his mind.

"Before you go, I don't believe that your name is actually Mr Material? Could you at least give us your real name so that we know who we are dealing with?"

"I go by many names. My Doctor friend here is indeed Mr Burr, but as you rightly conjecture, Material is not my name – just a name given to me by the community here, and which has suited me well. Everywhere I go, I am given, or take, new names. I have just returned from France where, as I recently informed your good Innkeeper here, I was given the name Daniel, and because they considered me stubborn and brave, I became Daniel de Lion. I am happy to keep that name for the time being. But if you wish to continue to call me Mr Material that is also perfectly acceptable. We will return very soon, I think." And with that, they both left.

Another silence fell over the assembled fae families. Eric sat down and re-immersed himself in his reading matter. The first to rise and break the silence was Mack Stout. He strode to the bar to demand the right to a belated last drinks order, and proclaimed to all who would listen.

"Well that just about beats everything. We've been mesmerised all evening by Dan de Lion and Doc Burr. I don't know about you lot, but after that I need this!" He raised his glass of Innkeeper's Choice, shouted 'cheers', and took a mighty gulp.

******

The morning of the day after his lunch with Derek Garner, Robert Hancock strode into the council offices. He noticed Ralph sitting near the steps, but was in too much of a hurry to acknowledge him or drop him a coin. Ralph in turn noticed Hancock and recognised him immediately. He made a mental note to check how long he stayed in the building and to mention his visit to Trixie and Robin as soon as they arrived for a progress report.

Robert Hancock took himself to Planning reception and signed himself in to see Jessica. He didn't have an appointment, but he made it plain to the receptionist that it was a matter of great urgency, and that Jessica would make time to see him. He sat for a few minutes, flicking through the paperwork he had brought with him, until Jessica came out of her office to welcome him and usher him in.

"Robert, this is unexpected. What can I do for you with regard to this matter, which is apparently so urgent?" Jessica had always attempted to be accessible to the public, but she placed just enough barb on her opening comments to make it clear to anyone sufficiently socially aware,[107] that she did not want to make off-the-cuff visits a normal feature of her working day. She sat down behind her desk and smiled, but in a less than friendly way. Hancock, oblivious to all of this, had already sat down and was laying out a plan and a report to show her.

"It probably won't surprise you, but it has to do with the Hill Farm site in

---

[107] Which did not, of course, include Robert.

Whimbury." He didn't look up, but merely turned the plan and report round to face Jessica and prepared himself to explain his situation.

"You're quite right, Robert. It doesn't surprise me. But it's not a new issue, so why has it become so urgent?" She glanced down at the Report and noticed that it was headed 'Tree Condition Survey' and prepared by the local Tree Specialists, Fell, Wood and Hyde.

"As you know, we have been negotiating fruitlessly with Eileen Robinson to get access to our site by the most direct, and least disruptive, route. Since we have no guarantees that this will be successful in the foreseeable future, we have also considered other routes, including punching through Whimbury Woods[108]." To illustrate his point. he gave a visual aid gesture of a punch, which he hoped appeared macho, but didn't. "Whilst studying the trees in the vicinity of the village, my consultants just happened to notice, while they were passing, that the old Royal Oak was showing distinct signs of ageing and disease. Since they were already there, they conducted a visual, photographic and physical survey, and concluded that several very large branches were in danger of breaking off altogether, which represents a great danger to the public, of course."

"Of course." Jessica was experienced enough to know what was coming next, and was interested in finding out how Hancock intended to present his suggestions. "Shouldn't it be our Tree Officer that you are telling this to?"

"Ordinarily, yes. But I rang his office before I came, and your reception said that he'd been called out on an urgent case."

"Yes, I saw him on the way out. He was off to check progress on some replacement planting scheme organised at the last minute by Fell, Wood and Hyde. Everything seems to be so urgent these days, don't you find. No-one has the time to plan things in advance any more, or so it would appear." Pieces of a mental jigsaw were assembling themselves in Jessica's mind, and a clear picture was emerging.

"That's the way of the business world, I'm afraid. Time is money, and devil take the hindmost – if I may mix my metaphors?" Jessica had to give

---

[108] 'Punching through' being a favourite phrase of Hancock and his fellow housing developer colleagues when attempting to present a dynamic and positive approach to felling woodland or otherwise destroying valuable wildlife habitats.

Hancock his due. He was very good at mixing his metaphors as a means of deflecting attention from the real business at hand.

"So, in the absence of my Tree Officer, you came to me instead?"

"Going to the very top seemed to be the only available option, given the severity of the situation. Also, if you're prepared to make a snap decision, I may be able to help out." Jessica rolled her eyes. In all the years she had known him, he had never helped anyone out unless there was something in it for him. She waved her hands in an acknowledgment of acquiescence and waited for the punchline.

"As it happens, my contractor friend has just finished a job a few miles away, and he has some metal security fencing on the back of his truck which he is prepared to put up around the tree until such time as the Council can decide what to do. It will, of course, prevent anyone getting near enough to be hurt by any falling timber. He doesn't want any recompense – just the satisfaction of knowing that he is performing a social service. He doesn't need the fencing for a few days anyway." Hancock looked pleased with himself, and made an elaborate show of pointing out to Jessica exactly where in the Tree Condition Survey it specifically stated just how dangerous the tree was to human health and safety.

"Under the circumstances, I suppose we need to prioritise health and safety. I'll get the Tree officer to deal with it formally in the morning. In the meantime, use the security fencing as your contractor thinks fit – but don't let him damage the tree putting it up or I'll bring down the full might of the council on him."[109]

"You can rely on me, Jessica, you know that. Discretion and Care are my middle names." [110] He folded up the papers and pushed them across the desk to Jessica. "Keep these for your nice tree man, and I'll look forward to seeing him sometime tomorrow to discuss the way forward. Just get him to ring me and arrange a time." He got up, hitched up his trousers, and walked away.

---

[109] The full might, in this instance, being approximately equal to being pecked viciously by a baby blue tit!

[110] Actually his middle names were St John and Peregrine, but he only advertised this amongst his closest friends.

"I'll do that Robert. And thank you for the very timely public-spirited actions." She watched as he left the room, and she then carefully placed the tree report and plans in her pending tray. She tutted to herself as she wrote a memo to herself to give the Tree Officer very clear instructions as to how to approach his meeting with Hancock the next day.

Out in the street, Hancock leant on the railings above where Ralph was sitting who, by now, had been joined by Robin and Trixie. He took his phone out of his pocket and found the necessary contact in his address book. He dialled and waited for a response, which came almost immediately.

"Hi, it's Robert Hancock here. Can you just tell Derek that it is all systems go for the security fencing round the Royal Oak? No need to disturb him if he's busy. Ask him if he'll arrange the necessaries and then get his lumberjack prepared for action, I'll meet him at lunchtime, usual place and time, and we can finalise the details." He put his phone away and hurried off[111].

Ralph looked down at Robin and Trixie.

"Did you hear that. That sounds highly disturbing and imminent. I just wish we knew more about what he's planning, then we could brief Barry." Chink. "Thank you!"

"We need to follow him and eavesdrop on his lunch appointment." Trixie stood up and flexed her wing muscles. "And I know just the person to keep up with him!" And with that she disappeared.

---

[111] Calling en-route at the Dry Cleaners to book his suit in for cleaning the next day.

Chapter Eighteen

"I THINK THAT YOU COULD become a faery very, very soon now." Percy sat with Milly in the front garden. Inside the cottage, Miranda was getting tea ready as Daisy played quietly with her 'Teddies'[112].

"Can I come to parties and play games in the Faery Tree?" Milly seemed genuinely excited.

"Yes, of course!" Percy was trying very hard to get round to explaining the dangers associated with the Crossover without frightening Milly and putting her off the idea. "But you have to really, really want to do it.[113] It might not work otherwise and then you might never be able to do it, and that would be sad for you and for the faeries."

"I really, really want to do it. But I want to play with Daisy and my friends as well. I can come back, can't I?"

"If you really, really want to be a faery, and you really, really want to be a little girl as well, then you can be both, provided we do the first change properly. It might mean that you have to do something without your mummy and daddy knowing – at least at first – but all of us at the Faery Tree will help you, and then it will be a lot easier afterwards." Percy paused for a few moments while Milly pondered what he had said, then he carried on. "What do mummy and daddy think about faeries?"

---

[112] Which, since many were originally Milly's, were actually rather more obscure members of the animal kingdom.

[113] Percy had very, very quickly learnt that doubling up of adjectives and adverbs worked really, really well at focussing Milly on crucial issues about the Crossover.

"They ask me a lot about faeries and animals. They know all about you – I tell them. I don't know if they believe me, they just tell me I'm special – but they like listening to my stories. They always laugh, though sometimes they shake their heads and look at each other." Milly did a passable impression of the somewhat incredulous expressions that passed between Miranda and Will when she told them who she had been talking to.

"Your mummy and daddy are special people too. After you have become a faery for the first time, you will have to tell them what you have done and how you did it. But don't tell anyone else, because they may not believe you. Leave it to your parents to tell people they like and trust. What you will do – very soon now – has never been done before by anybody, and your mummy and daddy will find it hard to keep doing the same things that they have been doing up until now. They will have to choose their best friends very carefully. And you will have to help them if they sometimes can't understand what you are doing. But they'll learn, the way you have learnt – and are learning," Percy was anticipating the question he most dreaded, and it came.

"What will I have to do to be like you?" In the end, it came in such a matter-of-fact way that Percy was temporarily knocked out of his stride. Later he kicked himself for not being prepared enough to answer immediately – after all, he had spent almost all of his spare time with her for over three years, and she had never shown any surprise or dismay about any of the topics that Percy had raised. She absorbed everything like a sponge and the time was getting near when she would need to wring herself out and let the knowledge tumble down the weirs and eddies of its own valley. When he finally responded, Milly was sitting, face in hands, waiting patiently for what he had to say.

"In truth, my precious little human, I'm not sure." Percy was being ultra-careful to choose his words for maximum simplicity and minimum disruption to her calm demeanour. "But I believe that, when the moment comes, you will know, and that we faeries will be in the right place to help you. All I can imagine is that you will need to want to be faery so much that you think and behave like one without even realising it. Can you do that?" For the first time since he took on the role of Crossover mentor, Percy was genuinely nervous about whether he had, indeed, been the right person for the job. What he had just said didn't, in the cold light of day, sound very profound or useful.

"Is that all? Oh yes!" Milly perked up – wanting to be fae was no problem at all. She was desperate to experience what they experienced, and if by doing so she could help them with their problem, she really couldn't wait. There are times when simplicity and even a little naivete are all that is needed to achieve the greatest things, if the motive is right and the desire strong enough. Percy began to understand at last why it was necessary for the Crossover child to be under the age of seven, when life had fewer hurdles and the world offered every opportunity for those with dreams. Milly was at that stage where her desire to experience the world of the fae was matched only by the faith in her ability to achieve it. She understood that it might involve danger, but had no fear of the unknown, so long as she had loving support beside her. All would be well!

Percy allowed himself the luxury of the one expression that only his closest friends and confidants were party to – a genuine, heartfelt smile.

"That's grand. I hoped that you'd say that. I even expected it in a way, though perhaps not expressed quite in the way that you did just then. But that's absolutely grand, yes indeed. When I tell the others what you've said, they'll be very, very happy. It will be important not only for us, but for all your human friends as well - and our animal friends. If you can do this, the future will be so much brighter for all of us." Percy exuded satisfaction with the whole situation.

"I like faeries! I like animals! I like my friends, and Daisy and mummy and daddy! I like the Faery Tree! I want it to always be here." Milly provided a succinct summary of everything that was important to her and, in the centre of her world, the one thing that linked everything together, was the Royal Oak.

"We all want it always to be here, my lovely, lovely girl. And I hope that if we all join together then it always will. But it may be hard, and it may hurt." Percy didn't want to encourage Milly to share in a potentially dangerous situation without first making it quite clear that it would not just be a bit of fun.

"My daddy says that I'm a brave girl. I had to have an injection once and I didn't cry. I'm not frightened."

"That's all I need to know!" Percy felt reassured, or at least as reassured as anyone could be who was relying on a 5-year old girl to rescue his community – local and global – from the might of the human property industry. "Either I, or one of the other faeries, or even maybe an animal, will contact you very soon, when it is the right time. If you are still ready to help us, you will need to come straight away when you are called, and you will need to want more than anything else to become one of us, even if it is only for a little while at first. I'll see you soon." And Percy walked away down the path.

"Bye Percy." Milly watched him duck under the gate, then she wandered back into the cottage, where the smell of tea was enough to draw her firmly back into her human world. Daisy was already in her straps at the table gnawing at a raw carrot.

"I was just about to call you." Miranda smiled as she dished out the baked beans. "Who were you talking to this time, princess?"

"Percy. I going to be a faery soon, but not for long. I'll be back to play with Daisy."

"Well, that's a relief!" said Miranda on behalf of Daisy, though deep down, and considering the bit about faeries, she wasn't entirely sure that relief was an adequate word to use.

****

In the Mission Church, the regular jumble sale was in full swing. All the decent stuff had already been snapped up and so it was the time when the stall-holders, the 'social-jumblers', and the 'tea and muffin' group were normally left to enjoy their more relaxed period. Except that, today, Eileen was organising a craft session to make banners and placards. On one table, some of the items of clothing that had been lying around for several jumble sales without attracting interest were being cut up and sewn onto pieces of old curtain that were of a colour that went out of fashion a generation or two earlier. On another table, dissected portions of large cardboard boxes were being written on in preparation for the making of placards. Such phrases as 'Save the Royal Oak', 'No Housing on Hill Farm', and 'Woods not Roads' were repeated many times, while one that simply said 'Save Whimbury Wool'

[114] was sticking out of a waste bin in the corner. Beside the waste bin, Eileen sat with her phone in conversation with Evadne.

"So we've got the makings of two good banners – and one not so good [115]. We've also got a lot of potential placards, so long as we can find enough poles to stick them on. Everyone's been very willing and, if nothing else, it means that there will be a lot fewer unsaleable products on the stalls at the next jumble sale." She went silent as Evadne responded.

"Good. But I think we need to be even quicker than we expected at first. I visited my contact at the local paper here in town, and she is geared up to cover any protest that we carry out, and she suggested doing it in the Town Square so that we get the biggest crowd, which will look good in their photos. But then, as I was walking past the council offices, I saw Ralph sat there by the steps. He was saying that the developer chappy had been in first thing and had some very imminent plans to discuss with somebody earlier today. So it looks as though what we thought was urgent, may just have become even more urgent." It was Eileen's turn to respond.

"Right. I'll get someone onto the poles issue immediately – might be able to get something from Green's, I'll check with Will."

"Yes, that sounds promising. Ralph did also say something about a Robin and a Trixie being on the job. I've no idea who he was talking about, and he very quickly changed the subject, but if he has other contacts helping out, so much the better. I'm just about to catch the bus, so I'll pop in and see you on the way back, if you're still there."

"I will be – with or without the rest of the Whimbury Arts and Crafts movement. See you later."

Both women shut their phones and carried on with the matters in hand.

****

---

[114] Written by Mrs Patterson from the 'Ever Been Fleeced' shop, who hadn't quite understood what the protest was all about.

[115] Eileen was hoping that she may not need to use the one being put together by two of her well-meaning neighbours, one of whom had forgotten her glasses and the other whose arthritic fingers were playing her up something rotten.

In the Fox and Hounds, Robert Hancock was briefing Derek Garner on his plans for the Royal Oak. Sitting on the corner of the table was Trixie, carefully memorising every instruction that he gave.

"I want to make it clear that it's not that I don't trust you, but it's my position and livelihood that's on the line here. That line of responsibility stops with me. So, if you don't mind, could you please repeat exactly what has to be done and when?" Hancock was a stickler for precision.[116]

Derek Garner took a mouthful of alcoholic beverage to wet his whistle before embarking on his task.

"Straight after the day's work finishes, I'm to put security fencing around the Royal Oak - at least as far out as the extent of its crown. Crown - that's quite appropriate for a Royal tree, isn't it?" He laughed nervously – alone - then resumed. "I need to use the 'high fencing with projecting pointy tops' – your description, but I know what you mean – so that no-one can climb over it. Anyone who engages in conversation regarding aforesaid fencing is to be told that it has been authorised by the Council on account of the tree being old and dangerous and needs making safe."

"And use those words exactly, don't get drawn into how much chopping needs doing. Just 'making safe' – remember that! Carry on!"

"Making safe. Yes. Got it! Then in the wee small hours of the morning, I return with Tyler and his chain saw, enter the compound silently and then get him to remove as much of the tree as possible before any of the locals manage to get assistance." Derek looked at Hancock for affirmation.

"Good, good – and your excuse for waking them up so early in the morning is?"

"My excuse is that I saw the weather report late this evening and it forecast high winds, so I thought it was best to make the tree safe before anyone got up and tried to get into the compound. But at least better safe than sorry, eh."

"Exactly – and if there aren't any forecasts of strong winds tonight?" Hancock was not about to let meteorological minutiae deflect his scheme.

---

[116] He found it had helped over the years when it came to discussing what exactly had gone wrong in regard to his various schemes and why it had done so, with various government inspectors, magistrates, lawyers, journalists, politicians, council officials and residents' groups.

"If there aren't any forecasts of strong winds, then I must have been looking at the wrong region, sorry. But no-one's got hurt."

"No-one's got hurt! And that's the key message. At the end of the day it's just a tree. There's lots more in the wood and a human life is worth far more than a tree. And this Taylor chap..."

"Tyler!"

"Tyler chap – he can get the tree down ultra-quick? You're confident of that."

"Absolutely. Without a shadow of a doubt. By the time any of the locals get dressed it'll be history[117]. And if they ring anyone up – assuming they can get anyone at that hour – there's no way they'll get to the tree before we're finished. Trust me – and Tyler!" Garner had considerable experience in matters such as these, and he knew the reliability of his sub-contractors. They were, after all, the secret of his success in delivering contracts on time, regardless of how it was achieved.

"That's exactly what I wanted to hear. And once the tree is no more, we have no further obstacles to the development at Hill Farm. Hit them hard and fast is my motto – no prizes for also-rans or the faint-hearted. By this time tomorrow the Royal Oak will be packaged up in bundles, ready to be delivered to the wood-stores and wood-burning stoves of Whimingham and beyond. About time it became something useful, eh?" Hancock raised his almost empty glass in a toast to the success of their venture, and then motioned to the bar for another bottle of his favourite beverage.

At this point, Trixie decided she had heard enough. Getting the message back to Whimbury was now priority. After a deep breath, she concentrated hard and left the building.

At approximately the same time or, given how urgent she considered the situation, it might have been a little earlier, Trixie entered the Royal Oak. As was usually the case in such circumstances, her sudden arrival scared the willies out of Barry, Robin and Damon.

"Can't you ring a bell or something to let us know you're coming?" Barry wiped up the slops from the tray he was cleaning out when she arrived.

---

[117] The fact that it already was history, and that was why it was now being protected, had not filtered into Derek Garner's brain.

"I could try it, but I think I'd still arrive before the sound.[118] Anyway, I'm here now and we need to get out thoughts together as a matter of extreme urgency. They're planning on chopping the tree down tonight." Trixie passed Damon a cloth to wipe up the slops from the tray he had just dropped at the other end of the bar.

"Tonight?" After a moment to take it in, Barry and Robin expressed their concern simultaneously. Barry then waved his finger around to emphasise his view that this should not happen.

"No, no, no, no, no, no. no!" He paused and waggled another finger from the other hand. "Oh no, no, no. no, no, no, no." The use of fingers from both hands in opposite directions did not seem to send his dilemma away. Nor did resting his elbows on the bar and placing his head in his hands. Robin took charge of the situation.

"OK Bro. It's now or never, we have to decide whether to involve the child in this. Messrs Dan de Material and Burr told us it was up to us, but they seemed clear that this was the moment for the Crossover. We need a meeting of the whole community here this evening to decide one way or the other – and if Milly's readiness is to be tested, we need a plan that's as safe as we can possibly make it."

"Well, plans are your strong point, Robin." Barry looked up and took a deep breath. "if you've got the makings of one, let's get talking." He motioned to Trixie and Damon to sit at a table with Robin and himself. Once all were seated, uncomfortably and shuffling their bottoms in a vain attempt to feel at ease, Robin spoke.

"I've had a vague idea for some time now, but a lot is going to depend on what else Trixie can tell us about the evil scheme currently being hatched. Then, as soon as we've finished here, I think I will need to hurry down to the child's home and make sure she knows to have her bedroom window left open tonight. Whatever the final plan, we'll need to act immediately when the time is right, and she'll have to be able to leave the house at a moment's notice."

There were nods of agreement, and Trixie began to elaborate on what she had heard earlier in the Fox and Hounds.

---

[118] At least that was the theory, as passed on to her by her relative, Uncle Albert.

****

In the early hours of what was becoming a very pleasant evening, Evadne took Spot for his routine ablution walk and exercise. As she passed Over Cross View, she saw Will filling the birdfeeders and paused for a chat. Spot was used to his walks being interrupted several times for chats and had learned that straining at his leash made no difference to the situation. Instead, he stood with his paws on the top of the gate and looked up at the first-floor window above and to the left of the floor door. This he knew was Milly's bedroom and he was very pleased to see that it was part open, as Robin had hoped it would be. He barked his pleasure.

"Quiet Spot, you'll wake Milly." Evadne smiled apologetically in Will's direction and stroked the dog's head to calm him down. "Sorry about that, Will, but he does get somewhat excited at the beginning of his evening walk. He'll be quieter after a good run across the field."

Will put down his tub of suet balls and walked casually to the gate.

"No worries Evadne, she went to bed early tonight and fell asleep really quickly. I think she got a bit hot and bothered at school and that must have tired her out. She said she wanted the window open for some reason and kept looking at it all the while I was reading her story. Then she went off and we haven't heard a peep out of her since. Have you seen Eileen and the placards and banners her little bunch of eco-warriors made today?"

"Yes, she showed me when I got back from town. Perhaps a little rough and ready, but I'm afraid we might need them any time from tomorrow on, so haste was of the essence. Thanks for sorting out the poles for them."

"No worries. Glad to help. Miranda is the political one in our family – I'm a bit naïve on such matters, so any chance I get to lend a hand in an unthinking, practical way, I'm happy to oblige. Do you really think the developers might do something as soon as tomorrow? Surely they can't do anything before they get permission?" Will had a tendency to believe that business ventures always played by the rules of their game. In this respect, he had an endearing[119] habit of

---

[119] If occasionally infuriating.

trying very hard to see the good in everyone, until proven otherwise – by which time of course, it was usually too late to change matters.

Evadne had a much more pragmatic approach to matters of business and politics, but accepted that folk like Will were essential around the place to provide a balance, and to help build a representative range of views. Nevertheless, on this matter she felt obliged to tell him exactly what she believed.

"Unfortunately, yes, I do really think they might well do something drastic tomorrow. It's not the normal way of operating, I'm pleased to say but, from my experience, that's the way people at their particular end of the business spectrum do tend to operate. And yes, they surely would do just that – to them money has a habit of talking more loudly than rules and principles."

"All money has ever said to me is 'now you see me, now you don't!'" Will tried to lighten the mood of the conversation, but he saw the genuinely worried look on Evadne's face. "Right! I'd best finish off what I was doing. I hope tomorrow goes OK. I'm sure Miranda and Daisy will do their bit with a placard or banner, provided the revolution starts during school time. Nice to see you – and you Spot!" He patted the dog on the head. Spot in turn looked up at Will and then across to Milly's open bedroom window. He remained silent and walked off in docile fashion as Evadne gave his lead a gentle tug, a silence and docility that took her very much by surprise.

****

In the Royal Oak, the early arrivals for the evening session[120] were enjoying a complimentary first drink while Barry explained the significance of what was likely to happen during the evening and overnight. When he got to the part where the tree was to be chopped down, a stunned silence hit the rooms. Other than a discernible 'clunk' as a large number of half-full glasses were put back down on the tables, there was no other indication of the presence of a large number of patrons. Barry waited while the news sunk in. Having well and truly sunk in, a flurry of questions was fired back.

---

[120] Which normally comprised around 90% of the total community, with the rest cursing at whatever it was that had held them up.

"The whole tree?"

"What happens to the Inn?"

"What happens to us?"

"Including the roots?"[121]

Barry held up his hands for order and shouted over the hubbub.

"One at a time, please, and raise your hands before shouting out!" A comprehensive show of hands appeared in unison. "In answer to the questions I've heard so far, it would appear that the whole tree would go – including the roots – and it would be replaced by a large road that would carry on through the woods to the bottom field at Hill Farm. The people responsible are clearly not supposed to be doing this, and that's why it's being done in secret, under cover of darkness. So now, first question! Inigo?"

"Chopping down the whole tree overnight is going to need some hefty equipment and expertise. How can we stop something like that?" Inigo Happling, glanced around at a sea of heads nodding in agreement.

"A very good question, and the answer, Inigo, is that we are going to need a very special plan, which I will come onto in a moment. Trevor? Ah yes, silly of me – of course you can, you know where it is. Everard?"

"Moight this 'ere plan involve the girl that Percy 'ave been preparin' these last three year? Seems to me loik there ain't goin' ter be a better toime to see what she can do! Oi reckons Perce 'ave done a moighty fine job so far and, in all 'onesty, oi can't see as 'ow there be much we can do without 'er!" Everard gave Percy a supportive nod of the head.

"As it happens, the plan does involve the girl. Percy knows her as well as any of us. What do you think Percy?"

"It would be impossible to take her through the whole history and society of Faeries during her whole lifetime, let alone her first five years or so. But I genuinely think that she has enough understanding to be able to complete the Crossover now, if needs be. I agree that there is little we can do without her. Tell us the plan and let's see how she fits in." There were murmurs as he made his final point, though neither he nor Barry could tell whether they were of assent or dissent.

---

[121] This question was from Junior, for whom the cellars had become almost a home from home.

"Thank you, Percy. OK everyone, here is the plan…. Eric, you have your hand up! What would you like to say?" Barry feared the worst and his fears were realised.

"This is madness! I don't want to belittle what Percy has done, but a five-year old? We're talking here of a tree. I know it means a lot to us, but it's just a tree. We can't possibly risk the Crossover child for this. It's hardly a matter of huge significance to both humankind and faekind. We need to wait until the right issue appears and when she is better equipped than now. Each of you needs to ask yourself how you will feel if it all goes wrong and the child is harmed. I can't support any plan that involves her at this stage of her development. Sorry! I blame the strangers for the unpleasant situation we now find ourselves in." Eric had always spoken plainly, but this time there was something approaching venom in his words. He felt strongly and he wanted everyone to know. Barry knew that the time had come where he had to stand firm and hope enough of his community would stand beside him.

"Eric. You've made this point before, and I appreciate your concerns, but I have to disagree. This is an important issue that affects both humans and faeries in the same community. It may not have worldwide implications, but I doubt we will ever find a situation like that – at least, not around here, and not before the girl reaches seven. I'm going to recommend a plan that I hope everyone here will support – and it involves Milly, and it involves the Crossover event taking place, here, tonight!" As one, the patrons of the Royal Oak lifted their glasses and took a very big swig of Innkeeper's Choice. As one, that is except for Eric, who stood up, holding his books, and stated:

"I can't stand by and be a part of this. It goes against everything I believe. I'm off!" And he left the Inn. Barry beathed a heartfelt sigh; part relief, and part fear. He continued from where he had left off.

"Do I have everyone's support? If anyone wants to leave with Eric you are welcome to do so and no-one will think any the worse of you. This is the most difficult decision we have ever had to make." No-one moved. "Right! Trixie, you know the plan already and we are going to need Ralph here. Can you get a message to him to come as soon as he can while I go through things with the folk here?"

Trixie exited in a blur and Barry outlined his plan. As he finished, Trixie reappeared in another blur, but this time looking flustered.

"I've been to town and found Ralph. He'll come over immediately, though it'll take him a good hour or more."

"Good." Barry was, in general, pleased with the news but could see trouble in Trixie's demeanour. "What's the problem?"

"There's a very large vehicle just appeared outside with some very large equipment on it. It looks like metal fencing. I think maybe we should take a look?"

Robin led the way out and as each of the crowd adjusted their eyes to late evening sun, they gasped. A number of humans were already beginning to erect a metal fortification around the tree, with a slickness that indicated they had done it, or something similar, several times before.

Further up the road, Evadne was returning from her walk with Spot when she saw also the activity around the Royal Oak. She shielded her eyes and shook her head. Then she knelt beside Spot and said simply:

"So now it begins, eh boy?" Spot turned his head to a 45 degree angle and growled softly but angrily.

Chapter Nineteen

HIGH IN THE TREETOPS OF Whimbury Woods as, below them, the human community of Whimbury slept, faery lookouts scoured the horizon in all directions. On the horizon, other faery lookouts concentrated their gaze on the roads leading into Whimbury. In the woods immediately behind the Royal Oak,[122] Ralph sat with Barry, outside of the protective fencing, awaiting the arrival of the demolition gang. Robin, Trixie, Percy, Damon and Junior remained in the bar, awaiting instructions. An air of nervousness pervaded the whole area.

"Well, they've certainly made a good job with the security fence." Ralph found himself having to make small talk to take his mind off things. "You'd have more chance trying to get out of Whimburton Gaol than this." He gestured at the metal barrier around the Royal Oak.

"Getting in is more the issue at the moment. If the plan is going to work, everyone, including Milly, is going to have to be inside when they arrive." Barry was agitated. He and Ralph had been sitting in the same spot for several hours, from time to time looking up to the tree canopy where Mack Stout was twiddling his thumbs and focussing with rare concentration on that part of the horizon allocated to him. In the distance, illuminated by the full moon, he could see both Inigo and Lancelot Happling, a few trees apart from one another, staring west towards Whimburton. He felt his eyelids droop and gave himself a slap around the cheeks in an attempt to keep awake. He sat up

---

[122] Or 'Operational Headquarters' as it was known for the duration of the plan.

straight, stretched and yawned, and waggled his feet, just as both Inigo and Lancelot began to wave frantically in his direction. He waved back and made a number of rude gestures until he remembered why it was that they were so animated, at which point he descended the tree rather more quickly than he had anticipated.

Barry and Ralph leapt as one from the sitting position to the standing position as Mack suddenly appeared from above them in a flurry of limbs and leaves. Mack instantly brushed himself down and hurriedly passed on the information that Inigo and Lancelot had just given him the signal that the humans were on the way.

"Right, that gives us around 20 minutes, maybe a few more if we're lucky" Barry turned to Ralph who knelt down to listen to what he had to say. "You stay here out of sight, Ralph, until the humans are inside the fencing, then you know what to do!"

"I do. Trust me!" Ralph stepped back into the undergrowth.

Barry slipped back through the security fencing and raced into the Royal Oak. He uttered the two words "We're on", and Trixie disappeared immediately. Robin, Barry and Percy walked out to that part of the fence adjacent to the road and waited.

Trixie niftily reappeared on the window-sill outside of Milly's open bedroom window. As she re-orientated herself, she found herself, unexpectedly, face-to-face with Eric O'Shy.

"Hi Eric. What are you doing here?" Trixie moved to enter the bedroom, but Eric stood tall in her way. She hadn't realised before quite how big he was.

"I might ask you the same question!" His voice sounded uncharacteristically cold and harsh.

"It's time." Trixie was temporarily confused. "Time for Milly to fulfil her destiny!"

"I can't allow that!" Eric seemed to uncoil and his eyes began to glow. "It is too dangerous for her. Please go back and tell the others the child is not ready. It would be best for them to devise a new plan."

"Sorry, Eric, but I'm going in. It's what the community decided and you can't overrule them." Trixie tried to sidestep him, but he held her in his gaze and she found herself unable to move.

"You will do as I say!" Eric's shouted his command as his eyes began to emit a purple shaft of light. Trixie felt a tightness all around her body, constricting her airwaves and restricting all movement. Her arms remained firmly forced against her side; she couldn't turn her head; and her legs and feet resolutely refused to move. Eric took a step towards her and then suddenly fell off the sill. Trixie's body returned to normal and she looked down into the garden where Eric lay breathless, panting and trying to flex his muscles. She turned back to the window where Milly stood on the roof of a doll's house, flicking her fingers, looking at her and smiling.

"Bad faery. Are we going to the party now?" Milly stepped off the doll's house and wrapped her dressing-gown around her "Insects in your garden" pyjamas[123]. Trixie landed on her shoulder and whispered in her ear as she wandered out of the bedroom and began to descend the stairs.

"You do know that you will have to do something very special before you can join in the party don't you? And it won't be easy!" Trixie didn't want to lead Milly into something for which she was unprepared.

Milly was aware that going out in the middle of the night in her pyjamas and dressing gown to turn into a faery and join in with faery fun in the base of a large oak tree was somewhat irregular behaviour, even from a five-year old like her. Accordingly, she crept down the stairs very quietly, keeping to the side to avoid the creaky ones, and whispered her reply to Trixie.

"I know. Percy told me and Barry told me and Larry and Junior told me. They all told me. I really want to be a faery, but I want to come back home afterwards. Will the bad faery be waiting outside?"

Trixie followed the stream of consciousness and realised at the end of it that she hadn't factored in the likely presence of Eric in the front garden. He had seemed frighteningly powerful before being ushered off the window-sill by Milly, and if he had recovered from the surprise of his fall, he would almost certainly be less than welcoming when they left the cottage. His inability to engage in flight mode during his rapid descent would have been due to shock, but he appeared to be recovering when Trixie looked down into

---

[123] Will had spent many minutes on his phone prior to the previous Christmas persuading the sales assistant that he didn't want the butterflies or birds or cuddly animal versions, despite the fact that they were still in stock.

the garden immediately afterwards. That worried her, but there was no time to waste, and she just had to trust that Milly was able to look after herself as far as 'bad faeries' were concerned. As for her own safety, that was secondary, and she would just have to do what a pixie had to do if and when the time came.

"Possibly! When we get outside, you must go straight to the Royal Oak and meet up with Barry, Robin and Percy. Don't stop for anything – although be careful crossing the road, of course. But don't wait for me, I may have things to do."

Milly looked across at her shoulder and fixed Trixie eye to eye. "I will go quickly and not stop, and I will look both ways when crossing the road. Now you must turn the key as I pull the handle."

Milly gave her instructions in a matter-of-fact way, with no intent or attempt to exercise authority. Nevertheless, Trixie complied immediately by leaping across to the door, and perching on a cross-member beside the key. Then she waited as Milly reached up as high as she could and pulled the door-lock handle down. At the same time Trixie dropped onto the key and spun it round with all the force she could muster. The door clunked open and Milly pulled it back sufficiently to peer around the frame. She slid back into the hallway and reported back on what she had seen.

"Bad faery standing in garden. He looks angry. His eyes are purple. I don't like him. I don't think the other two faeries like him either. Shall I run now?" Milly hitched up her dressing gown and prepared to leave.

"Just a moment. I'll go out first to attract his attention, then you follow me and…." Trixie had a sudden thought. "The other two faeries? Which other two faeries?"

"The two faeries standing by the gate looking at the bad faery. They looking at him like mummy looks at daddy when he forgets to bring the washing in from the rain."

Trixie stuck her head round the door and saw Messrs Material and Burr at the front gate. Now she really was confused. The three faeries in the front garden were engaged in a war of hard looks. Eric had an appearance of intense dislike and contempt. Mr Material stood tall, unyielding and authoritative. Mr Burr, perhaps uncharacteristically, stood beside Mr Material and assumed an air of confidence and belief that had not before been evident. It was clearly a stand-off, and Trixie had to make an instant decision as to how to get Milly through it and off to the Royal Oak. She took a deep breath, and stepped into the garden, followed by Milly who, by now, was in no mood to let a fae squabble that she didn't understand get between her and a good party.

"Right, I think it was decided that Milly should be given the chance to fulfil the Crossover legend…." Trixie adopted her most commanding tone of voice to address the front garden in general, taking great care to avoid the direct gaze of Eric, "….and we don't have time to argue. So, I suggest…."

Before she could get any further, Milly walked past her, ignoring the other faeries completely, and exited the garden by the front gate. The fae contingent all gaped in unison as she stood at the kerb, looked left and right and left again and then walked steadily and surely across the road, at which point she turned back, waved to those she had left behind and ran her way down towards the Royal Oak. Trixie picked up where she had left off.

"So, I suggest we accept that she's made up her own mind on this matter, and offer her all the help we can muster." She looked across in the general direction of Eric and then back to Messrs Material and Burr.

"There is no more help that we can give her." Mr Material continued his gaze down the road where Milly was rapidly disappearing into the distance. "It is now all down to her and those waiting for her at the tree. If she is ready it will happen – she will make it happen."

"How can she be ready?" Eric shouted his disagreement with a vehemence and vitriol that frightened Trixie. "She is only five and you are sending her into a situation that can only result in failure. I will stop her and you will not stand in my way!"

Eric released a beam of intense light and malevolence from his eyes in the direction of Mr Material. To the surprise of everyone except Mr Material himself, the beam stopped short and shattered into a swarm of harmless stars and crackles that vanished quickly into the air around the cottage. Trixie and Mr Burr looked on in admiration and awe. Both had had limited experience of Nixies, but from what they knew and, in the case of Trixie, had seen, the power of a Nixie stare was not normally repelled.[124] Eric had, after all the time he had spent in Whimbury, at last shown his hand and displayed who he really was – and his power was not enough to defeat Mr Material. Eric howled in the agony of a failed plan that had been meticulously worked out and which had occupied many years of his life. The return stare from Mr Material was more terrifyingly threatening, if less explosive.

"I think, Mr O'Shy, that it is now the time when you should be thinking of returning to wherever it was that you came from. Your intention is evil and your motive duplicitous. You have manipulated the friendship of these generous fae-folk in an attempt to further your own ambitions and those of your people. The future of fae- and human-kind across the earth is now, I'm pleased to say, out of your hands. Go home and tell those who sent you that they are not, and will never be, welcome in any fae community that keeps the principles and customs that the rest of us hold dear. Go!"

And with a shriek of anger that emanated from the pain of defeat, Eric O'Shy was indeed gone. Mr Material smiled the smile of a job well done and gestured to Trixie and Mr Burr that they should follow Milly and watch the upcoming events unfold.

****

At the security fence, Milly was kneeling on the ground talking earnestly with Barry, Percy and Robin.

"Where is the party?" Milly immediately got to the crux of the issue.

"The party will be in the tree." Barry pointed to the base of the Royal Oak where, to human eyes, there appeared only bark, grass and other wild flora. Milly placed her hand through the fence in a gesture of disappointment. She stared at the top of the fence and across to the heavy chain and padlock that held it together. She stood and attempted to squeeze through the narrow uprights, then sat again, dejected, as she realised the impossibility of the situation. Percy slid through the fence and sat beside her. He spoke gently and calmly.

---

[124] Mack Stout had direct experience of that from the day of the Crossover ritual, when he was a victim of a Nixie eye-missile and only re-appeared in the Royal Oak, totally disorientated, the next Wednesday.

"Now is the time, Milly! To come into the tree, you must become like us. No human being can join us, and we can't start our party until you are able to come as well. The tree is in great danger from bad humans and if they damage it, there will be no more parties and, maybe, no more faeries either. We need you to help us – and so do all your family and friends here in the village who love the tree. You can do it, Milly. Remember all I've told you. Do you really want to be able to become as one of us?" Percy was not going to plead or try to force the issue. It had to be Milly's decision.

"Yes!" was her simple and honest reply. It was what she had wanted above all else from the moment she had first become aware of her fae friends. She now wanted them to become her fae family also.

"Good. Now I want you to look hard at the bottom of the tree. Can you see a door?"

"No." Milly looked hard with the eyes of a human child, but even a human child with the ability to see beyond and through the constraints of a human adult, could not see the door.

"You will, Milly. You will, if you want to. Concentrate hard on the base of the tree and think of all the things I've told you. Look at the tree and think like a faery. Good girl. You can do it." Percy focussed all his powers of encouragement and support into Milly's actions and thoughts. From inside the compound, Barry and Robin silently urged the child on. As each moment passed and the effort etched itself into Milly's face and body, they looked anxiously at the nearby road junction, praying that the vehicle of the human destroyers would not appear.

Suddenly all of the strain around her eyes and chest and fists eased. Percy, Barry and Robin took a deep breath, fearing the worst.

****

As she passed the Potts' house, on their way to the Royal Oak, Trixie stopped Messrs Material and Burr and pointed to the downstairs front window, where Spot was standing, eyes sparkling and tongue flapping, showing himself ready to play his part in the plan. Trixie motioned in his direction and he ran out of sight, barking with all his might.

The trio moved on towards the tree and for the first time saw Milly standing outside of the compound. As they stood and watched, she slowly and deliberately raised her arms until they were horizontal to her shoulders. Her arms then turned forward as if to touch the fence and, with a squeal of delight, she was gone. In the gloom, they could see Percy skipping with unallayed joy through the fence and towards the tree, where he appeared to join three other faeries. The door to the Royal Oak opened and all hurried inside.

"It is done!" Mr Material announced the completion of the Crossover. His body took on a shimmering glow as his face assumed a look of what Trixie could later only describe as ecstasy. He took the deepest of deep breaths and turned to Trixie and Mr Burr, both of whom were doing their best to take in what they had just seen. "It is done!" he repeated, "you have just witnessed the most important event in the history of humans and faeries since our creation itself."[125] Neither of the other two had ever experienced Mr Material in such an expansive mood before, and his joy was infectious. However, it was also short-lived as, at that exact moment, a large lorry came slowly and quietly round the corner into High Street and pulled up outside the compound. The three of them rushed across the road and leapt through the security fence. They made straight towards the door in the Royal Oak and entered.

Inside, they found Milly with Percy, Barry and Robin. Milly was running around the bar in wild abandon and excitement as Barry pointed out the dartboard in one corner and sets of dominoes on the tables in the snug. Junior sat on the damp towel beside the pump that served the Innkeeper's Choice and watched delightedly as Milly turned this way and that, taking everything in. As she turned towards the door, she noticed Mr Material and ran to him, laughing that he was now bigger than her.

"Have you come for the party?" She addressed her question to Messrs Material and Burr with a look that embraced them both. Barry, Robin and Percy were bemused by her response and by the very fact that the two strangers were there at all. Milly turned back to the three of them.

"They are good faeries. Eric is a bad faery. I don't like him. I don't want him at the party." Now Barry was totally confused.

---

[125] This is detailed in the Fae Chronicles.

"Eric? What's Eric got to do with anything?"

"It's a long story! Trixie stepped into the conversation to hurry it along. "We won't be seeing Eric around again. But what's more important at the moment is that the human destroyers have arrived and we need to get moving now with whatever plan we have in place."

"Ah. Right. OK. Good. Yes. I see. Well then. Erm!" Barry tried desperately to get his brain out of 'Party Time' mode and into 'Full Security Alert' mode. "Percy, I think you need to explain the plan to Milly."

Percy sighed the sigh of a gnome who knew it was for the best that he was the one to tell Milly that the party would have to wait, but he didn't really want to do it. He had been building her up to completing the Crossover ritual, and now he had to hope that a 5-year old faery who was excited beyond belief would be prepared to revert back to a 5-year old human within just a few minutes of her transformation. He put his arm round her shoulders – still a very strange experience – and began to talk.

"Milly, I'm afraid the party will have to wait until another time." He saw the beginnings of a tear appear in her eye, but carried on as gently as he could as a matter of urgency. "Now that you know how to become one of us, you can do it again whenever you like, but there are some nasty men outside who want to chop down this tree, and only you can stop them. We need you to help us. If we can keep this tree, then we'll have a big party another day and you can play all of our games with us. If we lose the tree, I don't know where we will go, or even if we can stay in the village." Milly wiped away her tear and put on her bravest voice.

"I like the faery tree. I want to come here for the party. I don't want it chopped down. I'll go and stop the nasty men."

"You are a wonderful faery, Milly Hope. But now we need you to go back outside and concentrate very hard on being a little girl again. That's the only way we can stop them. Can you do that?" He smiled his biggest, softest, uncle-est smile and gave her a hug as she nodded her affirmation. From inside the bar, they heard the sound of a padlock clanking, a chain rattling, security fencing being opened, and men talking. Percy walked Milly to the door, passing Mr Material as they did so. Mr Material bent over and whispered in Milly's ear. She nodded, smiled and walked out of the Royal Oak with Percy.

Outside, they saw Derek Garner and 'Tyler the Chainsaw' talking softly as Garner slowly pushed the security fencing shut and glanced anxiously beyond the compound up and down the road. Percy looked Milly squarely and seriously in the eye.

"I know this is all very new to you, Milly, and you have never done this before, but it is really important that those men see you before they start their work. As a faery they can't see you at all. Do you think you can become a little girl again right now?" Percy hated putting such pressure on her, but the future of the Royal Oak now depended on Milly performing the reverse Crossover very, very quickly.

"Yes. Mr Material told me what to do – it's quite easy. Watch me!" Percy watched amazed as Milly turned in the direction of her home, raised her arms to point in front of her and concentrated intently on her bedroom and toys, her mother and father, her sister and all things dear to her. In an instant, the faery version of Milly was transformed back to the 5-year old human who had left her bed just a few minutes earlier. She shook her head a little to re-orientate herself to her new scale, and stood in front of the tree, looking straight at 'Tyler the Chainsaw'. Tyler had been putting on his safety harness and priming his saw, as Derek Garner checked the road for activity. As the saw blasted into life, both of them turned, only to be confronted by a 5-year old girl with attitude, looking very sternly at them. Tyler immediately switched off the saw and put it down.[126]

"You are not to hurt the tree. You are very naughty!" Milly adopted an angry adult pose and did her utmost to sound mature and upright.

Tyler and Garner looked at each other in total bewilderment. Neither could think of how to open any meaningful conversation with the other. Milly crossed her arms menacingly, tapping her foot as she did so.[127] Tyler asked Garner a wordless question with a point of the finger and nod of the head in Milly's direction, a shrug of one shoulder, and a deep, inquisitive look of utter

---

[126] Whilst he was lightning at chopping down trees, he was also very safety conscious, particularly with small children in the vicinity – especially unexpected ones who appeared from nowhere.

[127] Adults really do need to take care with regard to their defining mannerisms, which can often come back to haunt them at a later date.

confusion. Garner replied with a wave of both hands that ended up as a slap on each thigh and an equally deep look of confusion, followed by a shake of the head and a throaty gurgle. He took a step towards Milly before being halted by another human voice.

"I wouldn't advise going any nearer to that little girl, if I were you. And maybe you could explain what your business is being here inside that compound with that contraption." They jumped and turned in one movement to see Ralph deftly replacing the padlock between the chain links, and holding it with one hand away from the fencing such that there was no way they could get out. With his other hand, Ralph pointed disgustedly at the chainsaw. "And what exactly were you planning on doing with that? I suspect the obvious!"

"This tree is dangerous. We've come to make it safe before anyone gets hurt." Derek Garner rattled through the planned excuse in robotic fashion, as he tried to make sense of what was going on.

"In the middle of the night?" Ralph was beginning to enjoy himself.

"We're expecting a violent storm!" Even Derek Garner himself found it difficult to keep up the pretence.

Ralph looked up into the cloudless, still, moonlit sky and just shook his head with a mildly malevolent grin. From further up the road a dog came barking towards the compound dragging a pyjama clad Adrian along with him, and chased from further behind by a puffing Kenneth. As they reached the security fence, Spot stopped and barked loudly at the two men inside, then bared his teeth in what he mistakenly assumed was a fearsome sight. Nevertheless, even the appearance and sound of a poodle in those circumstances were enough to keep Garner and Tyler on the back foot. Kenneth puffed a greeting to Ralph.

"Good morning! You are Ralph I presume?" He proffered his hand which Ralph shook awkwardly.

"I am indeed, and you must be the family of Evadne Potts?"

"Yes, we are. This is Adrian, and the wolf doppelganger here is Spot, or "Fang" as he prefers to be known."

"Pleased to meet you." Ralph was genuinely happy to make their acquaintance. He had come to like and respect Evadne.

"Evadne has just gone up the road to fetch Will as additional support. I doubt he will have any idea what is going on here. Miranda will have to stay with Milly of course."

"I doubt it!" Ralph pointed to the tree and the little girl standing defiantly in front of it.

Kenneth and Adrian stood dumbstruck as their gaze moved in synchronised fashion between Milly and the terminally confused Tyler and Garner. Kenneth wafted his finger around in their general directions, then looked at Ralph for some clarification.

"How did she....? What are they....? Go back and get my camera Adrian! We need some pictures." He took Spot's lead from Adrian, who rushed back to the house.

"The answers to your two questions are, firstly, I think I know how she got there, but you wouldn't believe me if I told you, and secondly, they are intent on chopping down the Royal Oak because it is dangerous to passers-by and there is a violent storm coming." Ralph raised his finger to the clear and bright night sky, and left Kenneth to come to his own conclusion on the likely meteorological accuracy of Garner's excuse.

"When you've quite finished talking about us as if we couldn't hear, when are you going to let us out?" Garner walked menacingly towards the fencing, while Ralph pulled the padlock and chain as far out of reach as he could. Spot barked again suddenly and Garner stepped back in surprise, which pleased Spot to the extent that he felt another snarl was called for. It wasn't, but he enjoyed doing it.

"Patience, Patience!" Ralph knew the importance of letting the whole scene play itself out for as long as possible – or at least until the appropriate reinforcements arrived. "We'll let you out just as soon as we get some straight answers as to what you are doing with a chainsaw, a maple-leafed lumberjack, and a 5-year-old girl inside the security fence before dawn on a beautiful, calm starlit night. From where we're standing it's not looking good for you once the police get here."

"We've every right to be here. The Council gave us permission to put the fencing up and keep an eye on the tree. We can do what's necessary to keep the place safe." Garner felt that attack was the best form of defence. Tyler kept looking alternately between his saw and Milly, but failed to make any sense of the situation.

"I find it hard to believe that the Council gave you permission to hold a 5-year-old child hostage?" Kenneth joined in with the argument and did his utmost to keep a straight face whenever Spot let out a threatening growl.

"I've no idea where she came from. She's trespassing. And what are her parents doing, letting her come out at this time of night?" Garner's attack became seriously undermined by his utter confusion. His confusion became even more utter when Adrian arrived back with a camera and asked Garner, Tyler and Milly to smile, which they all did out of habit. While they all slowly recovered their sight after the camera flash, Adrian asked Tyler to pick up the chainsaw and point it menacingly at the tree. Without thinking, the champion lumberjack did so, still smiling at Milly in a totally benign way.[128] Garner sat down with his chin in his hands and awaited the inevitable. Adrian took a few more random photographs of the scene inside the security fence as Will and Miranda came racing down the High Street with Evadne.

"Where is she? What's happening? What are you two doing in there with our daughter?" Will raced through the questions in panic mode and not really interested in the answers, since he could see Milly and that she was alive and well, if not in the expected location. Milly rushed to the fence and thrust her hands through to hold Will's and Miranda's.

"I've been with the faeries! Next time we can have a party with games, if the tree is safe." Milly extricated one of her hands to point back to the tree.

"Oh, it's safe alright!" Ralph smiled down at the little girl and then at her bewildered parents. "These nice gentlemen are about to leave and take their fence away, isn't that right gentlemen? Because if they don't, there will be a lot of photos zooming through the media very soon which will require some very complicated explanations." He transferred his smile, which now had something of a cutting edge, to Garner and Tyler, and gestured that they might like to agree to his expectations of them.

"If you'd be so kind as to let go of the chain and padlock, we'll leave quietly. The fence will be gone by lunchtime." Garner knew when he was

---

[128] Tyler was massive in all dimensions and exuded raw power, but he loved children.

beaten and how to retreat with minimum harm to himself. Ralph opened the fence and Garner and Tyler walked back to their vehicle with maximum haste. Milly rushed over to Miranda and Will and gave them a hug as they knelt down to receive her. Around the Royal Oak, the representatives of the human and fae communities of Whimbury, independently of each other, watched in silence and then embraced as Garner drove off hurriedly, with Tyler waving an innocent farewell through the window.

Will picked Milly up and asked her, not unreasonably, why she was where she was and how she had got to where she had been. Her answer did not clarify matters to any great extent.

"Eric was a bad faery. He wanted the tree chopped down. I didn't want the tree chopped down. Nor did Trixie or the two new faeries. The big new faery chased Eric away. I went to help save the tree. I tried very hard and became very small and got to the tree. And Barry and Percy and Robin were there and they showed me where the parties are. But then I had to get big again when the nasty men arrived. When they saw me, they were very surprised, and couldn't chop down the tree. Then Ralph came and locked them in. Then Uncle Kenneth and Adrian came with Spot and they helped Ralph to protect the tree. Then you came and the nasty men went away, and the tree is safe." She ended the tale with a final flourish that signalled a job well done, but did little to help Will or Miranda fully understand what had just happened.

"I think for now, you might be as well taking the girl home." Ralph spoke gently to Miranda. "One day, all this will become crystal clear and you'll know precisely just how special your daughter is. If I understand things correctly, there's no-one else quite like her anywhere in the world, and I suspect that she will give you joy and worry in equal measure. She is destined for great things, and this morning is merely the start. I don't fully know how all this happened and maybe never really will, but I'm proud to be associated with you all – the way you care for each other and have even accepted me for who I am. That means a lot. And now, it's time to get back to town before I lose my place outside the Council Offices. I think the next day or so might be quite interesting in there, and I would love to be a fly on the wall." And with a jaunty wave he walked away before anyone could ask any questions.

"We'll be your fly on the wall!" Trixie landed on Ralph's shoulder as he rounded the corner. "Robin and I will report back on what goes on. See you later!" Trixie disappeared and Ralph continued his long walk back to Whimburton with more bounce in his step than he had known for a long while.

Chapter Twenty

THE SUN SHONE WARM AND undimmed by cloud over Whimbury. In the front garden of Over Cross View, Miranda and Evadne sat in camping chairs enjoying the stillness. Spot lay in the shade against the side wall, his tongue flapping, watching the wildlife in and around the bushes and occasionally barking snippets of conversation to Barry and Percy who were positioned on the gatepost. Despite being up for much of the early hours of the morning, Milly had insisted on going to school. Will was at work, not knowing quite how to explain to his colleagues why he was perpetually yawning. Kenneth was in the shop trying to keep himself occupied by arranging and re-arranging the limited fruit and vegetables that were laid on tables out the front.[129] In these respects, it appeared a normal day in the village. But it was very much nothing like the normal of the previous decades – or even centuries. 'Out of the ordinary' would become the new normal, though the Hopes, Potts and their friends were yet to fully appreciate that.

"I still don't understand how she got out – or why she decided to go out at all?" Miranda was perplexed, upset and relieved all in one giant mixed emotion. "I've never been so fearful in my life as when we realised the front door was open and she wasn't in bed. She can't open the door by herself when it's locked. And how she ended up inside the security fencing, I have absolutely no idea. She was obviously there before the chainsaw gang arrived

---

[129] Which he, but not Evadne, believed to be a work of art. Nevertheless, she indulged him.

and opened up. It's not possible – is it?" Miranda sipped her tea, leaving the question with Evadne to ponder.

As Evadne pondered, Spot continued to bark at intervals, seemingly for no reason.

"You know," Evadne spoke at last, "Spot has been acting strange as well over the last few days. I know dogs and children are supposed to have a special bond, but the way Spot and your Milly interact, and seem to be affected by the same events, is quite remarkable. I could swear he's not barking randomly, but there's nothing here in the garden to provoke him. Maybe there's just something in the air that they both react to in their own separate ways."

"She speaks to animals, insects, nothing and nobody in particular, and the fairies of course. Most of all to the fairies." Miranda laughed. "Barry and Percy and Trixie and Robin and... I lose count. And now Eric the bad fairy, and strange new fairies. I mean, we've always encouraged her imagination, but ... well, it goes beyond anything I can comprehend. They are all so real to her. It's almost as if the Vicar was right and that there are realities out there that only some of us can experience. Perhaps Milly is super-sensitive?"

Before Evadne could respond, Spot gave a final farewell bark to Barry and Percy, as they headed back to the Royal oak, and then wandered over to her, putting his head in her lap. She stroked his head and wiped his saliva off her trousers.

"And then there's Ralph. I'm sure he knows more than he's letting on." The more Evadne thought about it, the more complex the situation became, and the greater the number of players who had their parts to play. "Next time I see him, I'm going to want some answers as to how he just happened to be in the vicinity at the right time to keep the compound secure until we all got there to sort things out. I've a suspicion that we're all going to have to suspend disbelief in things that we once held as fanciful, and open our minds to new ways of looking at them. Your Milly could yet end up as the one to lead us into those new realities you mentioned!"

"Just so long as they are realities and not some weird fantasies." Miranda had always believed that there was something extraordinary about Milly, but she didn't want her to miss out on being a little girl, with all the joys available to her. Nevertheless, if there was something very different out there in the ether, maybe connecting with that would help to expand all their horizons and give her daughter new and important experiences to enhance her development. But fairies?

"No, I don't believe they're fantasies at all, Miranda. Milly is more grounded in the environment of Whimbury – and beyond – than most adults around here. And her imaginary world seems to be a logical development of that. I think we may all have a lot to learn from her, and I wouldn't be at all surprised if it was very important that we do." Evadne turned the tiniest bit teary, just enough for Miranda to notice and be a little shocked. "I genuinely feel immensely proud to have been present at her birth, and I look forward to watching her continue to grow up. I hope you'll let me continue to play a small part in that – it will be a privilege."

"Of course, Evadne, of course!" Miranda reached over and placed her hand gently on Evadne's. She had the feeling, after the events of that night, that she and Will might just need all the help they could get.

****

In the Planning Department at Whimburton council offices, Jessica Huntly-Philips was briefing her Tree officer on her meeting with Robert Hancock the previous day. She was also briefing Robin and Trixie, though she didn't realise it.

"Off the record, but as everyone knows, I wouldn't trust Hancock any further than I could throw him. But he showed me a tree survey and it clearly stated that the Royal Oak at Whimbury was exhibiting signs of decay and was a safety hazard. As I understand it, one of his contractors has put security fencing round it and I gave him strict instructions that the tree was not to be harmed until you had had the chance to discuss the issue with him. I think you need to do that as soon as possible."

"This would be the tree that stands in the way of potential access to Hill Farm?" Sam Williams had a long history of 'discussions' with Robert Hancock and his contractors regarding trees on or around development sites, and the trees rarely if ever came out of the situation in better shape than before the discussions had begun.[130]

"The very one!" Jessica had recognised the urgency of the matter from the moment Hancock had mentioned it and had organised the meeting with Sam at the earliest opportunity. "Which is why I have fears for its future, and would like you to give it the once over and take control over what happens to it. Are you free enough this morning to......" Jessica was interrupted by the appearance of her secretary, who indicated that there was an important telephone call that she should take. She gestured to Sam to wait a moment while she dealt with the call.

Sam Williams watched as Jessica looked shocked, then confused, then amazed, and finally highly amused. She said little, but Sam gathered it related to the Royal Oak. She put the phone down, turned to Sam with a smile and explained the substance of the conversation.

"It appears that there was a disturbance at Whimbury in the early hours of the morning. Two men and a chainsaw were interrupted from what was apparently an attempt to chop down the Royal Oak. The caller, who is a resident of the village, tells me that some of the locals disturbed said men and politely requested that they remove themselves from the vicinity before incriminating photographs of the event were published. The two men left quietly and, even as we speak, the security fencing around the tree is being dismantled. She wouldn't give me the full story but I think the immediate danger to the tree has passed."

Sam laughed out loud. "Excellent. I'd love to know how it all panned out. I've been waiting for that lot to over-stretch themselves for a long while now. Well done the locals of Whimbury, that's all I can say. So, what now?"

"I think the meeting with Robert Hancock's cronies should still take place – at the Royal Oak – where they can show you the supposed issues with the tree, and you can deal with them – issues and/or perpetrators - in any way you think fit. Can I leave that with you?" Jessica folded away her file, sat back and sighed a contented sigh.

"It'll be my pleasure! I checked the tree myself a few weeks ago and it's

---

[130] In fact, they rarely came out of the situation more than a few centimetres above ground level.

absolutely fine. I'll phone them now and arrange a meeting." Sam left the room, consulting his phone as he did so.

****

"What do you mean, they chased you off?" Robert Hancock was turning a very unhealthy shade of puce as he enunciated each word carefully and purposefully in an attempt to indicate the seriousness of the question. His early morning meeting over coffee with Derek Garner was already not going as planned, and they had only just ordered the cappuccinos.

"I'm not sure you'll believe me if I tell you, but I'll tell you anyway." Garner twiddled a sachet of sugar over and under his fingers and thumbs as he attempted to work out how to explain what had happened a few short hours ago. He decided not to start at the beginning because at that point there was no indication of what was to happen soon after, and how that happening somewhat upset all the plans he had made with Hancock previously.

"Tyler was all ready with his chainsaw inside the security fence." He began the tale from the last moment that he could understand what was actually going on. It was how to move on from there that was giving him difficulties. "Then we suddenly noticed a small girl standing beside the tree." He realised that he had maybe reached this stage of the proceedings rather too quickly for Hancock's level of understanding to accommodate. This was made clear by virtue of the way that Hancock's jaw dropped and eyes bulged, followed by an incredulous clicking of the tongue and a barely controlled exclamation.

"What?"

"A girl beside the tree." Repetition did not make it any easier for Garner to make his point. "We didn't see her as we went in, and we hadn't seen her until Tyler started moving towards the tree. It was as if she popped up out of nowhere .... I mean, it was still pretty dark – what on earth was she doing there at that time of the morning. And how did she get in there? The fencing is 2 metres high with spikes and the gate was padlocked. It makes no sense!"

"You're right there. I can certainly make no sense of it." Hancock shook his head in disbelief. "And this girl chased you off?"

"Not the girl – at least not just the girl. Other residents started appearing, one with a massive snarling dog.[131] They were taking pictures and threatening us. In the end we just had to get away as quickly as we could. It was totally weird – almost as if they were expecting us and fully prepared for action." He paused as their coffees arrived. He was putting the sugar in when his phone rang suddenly, causing him to spill much of it all over the table.[132]

Hancock dropped a napkin onto the coffee spill and then stirred his coffee in agitated fashion as he waited for Garner to finish his conversation. The somewhat deferential tones with which Garner repeated the words 'Yes' and 'Right' and 'I understand' at frequent intervals did not fill him with confidence.

"I take it that was not the good news that everything was going to be fine and that last night was just a minor hiccup?" Hancock was now in full upset-beyond-words mode and sat back to await clarification.

"Not exactly!" He finished stirring the remains of his coffee, blew on it, took a large sip and cursed as it burnt his tongue. "I'm going to have to go. I have a meeting with Sam Williams in a few minutes in Whimbury. He sounded disgustingly victorious. I need to sort a few things out!" He blew again and tried to take another sip before standing up and wiping his mouth with a clean napkin.

"Yes, you do! This scheme has a great deal of money resting on it. Your antics last night are threatening to scupper it entirely. So for both our sakes, I hope you can calm the troubled waters enough for us to work out a Plan B. Ring me after the meeting!" Hancock angrily picked up his coffee, waved Garner away, took a sip and cursed as it burnt his tongue.

****

Outside the Council Offices, Ralph was sitting in his usual spot, waiting patiently for a report from Robin and Trixie. He was having trouble staying awake and had taken to singing in an attempt to maintain concentration.

---

[131] Garner was a bit on the defensive at this point.
[132] Probably not helped by the fact that he had chosen the opening bars of Beethoven's 5th Symphony as his ring tone.

Although his lifestyle involved much walking and irregular hours, the hurried walk to Whimbury the previous day and the walk back that morning had taken a lot out of him – that and the fact that he had no sleep at all while awaiting the arrival of the 'Tree Surgeons'.[133] Ralph was not known for his singing skills[134] and after several verses of unrecognisable, though supposedly popular, songs he had still only acquired a single copper coin for his troubles – and that was accompanied by a request from an elderly woman that he stop singing immediately as it was setting her Jack Russell off.

At last, he saw Sam Williams skipping down the steps followed by Robin and Trixie. Sam was texting rapidly on his phone and looking at his watch. Robin sat down next to Ralph and pointed at Sam as he disappeared down the road.

"Apparently, he's a Tree Officer – whatever that means, and he's off to meet the Chainsaw Gang at the Royal Oak. He's obviously come across them before and I've a suspicion he's looking forward to making things uncomfortable for them." Robin rubbed his hands in glee.

"Well, it's no more than they deserve." Ralph smiled. Chink! "Thank you!" He pondered over the events of the night. "My only hope is that the embarrassment and the threat of exposure in the media leads them to the conclusion that it's best not to try to explain it away. If it all dies down naturally, then the story of the 'now you don't see her, now you do' little girl won't come out into the open. If it does, it's going to bring the Press down to Whimbury and all kinds of stories will appear. Whimbury could end up as a tourist attraction, which might not be the best outcome!"

"I hadn't thought of that." Trixie looked suddenly concerned, but continued in positive vein. "Though I suspect that a story involving the possible kidnap of a five-year-old girl as part of a covert operation to chop down a protected tree under cover of darkness would not enhance their corporate image. No! I think we're safe on that score. At least, I hope so."

---

[133] In this case, 'Surgeons' with similar results in terms of the recovery chances of their 'patients' to those of Dr Frankenstein and Dr Knox, along with their body-snatchers.

[134] In fact, he was barely known for anything at all other than just being there from time to time.

"So do I! So do I! It's going to be hard enough for Milly to continue her role without mass media coverage. She's going to need time to adjust and learn when and how to use her powers."

"Yes! Well, she'll have us all to help her on that one – and at least the tree is safe and the housing developers have been seen off." Robin maintained the positive approach that was his trademark.

"For the time being, Robin! For the time being!" Ralph never liked to dampen Robin's spirits, but he knew the way that certain human beings operated, having had more previous experience of their capabilities than the Fae community of the area. "We may have won the battle, but the war continues. Schemes like the one planned for Whimbury don't tend to just go away. We can celebrate now, but we have to remain on our guard – and I think out little Crossover miracle will need our love, attention and support for a good while to come yet!" Chink. "Thank you."

****

Later in the day, as dusk fell, Messrs Material and Burr found themselves sitting at a table in the bar at the Royal Oak enjoying a drink. They were unusually relaxed and engaged in social conversation with Barry, Robin, Trixie and Percy. In the opposite corner, Lancelot and Inigo were preparing for a quiz night without Eric's participation, which at least would open the way for more teams to experience some success. On the adjacent table, Mack and Trevor were singing tunelessly at the top of their voices:

O the summer time has come
And the trees are gently swaying,
The sheep are in the fields
With their lambs a-sweetly playing
Shall we go Laddie go? ……

"You should all feel very proud and satisfied with the role you have played in this momentous event." Mr Material was gushing and genuine in his praise. "On one level, I never doubted your abilities and willingness, but when the time arrives, it is a different matter to be able to carry the process through to its conclusion. The girl was ready. In her own mind and body, she has always been ready, but to fulfil the Crossover itself required you all to prepare her for Faedom, and that you have done magnificently. Percy, you have been a model of patience and wisdom. Robin, Trixie – your energy and preliminary work have been essential elements. Barry, your oversight and organisation – along with Ralph's input – was inspiring. And the support of all of your friends here in Whimbury – fae and animal - ensured it all could happen. The world will not be the same again. There is hope – though never certainty – that humans and faeries can work together for the good of the Earth."

To cause a bit of bother:
Tis the wild mutton time,
See them roam around the heather,
Shall we go Laddie go?......

"Mr Material and I have been travelling for a long while, often coming back here to see how you were getting on. Sometimes we made ourselves known, sometimes we just watched from a distance. Seeing you all operate together with one goal has never been short of a great pleasure." Mr Burr emerged from the shadow of his more forthright colleague, seemingly now more confident and more sure of his own position – less the student now and more the fellow traveller. "At first, I learnt from Mr Material here and hung on his every word and action. More recently I have learnt also from you – other values and gifts, including how to live and work together. Yes, I've laughed at your sparring and your arguing, but that is the surface. The community here is deep, and that is the basis of your success. I toast you all."

Mr Burr raised his glass of Innkeeper's Choice, which was not his normal drink of choice, and took a large celebratory swig. After a prolonged coughing fit and finally regaining his voice, he proposed that Robin and Percy join the two, no-longer-strangers, in a quiz team, while Barry and Trixie resumed their duties at the bar with Damon. Percy, who had never before been part of a team containing anyone other than another member of the Family Grump, winked at the other three, before launching into a tirade of grumpiness designed to protect his image. Having indulged himself to an extent he deemed to be sufficient, he loudly pronounced his agreement under great sufferance. This was, after all, an unprecedented day and promised to be an evening like no other before.

Epilogues

Later that same evening

BARRY, TRIXIE AND DAMON WERE wiping down the tables at the end of the quiz night. In the corner, the victorious team of Messrs Material and Burr, along with Robin and Percy were reliving some of the more obscure answers that they had been able to dredge up from the dim recesses of their collective memories. Mr Material was in exceptionally high spirits while Mr Burr was mentally preparing himself for the rigours of the following morning after an evening of excessive consumption of Innkeeper's Choice. Barry called across to them from the other end of the room.

"Masterstroke of yours, if I may say so, Mr Material, to donate your prizes back to the team who came second. That's gained you at least four new best friends in the whole world. And as for buying the whole assembled masses a drink, Mr Burr, well that was generosity beyond their wildest dreams. That guarantees you the warmest of welcomes next time you come back."

"Did I do that?" Mr Burr gazed imploringly across to Mr Material, hoping that he wouldn't confirm what Barry had said. Unfortunately, Mr Material merely nodded in agreement. "Oh dear – I'm really not used to drinking that stuff – this stuff!" He looked down at his nearly empty glass and tried to remember how many such drinks he had had that evening. He gave up when he ran out of fingers and just moaned lightly.

"It's been one of the most pleasurable evenings it's been my privilege to share, Mr Innkeeper. And following on from the incredible events of the night before, it marks the beginning of a new era. You should all be proud to have been a part of it. And now, I think it is time to go. Come along Mr Burr, it's time to leave these good folk in peace – but we'll be back to see you – and the Crossover girl from time to time. Thank you for all you have done." Mr Material stood and waited for Mr Burr to do the same. After a few false starts, Mr Burr was able to join him and they wandered over towards the door, one rather more steadily than the other.

"It's us who should thank you!" Barry waved a fond farewell. "Hope to see you soon Mr Material – or should we call you Daniel?"

"I answer to many different names. You may call me whatever feels right for you!" And with that, Mr Material walked out. Mr Burr made to follow and then returned unsteadily to the bar, where he leaned over to whisper in Barry's ear.

"Before we came back a couple of days ago, Mr Material invited me to his home to meet his wife. Quite a dramatic and forceful woman. She calls him Oberon. Just thought you ought to know!" Mr Burr touched the side of his nose in conspiratorial fashion and made his erratic way out of the Royal Oak.

****

Mid-morning the next day

Evadne stood by the gate of Over Cross View, watching Daisy running around energetically in the front garden. Miranda was doing a bit of weeding – more as an excuse to keep an eye on her No 2 daughter than to keep the garden under control.

"They grow up so quickly these days don't they?" Evadne smiled as Daisy kept running round and round what appeared to be a mini-assault course or obstacle race. "She's a bit more lively than Milly, isn't she!"

"Just a bit! Mind that log!" Miranda was a little late in her warning and Daisy tripped over the log, but then got straight up and continued where she left off. "She's got an imagination like Milly, but channels it in different ways. She'll either be an athlete when she grows up or a member of the SAS. Pity her teacher when she goes to school."

"Ah well, make the most of her while she's still here every day. Once she gets to school it'll be having friends round, sleep-overs, pre-occupations with bodily functions – especially rude ones. Though each stage is lovely in its own way – usually!" Evadne and Miranda paused momentarily to take in what Daisy was doing and shouting.

"I suppose, now that the housing issue has been sorted out and the tree saved, I'll be able to concentrate on Daisy that bit more – though I'll no doubt be spending much more time in future worrying about what Milly is getting up to instead. I've no idea how we're going to get to the bottom of what happened the other night."

"It might take some time to fully find out. In the meantime, indulge her a bit. I doubt she knows herself exactly what happened – maybe she was sleepwalking?" Evadne had her suspicions but was keeping them to herself for the time being. "And as for the housing thingy and the tree, I wouldn't be so sure that it's sorted out. In my experience, people like them don't give up easily, and I doubt it'll be long before they're back with another cunning plan. I hope I'm wrong, but – don't hold your breath!

****

The same

In the Nixie Rehabilitation and Re-programming Centre, known affectionately by its inmates as R and R[135], Eric was peeling potatoes and ruminating on how his plans could have gone so wrong when he had been so meticulous in his preparations. Had he not read and re-read the Fae Chronicles till they were engraved into his psyche? Had he not spent months perfecting the character and lifestyle of the Bashful Tribe of gnomes? Had he not ingratiated himself with the hated enemies of the Nixies, with all the angst and discomfort to himself that it involved? Had he not sacrificed several years of his life in the cause of trying to prevent the Crossover from taking place? True he had failed, but he hadn't been trained for a direct confrontation with the mysterious Mr Material – and he was sure that he knew exactly who the tall stranger really was. It was unfair to treat him as a failure.

---

[135] Some of the Nixies there, who didn't conform to the norms of Nixie society and beliefs, could, on occasion, display something approaching ironic humour. Most of them had had it knocked out of them by the time they were released.

"Hey, Greeny!"[136] A very large, uncompromising deep purple Nixie walked over to Eric and put his hand on Eric's shoulder. "Just a word from a long-suffering inmate of this here luxury spa." He turned to acknowledge the howls of laughter from his companions.[137] "You'd better get a move on, cos if you haven't peeled all them spuds by the time the cook needs them, you'll have had your chips!"

He walked away from Eric and back to his adoring audience. Eric had remained impassive throughout the interlude and now focussed his attention quietly on planning the downfall of his newly acquired nemesis – along with speeding up his work of peeling the potatoes.

****

Two years later

Milly raced through her tea and jumped down from her chair.

"Don't you want ice cream?" Miranda recognised the signs, but still felt obliged to try to slow her daughter down and get her to finish her evening meal.

"I'll be late for the dominoes competition. I'm playing doubles with Percy. It's a special event." Milly put on her cardigan and ran to the front door. Daisy also left the table and followed her. Miranda called Milly back to give her final instructions.

"You're to come straight back. You've school in the morning. And don't whatever you do, stay there till it gets dark." Miranda still couldn't believe what she was saying. She shook her head in disbelief that she was actually telling Milly not to be late back from a faery gathering in the base of a large oak tree. It had taken her a long time to accept that all Milly's explanations of what had happened the night of the Crossover were, in fact, true, and that Milly was even more special than she or Will had ever dreamed she could be. And now Daisy could also communicate with the faeries, although communication was as far as she would ever be able to go. 'You just have to

---

[136] Nixies were certainly not above regular usage of discriminatory language, especially those in the R and R centre.

[137] While not all of them were blessed with the gift of cutting wit.

believe it with all your heart', Milly had told them all, and you can see and hear them. She and Will could not quite go so far as yet, but they were getting there – they had to, in order to understand what Milly was doing when she went rushing off to join in some special fae activity.

I'll come straight back, I promise." Milly and Daisy ran off to the front gate. "Percy and Mack will come back with me to see me home safe." She hurried down the High Street in the direction of the Royal Oak and, as she approached it, she disappeared – literally.

Back at the front gate of Over Cross View, Daisy looked down the road in the direction that her sister had just gone. Then she waved her hand in the air.

"Hi Robin. I'm going to have Milly's ice cream." And she ran back into the house.

THE END

www.ingramcontent.com/pod-product-compliance
Lightning Source LLC
Chambersburg PA
CBHW060423030726
47495CB00003B/716